LUCY KING

LOST SONS
OF ARGENTINA

LUCY KING

LOST SONS
OF ARGENTINA

MILLS & BOON

LOST SONS OF ARGENTINA © 2024 by Harlequin Books S.A.

The publisher acknowledges the copyright holders of the individual works as follows:

THE SECRETS SHE MUST TELL
© 2020 by Lucy King
Philippine Copyright 2020
Australian Copyright 2020
New Zealand Copyright 2020

First Published 2020
Second Australian Paperback Edition 2024
ISBN 978 1 038 91799 7

INVITATION FROM THE VENETIAN BILLIONAIRE
© 2021 by Lucy King
Philippine Copyright 2021
Australian Copyright 2021
New Zealand Copyright 2021

First Published 2021
Second Australian Paperback Edition 2024
ISBN 978 1 038 91799 7

THE BILLIONAIRE WITHOUT RULES
© 2021 by Lucy King
Philippine Copyright 2021
Australian Copyright 2021
New Zealand Copyright 2021

First Published 2021
Second Australian Paperback Edition 2024
ISBN 978 1 038 91799 7

MIX
Paper | Supporting
responsible forestry
FSC® C001695

Published by
Harlequin Mills & Boon
An imprint of Harlequin Enterprises (Australia) Pty Limited
(ABN 47 001 180 918), a subsidiary of HarperCollins
Publishers Australia Pty Limited
(ABN 36 009 913 517)
Level 19, 201 Elizabeth Street
SYDNEY NSW 2000 AUSTRALIA

Printed and bound in Australia by McPherson's Printing Group

CONTENTS

Lucy King spent her adolescence lost in the glamorous and exciting world of Harlequin when she really ought to have been paying attention to her teachers. But as she couldn't live in a dreamworld forever, she eventually acquired a degree in languages and an eclectic collection of jobs. After a decade in southwest Spain, Lucy now lives with her young family in Wiltshire, England. When not writing or trying to think up new and innovative things to do with mince, she spends her time reading, failing to finish cryptic crosswords and dreaming of the golden beaches of Andalucia.

The Secret She Must Tell

MILLS & BOON

PROLOGUE

SHE COULDN'T TAKE her eyes off him.

Sitting on the crimson velvet banquette that curved around a table upon which sat a bottle of bubbles chilling in a bucket, Georgie Wallace took a sip of champagne and felt it fizz down her throat to join the unfamiliar buzzing in her stomach.

Her pulse thudded in time to the beat of the sultry music drifting over from the dance floor. The blood pounding through her veins was thick and hot. This pull, this dizzying breathlessness, this inability to concentrate on the conversation going on around her had never happened to her before.

But then, she'd never seen anyone quite like *him* before either.

She'd noticed him the moment he'd entered the room what felt like an eternity ago but could only have been a matter of seconds. One minute she'd been laughing at something one of her friends had said, the next the air had started vibrating with a strange sort of electric tension that had sizzled straight through her, igniting her nerve-endings and robbing her of all coherent thought. Her gaze had located the source of it with the precision of a heat-seeking missile, and the impact of seeing him had dealt a blow to her senses from which she'd yet to recover.

Now he was striding across the floor away from her, dominating the space as if he owned it, all towering height, confident authority and purposeful intent. Anyone in his way instinctively stepped out of it. No one appeared inclined to inform him of the club's no-jeans policy.

'Magnificent,' Georgie murmured to herself, watching transfixed as he slid onto a stool at the far end of the busy bar and summoned the bartender with nothing more than a barely perceptible lift of his head.

That was what he was.

In command.

Compelling.

And clearly in need of a drink, if the way he knocked back the one that appeared in front of him was anything to go by.

'Huh?' said Carla, her oldest and best friend, who was sitting beside her and who she could see out of the corner of her eye was bopping to the music while plucking the bottle from the bucket to refill her glass.

'The guy at the bar,' Georgie said, unable to wrench her gaze away.

'Which one?'

Wasn't it obvious? 'Far left. Dark hair in need of a cut, checked shirt.'

'Big and broad with his sleeves pushed up?'

'That's him.'

Carla replaced the bottle in the bucket and sat back. 'A bit dishevelled for my liking,' she said after a moment's consideration. 'Nice back, though. Good shoulders.'

'Very.' With muscles clearly visible beneath the cotton that stretched across them, they were possibly the finest set of shoulders Georgie had ever seen.

'Did you get a look at his face?'

'Not properly.' Just a tantalising glimpse of a strong masculine jaw and straight nose as he'd stridden past her.

'It would be helpful if he shifted round a bit more.'

'True,' Georgie said with an assessing tilt of her head. 'But even if he did, he'd still be too far away to make out the details.'

'Shame.'

It was indeed, because just imagine if his face matched up to the promise of his body. He'd be breathtakingly gorgeous and that was something she wouldn't mind taking a good, long look at.

But, intriguingly, what was equally as arresting as his physique on the move was his stillness and his containment as he sat alone at the bar. Now furnished with another drink, which he was taking more slowly than the last, he seemed to be utterly lost in thought, an island of immobility in a sea of activity, his bleak sobriety a sharp contrast to the hedonistic atmosphere of the club, and oddly desolate.

Who was he?

What was he doing here?

And would he like some company?

At *that* distantly familiar thought, Georgie inwardly stilled, her heart skipping a beat before racing.

Oooh, how *interesting*.

Once upon a time, as an out-of-control teenager desperate for parental attention and discipline, she hadn't thought twice about approaching good-looking men in bars for a spot of light flirting or dirty dancing, and she'd been extremely good at it.

But ever since she'd come to the distressing realisation at the age of sixteen that if she wanted boundaries she'd have to set them for herself, she'd given up that sort of reckless, impulsive behaviour and had knuckled down to the serious business of adulting. With a love of rules that had been missing from her upbringing, she'd pursued a career in law—much to the horror of her hippie parents—and had slowly built the structure she craved into her life.

She'd had dates, of course, relationships even, but they were casual affairs with guys at college or, later, with men she generally met at friends' dinner parties, men she already faintly knew instead of random strangers picked up in bars.

And, while she'd liked and respected and fancied all of them, none had made her heart race particu-

larly fast. Her last relationship—six months with a
perfectly nice but ultimately unexciting banker—had
fizzled out over a year ago and she'd neither lamented
its demise nor been on the lookout for another.

For the last twelve months, in fact, she'd become
so engrossed in the job she loved, so determined to
get the promotion she'd been after, that she hadn't
given the opposite sex a moment's consideration.
She hadn't wanted the distraction. She hadn't needed
the hassle.

Tonight, however, with her promotion in the bag
and her foot easing off the accelerator a fraction, it
appeared she wouldn't mind some of both.

'Good *song*,' Carla said in response to a shift in
the music as she bopped about on the seat a bit more
energetically. 'Want to dance?'

Not particularly.

In fact, Georgie wanted something quite different. Because, while hitting the dance floor with her
friends and forgetting all about the brooding hunk
at the bar would be by far the safest, most sensible
option, she didn't *want* to forget about him. And for
once she didn't *want* to be sensible. She wanted to
meet him. Talk to him. Flirt with him. She wanted
to give in to the scorching heat and the dizzying lust
rushing through her and see where they took her.

She couldn't remember the last time she'd experienced such an intense and immediate attraction,
or felt so alive. She hadn't realised how much she'd
missed the heady thrill of sexual excitement, how

long she'd been treading water. Besides, it was her birthday. If she couldn't let her hair down tonight of all nights, when could she?

'Maybe later,' she said, her stomach tightening and her pulse racing at the thought of what could happen if she went for it.

Beside her, Carla stilled, her eyes wide. 'Oh? But you usually love dancing.'

'I think I might go over and see if I can't cheer him up instead.'

There was a moment of stunned silence, and then an incredulous, 'Seriously?'

'Why not?'

'Because he does *not* look like the sort of suave, sophisticated professional you usually go for these days. He looks…untamed.'

'I know.' And that was the attraction.

'Are you certain?'

'Yup.' Ish. Her chatting up skills were a bit rusty, and not only might he not be in the mood for company, he might also be spoken for. But what was the worst that could happen? If she crashed and burned, she could always give a nonchalant shrug and leave. If, on the other hand, she didn't, and the attraction she was experiencing turned out to be mutual… well…the outcome could be explosive.

'I thought you'd given up doing that sort of thing.'

'It's only conversation,' she said while thinking, Well, maybe. To start with, at least.

'Sure it is,' said Carla with a wry grin that Georgie couldn't help returning as she put down her glass and got to her feet, her stomach churning with nervous excitement.

'Wish me luck.'

'Good luck. Not that you ever needed it. One thing, though…'

'What?'

'Just in case it *isn't* only conversation and you leave before we're back from the dance floor, message me his name and a photo, and call me in the morning.'

Oblivious to the energy and buzz surrounding him, Finn Calvert stared unseeingly into his drink, his usually ordered thoughts a jumble, his legendary focus blitzed.

Twelve months. Eighteen at most. That was how long his father had left.

Details of the phone call he'd received an hour ago, which had ripped him apart and shattered his world, ricocheted around his head.

Four weeks ago, unbeknownst to him, his father had gone to his doctor complaining of a prolonged cough and shortness of breath. Subsequent tests had revealed lung cancer. Metastasised. Incurable.

Devastating.

Ever since his mother's death when he was young his father had been his only family. He'd been the one who'd brought him up and who'd fished him out of the trouble he'd got into as an angry teenager.

When, at eighteen, Finn had announced he wanted to buy the bar where he'd been working and which was up for sale, his father had been his initial investor. Over the years he'd subsequently proved a solid sounding board and his staunchest supporter, and the bond they shared was deep and unassailable.

Now he was dying, and there wasn't a thing he— Finn—with all his wealth and influence, success and power, could do about it.

His jaw clenched and his fingers tightened around the glass as he fought back a hot surge of emotion, a tangle of helplessness, injustice and rage. Why had his father waited so long before seeing his GP? Why hadn't ever he said anything about not feeling well?

And how had *he* not noticed that anything had been wrong? His father could be guarded at times and had practically invented the stiff upper lip, but that was no excuse. Nor was the acquisition of a hugely grand yet derelict Parisian hotel, the renovation of which had become so complex that Finn had barely had a moment's thought for anything else. He should have made time. He should have visited his father more often. Then he might have seen that something wasn't right.

But he hadn't and now it was too late, and the guilt and the regret were crucifying him in a way that, contrary to his hopes, alcohol was doing nothing to dull. All he wanted from the whisky he was drinking was oblivion. Just for tonight. There'd be time for stoicism and practicality in the morning. But the whisky might as well have been water because the pain was as excoriating as it had been an hour ago and his chest still felt as if it were caught in an ever-tightening vice.

By coming here he'd chosen the wrong place, he thought, downing the remainder of his drink and feeling the burn momentarily scythe through the turmoil. It was convenient, certainly, but it was too loud, too damn full of fun and laughter. He ought to leave and go in search of a darker, quieter, harder bar, one where he could sit on his own in the shadows and the alcohol would flow without question.

And he ought to leave now.

'Hi.'

The soft voice came from his right, puncturing the fog swirling around in his head and freezing him mid-move. The sexy, feminine timbre of it hit him low in the gut and wound through him from there, heating the blood suddenly rushing through his veins and reigniting sensation everywhere.

Automatically, Finn lifted his head and turned it in her direction. She was standing a foot from him, enveloping him with an intoxicating combination of heat and scent, confidence and vibrancy. His gaze locked onto hers, and in that instant the overall impression he had of dark, tousled hair, dazzling smile and a short black sequinned dress was pulverised by a punch of lust so strong it nearly knocked him off his stool.

Lost in the soft brown depths of her eyes and unable to look away, he felt his pulse slow right down. The noise and activity of the club faded. His surroundings disappeared. His head emptied of everything but a strange sense of recognition.

Which was absurd, he told himself, getting a grip and blinking to snap the connection. His foundations had been rocked. His defences were weak. Recognition? No way. They didn't know each other.

But they could.

They could get to know each other *very* well.

Because the intense attraction that had hit him like the blow of a hammer was not one-sided, he realised as he let his gaze drift over her in a leisurely assessment. She felt it too. Quite apart from the fact that she'd been the one to approach him, he could see it in the dilation of her pupils and the rapid rise and fall of her chest. In the flush on her cheeks and the accelerated flutter of the pulse at the base of her neck. He could hear it in the hitch of her breath and feel it in the way she was now very slightly leaning towards him.

And it occurred to him then that perhaps there were other ways to achieve the mindlessness he craved. Perhaps a night of hot sex and dizzying pleasure would succeed where alcohol had failed. Just the thought of it was pushing aside his father's devastating diagnosis and his own reaction to it. Imagine the reality. If he switched his focus and put his mind to it he wouldn't even have to imagine.

'Hello,' he said, giving her a slow smile that had

felled many a woman over the years and was clearly
no less effective tonight, if the sparkle that appeared
in her eyes was anything to go by.

'Would you mind if I joined you?'

'I can't think of anything I'd like more.'

CHAPTER ONE

Fifteen months later

STILL NO NEWS.

Oblivious to the faint thud of music coming from the club below, Finn tossed his phone onto his desk and stalked to the window, frustration boiling through him as he stared out through the Georgian sash window into the dark London night.

It had been two months since he'd found the adoption certificate amongst the papers left behind by the man he'd always considered to be his father, and he was no closer to discovering the truth surrounding his birth now than he had been the moment he'd figured out what he was holding and his life, already shattered by grief, had blown fully apart. The only people who could shed any light on anything were no longer around to ask, and the investigation agency he'd hired—allegedly one of the best in the country—had hit a dead end with every lead.

The paralysis was driving him demented. All he

wanted was answers. All he needed was clarity. He'd thought the sorrow and emptiness that had consumed him in the days following his father's—no, *Jim's*—death and the realisation that he was now all alone in the world had been harrowing, but at least there'd been a feeling of closure. At least there'd been a logical, if agonising, process to get through.

Now there was nothing but chaos. Where order and certainty had once ruled Finn's world, confusion and doubt now reigned. He no longer knew what to believe; facts he'd never once had cause to examine now tormented him day and night. Who was he? Where did he come from?

The questions that spun around his head and left scorching trails of betrayal in their wake were many and relentless. Why had he been adopted? Where and who was his real family? Had he been abandoned? How had he ended up where he had?

And, most crushingly, why had he never been told the truth? There'd been eleven thousand opportunities to explain the circumstances surrounding his adoption, give or take a day or two, and eleven thousand opportunities missed. Why keep it a secret? His father, the man he'd so admired and looked up to, who'd circled the wagons when his mother had died and to whom he'd turned for advice and support back in the early days of his business, had become a stranger overnight.

As a result Finn had no idea how much of his thirty-one years on the planet had been genuine and how much hadn't. In the absence of fact, his previously staid imagination ran riot. In the darkest moments, when he couldn't sleep and prowled around his penthouse apartment unable to stop the constant churning of his mind, he found himself revisiting the circumstances of his mother's death. He'd only been ten when she'd stepped out into a road and been hit by a bus. The driver had sworn she'd seen him coming, had even looked him straight in the eye, but why would she have done it deliberately, a pale-faced, tight-jawed Jim had immediately countered, when she'd had no reason to take her own life and everything to live for?

The coroner had ruled her death an accident and Jim had always unflinchingly maintained this verdict, but in the cool, calm quiet of the early hours of the past couple of weeks the doubts had crept into Finn's head and taken root. Jim had lied to him about his birth, had lied to him his entire life, and now he couldn't help thinking, what if he'd been lying about that too? What if his mother's death *hadn't* been an accident? What if every time she looked at him, her *adopted* son, she was reminded of what she'd never been able to create for herself? What if that had finally become too much to bear? What if she'd deliberately stepped in front of that bus because of him, because in some way he'd failed her, because he'd behaved too badly or somehow hadn't been a good enough son?

If he'd been able to think logically, rationally, he

might have seen this extrapolation for the unlikelihood it was, but logic and reason were long gone. His identity, his history, his entire belief system had been decimated and he didn't know what to think or who to trust any more. He couldn't even trust himself. He'd been taken for a fool and deceived his whole life, yet had never suspected a thing. The instincts he'd always considered rock solid and uncannily reliable were clearly worthless, and as a result his ruthlessly efficient decision-making ability had vanished. His concentration was shot and his attention to detail was history. His usually long fuse was now microscopically short, and he was snapping and snarling at anyone who had the misfortune to cross his path.

He neither recognised nor liked the man he'd become, a man who no longer knew his place in a world he'd always dominated, but there didn't seem to be a damn thing he could do about it. The armour he'd taken for granted had been brutally stripped away and he was all at sea, unanchored and rudderless, and it was hell.

'Boss?'

Shaking free of his tumultuous thoughts, Finn turned from the window to see the club's doorman standing in the doorway.

'Yes?' he all but growled.

Bob, built like a tank and in possession of an attitude to match, didn't even flinch. 'There's someone looking for you.'

'Who?'

'No idea. But she's outside, asking if anyone knows you.'

'She?'

'Brunette. Mid-to-late twenties, I'd say. Slim. Could be stunning if she tried. Not really dressed for partying. She's saying she met you in the bar the October before last. She sounds like a fruitcake if you ask me, but I thought you should know in case she turns out to be a crazy stalker or something.'

Finn's brows snapped together. 'CCTV?'

'Sure.'

The doorman pulled a device from the inside of his jacket and hit a couple of buttons. 'There she is,' he said, pointing at a figure on the screen.

Finn took the device, examined the live feed and froze, his entire body clenching with recognition and an unwelcome punch of heat.

Georgie.

Once met, never entirely forgotten, much to his irritation.

If he chose to, he could recall the night they'd spent together as clearly as if it had been yesterday. The heated looks they'd exchanged at the bar, the heavily laden conversation, the bizarrely intense connection… The chemistry between them had been incredible. The sex had been hot and wild, the best he'd ever had. Over and over again that night she'd given him the oblivion he'd craved, and for a brief mad moment as dawn had broken he'd been tempted to ask for her number before remembering that they'd agreed to one uncomplicated night only, and, in his case, why that was. He'd had enough on his plate with Jim's illness. He'd been in no way looking for anything more. But that hadn't stopped her invading his dreams and giving him uncomfortably sleepless nights for weeks afterwards.

'What does she want?' he asked, ignoring the heat and handing the device back with an odd sort of reluctance.

'She won't say. Just keeps flashing around this photo of you on her phone.'

The same photo she'd taken outside his club, *just in case*, she'd said with a foxy smile that had thumped him square in the chest? Had to be. She wouldn't have found one anywhere else. Despite owning a company whose portfolio boasted seven-star hotels, top-end bars and clubs, and restaurants with six-month waiting lists, he rarely appeared in the media. He didn't need to; the firm that dealt with his PR was outstanding.

'What would you like me to do?'

Good question, thought Finn, shoving his hands in his pockets as he searched for the answer that not so long ago would have come to him instantly. If Georgie had come looking for him before his entire life had been turned upside down he'd have wondered if perhaps she'd been having as much trouble forgetting him as he had her, and whether she might be up for a repeat performance.

But now he didn't know what to think and because

he didn't, because his behaviour was currently so unpredictable, he ought to have her sent on her way and put her out of his mind. Besides, he didn't need to know why she was here. They were done months ago and the last thing he wanted was potentially even more chaos and complication.

And yet for some unfathomable reason, despite his better judgement, he *wanted* to know why she was looking for him, now, after all this time. It intrigued him, shifted his focus and gave him a welcome respite from the turmoil. Frankly, her reason for showing up here couldn't be any more destructive than anything else that had happened to him over the last couple of months, could it? 'Send her up.'

With a heavy heart, Georgie locked her phone and stuck it back in her bag, weariness and despondency washing over her in a great, drowning wave. Coming to the club where she and Finn had met all those months ago had been a long shot, but she hadn't known where else to try.

She'd spent two days trying to track him down with nothing to go on except his first name and a photo. Unsurprisingly, the internet had yielded nothing. The records held by the hotel in which they'd spent the night were data protected, and her enquiries here had met with blank stares and stony silence.

Which meant she was all out of options and back at square one, she thought, anxiety churning around in her gut as the hopelessness of her situation hit

her all over again. She had no job, little money and
home was, for the moment, a tiny, damp bedsit in a
crime-ridden part of London. Because of what had
happened, she was unemployable. Her prospects
were nil. Her confidence had hit rock bottom and
her judgement was unreliable. How she was going
to manage going forward she had no idea.

Digging deep to stave off the relentless despair,
Georgie turned to leave, only to freeze when she
heard a brusque, 'Stop.'

She swung round, her heart banging against her
ribs, to see the man with the muscles and the un-
promising attitude, he of the stony silence and blank
stare, bearing down on her.

'Don't worry, I'm going,' she said, lifting her
hands and backing off as he came to a halt in front
of her.

'Wait.'

She blinked. 'What?'

'The man you're looking for,' he said curtly. 'He's
upstairs.'

At the unexpected information, Georgie's stomach gave a great lurch and her pulse leapt. 'Really?'
she said, glancing up and seeing nothing but dark
windows and an absence of movement.

'Follow me.'

He turned smartly on his heel and, for a moment, she dithered. Was it true? Could she really
have found him at last? On the other hand, how likely
was it that Finn was indeed up there? Why would

he be? What if Muscles was part of some dastardly
trafficking scheme or something and taking her to
a place from which she wouldn't return?

No.

Ridiculous. That was what she was being. Utterly ridiculous. She was in no danger. She needed
to banish the wreck she was these days, beat back
the paranoia and channel the fearless Georgie of the
October fifteen months ago, who hadn't hesitated to
go for what she wanted and watch out anyone who
got in her way. The old her was in there somewhere.
She had to be.

Gritting her teeth, Georgie determinedly shook
off the frightening darkness that was gathering at the
edges of her mind in an all too familiar way and the
memory of the confusing, terrifying thoughts that
had consumed her for much of the last six months,
and set off in the doorman's wake. She stepped
through the door and into the club, and was immediately hit by a wall of noise, a burst of heat, and a
deluge of memories that had her momentarily stopping in her tracks with their vividness.

There was the bar where she'd walked up to Finn
and asked if she could join him, she thought, recalling the desire that had swept through her when she'd
looked at him and realised he was as breathtakingly
gorgeous as she'd hoped. Where he'd given her that
devastatingly wicked smile and she'd known in that
instant that they'd be leaving together. Where they'd
sat close and flirted, their gazes locked, their bodies

communicating on an entirely different level, their off-the-charts chemistry sizzling and soaring until they hadn't been able to take any more.

When she'd breathed into his ear that she wanted to leave—with him—he'd taken her hand and led her out of the club with flatteringly indecent speed. He'd pulled her into a dark doorway and kissed her until her knees went weak and her stomach dissolved into a puddle of lust. He'd then taken her back to his hotel room where they'd spent hours burning up the sheets of his bed before parting in the morning with no promises and no regrets.

It had been everything she'd been hoping for.

It had been perfect.

And then, a while later, not so perfect.

With a sigh, Georgie let go of the memories, and resumed her progress across the room, aware of the curious glances she was attracting, which were hardly surprising, since her appearance gave a whole new meaning to the phrase 'dressing down'. She hadn't dressed up for this meeting. She hadn't dressed up for anything in a long time. Would her zest for life, her energy, her libido, ever come back? Would *she* ever wholly come back? Who knew?

As she followed the doorman up the stairs at the back of the club her heart began to thump, not with excitement, as it had the last time she'd been here, but with nerves. How was this going to go? She didn't have a clue. On one level she was sure that seeking Finn out was the right—the only—thing to do. Yet, on another, she didn't know him, she didn't know how he was going to react, and therefore the outcome was scarily unpredictable.

At the top of two flights of stairs Muscles rapped on a door and opened it. He stood to one side and gestured for her to go in. Georgie took a deep breath in through her nose that she let out slowly through her mouth, and, on legs that felt like jelly, stepped forwards.

And there he was. Standing at the window in the shadows with his back to her, the same broad, muscled back she'd raked her nails down while gasping his name and writhing with pleasure.

The door closed behind her. Finn turned and her breath left her lungs. She'd forgotten just how attractive he was. How breathtaking the impact of his indigo gaze on her could be. The intensity of his focus sent an unexpected bolt of heat shooting through her that for the briefest of moments sliced through the icy numbness she'd lived with for what felt like for ever and made her wish she had the energy to care about the whole make-up-hair-clothes thing.

As the seconds stretched and the silence throbbed she dragged her gaze from his and ran it over the rest of him. He looked harder than she remembered, as if life had knocked him about a bit. Less forgiving too, which perhaps didn't bode well for this meeting. Possibly even a bit wary about why she was turning up out of the blue like this. None the less compelling, though. None the less in command as he stood there utterly still, utterly in control, his feet apart and his hands in his pockets. And if he seemed bigger and broader than she remembered…well, maybe that was because she'd shrunk.

She lifted her eyes back up to his and she thought she saw a flicker of heat, of shock, in the depths of his. But it disappeared before she could work out if she was right, and whatever he'd been thinking was now hidden behind a mask of neutrality. She couldn't gauge how he felt about her being here. Or if he felt anything at all, for that matter. Not that he had any reason to. What they'd had had been a mutually agreed one-night stand, nothing more. She'd hardly expected the same laid-back, full-on seduction she'd been on the receiving end of when she'd initially approached him all those months ago. She wasn't expecting anything. Hoping for, yes, but expecting, no.

'Hello,' she said hoarsely, her heart pounding and her mouth dry. 'So you probably don't remember me, but—'

'I remember you.'

'Good,' she said with a shaky attempt at a smile. That made things slightly easier. At least she didn't have to first explain how they knew each other. 'How have you been?'

A shadow flitted across his expression. 'Fine. You?'

Not quite so fine, actually, although there was no way she was telling him how not fine she'd been. She had far too much to lose. 'Couldn't be better.'

'I'm delighted to hear it.'

'I can't believe I found you.'

'How hard have you been trying?'

'Very. I didn't have much to go on. Just your first name and the photo I took when we left here that night.'

He gave the briefest of nods. 'Just in case.'

'It seemed sensible.'

'You kept it.'

'As a memento.' Which, in hindsight, was deeply ironic when she'd ended up with a memento of a totally different kind. 'Anyway, I remembered that you looked comfortable at the bar. You didn't pay the bill. I wondered if you had a tab and, if you did, whether you might be a regular. Now I know differently.' She glanced around the softly lit space that contained a mahogany desk, a couple of chairs and sage green walls lined with books. 'Do you manage the club downstairs?'

'I own it.'

Right. That made sense. He'd said he worked in hospitality and he hadn't struck her as the type to take orders. 'No wonder no one threw you out for wearing jeans.'

His dark brows snapped together in a deep frown. 'What?'

'Nothing.'

'As fascinating as this trip down memory lane is, Georgie, I'm busy. So get to the point. What are you doing here? What do you want?'

He was right. The time for dithering was over. Finn had a right to know and she badly needed any support he might be prepared to offer. She stuck her hands into the back pockets of her jeans to hide the trembling and took a deep breath. 'Well, the thing is, you…we…well, basically, Finn, our one-night stand left me pregnant and as a result you have a son.'

CHAPTER TWO

WHEN FINN HAD instructed Bob to send Georgie up he hadn't given much thought to what he was expecting with regards to her appearance. On the rare occasion he'd allowed the memory of her to flow unfettered through his mind, she either sat at the bar, exuding confidence and vibrancy and dazzling him with flirty banter and smouldering smiles, or lay sprawled across his bed as morning dawned, looking flushed and tousled and sleepily sexy.

He barely recognised the on-edge, wary version standing in front of him. Her dark hair was scraped back from a face that was ghostly pale. Her eyes were dull and her cheeks hollow. Her clothes were hanging off her. Above the neckline of her white T-shirt, her collarbones stuck out, and her jeans hung loose on her hips despite her belt being tightly buckled. It was as if someone had switched off her light, and once he'd got over his shock he'd found himself wondering what had happened to her.

Now, with the bombshell she'd just dropped, he

couldn't think at all. His mind had gone blank. His pulse was thundering and a cold sweat had broken out all over his skin. His vision was blurred. The room seemed to be spinning.

'What?' he said roughly, his voice sounding as if it came from far, far away while the disorientation intensified.

'You, well, *we*, have a son,' she said. 'Josh. He's six months old.'

A son.

Josh.

Six months old.

The words flew through the air, bulldozing a path through the chaos and hitting his brain like bullets, where they pulverised the fog and cleared the way for indisputable logic and instinctive denial.

A baby?

His baby?

It was impossible.

Or at the very least improbable.

'We can't,' he said thickly, grappling for some kind of hold on this.

'We can. We do.'

'You said you were on the pill.'

'I was.'

'So what happened?'

'I don't know,' she said with a slight frown. 'I might have been sick. Or on antibiotics. I don't remember.'

Disbelief barrelled through him. 'You don't remember?'

'No.'

How could she be so cool, so calm? Could she possibly have done it deliberately? At the thought his blood chilled and his gut churned. 'How convenient.'

Her eyes narrowed. 'What are you suggesting?'

'What do you think?'

Her chin came up. 'Believe me, I did *not* plan it. I did not plan *any* of it.'

'What makes you think he's mine?'

'You're the only person I slept with at the time. The last person I slept with actually.'

'Do you expect me to believe that simply because you say so?'

'Well, yes. But it doesn't matter. I have photos,' she said, twisting slightly to rummage around in her bag before extracting her phone and fiddling with it for a moment. 'Here.' She walked over to him and held out the device. 'Take a look. Swipe left. There are lots.'

For a moment Finn stared at the phone as if it were a live grenade. His heart hammered against his ribs. He went hot, then cold. He wanted to look. He didn't want to look. He didn't know what he wanted, but it didn't seem to matter because, with a hand that wasn't entirely steady, he was reaching for the phone anyway and lowering his gaze, and one glance at the screen was enough to detonate what remained of an already shattered life. Because the baby in the photo, with his shock of thick, dark hair, laughing blue eyes, and rosy, chubby cheeks was the spitting image of him at a similar age.

The blow of recognition winded him so hard he couldn't breathe. The floor tipped beneath his feet and his knees nearly gave way. But somehow he remained upright and somehow he managed to blindly swipe through the pictures that followed, the overwhelming sense of familiarity intensifying with every passing second.

The truth of the child's parentage was undeniable.

Which meant that he was a father.

A violent rush of emotion rocked though him then, tangling up with the issues surrounding his own parentage and his feelings about Jim and Alice, which he couldn't even *begin* to unravel. And quite suddenly, out of the hot, bubbling chaos roared a protective instinct he didn't know he had and a clamouring primitive need to claim what was his above all else.

He could forget for now that Georgie had kept the existence of this child from him. He could ignore the myriad questions bombarding his head, adding to the confusion and turmoil. There'd be time for explanations and answers and analysis later. Right now he wanted—no, *needed*—to see his son.

'Where is he?' he said, handing her phone back and knowing the images on it would remain imprinted on his memory for ever.

'With a friend.'

'Take me to him.'

She stared at him for a moment, her eyebrows shooting up. 'Now?'

'I've missed all six months of my son's life,' he said, his jaw tightening and his tone chilly as he thought briefly of how much she'd denied him even if he didn't yet understand it. 'I don't intend to miss a moment longer. So yes, Georgie. Now.'

In an ideal world, Georgie would have chosen to introduce Finn to his son on neutral territory, such as a park or a café, or, really, anywhere other than the dingy bedsit she now called home. However, she hadn't thought it wise to suggest they wait until morning. Once he'd recovered from the shock, Finn's stunned disbelief had very obviously turned to simmering anger, and why would she want to provoke that?

Sitting in the passenger seat of the top-of-the-range car that he was driving through the dark streets of the city and feeling the tension still radiating off him in great waves, Georgie could understand his animosity and resentment. From his point of view, she'd deliberately kept her pregnancy and his son from him. She'd denied him key moments in Josh's life. He didn't know that she hadn't even realised she'd been pregnant until she'd given birth. He didn't know that, subsequently caught in the terrifying grip of post-partum psychosis, she hadn't had the capacity to track him down. Nor did he know that as soon as she'd recovered enough to be able to make a choice about what to do next, she'd gone about rectifying that.

Nevertheless, despite Finn's stony silence and tightly leashed displeasure, she was glad she'd managed to find him, and unbelievably relieved that he appeared to want to be involved. His reaction to her blurted revelation could have gone either way. They barely knew each other. When they'd originally met it had been all about the sex. Neither had been looking for an in-depth character analysis of the other and, while she had felt an odd sense of connection, conversation had been sparse. So, upon hearing about Josh, Finn could easily have simply handed her phone back, told her he wasn't interested and thrown her out. But he hadn't, and for that she was inordinately grateful.

She was also more than a little nervous, she had to admit as she laced her fingers tightly in her lap while her stomach began to churn. At the moment he looked to be too busy absorbing the shock of fatherhood to question why it had taken her so long to contact him, but there'd come a point when he'd ask. And when he did, what would she say? He didn't seem the sort to be satisfied with a vague 'it's been a busy time' kind of explanation, yet she'd never told anyone the full extent of what she'd been through, not even Carla.

So should she tell him? As Josh's father, he deserved to know the whole unvarnished story, and as part of her recovery it had been recommended she share it. But if she did, what would he think? What would he do? There were so many possible outcomes to this thing she'd set in motion, she thought, her stomach knotting as she stared out into the damp night. Some she could only hope for, some she dreaded, some remained unknown.

But one thing *was* certain.

While she couldn't avoid telling Finn the truth for ever, she could at least put it off until he actually asked. Maybe even beyond that. She didn't have to share it all *now*. And so, until the moment of reckoning came, until she had no option but to confess all and hope for the best, she was saying nothing.

If Finn had been asked to describe the route he'd just driven or name the neighbourhood in which he now found himself he'd have drawn a blank. The moment he'd registered the fact that he was on his way to meet his son, everything had become a blur, a great maelstrom of emotions and thoughts that he could barely absorb, let alone process. He'd had to shut down in order to be able to concentrate on driving and that was how he'd remained during the entire half-hour journey.

Now, however, as he stood in a room that was smaller than his en-suite bathroom yet apparently incorporated a bedroom, kitchen and living area, his brain was waking up and his senses were returning. He could hear the sink tap dripping rhythmically. The musty smell of damp invaded his nostrils. Behind him, the door opened and then closed behind the friend he distantly recalled being introduced to as Carla Blake, who'd been minding Josh while Georgie pitched up on his doorstep and exploded a world already off kilter.

Yet his focus was all on the cot in the corner and the child lying within it.

As he slowly walked towards it, his pulse pounded and his mouth went dry. He gripped the top rail, his knuckles white, and looked down. At the sight of the baby, lying on his back with his chubby arms out and his tiny hands curled into loose fists, his breath caught and his chest clenched.

'Do you want to pick him up?' he heard Georgie say quietly in the gloomy darkness that was illuminated by one bare lightbulb.

No. Yes. More than anything. 'I don't want to disturb him,' he said gruffly, mesmerised by the gentle rise and fall of the blanket that covered the little body.

'You won't. He takes a while to settle but once he's out, he's out. Just make sure you support his head.'

He reached down and lifted the bundle of warm baby and bedclothes to him, his throat tight. Josh snuffled and then settled against his chest, and he felt the warmth of his son's body seep into every inch of him, filling him with an emotion he didn't recognise and couldn't begin to describe.

He was so tiny, so vulnerable. And only six months old. The same age as Finn had been when he'd been adopted. Who could give up something so precious?

And why would someone want to? Had he been too difficult? Too demanding? Had his biological mother needed help in the same way it seemed Georgie did, if her descent from glorious, kick-ass girl-about-town to nervous, ghostly wreck was anything to go by? Had his own mother not had it?

Yet more unanswerable questions.

But this wasn't about him right now. This was about the baby he was holding. Already, there was nothing he wouldn't do for this child, he thought with a burning conviction he could hardly comprehend. Nothing. Never mind that he had no experience of babies. Never mind that he hadn't ever wanted responsibility of this kind before. He had it now and, whatever the circumstances, he would never abandon Josh. He would never give up responsibility for him. His son would never have cause to wonder who he was or where he came from. His son, his flesh and blood and, as far as he knew the only relative he had left in the world, would have everything that was in his power to give. And be. Because Finn may or may not have been good enough for either his biological or adoptive parents, but he'd do his damnedest to be the best for his son.

Here was his chance to right past wrongs. To try and move on from the still raw sense of betrayal and rejection he felt. To plan and to build and to focus on something greater. He was no longer alone. He now had a purpose beyond work and an escape from the chaos. And as he bent to settle the baby back in the cot, missing his sweet smell and soft weight already, he realised that, for the first time in months, the way forward was crystal clear. On this, at least, he knew exactly what to do.

Pushing aside messy, incomprehensible emotion and replacing it with easier to understand practicality, Finn straightened and turned to face Georgie, who was leaning against the one kitchen unit that the bedsit contained, looking oddly flushed and on edge.

'Here's what's going to happen,' he said, watching as her chin came up and her eyes narrowed slightly at his tone.

'Oh, yes?'

'Josh is coming home with me.'

She blinked. 'What?'

'This place isn't fit for habitation.'

'I know.'

'It's a health hazard.'

'I know.'

'He's not staying here.'

'Well, he's going nowhere without me,' she countered, and for the briefest of moments Finn toyed with the idea of telling her that he could easily take Josh without her. That he had the power and resources to remove her from the picture altogether, especially in view of her straitened circumstances, and could do so with a click of his fingers.

But he knew what it was like to grow up without a maternal figure and the gaping hole that had left in his life. The man he'd considered his father had done his best, but Finn had no doubt that much of the trouble he'd got into as a teenager had been an outlet for the delayed rage and injustice he'd felt at his mother's loss.

And then there was the situation he was currently in. He'd been denied the truth about his parentage and as a result now seethed with resentment and frustration. He wouldn't wish the torment he'd experienced as a boy and was now experiencing all over again on anyone, least of all his own child. Therefore, while Georgie was an added complication, she was a necessary one.

'Alright,' he said. 'You come too. Get what you need for tonight and I'll have the rest of your things moved to my place in the morning.'

'For how long?'

'Until we figure out what happens next.'

'We?'

At the question in her voice, Finn inwardly tensed. He'd never been part of a 'we' before. He'd never had to be, never wanted to be, had no clue how to be. But so much of his life had become uncharted territory recently, what was one patch more? 'We,' he confirmed with a brief nod before stalking over to the cupboard and reaching up to pull down a bag that had been stashed on top of it. 'Start packing. You have five minutes.'

Since her bedsit was minuscule and the possessions she had with her meagre, Georgie took only four minutes, and one of those she spent arguing with herself.

The old her would have protested loudly at being ordered around in such an autocratic fashion. She'd have demanded to know who Finn thought he was and what century he was living in before telling him where to go and shoving him out the door. But, while part of her wished she had the energy to conjure up that version of herself, the other part of her, the current Georgie, the one that was exhausted and desperate, whose judgement was skewed and who couldn't trust herself, was too grateful to put up any kind of a fight. To have someone else make the decisions and take responsibility was such a relief. Finn's authority and decisiveness imbued her with the confidence that if something should happen to her, her son would be safe. After months of not being able to make choices, she'd finally made the right one. She and Josh badly needed rescuing, and Finn being the one to do it was absolutely fine with her.

Besides, he clearly wasn't planning to leave without them and the last thing she wanted was a stand-off leading to more time spent in this place. The flat was small enough without Finn in it. With him in it, it felt even more claustrophobic. There was just so much of him too close. His size and proximity and sheer presence made her aware of him and the narrow bed in a way she hadn't expected and definitely wasn't comfortable with. When he'd lifted Josh out of the cot, and held his son's tiny body against his big, broad chest, her stomach had clenched and her entire body had flushed.

Now, as she moved around the space, around *him*, gathering the things she and Josh needed, she could feel his cool, assessing eyes on her, and his scrutiny caused her skin to prickle and a strange heat to seep through her. Not that it mattered how Finn made her feel. Even if he *had* been interested in her in the way he once had been, which clearly and thankfully he was not, she was far too fragile for that sort of thing these days, so it was just as well her libido had gone AWOL. And, besides, she had other, far more important things to focus on now.

Zipping up the bag, Georgie handed it to Finn and went to pick up their son. From above there came an ominous thud followed by a loud crash that made her jump. And as she locked the front door of the bedsit and followed Finn down the dimly lit stairs she thought that whatever his reaction when he eventually learned the truth, however precarious her position in all this, the future had to better than the past.

What a night.

A couple of hours ago all Finn had had to worry about was the frustrating lack of results the investigation into his adoption had generated. Now he had a son being tucked up in one of his spare rooms by an unexpected house guest, and he was pacing up and down in front of the wall-to-wall windows of his sitting room wondering what more the universe could possibly hurl at him. Battered didn't come close to describing how he felt about everything that had happened this evening. He'd been on the receiving end of one punch to the gut after another, and, quite frankly, how he was still standing he had no idea.

And that wasn't all he couldn't fathom. There was also the conundrum that was Georgie. What had happened to her? he wondered as he strode to the drinks cabinet and poured himself a large Scotch. When they'd originally met she'd been vivacious and sassy and intoxicating, out celebrating her twenty-fifth birthday with friends. She'd told him she worked as a lawyer specialising in defamation, that she'd just been promoted and had her eye on a partnership. She'd been living in Kensal Rise, and he specifically recalled her telling him, out there on the street in between hot, drugging kisses, that if they wanted privacy the flat she shared with three others was not the place to go.

Clearly she'd fallen on hard times, but how, and why? She'd had a baby, yes, but that wouldn't have felled the Georgie he'd met fifteen months ago. That girl would have taken a baby in her stride and carried on conquering the world.

And, on the subject of timings, why was he only finding out about his son now? Why had she taken so long to contact him? Why the secrecy? He couldn't stand secrets. Ignorance put a man at a disadvantage. It robbed him of control and rendered him powerless and weak, and he should know because he was living it.

Well, he'd had enough of being kept in the dark, he thought, knocking back half his drink and resuming his pacing. The issues surrounding his adoption aside, he had a multitude of questions to ask Georgie about Josh, and the minute she reappeared he was getting an answer to every single one of them, whether she liked it or not.

CHAPTER THREE

OBLIVIOUS TO THE drama going on around him and having remained asleep throughout, Josh handled the move to Finn's place with ease. Georgie, on the other hand, was having slightly more trouble adjusting.

She'd been too relieved to see the back of the bedsit to give much thought to where Finn might be taking them, but even if she had, the seven-star hotel where they'd spent that wild night together would not have crossed her mind. Yet here they were, in the penthouse, no less, which boasted a stunning sitting room, a state-of-the-art kitchen, a library and a terrace. The upper level comprised of three en-suite bedrooms—two of which were interconnecting—and a separate wing that had been presumably designed for staff. The chandeliers were crystal and the linen on her bed felt as though it had a thousand thread count. The walls throughout were painted a soft white, and neutral rugs covered glossy dark oak floorboards.

The whole apartment smelled divine and the sense of peace and tranquillity was like a balm to her soul.

She couldn't imagine a greater contrast to either the bedsit or the mother-and-baby unit of the psychiatric ward where she'd spent close on five months, and once again a wave of gratitude and relief washed over her, along with a hefty dose of curiosity. Who exactly was he, her knight in shining armour who owned a nightclub, drove a Lamborghini and lived in a seven-star penthouse?

Leaving the door to Josh's room ajar in case he needed her, Georgie went down the stairs, crossed the hall and stopped in the doorway to the sitting room. Finn was pacing up and down in front of the window, a near-empty glass in his hand and a deep frown creasing his forehead. When he saw her, he came to an abrupt halt. His jaw was set, his eyes were dark and intense, and something in his expression, in the way he was looking at her, sent a shiver down her spine.

'Is everything all right?' he said.

'Everything is very all right,' she replied, ignoring the shiver and mustering up her second smile of the day, which had to be a record. 'I just wanted to say thank you for everything you've done.'

'You're welcome.'

'You have no idea how grateful I am for your support.'

'Josh is my son.'

And what was she? An inconvenience? Undoubtedly. Finn didn't even want her here, she knew, remembering how he'd grudgingly told her she could come too when she'd swiftly disabused him of the idea that he'd be taking Josh without her.

'I didn't realise you actually lived here,' she said, dragging her gaze from his to sweep it around the room upon whose threshold she was hovering. 'When we met you said you were renovating. I assumed your stay was temporary.'

'I was, and in that room it was temporary.'

'But why live in a hotel?'

'Why not? I own it.'

Her gaze snapped back to his and her jaw dropped. 'You *own* it?'

'Yes.'

'As well as the club where we met?'

He gave a brief nod. 'Among other things.'

'Who *are* you?' she said, thinking that in hindsight it was a question she should have asked him last October. She still didn't even know his last name. She'd had to leave that space on Josh's birth certificate blank.

He muttered something that sounded remarkably like 'Good question', which made no sense all, but then added something that did. 'Finn Calvert,' he said. 'Look me up some time. Right now, though, we need to talk. Or rather, you do.'

As his gaze drilled into her Georgie went still, her pulse beginning to thud alarmingly fast. 'Oh, well, I really just came to say thank you and goodnight. It's been quite a day.'

'You're telling me.'

'I'm exhausted.'

'Too bad.'

'Any chance we could talk tomorrow?'

'No.'

She stuck her hands into the back pockets of her jeans and shifted her weight from one foot to the other. 'Because, ah, you know, I think I hear Josh crying.'

'No, you don't,' he said, the brusqueness of his tone reflecting the flint in his expression. 'Carry on prevaricating, Georgie, and I'll have a team of investigators looking into you so fast it'll make your head spin.'

Her eyes widened. 'Are you serious?'

'One phone call. That's all it will take. I have them on speed dial.'

Why would Finn have investigators on speed dial? was her instant thought in response to that, but it was a question for later. Because clearly the moment she'd been dreading had come. Would he really get her checked out? Or was he bluffing? Either way, it didn't really matter. She couldn't take the risk that he would do precisely as he threatened. She needed to control the narrative. She needed to provide context and detail to the cold, clinical facts. It was important that Finn understood exactly what she'd been through and sympathised. She needed him on her side. It wasn't going to be easy. In fact, it was probably going to be hell, but it had to be done.

'All right,' she said with a nod as her stomach began to churn.

'Sit down.'

On legs that felt as weak as water Georgie walked over to the sofa Finn indicated and perched on the edge of it, because to sink back into the soft cushions would result in an inadvisable degree of relaxation. She waited until he'd folded himself into one of the armchairs on the other side of the coffee table, then took a deep breath. She opened her mouth, then closed it and gave a helpless shrug. 'I'm not quite sure where to start.'

'How about by telling me why I am *only now* finding out I have a six-month-old son?'

She inwardly flinched at his tone, but it was as good a place to start as any, so she pulled herself together and mentally spooled back to the beginning. 'As I told you earlier this evening,' she said, deciding to start with the marginally easier bit, 'you're a hard man to track down.'

'You've had fifteen months.'

'Not quite.'

His brows snapped together. 'What do you mean?'

'I didn't know I was pregnant until I went into hospital with severe stomach cramps back in July and had Josh four hours later.'

The silence that suddenly fell vibrated between them, laden with astonishment and disbelief. The tick of the clock on the mantelpiece, marking the passing of the seconds that felt like minutes, was deafening.

'You didn't know you were pregnant?' he echoed eventually, the intensity of his gaze pinning her to the spot and making her squirm.

'No.'

'How is that even possible?'

'That's a question I've asked myself many times.'

'And?'

'I apparently had what's called a cryptic pregnancy,' she said, rubbing her damp palms down her denim-clad thighs. 'I carried on taking the pill, so I didn't miss a period. I didn't have morning sickness or any other signs. Because I was so busy at work I was exhausted anyway. Maybe I ate a bit more and gained a couple of pounds, but I put it down to stress-related comfort eating and cut back.' She paused to give him time to at least partly absorb what she'd said, then added, 'I realise how this must sound.'

'You can't have any idea how this sounds,' he said darkly. 'Implausible doesn't come anywhere near it.'

She couldn't blame him for his scepticism. If she'd been in his shoes she'd have dismissed the idea as ridiculous too. 'It's rare but it happens. To one in about two thousand five hundred women. I had an anterior placenta. If I ever felt any movements, I put them down to tummy rumbles. I really had no idea. When my waters broke and I started having contractions right in the middle of A&E, no one was more surprised than me.'

And wasn't that an understatement? Stunned and terrified was a more accurate description of the feelings that had stormed through her. She'd never felt physical pain like it. She'd thought she was dying. And then, when realisation had dawned, the awful, horrible confusion. How could she be pregnant? How could she not have known that she was? She wasn't stupid. She wasn't uneducated. Yet in those bewildering, petrifying moments she'd felt both.

'And subsequently?' he said bluntly, yanking her out of the chaos and confusion of the delivery room and back to the present. 'Josh is six months old.'

'The whole thing came as a massive shock to me,' she said, remembering with a chill how quickly and devastatingly her smooth, well-ordered life had been blown apart. 'I was totally unprepared. I hadn't been to any antenatal classes. I'd read no books and looked nothing up. I had no baby things and absolutely no idea what I was doing. I was thrown in at the deep end and expected to swim. It's been a busy time and insanely tough.'

His dark gaze held hers, not allowing her to look away, not letting her off the hook for one second. 'Still, Georgie. Six months.'

'I know.'

'Well?'

This was it. Her moment of reckoning. 'Could I possibly have a drink? I'm not prevaricating,' she added in response to the sharp arch of his eyebrow. 'Truly. I could just do with a bit of fortification.'

'That bad?'

Worse. 'Maybe.'

'What would you like?'

'Whatever you're having.'

'Scotch.'

'That'll do. Neat. No ice.'

With a brief nod, Finn got to his feet and strode over to the bar to fix her drink and refill his while Georgie tried to marshal her thoughts, her mouth dry and her heart pounding. How much should she tell him? What could she leave out? Was there anything she could do to make this easier? Unlikely.

'Thank you,' she said, accepting the glass he held out and taking a long, slow sip of the whisky. 'Delicious. Peaty.'

The look he gave her was forbidding, his patience clearly stretched. 'Georgie.'

Right. OK. She lowered her glass and braced herself for the guilt and shame and anguish that still crucified her even though she knew that none of it had been her fault. 'So, as I said,' she said, her voice shaking a little despite her efforts to control it, 'Josh's arrival was unexpected. It was also extremely traumatic. Not from a medical point of view—in those terms it was very easy apparently—but from a mental one. I'd left home that morning expecting to be given some strong prescription painkillers. I'd envisaged being back in time to finish the report I'd been working on. Instead, ten hours after being admitted, I went home with a tiny newborn baby.'

She looked at him, willing him to at least try to understand, however big an ask that was. 'The shock was cataclysmic. I can't begin to describe the weight of responsibility. Or the terror. I was all on my own and I had no clue what to do. I didn't know how to feed him or soothe him or anything. For forty-eight hours neither of us slept, which meant that nor did my flatmates, who were quick to point out I was now in contravention of the tenancy agreement and threatened to call the landlord.'

She glanced down at the glass she was turning in her hands, the amber liquid swirling continuously. 'I phoned my parents but they didn't answer, which I more or less expected, since we hadn't spoken for a while, so I rang Carla, the friend of mine you met earlier. She came over and scooped us up and took us back to her house. And that was great for a couple of days. I scoured the internet and read books and did a crash course in babies. And I got a bit better at changing Josh's nappies and feeding him and generally looking after him. But as the shock wore off, reality kicked in.' She looked up at Finn, who was sitting impossibly still, his eyes dark and his expression unreadable, although she guessed he wasn't missing a thing. 'Did I ever mention my five-year plan?' she asked with a slight tilt of her head.

'You mentioned having one.'

'Well, that went out the window. And so did all the structure and routine I'd created for myself and have always depended on. My life fell completely apart, and for the first time in years I had no idea where I was heading.' She shook her head, the memories swirling. 'It was all so overwhelming. I went into a sort of spin and it happened really quickly and really intensely. I wasn't sleeping much anyway, but suddenly I wasn't sleeping at all. My appetite all but disappeared. And then I started doing things that were really out of character. Like talking really fast one minute then not uttering a word for hours. I developed panic attacks and became convinced that Carla's neighbour was following me. I even called the police one night,' she said, biting her lip and remembering how scary it had been to realise on some level that what she was doing wasn't normal, wasn't right, but not knowing why she was doing it and not being able to do anything about it. 'Anyway, eventually I was admitted to the psychiatric ward of my local hospital, where I was diagnosed with post-partum psychosis.'

'Which is what?'

'Like postnatal depression but worse.' Far, *far* worse. 'I stayed there for a week and then a bed came up in a mother-and-baby unit a hundred miles away. Josh and I left there ten days ago,' she said, glossing over five intervening months, since Finn did not need to know how bad it had got before the medication had kicked in and the therapy had started to take effect. In any case she doubted she could even begin to explain how terrifying the delusions and the hallucinations and the disorientation had been, or how distressing she'd found it knowing that she wasn't well. The feelings she'd had for Josh, or, rather, the lack of them, were far too upsetting to put into words, and

Finn would never understand her gut-churning dread that the long, dark tunnel she'd been in had no end. He'd never fully understand any of it. No one could.

'And that's why it's taken so long for me to contact you,' she said, determinedly not letting those agonising memories descend but instead focusing on the man who was now looking at her a little as though he'd been slapped round the head with a wet fish. 'I wasn't in a position to do so. As soon as I was, I did. And that's it. Now you know everything.'

Everything? *Everything*?

He knew *nothing*.

Watching dazedly as Georgie finished her drink, set the glass down on the coffee table and sat back against the cushions, Finn could barely recall his own *name*. He was reeling too hard, too stunned and shattered to be able to make head or tail of anything. Whatever explanation he could possibly have envisaged, none would have come anywhere near the one she'd just given him.

That she was telling the truth was without doubt. He might have had suspicions initially—who wouldn't?—but not for long. No one would make up such a story, and no one could fake the emotion that had emanated from her, despite her attempts to contain it. When she'd been talking about what she'd been through, her voice had cracked and her eyes had become twin pools of pain. Her hands had trembled and her anguish had been palpable, and her obvious distress had cut right through him.

On one level he could identify with some of what had initially happened to her. He knew what it was like to have your life turned upside down and your plans destroyed. He'd experienced the sort of catastrophic shock that imploded your world, and the subsequent feeling of being utterly at sea. In that respect their recent histories were not unalike.

As for the rest, however, he couldn't *begin* to imagine what she'd been through. He thought he'd been having a rough time, but compared with her past six months, his had been a breeze. Giving birth like that must have been terrifying. Finding herself wholly and solely responsible for a tiny, helpless human being that came with no instruction manual must have been petrifying.

And then afterwards... God, he didn't even know what post-partum psychosis was. But it sounded horrendous, like hell on earth. Georgie hadn't gone into detail about her stay in hospital but what she *had* revealed had been harrowing to listen to, let alone to actually live through, so how had she got through it? *Had* she got through it? Well, clearly she'd recovered at least to *some* extent because she and Josh were here, not that it was any thanks to him.

He should have been there, he thought, a white-hot streak of regret and guilt suddenly burning through the defences he hadn't had time to shore up. He should have known. Never mind that he couldn't have. Never mind that her recent experience was no one's fault, not even his. And never mind that even if he *had* been around he probably wouldn't have known her well enough to recognise the out-of-character behaviour or any of the other signs that indicated she was ill.

What mattered was that he hadn't been there for his father, and he hadn't been there for Georgie and Josh either. History had apparently repeated itself and that ended right now because, while he hadn't been able to help his father or the Georgie of then, he *could* help her now. In whatever way she needed, whenever she needed it. He wouldn't let her, *them*, down.

'How are you doing now?' he asked gruffly, aware suddenly that she was looking at him with the expectation of some sort of response.

'Better. Much better.'

'And Josh?'

She released a long, slow breath and the troubled expression that flitted across her face made his chest tighten with renewed regret that things hadn't been different for her.

'I'd like to be able to say that I've totally bonded with him and everything's great,' she said carefully. 'But the truth is that, while I *am* getting there, it's a work in progress. For a long time I couldn't look after him properly. I couldn't even look after myself. He was cared for by hospital staff so we didn't get a chance to create that connection that everyone talks about and I missed many milestones.' She shifted on the sofa and frowned for a moment as if something had suddenly occurred to her. 'But maybe subconsciously I knew that there'd be a time when I was OK because I took photos and kept a diary. I did everything that was recommended. And I think it's working. Now I find him fascinating. I can't imagine not having him around, and when I think... Well... I'd rather not think about any of it actually.'

As she tailed off Finn could see the undeserved guilt and shame in her eyes, which deepened his regret, but he could also recall the fire in her expression when she'd stood there in her flat and told him that Josh was going nowhere without her. Perhaps the bond between them was stronger than she was able to recognise right now.

And, seeing as how he was now thinking about where she and their son had been living... 'How on earth did you end up in the bedsit?' he asked, seeking some sort of refuge from the emotions battering him by switching to practicalities.

Georgie blinked at the sudden change in subject and visibly shuddered. 'It was all I could afford.'

'What happened to your job?'

'A couple of weeks after I was admitted to hospital I got an email from my company saying that as a result of restructuring my position no longer existed.'

He frowned. 'A coincidence?'

'I doubt it. But I was in no state to object. The pay-off was pathetic.'

Bastards. 'What about your parents?'

She gave a wry smile. 'Even if we were on speaking terms, a hippie commune is the very last place I would choose to raise a child. Believe me, I have first-hand experience and it wasn't all that great.'

'Friends?'

'It's all been too much for many of them and I was too far away. And I couldn't ask any more of Carla. She'd already done so much…' She paused for a second, swallowing hard as a quick frown creased her brow, seemingly lost in thought, but a second later she'd rallied. 'Besides, she has her own life to lead. Her job is insane.'

'Remind me to thank her some time,' he muttered, not wanting to even think about how alone Georgie had been, how desperate she must have felt.

'She's going to be intrigued by this latest turn of events. If she wasn't going away for work tomorrow I have no doubt she'd be banging on the door first thing.'

'She's welcome any time.'

For a moment she didn't say anything, just looked at him, her eyes shimmering with gratitude that he did not deserve when his help had come so late. 'You have no idea how glad I am to have found you.'

His pulse thudded heavily and something shifted in his chest. 'Likewise.'

'You may not think that when Josh is screaming the place down.'

'The walls are soundproofed.'

'That's a relief.' She gave him a faint smile. 'So. Is there anything else you'd like to know?'

Probably. No doubt there were questions he hadn't even thought of. But in all honesty he couldn't take any more tonight. He was utterly drained. God only knew how she had the strength to smile after everything she'd just told him. But then, compared with what had come before, he supposed relaying an account of it would have been a walk in the park. Her courage was staggering. Her resilience was a thing of awe. He'd thought that he was pretty tough, but he had nothing on her. He had nothing at all. 'We'll talk more in the morning.'

CHAPTER FOUR

WHILE GEORGIE GOT ready for bed she reflected that, as she'd suspected, it hadn't been easy telling Finn her story. In fact, reliving events even on the most superficial level had been horrible and exhausting. But it had also been cathartic. The weight and severity of what she'd been through had been overwhelming and now that she'd shared some of it she felt slightly lighter, as if a socking great rock was beginning to lift from her shoulders.

It had helped that Finn was such a good listener. He'd offered no opinion and no judgement. He'd just sat there letting her talk. Of course, it was entirely probable that there'd simply been too much to take in for him to be able to respond with anything more than the most basic of questions, but nevertheless she was grateful for his restraint. And his involvement. It was such a relief to know that she was no longer in this alone, but who exactly was she in it with?

Remembering his suggestion to look him up, Georgie fished her phone out of her bag, then climbed under the gorgeously soft covers of the enormous bed. She tapped his name—complete with surname—into a search engine and spent the next fifteen minutes clicking on links and reading articles.

But, instead of cementing the feeling of safety and security that had been burgeoning inside her, what she discovered blew it wide apart. Because, while she'd already guessed that Finn was successful— what with owning a hotel and a club, driving a top-of-the-range car and living in a penthouse—never in her wildest nightmares would she have imagined that he was one of the richest men in the world.

Yet he was.

His company owned hotels and bars and clubs and restaurants and he was worth billions. He'd worked his way up from virtually nothing to become a top player in his industry. His power was immense and his influence was wide-reaching, and it was suddenly terrifying because now she couldn't help thinking that what if, once he'd had time to absorb the truth about where she'd been and what she'd been doing for the last six months and reflect on it, he considered her unfit to be a mother to his son? What if he tried to take Josh away from her in earnest? She wouldn't stand a chance. If it came to a custody battle, a judge would take one look at her with her recent mental health record and another at Finn with his billions and that would be that. Case closed. She was sure of it.

She'd gone into so much detail, she thought, a wave of nausea rolling up from her stomach to her throat. About her behaviour. About her conflicted feelings towards Josh. She hadn't told him the worst of what had happened, but it had been enough. More than enough.

Her vision blurred and a cold sweat broke out all over her skin at the thought of how much she'd revealed, how vulnerable she'd made herself. What had seemed such a relief a mere half an hour ago now felt like the biggest mistake of her life. What did he think about it all? What could he be plotting? How could she possibly sleep, not knowing what he intended to do next? Morning was too far away. She needed clarification now.

Throwing back the covers, Georgie leapt out of bed and crossed the hall. When she reached his room she didn't think to knock; all she could focus on was protecting Josh and herself and fighting her corner. She opened the door and strode in. Finn was standing next to the bed, wearing a look of surprise on his face and nothing but a towel wrapped around his hips.

'I have one more thing to say,' she said hoarsely, barely able to hear her own voice above the thundering of her heart, 'and it can't wait until morning.'

'What is it?'

'I am not perfect. I am still in recovery. But I can do this. And I am capable. I am not a risk to either myself or Josh and I never will be. I will not let you take my son away from me. I will *never* let you take him away from me.' She stopped, breathing hard, the force of the emotion swirling through her nearly knocking her off her feet.

'What are you talking about?' he said with a frown. 'I have no intention of taking him away from you.'

'You did earlier,' she fired back. 'In the bedsit.'

'Yet here you are.'

His dark, steady gaze was locked on hers and something in it, together with the very valid point he'd just made, calmed some of the wildness whipping about inside her. 'How can I believe you?'

'You have my word.'

'I don't know you well enough yet to know if that means anything.'

'Then you'll just have to trust me.'

'How can I?'

'My mother died when I was ten,' he said, a shadow flitting across his face. 'I know what it's like to grow up without one. It is not something I'd ever wish to inflict on my own son. Josh will always know both his parents.'

His words sank in and she swallowed hard. 'Do you really mean that?'

'I do,' he said with a brief nod.

'OK, then,' she said, letting out a breath as the tension and steam inside her eased. 'Good. Thank you.'

'Was there anything else?'

'Ah, no. Sorry to barge in like that. I didn't realise you were…' What? What had he been doing? Her gaze, which had been fixed firmly to his, broke away to travel over the rest of him. His hair was damp. The exposed skin of his broad, muscled chest gleamed in the soft golden light of the room. He'd clearly just come out of the shower, and, now that she wasn't all fired up with needing to say her piece, it hit her with the force of a freight train that she was standing in his bedroom and he was practically naked.

'…In the middle of something,' she finished lamely, feeling her cheeks burn as she dragged her eyes back up.

'Obviously not.'

'Sorry.'

'Next time, knock.'

There wouldn't be a next time. 'Right. Yes.' She cleared her throat. 'Of course. Sorry. Again.'

His dark blue gaze glittered. 'Goodnight, Georgie.'

'Goodnight.'

When Georgie woke up the following morning, it was with great reluctance. Not only was she so warm and cosy she didn't want to leave the cocoon she'd fashioned out of the duvet, but she was also still utterly wiped out.

It had taken her a long while to fall asleep. She hadn't been able to stop thinking about everything that had happened the evening before, starting with the moment Finn's bouncer had told her to stop and wait. She could scarcely believe any of what had subsequently unfolded was real, yet here she was, safe and warm and no longer wretched and desperate and on her own.

And then there were the dreams she'd had once she *had* managed to drift off, dreams that seemed to involve her and Finn and what might have happened if, instead of fleeing his room, she'd walked up to him and rid him of his towel. Details of what followed were hazy and the whole idea of it was absurd, of course, but nevertheless, why she should be going there, even subconsciously, was a bit baffling.

As was the fact that light was streaming in through the blinds, which, seeing as how it was January, meant that it must be late.

Too late.

And too quiet.

And then mid-yawn, mid-stretch, it suddenly struck Georgie that she'd woken of her own accord and she froze, panic coursing through her. Why hadn't Josh woken her as usual?

Something was wrong.

Icy cold and shaking, she threw back the duvet and leapt out of bed. She raced to his cot in the room next door, only to find it empty.

Where was he? Who had taken him? What had Finn done?

Terror gripped every inch of her. Her knees gave way and she had to cling to the rail of the cot to stop crumpling to the floor. Her heart was thundering and she felt as if she'd been cleaved in two. She couldn't have lost her son, having only just found him. Fate couldn't be that cruel. But where had he gone? What was she going to do?

And then a burst of sound pierced the fog of alarm and desperation, rooting her to the spot and pricking her ears.

A gurgle. A stream of giggles. A low masculine voice.

Slowly coming out of her daze, Georgie felt reason return and the terror subside. Josh was OK. Everything was all right.

Still trembling, her pulse still racing, she followed the sounds to the glossy kitchen, where she found Josh sitting in a brand-new pristine high chair, with Finn beside him, feeding him. Upon the black granite worktop that looked as if it had never met so much as a chopping board sat plastic bottles and tubs of milk powder, bibs and muslins, tiny plates and cutlery, all the paraphernalia an infant required and lots more besides.

Stunned into immobility, she watched Finn expertly spoon food into Josh's waiting mouth, with hardly any of it splattering onto the tray or the floor, and to her shame she felt a surge of resentment. Where had all this stuff come from? How did Finn know in less than twenty-four hours what it had taken her months to figure out? She'd found feeding her son unbelievably fraught. She'd been riddled with anxiety and uncertainty, convinced she was somehow going to poison him by getting the proportions wrong. She still was on occasion. Yet Finn made it look so easy. Unfair didn't *begin* to describe the situation.

'Good morning,' he said, shooting her a dark glance which he then raked over her, his jaw tightening minutely. 'Did you sleep well?'

Ish… 'Yes,' she replied, ignoring his obvious, if unfathomable, objection to her pyjamas. 'Did you?'

He muttered something non-committal and turned his attention back to Josh. 'Help yourself to some breakfast.'

She looked in the direction in which he'd nodded, and at the sight of the array of pastries and fruit enticingly arranged on a great silver platter her mouth watered and her stomach rumbled. God, it had been a long time since she'd come across anything so appetising. She filled a plate and then took a seat opposite him.

'How long has Josh been up?' she asked, pouring herself some coffee and taking a fortifying sip.

'A couple of hours.'

She frowned. 'I didn't hear him.'

'You were dead to the world.'

'But you weren't.'

'No. I was doing some research.'

No need to ask into what.

'And some thinking.'

'Oh?' she said, picking up a *pain au chocolat*. 'About what?'

'What happens next.'

'Which is?' She took a bite and nearly groaned with pleasure.

'Firstly,' he said, his gaze dipping to her mouth for a second and darkening, 'I've hired a nanny.'

Georgie nearly choked on a flake of pastry. A nanny? Why would he do that? Didn't he trust her? Didn't he think she could cope? Just because she'd had a lie-in this morning didn't mean she couldn't. And what else had he unilaterally arranged? Lawyers? Psychiatrists? What? Her heart was beating too fast. Her breathing was too shallow. She had to calm down.

'I said I could do this,' she told him, her mouth dry and the *pain au chocolat* turning to lead in her stomach.

'I don't doubt it,' he replied, all steady calm and cool self-assurance.

'Are you sure about that?'

'Yes. However, you've been ill. You need rest.'

'I need to be with Josh. We need to strengthen our bond.'

'I suspect your bond is stronger than you realise.'

At that, hot anger flared into life inside her. How dared he be so patronising? What did he know about anything? One night of research and he was an expert? She didn't think so.

'Another stranger in his life will be confusing,' she said, ignoring the tiny stab of guilt she felt when he visibly flinched. 'I don't want a nanny looking after my son. I don't need that kind of help.'

'Well, perhaps I do,' he countered with a bluntness that whipped the wind from her sails.

This wasn't just about her any more, she realised with a shock. She had to consider the situation from his point of view too. His life had irrevocably changed overnight. This was new territory for him. She had to give him a break. And maybe, on occasion, she *did* need the kind of help a nanny would provide.

'When does she start?'

'The day after tomorrow.'

'Full-time?'

'Days only.'

'OK, fine,' she said, a bit grudgingly nevertheless. 'But you should have discussed it with me first.'

He gave her a long look and then gave a brief nod. 'My mistake.'

'From what I read last night, you don't make mistakes.'

'This isn't business.'

'No.' Although quite what it was she had no idea. 'And secondly?'

'Secondly, I'm taking some time off work.'

Oh? At the thought of him being around to witness her struggles and her ineptitude, her skin prickled. But, seeing as how she'd requested his support and he'd supplied it, she could hardly protest. 'I read you were a workaholic.'

'That was before I became a father,' he said, glancing at Josh, who was banging a spoon on the tray of his high chair, his expression softening a fraction. 'I intend to get to know my son. Everything he is and everything he does. Nothing is more important.'

He meant it too, Georgie thought, her resentment morphing into wistfulness as she watched Finn watching his son with an intensity and interest she'd never had from either of her parents. It was silly and slightly shameful to be jealous of a six-month-old, but there it was.

'You'll need to show me what to do,' he added, sliding his gaze back to her, the lingering warmth in his eyes easing some of the numbness that filled so much of her.

'*You're* asking *me* for advice?' she said with a quick glance at the extensive baby kit he'd somehow masterfully amassed.

'You have a head start on me.'

'Not much of one.'

'Yes, well, I know nothing. Before last night I'd never been this close to a baby, let alone had to take care of one.'

Slightly taken aback by his frank admission, because in her experience rare was the man who confessed he needed help, although she supposed that, unlike many men of her acquaintance, Finn had nothing to prove, she asked, 'So where did all this come from?'

'My COO's off on maternity leave. I called her and she sent me a list of essentials. And that's it.'

It was strangely reassuring to know that she wasn't the only one at sea. 'Well, I'll *try*.'

'OK, then,' he said, flashing her a sudden smile that lit up his whole face and momentarily dazzled her. 'Let's do this.'

An hour later, Finn found himself in Josh's room, grappling with the concept of a wriggly, giggly child, a nappy that needed changing and not enough hands.

How could such a simple thing be so difficult? Georgie had told him what to do before heading off for a bath and it hadn't seemed that complicated, yet he'd been at it for ten minutes now with no success. His company tax returns were easier to get a handle on than this.

Nevertheless, there was absolutely nothing he'd rather be doing. One of the many reasons it was taking so long and proving so tricky was because he kept being distracted by his son. He'd only just managed to lay him flat when he'd found himself transfixed by the curve of his right eyebrow for a good thirty seconds, by which point Josh had kicked several crucial pieces of equipment to the floor and they'd had to start all over again.

At least Georgie had left him to it and wasn't around to witness his rare incompetence and his even rarer sentimental fascination with another human being. With any luck she had no idea either of how her brief but disturbing foray into his bedroom last night had affected him. In she'd barged, all stunningly fired up one moment and then staring at him as if she wanted to gobble him up the next. He'd caught a flash of hunger in her eyes and heard the breathlessness of her voice, and a reciprocal burst of hot, dizzying desire had shot through him. After she'd left he'd had to take another shower, a cold one, and he had the feeling that he'd be taking many more if his response to how she'd looked walking into the kitchen this morning, all warm and flushed and tousled, was anything to go by.

Finally achieving the impossible and sticking the nappy tabs in the right places and then somehow managing to guide two wriggling legs back into a pair of tiny trousers, Finn lifted Josh off the table. As he did so their eyes met and held, and as they stared at each other, stock still and fascinated, he felt something deep inside him twist. The physical similarities he and his son shared were startling. He hadn't resembled either Alice or Jim at all. And suddenly he wondered, did he look like either or both of his biological parents? Did he have his father's nose? His mother's eyes? A grandparent's mouth? Would he recognise them if he ever had the chance to meet them? Would they have the same connection he felt with Josh?

Would he *ever* find the answers he sought?

'How did you get on?' said Georgie, coming into what was now the nursery and snapping him out of his impossibly frustrating thoughts.

'It's harder than it looks.'

'You'll get the hang of it. If I can, anyone can.'

Hmm. 'Did you want something?'

'The rest of my things have just arrived. I was wondering if you'd like to see the photos of Josh that I took while we were in hospital.'

'I would.'

She took a couple of steps towards him until she was closer—too close—and shifted her glance from him to Josh. 'He looks so like you,' she said, her voice filled with warmth and softness.

He took a step back, his pulse skipping a beat. 'Yes.'

'Maybe we could compare pictures. Of both of you as newborns.'

Impossible. There weren't any of him at that age. When going through his father's attic he'd found a few photos of himself at six months old, and endless photos of himself older than Josh was now, but none younger, which he'd wondered about until he'd found the certificate of his adoption and it all made sense. 'Another time.'

'All right.'

'I'd like you to talk me through Josh's routine,' he said, carrying his son out of the nursery, which was far too small and claustrophobic with Georgie in it too, down the stairs and into the sitting room.

'To be honest, he doesn't really have one.'

'Do you want him to?'

'More than anything. What do you think?'

'I'm as big a fan of structure as you are.'

'Be still my beating heart.'

And, as his gave a great thud in response to the smile she flashed at him, Finn set Josh gently on the mat on the floor and thought that the least said about that particular organ, beating, thudding, lurching or doing anything else for that matter, the better.

The following morning, Georgie stepped through the front door of the apartment and dropped her bag on the console table. The therapy session she'd just had had been a mixed bag, as indeed had the last twenty-four hours.

On the one hand, as she'd told the therapist, she was now glad Finn had made her tell him some of what had happened to her. If she did inevitably have the odd day when things got a bit much, and her anxieties descended, it would come as no surprise to anyone, which in turn would ease some of the stress of it.

Furthermore, she'd discovered that a problem shared was literally a problem halved. Not that Josh was a problem, of course, but undoubtedly, on a practical level at least, parenting with Finn was a whole lot easier than doing it on her own. She hadn't realised how much she'd relied on the support of other people when she and Josh had been in hospital or how stressful she'd found having to be constantly on the alert without it.

And, although it was early days and she couldn't be certain the novelty might not wear off, Finn certainly seemed to be reliable. Last night he'd told her he'd take the night shift, since a grizzly Josh had a tooth coming through, and this morning at dawn she'd gone through to the nursery to find him sprawled in a chair with their son, arms out, draped across his chest, both fast asleep. One big hand had lain splayed on Josh's back, protective, warm and secure, and the sight had melted her heart.

However, warring with the feelings of relief, gratitude and warmth were the resentment and jealousy that she'd experienced over breakfast yesterday and which hadn't entirely ebbed. To her shame, despite Finn's generosity and support, she'd been relieved to see his initial uncertainty and clumsiness when left on his own to deal with the messier side of parenting. Not that it had lasted for long. His natural competence had soon risen to the challenge, and watching him interact with Josh subsequently, his ease and instant adoration highlighting her own failings, was like a twist of the knife in her chest, every single time.

Such as now, she thought, coming to an abrupt halt in the doorway to the sitting room, her breath catching in her throat. Finn and Josh were lying on their fronts on the floor, nose to nose. Josh was grabbing at Finn's mouth, giggling and squealing while Finn, resting his chin on his hands, was patiently letting him, simply staring back at him in awe.

She ought to be glad that he'd taken to fatherhood so well, she knew, taking in the scene and feeling an ache throb deep within her. She ought to be relieved

that he seemed to be taking his responsibilities so seriously. She shouldn't be jealous of a connection that
was instant and deep. She shouldn't feel bitter about
the fact that it was a connection she'd been denied.
She should be glad that Finn looked to be taking an
approach to parenthood that was so different to her
own experience.

She was all that, and she wished she could shake
off the negativity and focus on the positives, but she
couldn't and she lived in fear that at any moment
the ugly emotions swirling around inside her would
rise up and make her say or do something she might
regret.

'How did it go?' he asked, glancing up at her, his
eyebrows raised.

'All good.'

'Come and join us.'

She gathered her hair up and gave it a quick twist,
then with a small smile shook her head. 'Maybe later.'

CHAPTER FIVE

THE ARRIVAL OF the nanny went some way to easing the volatility of Georgie's emotions. Mrs Gardiner was a sensible woman of sixty with decades of experience and spot-on instincts, whom Josh adored. Discreet, non-interfering and non-judgemental, she knew exactly when to step in with a subtle suggestion and when to back off and leave Georgie to it.

As the days passed and they settled into a rhythm, Georgie's strength and well-being improved. Her belief in herself and her confidence grew, and gradually her insecurities and doubts lessened. The more she saw how Finn's continuing interest and involvement benefited their son, the less she saw him as a threat, and her resentment and jealousy started to fade.

Unfortunately, with this progress came a growing awareness of Finn not just as a father but as a man, a man with whom she'd once burned up the sheets. The excruciating moment she'd barged into his bedroom was becoming harder to forget. The dreams she'd had immediately afterwards were getting worse and more lurid in their detail, and now, alarmingly, during the day too the image of him standing there in just a towel, wet and semi-naked, kept popping into her head, sending her temperature soaring and stealing her breath.

That he was gorgeous went without saying, and it was true that she'd developed something of an obsession with his strong and capable hands that had once been so hot and skilful on her body but were now so infinitely careful and gentle when handling Josh. But it was more than his many physical attractions that tugged at something deep inside her. It was his endless patience, the wholehearted attention he paid Josh and his rock-solid dependability. His self-confidence and reassuring air of authority. For a girl who'd had none of that growing up, these traits of his were incredibly appealing.

As a whole, Finn was heady stuff and she found it all very confusing. She'd become increasingly tongue-tied around him and went bright red whenever she did manage to hold any sort of conversation with him, and it was a mortifying state of affairs because she'd never been the bashful sort.

It was therefore a good thing that in the evenings, once Josh had gone to sleep, Finn disappeared to catch up on work. At least she was spared agonising small talk over supper while trying to sort out how she felt about everything and trying not to remember the things they'd once done together, even if they probably did need to get to know one another better on a level other than the carnal.

However, things would settle down soon enough, she reminded herself for the hundredth time as she navigated the pushchair into the café where she'd arranged to meet Carla for an impromptu weekday lunch a week later. It was a period of adjustment, that was all.

And once they had adjusted she and Finn would discuss how to move forwards. Even though he'd already told her that he'd take care of both her and Josh financially, which was one less thing to have to worry about, at some point in the not-too-distant future she'd have to dip her toe back into the world of work and see if anyone would employ her. She'd loved her job. She couldn't imagine not ever working again. Mrs Gardiner had said she would stay as long as she was needed, so maybe she'd even go with them when Georgie and Josh eventually moved out of the penthouse and set up home somewhere conveniently near by.

Spying Carla sitting at a table in the corner that had plenty of space for a pushchair beside it and feeling a grin spread across her face, Georgie made her way over.

'Hi!' she said, giving Carla, who stood up, a quick kiss on the cheek.

'Wow, you look better,' said her friend with a smile.

'I feel better,' Georgie replied, taking off her coat

and sitting down. In honour of the outing she'd styled her hair for the first time in months and slapped on some make-up. This morning she'd looked at herself in the mirror and noticed with delight that the colour had returned to her cheeks and her eyes had regained the sparkle she'd missed so much. 'Practically back to normal.'

'Hotel penthouse life is clearly suiting you.'

'It is. I don't have to lift a finger, so I'm getting plenty of rest. Finn has food sent up and it's so delicious I've put on a stone.'

'You needed to.'

Georgie grinned. 'I know.'

'Any regrets?'

Only that she turned into an awkward teen with a crush whenever Finn was around. 'None at all.'

'I'm glad.'

'So am I.'

'And how's my gorgeous little boy?'

'Thriving.'

'Can I have a cuddle?'

'Of course.' Reaching down, Georgie unstrapped Josh, eased him out of the pushchair and handed him over. 'How was your trip?' she asked, watching as her son tried to grab Carla's necklace and feeling her heart squeeze when he giggled.

'Good,' said Carla, taking his chubby little hand and wiggling it instead. 'Exhausting. The usual obstacles to overcome but nothing I couldn't handle.

Far more interestingly, how's your hot baby-daddy flatmate?'

Eeew. 'Please don't ever refer to him like that again.'

Carla grinned. 'Is he as gorgeous as you remember?'

Every bit of it. And much more so now she'd caught glimpses of the man beneath the very attractive surface. 'Yup,' she said, automatically thinking about him in a towel and inevitably, irritatingly, feeling herself blush.

'Aha!' said Carla, who was extremely perceptive and knew her way too well. 'Intriguing. I sense a story. Once we've ordered, you need to tell me absolutely *everything.*'

Where the hell were they?

Listening to Georgie's voicemail recording click in for the dozenth time, Finn hung up and tossed his phone onto the buttoned ottoman that had once remained uncluttered but now served as a general dumping ground for things that hadn't existed in his life pre-Georgie and Josh.

He'd arrived home half an hour ago after a lengthy meeting, expecting to be greeted by the noise and activity that over the last two weeks he'd become used to, and that unexpectedly he'd begun to welcome, in fact, since it provided a distraction to the continued lack of progress the investigation agency was making in locating his real parents.

Instead, he'd been met with silence. Georgie hadn't left a note and she wasn't answering her phone, and it was Mrs Gardiner's day off. He had no idea where anyone was, and he didn't like it. He didn't like it one little bit, not least because it had just occurred to him that Georgie could waltz out of here taking Josh with her at any point. In fact, he thought as his pulse skipped a beat and he suddenly went icy cold, she could well have already done so.

When they'd first moved in she'd badly needed his support. She'd been in no fit state to take control and only too happy to let him dictate what was going to happen. Now, however, she was stronger, fitter. He'd watched the transformation happen—the hollows in her cheeks slowly filling out, a healthy pink replacing the grey tinge to her skin. He'd witnessed with a strange sort of pride her increased confidence and the growing ease with which she interacted with their son.

In response to the way she'd blossomed, he'd experienced an annoying and frustrating surge in attraction, which he had no hope of assuaging, since not only was she still incredibly vulnerable, but it was also blindingly obvious that she had absolutely no desire to explore the possibility that the chemistry that had once consumed them still existed. She could barely even look at him and when she did she clearly found it uncomfortable, which was why he absented himself every evening. He claimed he had to work, but he didn't because, despite being in total control of his company for the last thirteen years or so, he'd recently discovered that he had no problem with delegation.

Instead he spent the time in the basement of the hotel, either whipping up a storm in the gym or ploughing up and down the pool to ease the need and frustration pummelling through him. How could she not share the attraction he felt so strongly? he found himself wondering. Exactly how fragile was she still? And then, why the hell couldn't he seem to stop thinking about his son in relation to his father?

The longer he spent with Josh, the greater the connection that built and the deeper the fascination that grew, the more he regretted the fact that the two had never had the chance to meet. Would his father's illness have been easier for them both to handle if they'd known about Josh? Would it have brought happiness? Would it have bought them both more time? It was a regret that was irrational and made no sense. His so-called father deserved no sympathy and no forgiveness. Yet that didn't stop the insidious wistfulness creeping into his head and taking root.

Frustratingly, no amount of exercise seemed to clear his head or calm his body, and Georgie's un-explained absence this afternoon was making things worse. Although he could work out from the fact that nothing seemed to have been taken that she probably *hadn't* gone for good, as she got even better there'd be less keeping her here, and that was a concern.

He wasn't losing Josh, he thought with a touch of

grim desperation as he stalked into the kitchen to make himself some coffee. Not now. Not ever. He was loving the time they were spending together getting to know each other. He found him utterly intriguing and was continually staggered by the depth of the bond he shared with this tiny person, for whom he would willingly die.

Yet how could he stop Georgie from walking out and taking Josh with her? With what she'd been through he had some leverage but using it did *not* appeal. The legal route would take months. Realistically, there was nothing he could do.

Unless…

He froze suddenly, his pulse racing and his head spinning.

There was one way. A bit dramatic possibly, but, without doubt, binding.

Commitment had never held any interest for him before. He'd witnessed Jim's grief when Alice had died, all the more potent for his restraint, as well as the lingering sadness that had tinged his life for the remaining twenty years he'd had of it. Finn had no desire to experience any of that for himself, regardless of the examples of happiness set by the one or two of his friends who had married. To date he'd never met anyone who'd threatened the status quo and right now, with the frustration and confusion he felt over his identity, he was not in any position to enter into a relationship with anyone.

Apart from his son.

During the two months following Jim's death, he'd found himself dwelling increasingly on the idea of love and what it meant, and finding it tainted because surely lying and betrayal formed no part of it. But Josh had made him reconsider. The strength of his feelings for this tiny person, *his* tiny person, blew him away. He was *not* losing him and he was *not* having Josh growing up not knowing him. So if hitching himself to Georgie was the price he had to pay to secure Josh then that was what he'd do and to hell with the X-rated dreams it might give him and the additional discomfort it would no doubt cause her.

His swift but absolutely right decision had nothing whatsoever to do with a subconscious desire to create the family that deep down he might possibly crave. Or the fact that he'd got used to having them around and couldn't stomach the thought of the silence and emptiness their absence would bring. And of course he wasn't worried about abandonment and rejection and being left all alone again. What he'd come up with was a purely practical solution to an unthinkable possibility and a means to eliminating a very great risk, and he'd implement it just as soon as she turned up.

Which, *finally*, he thought darkly as he heard the sound of the front door opening and closing and abandoned the coffee to stride towards it, was now.

'Where have you been?' he said curtly, relief, a shot of unwanted desire and something else undefinable making him sound short.

Having parked the pushchair just inside the door, Georgie glanced up at him, her eyebrows raised no doubt in response to his tone. 'Out,' she said, turning her attention to Josh, unbuckling him and lifting him free.

'Where?'

'We had lunch with Carla.'

'I called.'

'My phone ran out of battery.'

'It's late.'

'We were chatting. I lost track of time.'

'You should have left a note.'

As she fitted Josh to her hip, she turned to him, her eyes narrowing minutely and her chin jutting up. 'Are you implying I'm somehow accountable to you, Finn?'

No. Yes. Dammit. 'No.'

'So why are you so cross?'

'You weren't here when I got home. That's never happened before. I was worried.'

She froze, tension suddenly pouring off her as the colour bled from her face. 'Josh is fine,' she said, her voice tight. 'Truly. Look.'

What? No. She couldn't believe that he'd think she'd hurt him, could she? Hell, just how bad had things got? 'That wasn't what I meant at all.'

'Really?'

'No,' he said with a decisive shake of his head.

'Then what did you mean?'

There was no way he could explain the emotions

that had ripped through him when it had occurred to him that she and Josh might have gone for good. He wasn't entirely sure he fully understood them himself. Perhaps it would be best to get to the point. 'I have a proposal.'

Her gaze turned quizzical, wary. 'What kind of a proposal?'

'A way forward that will suit us all. Permanently.'

She frowned. 'By "proposal" you don't mean marriage, do you?'

'No.'

'Phew. Thank goodness for that.'

'I wouldn't go thanking goodness just yet.'

'Why not?'

'Because instead, you and I are going to enter into a civil partnership.'

If Georgie hadn't been holding on quite so tightly to Josh she might well have dropped him in shock. A civil partnership? Was Finn being serious? He couldn't be. And yet he didn't look as if he was joking. His jaw was set and he wasn't smiling. His gaze was fixed on hers with an intensity that was both unnerving and oddly exciting. He clearly meant every word.

'What on earth makes you think *that's* a good idea?' she asked, ignoring the little leap of her pulse and concentrating on the fact that a civil partnership may not technically be marriage but it was just as much of a commitment and equally unnecessary.

'It will provide security for Josh.'

Not 'would' but 'will', she noticed. So this wasn't a hypothetical proposal. Finn had given it quite a bit of thought already and evidently considered it a fait accompli. Too bad for him that she didn't. 'He already has security without it,' she pointed out. 'We've added your name to his birth certificate and he now carries your surname instead of mine. Plus financially you've set him up for life.'

'That's not enough.'

Of course it was enough. It was more than enough. So what was going on? What more security could Josh have or need? Unless it wasn't only Josh Finn was thinking of. 'Is this in some way about you?' she asked, since there was absolutely no chance it was about her.

Something flickered in the depths of his eyes, something that suggested she'd hit the nail on the head. 'Why would it be about me?'

Hmm. 'You do know that I have no intention of ever preventing Josh from seeing you or vice versa, don't you? Even if I wanted to, which I don't, I don't see how it would be possible.'

'I have no doubt you mean that at the moment.'

Ouch. 'Don't you trust me?'

'It's early days.'

'I'm well aware of that,' she said coolly, still stinging at the realisation he didn't see her progress in the same light as she did.

'Then you'll understand why a formal arrangement is necessary.'

'I can understand why you think it might be, but I don't agree.'

'It will benefit you, too.'

Oh? 'In what way?' she asked, transferring Josh to the other hip.

'Commit to me and you'll have the stability you admitted you need. You'll never want for anything again.'

Well, materially that might be true, yet he'd promised her that already. And what about him? What advantages would it have for him? Was he somehow hoping for a friends-with-benefits sort of thing? He'd better not be. 'What would you get from it?'

'Peace of mind.'

'Anything else?'

'No.'

Right. So not sex. Obviously. Stupid of her. Why would she even have thought it when he showed absolutely no interest in her like that? Damn those scorchingly hot dreams she'd been having about him.

'What would happen if either of us met someone else?' she asked, thinking that, while she couldn't imagine ever doing so herself, Finn was gorgeous and a billionaire and presumably had women flinging themselves at him left, right and centre. She'd seen zero evidence of it to date, but that could well change once things settled down.

'We'll cross that bridge if and when we come to

it,' he said, which wasn't exactly a denial. 'Think about it, Georgie. What do you have to lose?'

The hint of arrogance and condescension in Finn's voice annoyed her even more than the tiny irrational stab of jealousy she felt at the thought of him with another woman, but actually none of this was about her, was it? This was about Josh. Too much of his short life had been taken up with her illness and she owed it to him to make amends. Goodness knew she hadn't been the best of mothers. In fact, she must have been among the worst.

Surely he'd be better off with two parents together. Didn't the statistics suggest precisely that? The inconvenient and all-consuming attraction she felt for Finn would fade to a manageable level eventually. It already had done a bit. Look at the way the shock of his suggestion had rid her of her ridiculous embarrassment around him.

And they were hardly strangers any more. She'd even go so far as to say that they had a weird kind of connection that had nothing to do with Josh, an odd sense of recognition that made her think 'oh, that's right, it's you', which she'd felt the night they'd met, and which hit her with increasing regularity now.

And really, how bad would such a situation be for her? she thought, on one hand barely able to believe that she was even considering Finn's preposterous suggestion yet on the other totally seeing the sense of it. They got on well enough. And he was right. She *would* have the stable family unit she'd always yearned for, along with the security that Finn could provide.

If they were joined in partnership he wouldn't be able to just get up and leave, would he? Should she have a relapse he wouldn't abandon Josh, and therefore he wouldn't abandon *her*. They'd be safe. He'd told her she'd always have his support, which she believed, and she wasn't going to get anything like it anywhere else. She wasn't exactly an attractive prospect and it wasn't as if there was anyone else waiting in the wings.

Ultimately, despite his arrogance and condescension, Finn had a point. She really did have nothing to lose. In fact, she had everything to gain, and so, to ensure the best future for Josh in particular, it really was a no-brainer.

'All right,' she said with a brief nod. 'If it's a civil partnership you want, it's a civil partnership you shall have.'

CHAPTER SIX

THE CEREMONY TOOK place in a register office a stone's throw from Finn's hotel a week later, the usual lengthy bureaucracy associated with such an event magically disappearing the moment he produced an enormous cheque, which only went to demonstrate yet again that once he wanted something he didn't stop until he got it.

The arrangements hadn't been complicated in any case. Georgie had only wanted Carla there, and, apart from their son, Finn had no relations. His mother had been hit by a bus when he was ten, he'd told her, his father had died of terminal cancer around three months ago, and he had no siblings. He was as alone in this world as she was, and when she'd discovered this she'd had the fanciful notion that by hitching her wagon to his she might be rescuing him as much as he'd rescued her.

Faintly unsettled by that thought and unwilling to acknowledge what the accompanying squeeze of her heart might mean, Georgie had joked that it was going to be a small ceremony, and indeed it was. She wore a knee-length ivory dress and matching coat. Finn had on a dark suit that fitted as if made for him, which it probably was, and a snowy white shirt open at the collar that drew attention to the firmness of his jaw and strong planes of his face.

She didn't know quite why they'd dressed up. There was nothing remotely weddingy or romantic about either the venue or the occasion. But that didn't douse the flicker of warmth that uncurled deep within her when they stood together with a thankfully beautifully behaved Josh in Finn's arms while Mrs Gardiner, who'd doubled up as the second witness, took the photo she'd insisted on taking after they'd all signed the register. Nor did it stop her noticing how smoulderingly hot her new... What? Not husband... So partner...? How smoulderingly hot he looked and how delicious he smelled close up.

Not that any of that mattered, any more than the weird idea that the ceremony was somehow special did. She'd get over that nonsense. Nothing had changed. And, while the way Finn made her physically feel was going to continue to be hard to ignore, it wasn't impossible. She was made of stern stuff. If she could get through the insanely tough initial stages of post-partum psychosis, she could handle this inconvenient attraction, however insistent. It wasn't as if there was any other option when how she felt was so clearly one-sided. She was hardly going to throw herself at him and suggest a repeat of that wild night they'd spent together. Heaven forbid. His likely rejection would be mortifying.

However, for the sake of their son, she and Finn could be perfectly civil and mature about all of this, and she, at least, intended to start with the lunch they were about to embark upon to mark the occasion. Carla had gone straight back to work after the ceremony and Mrs Gardiner had taken Josh back to the apartment for his customary nap, which left her and Finn in one of the many restaurants in his company's portfolio, together and on their own for the first time in weeks.

'What shall we toast to?' she asked, once they'd sat down at their table and a bottle of champagne had been delivered and poured.

Finn arched one dark eyebrow. 'Is there any need to toast anything?'

'I think so… Ooh, I know. How about to no longer being alone?'

He didn't say anything, merely carried on looking at her steadily, his gaze unwavering and unfathomable, and for one horrible moment she thought she'd got it all wrong. But just as she was beginning to feel a bit of a fool sitting there with her hand outstretched, he touched his glass to hers and gave her the faintest of smiles before lifting the glass to his lips and tipping half of its contents down his throat.

'So why didn't you want any of your friends to be a witness?' she said, taking a sip of her own drink and for some reason feeling ridiculously pleased that she hadn't got it wrong after all. 'Come to think of it, do you *have* any friends?' She hadn't heard any mention of any.

'Of course I do,' he said, setting his glass down and twirling the stem between his fingers and thumb. 'One of them's on honeymoon, and it didn't seem worth bothering any of the others for something that was merely a formality.'

Oh. Right. Well. That told her. Just as well she hadn't been harbouring any ideas of their civil partnership being anything other than purely practical.

'Do they know about me and Josh?' she asked, slightly distracted by the mesmerising movement of his fingers, as so often happened whenever she looked at his hands.

'If they do it'll have been via the press.'

So he wasn't exactly shouting the news of their union from the rooftops. Which was fine. There was absolutely no reason why he should, she told herself, lifting her gaze and getting a grip. 'Will I ever meet any of them?'

'I imagine so.'

'I look forward to it,' she said, realising with some surprise that it was true. She wanted to know more about this man and, weirdly, not just because he was the father of her child.

'Why didn't you want your parents there today?'

With a jolt she refocused and, as usual whenever she thought of her parents, a tight knot of anger and resentment and God only knew what else formed in her stomach. 'There wouldn't have been any point,' she said, hearing the faint note of bitterness in her voice and inwardly cringing. 'They wouldn't have come even if we had been on speaking terms. Marriage and civil partnerships are far too conventional for their way of life.'

'You mentioned they live in a commune.'

'That's right. They do.'

'Where?'

'I have no idea. They travel around. They always have.'

'Even when you were young?'

'Even then.'

'What was it like?'

'Great in some ways, awful in others,' she said with a casual shrug designed to hide the strange combination of pain and happiness that accompanied memories of her childhood. 'When I was very young, not having to go to school was fantastic. I had no set bedtimes and I could eat what I liked, although, since we only really had lentils and vegetables, I guess that wasn't such a luxury. The first time I had a grilled tuna steak I thought I'd died and gone to heaven. It's still my favourite thing to eat. Anyway, there were no boundaries and zero discipline. In hindsight, I must have been totally feral. We all were, really.'

'All?'

'Wherever we lived and however many families we lived with, there were always *lots* of children.'

'It sounds idyllic.'

'I know,' she said, considering it from the point of view of growing up with only one parent and no siblings. 'But it wasn't.' Not for her, and definitely not for Carla. 'Not for a teenager, at least.'

'Why not?'

She frowned for a moment. 'I think subconsciously I really needed those boundaries to prove that I mattered. That my parents did actually care about me. And because I didn't have any, I went looking for them.'

'How?'

'I became a classic attention-seeking teen. I used to dress up and hang out in bars and order drinks while underage and flirt with all sorts of inappropriate people, desperate for someone to come and haul me home and ground me after some stern words.'

'And did they?'

'Nope,' she said with a sigh of the deep disappointment that annoyingly she still couldn't seem to shake even now, a decade later. 'Never. Once I got caught shoplifting and was delivered home by the owner of the shop with a warning and the only thing my parents were cross about was that the face cream I'd nicked wasn't organic. Eventually I figured that the only person who was going to look out for me was me and so I decided to take control of my own life. I managed to blag my way into a sixth-form college and then got into university. As if that wasn't conventional enough, I became a lawyer, at which point my parents pretty much disowned me. We haven't been properly in touch much since.'

'Do you miss them?'

She stared at him, for a moment completely taken aback. What an odd question. She'd never thought about it like that. She'd always been too stuck in a rut of simmering resentment and disappointment to allow herself to grieve for the loss of what could have been.

'I think I miss the *idea* of them,' she said after a few moments of consideration. 'I envy families. I never really had a proper one. The commune was no substitute. I was angry with my parents for a long time. Maybe I still am a bit. They let me down in every way possible. They failed at everything. No child deserves to feel unloved and unwanted. They should have been responsible. They should have been *better*. It's kind of in the job description.'

A job description that was hers now, she thought, making a silent promise to be the best parent she could for Josh. She might not have got off to a good start on the motherhood front but she would now do everything in her power to prevent her son *ever* feeling the way she had. Josh would never have to question whether he mattered. Whether he was truly loved. He'd never feel he had to find support else-where. He would never have to seek the attention he craved by hitting bars and clubs and engaging in unsuitable flirting.

'Do they know you've been ill?'

She shook her head. 'I didn't see the point of telling them. They wouldn't have been any help. They'd have just boiled up some hemp and sung a song or something. They've had the luxury of never being properly ill. At least, as far as I'm aware.'

'Have you told them about Josh?'

'I emailed my mother and got a reply warning me about the dangers of disposable nappies.'

'Their loss.'

And so it was, she realised as those two simple words sliced through the complex emotions she felt about her upbringing and pulverised the resentment and the pain. Finn was right. Her parents would never know her or him and they would never know their grandson, and that *was* their loss.

It wasn't her fault that they'd been so undeserving of the role. However much she might have wondered over the years what she'd done wrong or what she could have done differently, the answer to that was nothing. The responsibility for her well-being had been entirely theirs.

Well, she was done with them and with looking back. She had to look forward. Her family was Josh now. Maybe even Finn too, who was perceptive and clever, who'd just shone a spotlight on the knotted mess of emotion she'd lived with for years and unravelled it in an instant and who was not a man to be underestimated. In any department.

Feeling strangely lightheaded while at the same time all warm and fuzzy, Georgie sat back and watched as he drained his glass, her gaze snagging on the strong column of his throat and the tantalising wedge of flesh that his open-necked shirt revealed.

'So what was growing up like for you?' she asked with a touch of huskiness that she cleared with a tiny cough. 'It must have been tough not having a mother around.'

As he lowered his glass she saw a shadow pass over his face and a flash of bleakness in the depths of his eyes. 'It wasn't the easiest of times.'

'Before that?'

'I don't really remember.'

'How did your father cope?'

'As well as could be expected.'

'Do you want to talk about it?'

'I'd rather not.'

Fair enough. She was more than happy to back off. The afternoon was far too sunny for such sombre conversation and there was no need to push a topic that was clearly off limits. She and Finn had plenty of time to talk about histories and dreams. Years, in fact, she thought, the reality of what she'd agreed to hitting her suddenly and making her head swim for a moment. 'Will you tell me about your business, then?'

'Which bit of it?'

'Well, how did it come about?' she asked, thinking that, honestly, getting him to open up was like trying to get blood from a stone.

'When I was eighteen and had left school I started working behind the bar of a club in the centre of the city.'

'I bet you were good at it.' With his darkly devastating looks and brooding charisma she had no doubt that people—well, women mainly—would have been tripping over themselves to be served by him.

'I was,' he said with the glimmer of a smile, the tension she could see gripping his shoulders easing a little. 'I was very good at it. And more importantly I got a massive kick out of it.'

'You didn't want to go to university?'

'I had a place at Oxford to read Maths but I gave it up.'

'That was brave.' University for her had been a lifeline and she'd loved it.

'It was the arrogance of youth.'

'Which in your case was justified.'

'So it turned out. Six months later the club had become a go-to destination and hit all the A-lists. Soon after that the manager, who also owned it, fell ill. He had to take some time off and I stepped in. I started doing the books, figured out where savings could be made and margins improved, and wound up increasing the profits by fifty per cent. When it eventually came up for sale I bought it. I worked bloody hard and I expanded and diversified and things went from there.'

Admiration and awe surged through her. 'And you did it all on your own.'

'With the support of my father,' he said, his mouth twisting slightly as his smile faded. 'He lent me the money to buy the club in the first place, and gave me endless advice. He was an accountant and very shrewd.'

'You must miss him.'

He didn't answer, just looked so tortured for a moment that it tugged on her heartstrings. 'Was it quick?'

'It took around a year,' he said, his voice oddly flat. 'I received his diagnosis the night you and I met.'

She gave a slow nod of understanding. 'That was why you looked so sad.'

'Did I?'

'Well, desolate really.'

'I was drowning my sorrows.'

'And then I rocked up and intruded. Sorry about that.'

'Don't be,' he said. 'You were the perfect distraction.'

Her breath caught and a hot shiver ran through her. 'You were the perfect birthday present,' she said huskily. 'It was a good night.'

'It was better than good.'

His dark, glittering gaze remained locked onto

hers and scorchingly vivid memories suddenly poured into her head. The air surrounding her thickened. The hustle and bustle of the restaurant faded. Up until this point she hadn't realised how much of a chaperone, a shield, Josh had been. Without him, she felt wild and carefree and she suddenly wanted to stand up and lean over and kiss the man sitting opposite her looking at her so intently. Her mouth was dry and her heart was pounding, and deep inside she ached. She wanted to grab his hand and take him home and have him seduce the hell out of her all over again.

But none of that would happen. It couldn't, even if the heat and desire *had* been mutual, which it clearly wasn't. What with the risk of pregnancy and the chance that it might induce another psychotic episode, she was never having sex again. It was vaguely ironic that her libido had returned when it was of least use but she had to ignore it. Starting now, she thought, shifting to alleviate the ache only to accidentally knock his knee with hers and jolt as though electrocuted.

'Sorry,' she muttered, blushing fiercely while mentally throwing her hands up in despair.

'No problem,' Finn replied, unlike her, completely unmoved by the moment, if the inscrutability of his expression was anything to go by. 'We should order.'

Despite appearances, Finn was anything but unmoved by his brand-new civil partner. Theoretically, the ceremony should have changed nothing. The whole event had been a legal and bureaucratic process designed to bind Josh to him permanently, and that was it. He hadn't given Georgie a ring or planned a honeymoon and the lunch they'd had afterwards had hardly been a celebration.

However, for some baffling reason things *had* changed. A week in and there now seemed to be an inexplicable intimacy about living with her that somehow hadn't existed before. At night he'd started imagining her in bed and what he might do to her should he find himself ever in it with her. In the mornings, when he heard the sound of the shower running, he now envisaged her in it, wet and naked.

He seemed attuned to her every movement. Her scent lingered even when she wasn't around. When home, she'd taken to wandering around the apartment in tiny shorts and T-shirts that drew his gaze to her long legs and spectacularly returning curves. When going out she did at least put on proper clothes, none of which were either particularly tight or revealing, but that didn't provide much relief. He knew what lay underneath regardless, and to his immense irritation he couldn't stop thinking about it.

And then there were the little things that he'd noticed and now couldn't un-notice, such as her habit of nibbling the end of the pen that she used when writing in her diary. The extraordinarily expressive delight with which she savoured the food she ate. The way she gathered her hair up and then with a sort of flick of her fingers twisted it once before letting it go.

He couldn't stop thinking about *any* of it and he existed in an agonising, limbo-like state of wanting to back her up against a wall and slake his desire yet not being able to do one damn thing about it, of yearning to escape her mind-scrambling orbit but needing to be as close to his son as possible. At least she had no idea of the battle raging inside him. She couldn't. If she did she'd never prance around the place so scantily clad. She wasn't that foolish.

Nevertheless, everything else about the situation was driving him demented, and despite his best efforts to contain it his mood of recent days had not gone unnoticed. From time to time he'd caught her looking at him, her eyes on him searing his skin and burning through him, as if deliberating whether to question him about it.

She was doing it now, sitting out here on the terrace that overlooked London, staring at him from over the rim of the mug she drank coffee out of every morning, which had 'world's sexiest lawyer' emblazoned across it, as if he needed a reminder.

'If you have something to say, just say it,' he snapped, unable to stand the scrutiny and the suspense any longer.

'All right,' she said, putting her mug down. 'I've been thinking. What would you say to spending your evenings up here with me instead of disappearing off to wherever it is you go?'

What? No. No way. He barely trusted himself with her in the presence of their son and Mrs Gardiner in broad daylight. He and Georgie in the evening alone with soft lighting and an even softer sofa was *not* happening. 'Work needs me,' he said, which was a big, fat lie, since the team to which he'd delegated everything was doing just fine.

'It would be good to spend some time together without Josh.'

'Why?'

'There are things we should discuss.'

'Like what?'

'How we move forward.'

'Josh is having a nap. We can discuss that now.'

'He's due to wake up any moment and I'd like to know more about you without distractions.'

That wasn't happening either. Talking about himself wasn't something he was particularly fond of doing at the best of times. Right now it was the last thing he wanted to do. And she *was* the distraction. 'You know everything there is to know.' Everything that was relevant, anyway.

'OK, fine,' she said with an exasperated huff. 'You know what? Forget it. I do think we need to talk about the future, but really, I'd just like the company. It's lonely up here on my own every evening. It's quiet.' She gave a careless shrug. 'I dare say I'll survive, though.'

Well, now, how was he to respond to that? Just when he thought he'd successfully shut her down, along came guilt to hit him in the gut like a ton of bricks. He had no excuse really, and to persist with pretending he did would simply be cruel. He wasn't having her feeling lonely because he had an issue with self-control. He'd just have to cope. Because hadn't he vowed to provide her with what she needed whenever she needed it?

'All right,' he muttered, nevertheless slightly wishing that he had less of a problem with breaking promises. 'I'll make some adjustments.'

'Thank you,' she said with a smile so dazzling that it blinded him to the realisation that she'd got up and was walking over to him.

By the time he did register what she was doing it was too late. Before he could brace himself, she'd come to a stop right in front of him and bent down, her scent and her warmth scrambling his senses. The world skidded to a halt and every inch of him froze. Then she reached out and touched her hand lightly to his head, threading her fingers through his hair, and for one heart-stopping, delirious moment he actually thought that she was going to lean in and kiss him.

'What are you doing?' he said hoarsely, his mouth dry and his body aching unbearably.

'You have a piece of toast in your hair.'

She removed her hand and stepped back and he didn't know whether to be gutted or relieved, what to think or what to do, although breathing would be a good start. Followed by getting the hell out of here before he completely gave in to temptation and turned some of his wilder imaginings into reality.

'Where are you going?' she called as he leapt to his feet and stalked back into the apartment as if he had the hounds of hell at his heels.

'Meeting.'

CHAPTER SEVEN

EYEING FINN WARILY as he paced up and down his sitting room one evening several days later, Georgie frowned. Up until a few days ago she'd thought that everything was going really rather well. He seemed pleased with their civil partnership and, although it was a struggle, she was just about keeping a lid on the attraction that she felt for him. She'd had a slight blip when she'd discovered that he'd added tuna steak to the menu of dishes that continued to be sent up, and gone all breathless and gooey inside at the realisation he'd remembered what she'd told him at that lunch, but she'd recovered well enough. It hadn't meant anything. She needed building up, he'd told her when she'd thanked him. She needed the protein. That was all.

Lately, however, Finn had become weirdly distracted, frequently grumpy and anything but friendly. Physically he was around as much as ever, more so now he spent the evenings with her, but spiritually and emotionally he seemed to be on a whole other planet. He volunteered little in the way of conversation and his answers to her questions were monosyllabic.

The tension that now radiated off him had to come from somewhere and she didn't think it was caused by Josh, since being with him was the only time Finn didn't seem stressed. So maybe it was her, she'd begun to think. Maybe he was more annoyed by her habit of leaving the milk out than she'd realised. Maybe she was doing something else wrong. It wouldn't exactly be a first.

Whatever it was, though, Josh was picking up on it now and she'd had enough.

Closing the journal she filled in nightly, and setting both it and the pen she used on the ottoman, Georgie tracked his restless movements for a moment and then pulled her shoulders back and went for it. 'OK, Finn, what's wrong?'

'Why would anything be wrong?' he said, shooting her a glare, which did rather prove her point.

'You're wearing a permanent scowl these days and you've taken to prowling around the apartment like a caged animal.'

He stopped mid-pace and with what looked like a Herculean effort cleared his expression and shot her a tight smile. 'Everything's fine.'

'Hmm,' she said with a sceptical frown. 'Is it work?'

'No.'

'Is it me and Josh?'

'Why would it be you?'

'I'm very aware that this has all been a huge upheaval for you. The noise and the mess, I mean. It would be completely understandable if you were finding it hard. Your life has changed immeasurably.'

'That's nothing new.'

Her eyebrows lifted. 'Sorry?'

'Nothing,' he said curtly. 'Everything's fine.'

'Are you sure?'

'Yes.'

'Anything you want to talk about?'

'No.'

In the face of such intransigence Georgie gave up. She could try till she was blue in the face and she wouldn't get anywhere. 'OK,' she said. 'It's your call. I rather feel that if you carry on like this sooner or later you're going to burst a blood vessel, but have it your own way.'

'Have it *my* way?' he said with a bark of humourless laughter. 'You have no idea.'

'Then tell me.'

She shifted to make herself more comfortable, just in case he did want to talk, and suddenly something inside him seemed to snap.

'All right,' he said, his eyes blazing and his hands curling into fists. 'You're right. There is something.'

'What?'

'Do you think, for once, you could put on a bloody dressing gown?'

And with that he turned on his heel and strode out, leaving Georgie staring after him, reeling and agape.

What on earth...?

What was wrong with what she was wearing? There was nothing immodest about the baggy T-shirt or the board shorts that she had on, yet what he'd just said and the way he'd glowered at her while saying it implied that not only did he consider it to be the skimpiest outfit he'd ever seen but also that it bothered him.

However, why would it? He wasn't affected by her. Unless he was, of course, and that tension he was obviously feeling could actually be some kind of sexual frustration because, contrary to what she'd assumed, he *was* still attracted to her.

But no. He couldn't be. She'd seen no evidence of it. There'd been no long, heated looks, no off-the-charts chemistry and no sizzling subtext to their conversations. If that was the case, surely there'd have been signs...

But maybe there had been, she thought suddenly, her heart quickening as the clouds in her head parted to reveal possibilities that had hitherto been hidden. What if some of the looks Finn had given her over the last few weeks, some of his expressions that she hadn't been able to decipher and some of the strange things he'd done, were in fact cases in point?

Take, for example, the way his gaze dropped to her lips pretty much every time they ate together. She'd always vaguely assumed he'd been staring at a stray crumb or perhaps a bit of parsley stuck between her teeth. But what if instead he'd been bombarded with thoughts of kissing her the way she always thought about kissing him whenever she caught herself looking at his mouth? And what about his habit of taking a step back whenever she approached? Could he be doing that because he found her proximity somehow disturbing?

He appeared to have such a tight grip on his control, but maybe the absence of a reaction hid a very different kind of response. What if when she'd barged in on him that night and found him naked save for a towel he hadn't been as unmoved as he appeared? What if when her knee had brushed against his the day they'd had lunch, he'd been as affected as her? And what if his disappearance every night was less about catching up with work and more about avoiding her?

Or was she seeing signs where there were none?

It was entirely possible, but, if she was right and these were signs that she'd missed, then she was not only an idiot but she was also not as back to her old self as she'd imagined because that Georgie would never have missed anything.

But that wasn't important right now. Assuming she hadn't got things completely wrong, Finn appeared to want her and she might as well admit that she wanted him. She'd tried to ignore it and treat him like a flatmate, as if she were back in her old flat in Kensal Rise that she'd shared with three others, two of whom had been men she'd had no interest in, but that hadn't exactly worked. Despite her best intentions, she hadn't been able to entirely stop fantasising about him naked, about what they might get up to if she should happen to find herself in his vicinity naked too.

So what was going to happen next?

They clearly couldn't carry on like this. Things would eventually come to a head and erupt. And what was she going to do when they did? Well, she was never having sex again obviously, but, assuming Finn was amenable, there was no reason they couldn't do other things. From what she remembered he'd been spectacularly good at those other things and he hadn't exactly complained about her skills either.

Did she have the courage to tell him what she now quite desperately wanted, she wondered, her heart beginning to pound with excitement as her stomach churned nervously. Once upon a time she wouldn't have hesitated, but now… On the other hand, while she *had* been scarred by what had happened to her, it didn't have to define her going forward, did it?

So how hard would it be to go to Finn and tell him what she wanted? All it would take was guts, and heaven knew she had plenty of those. If she tried her hardest and he still sent her away, if she'd read too much into things and got completely the wrong end of the stick, then so be it. After everything she'd been through she could handle a spot of mortification. She could handle anything.

* * *

Cursing himself for what he'd revealed, and deeply regretting his momentary loss of control, Finn stormed into his room and slammed the door. If only Georgie had backed off and left him to stew. Instead she'd pushed and prodded and told him to have it his way, which was an absolute joke since his way involved her being horizontal in his bed, sighing and gasping beneath his hands and mouth, a scenario that wasn't going to happen. As if that wasn't enough she'd then leaned back and lifted her legs to tuck them under her, a movement that made the fabric of her tiny T-shirt tighten enticingly against her breasts, and he'd lost it, any hope he might have had of making it out of there with his pride intact history.

His movements jerky, Finn yanked his T-shirt over his head and tossed it on the bed, only to spin round at the sound of his bedroom door opening. Georgie stood there, silhouetted in the space, and as a bolt of desire shot through him, nearly taking out his knees, he swore beneath his breath.

He should have known she wouldn't let his parting shot go. He should have known she'd follow him. That perhaps he subconsciously *had* known and had wanted her to do so, so that they might continue where they'd left off that first night she'd barged into his room, wasn't something he wanted to contemplate ever. Because if that *did* turn out to be the case it would mean his attempts to get a grip on his unpredictable behaviour had utterly failed.

'What is it with you and knocking?' he said, practically at the end of his tether with his inability to control the futile attraction he felt for her.

'Sorry.'

She stepped forward into the light, into his territory, and he saw that she didn't look sorry. She didn't look sorry in the slightest. 'What do you want?'

'To continue our conversation.'

'We're done.'

'I don't think we are.'

Before he could even think about striding past her and getting the hell out of his room, with its huge bed squatting there like some giant neon sign advertising sex, she'd walked towards him and planted her palms flat on his chest.

'What are you doing?' he said, every muscle in his body freezing while he burned where she touched him.

'I'd have thought it was obvious,' she murmured, moving her hands up over the muscles of his chest while staring at his mouth.

His jaw clenched and his fists tightened. 'I'd advise you to stop.'

'Why?'

Yes, why? his body screamed while his brain fought to be heard. 'Because you're playing with fire.'

'I'm more than happy to be burned.'

'You've been ill.'

'I'm much better now.'

But she still had some way to go. He'd done the research and witnessed her occasional off day. She was by no means totally well yet. 'That's irrelevant.'

'All that's relevant right now is that I want you and you want me.'

Not much point in denying it, really. He needed her so badly he was in physical pain and it was becoming blatantly obvious. Nevertheless...

'What I want doesn't come into it,' he muttered though gritted teeth.

'Yet here we are, all partnered up.'

'For the sake of our son.'

She tilted her head as she lifted her gaze to his, her brown eyes shimmering in the soft light. 'Are you sure about that?'

He had been once. Right now he wasn't sure he could even remember his own name. Her scent and her warmth were destroying his faculties. All he could think of was how good it had been between them and how desperately he wanted to find out if it still could be. 'One hundred per cent.'

'So selfless,' she said with the hint of a smile.

'Don't patronise me.'

'The tension is driving you nuts, isn't it?'

'What tension?' he ground out.

'We could make it go away. *I* could make it go away.'

She ran her hands along his shoulders and down his arms and he shuddered. He had to take a step back, out of her orbit. He had to break the spell she was weaving around him. His thundering heart couldn't take much more and his self-control was fast unravelling. But he couldn't move. His feet appeared to have taken root. And his grip on his sanity, already loosened by weeks of frustration, was slipping away.

'Leave me alone, Georgie,' he said, but the protest was weak and he knew she knew it.

'Give me one last shot and, if you really insist, then I'll go.'

He couldn't speak for trying to drum up the will to insist she leave, regardless of what she did next, and she seemed to take his silence as assent, which maybe it foolishly and recklessly was, because before he knew what she was planning, before he could brace himself for what she might say or do, she'd let go of him, reached down, and gripped the hem of her top.

And as she whipped it off and tossed it to the floor, exposing her lace-covered breasts and inches of beautiful, creamy skin to his ravenous gaze, Finn felt what was left of his resistance crumble and the last remaining vestiges of his self-control shatter.

When, suddenly galvanised into action after minutes of rock-solid stillness, Finn hauled her into his arms and his mouth crashed down on hers, Georgie's first thought was, oh, thank heavens for that. She hadn't known what she would have done next had he rejected her bold move. Back away and flee, most probably, because there was taking a leaf out of his book and not stopping until one got what one wanted, and then there was harassment.

Now, though, as he held her tightly and kissed her as if his life depended on it, she couldn't think at all. Her head was swimming and the electricity zinging through her as a result of his chest hair rubbing against her sensitised skin was enough to power the national grid. She'd forgotten how very good he was at this, how good they were together, and she kissed him back with equal fervour.

When at last Finn lifted his head, his eyes were so dark they were almost black and his breathing was as ragged as hers. 'You really don't play fair,' she heard him murmur harshly over the thunder of her heart.

'You're a hard man to crack.'

'You have no idea how hard I've been.'

She arched her back, pressing her hips more firmly to his, and gave him a quick grin. 'I think I may have some.'

His gaze bored into hers and she shivered. 'Are you sure about this?'

'Yes.'

'What exactly do you want from me?' he persisted.

'Not sex.'

He stilled for a moment and eased back, his expression tortured. 'OK, then,' he said, clearly grappling to contain his surprise and disappointment. 'OK.' And then, hoarsely, 'Out of interest, why not?'

'It's too risky,' she clarified swiftly to put him out of his misery. 'We were careful the last time and look what happened. I can't get pregnant a second time. I can't go through the last six months all over again. Ever. We can do everything else though.'

As her words sank in he shuddered with visible relief. 'Thank God for that.'

'I'm sure you know things I've never even heard of.'

'Based on past experience, I very much doubt that.'

'Is that OK?' she added, suddenly worried that it might not be enough for him.

'I'll take anything you're willing to give.'

Phew. 'Then we're going to be busy.'

'Fine by me.'

He turned with her still in his arms and backed her up towards the bed until her knees hit the edge of it. Together they fell onto the mattress, his hard-muscled weight pinning her down in the most breath-takingly lovely way.

'That's better,' he muttered, lowering his head and capturing her mouth with his in a kiss that blew her mind all over again.

Caught up in a maelstrom of soul-shattering sensation, Georgie gave up thinking and let instinct take over. She lifted her hands to his shoulders, smoothing them over his muscles, feeling them bunch and flex as he held himself off her just enough to prevent crushing her.

He dragged his mouth along her jaw to her ear, nipping at a spot that made her groan as heat sizzled through her, and she gasped, 'You remembered.'

'I remember everything.'

Shifting slightly onto his side, Finn put one large, warm hand on her waist, making her jump and shudder, and then slid it behind her back to unclip her bra. After slipping it off her and throwing it aside he cupped her breast, and with a soft moan she instinctively arched her back to press herself further into his hand. He bent his head and caught one tight nipple between his lips and she whimpered as sparks shot through her. Her hands tightened in his hair, although whether to hold him still or push him lower she couldn't tell. She didn't want the exquisite torment he was subjecting her to to stop but on the other hand she wanted that clever mouth of his all over her. It was the most delicious of dilemmas.

Abandoning her breast, he slid his hand lower, easing beneath the waistband of her shorts and knickers, and she lifted her hips to help him push them down.

'Beautiful,' he muttered gruffly, his gaze singeing her skin as he moved his hand back up her calf, her knee, her thigh, taking his time and lingering in places that had her quivering. When he reached the juncture of her thighs and covered her where she was so hot and needy she cried out. He parted her with his fingers and stroked, and jolts of excitement streaked through her. Her breath caught and her heart thundered and when she reached down to touch him through his jeans his breath shot out in one long hiss.

Unable to lie there impassively while Finn was still partly clothed and doing everything, and desperately wanting to feel him without denim between them, she nudged him to encourage him to roll over, but he stopped her.

'No,' he said roughly, his entire body vibrating with tension. 'You're first.'

Noble, she thought with a shudder at the thought of the pleasure to come. But no. That wasn't happening. Not when she owed him for the whipping-her-top-off moment. 'Who said we have to take turns?'

He went still for a moment and then his eyes darkened and his mouth curved into a slow, smouldering smile. 'Good point.'

He flipped onto his back, taking her with him, and she wriggled down his body. Her hands were trembling as she unbuckled his belt, so much so that she couldn't actually undo the buttons of his fly. He batted her aside to do it himself and the sight of his capable hands with their strong fingers that could cause so much devastation within her liquefied her stomach.

He kicked off his jeans and shorts and then planted his hands on her waist to manoeuvre her into a position in which she was facing his feet and he was gripping her hips and lifting her to where he wanted her and where she wanted to be. Supporting herself on her elbows, she wrapped her fingers around his long, thick, hard length and heard him groan, and then gave a reciprocal one of her own when his tongue touched her sensitive flesh and sent sensation coursing through her.

As she moved her hand up and down the velvety steel of him, and he found her clitoris and licked, her eyelids fluttered shut, her entire body filling with molten heat. She was shaking all over, but not nearly as much as he was when she took him into her mouth. When she started moving her head he moaned against her, and the vibrations sent tiny shock waves shooting through her.

His response stoked hers, making her move faster, which drove him to increase the pressure and the intensity of what he was doing to her and she was fast spiralling out of control. She could feel the tension building inside her, the heat and pleasure winding tight and scrambling her senses, and she seemed to be in synch with him because he was now shifting his hips and thrusting into her mouth as she moved, and his breathing was hot and ragged against her.

Desire soared within her, igniting a desperate ache, and she was just about to reach a hand down to where his tongue was buried to hurry him along, when, as if able to read her mind, he held her still and thrust two fingers inside her and curled them so that they hit that exact spot, and that was it. She flew apart, her orgasm crashing into her, a white-hot burst of pleasure spinning through her like a Catherine wheel. And as stars whirled round her head she took him deep, and with a harsh groan he grabbed her head, tensed and then pulsated hard, spilling into her mouth until neither of them had anything left.

Feeling utterly drained, Georgie eased herself off him and flopped back, lying top to tail against him while waiting for her heartbeat to regulate.

'God, we're good at this,' she said when she had enough breath to speak.

Finn rolled onto his side, and regarded her, his gaze dark and glittering and his face flushed. 'Just think how much better we could be with a bit of practice.'

A sharp shiver raced through her, electrifying her nerve endings all over again. 'I don't know if I'd survive.'

The smile he gave her was slow and full of wicked promise. 'Oh, you'll survive.'

CHAPTER EIGHT

THEY PRACTISED A LOT, and got so good that a week later Georgie thought it was just as well that the walls were soundproofed. Finn was very inventive and, as she'd suspected, he knew things to do with positions and accessories and devices that she'd never even seen before, let alone deployed.

He just had to look at her and she became flushed and aroused. Every night as soon as Josh had been put to bed—indecently soon, actually—Finn took her hand and led her into the nearest bedroom, where they stayed until either day broke or their son woke. She'd lost count of how many orgasms she'd had and she was fast becoming addicted to the things he could do to her.

She wasn't just surviving the way he handled her body, she was thriving on it, as the entries in her diary detailed, which only went to show that oxytocin and dopamine and the endorphins that accompanied them really were good for the brain. And if something was occasionally missing, if she sometimes felt a bit hollow on her way down from the bliss and sort of wished she could have all of him, well, that was the compromise she just had to make, in the same way that all this lovely nocturnal activity came at the cost of the conversation she'd been so keen to encourage.

Her days now had structure and routine and she and Finn were getting on splendidly, and she had absolutely nothing to complain about. However, in the absence of stress and anxiety and sexual frustration, she found that now all she had to wonder about was if and when he was going to introduce her to his friends as promised. He'd shown no indication of it so far, and she couldn't help wondering why not. They were in every night, so it wasn't as if a hectic schedule prevented it. So was it something to do with her, then? With their situation? Or did he see her as unfit for anywhere other than the bedroom?

There was only one way to find out.

'So when am I going to meet your friends?' she asked him one night as they lay sprawled across his enormous bed, the moonlight streaking through the windows and bathing everything in a silvery glow. 'It's been weeks. Are you in some way ashamed of me?'

'What?' he replied, his words muffled by the pillow he'd flopped onto only moments ago. 'Don't be ridiculous.'

Hmm. That wasn't exactly an answer. 'Don't get me wrong,' she said, trying to keep her voice light, 'your attention is very flattering but a girl could get a complex.' Especially a girl like her, with anxieties and insecurities that she knew could pop up at any time.

'She shouldn't.'

'She might.'

He turned his head to the side and levelled her with a long, hot look. 'Really?'

She nodded. 'Really.'

'I'll set something up.'

'Thank you,' she said with a grin.

'You're welcome.'

'I shall cook.'

'There's no need. We'll go out. Or have something sent up.'

'No, I'd like to. I used to love cooking and I can't keep eating all the food the kitchens provide. It's too easy, too convenient and way too delicious. Much more of it and I'll be as big as a house.'

His gaze slowly roamed over her, setting her on fire wherever he let it linger. 'You're fine,' he said, his smile fading and his eyes darkening as he reached for her yet again. 'You're beautiful. And I am in absolutely no way ashamed of you.'

And that was how, the following Friday evening, she and Finn played hosts to his friends, Theo and Kate Knox, and her friend Carla. Finn and Theo had known each other professionally for a couple of years, and socially for one of those, more so since Theo had met Kate and settled down. Kate, his wife of three months, was tall, statuesquely beautiful and heavily pregnant.

Over drinks and nibbles, a starter of salmon and asparagus and a main course of slow-roasted lamb, Georgie listened to the conversation that flowed easily, picking up anything she could about Finn, however tiny, and filing it away for later consideration. She smiled and laughed and made contributions where necessary, but for the most part she found herself surreptitiously watching Kate and trying not to envy her.

The other woman's clear enjoyment of her pregnancy and the serenity and radiance that she emanated were things that had been denied to Georgie, and that filled her with regret and sadness. If only she'd known she was pregnant, things could have been so different. It was hard not to feel cheated.

And then there was the immense love that Kate was lucky enough to bask in. In all honesty Georgie found Theo faintly aloof and more than a bit intimidating, but when he looked at his wife the hard lines of his face softened and the blazing emotion that warmed in his eyes stole her breath. What would it feel like to be on the receiving end of such love and such passion? Would she ever know? It didn't seem likely, given the hand of cards she'd been dealt.

'So how did you and Theo meet?' Carla asked, and Georgie made herself shake off the gloom and focus.

Kate put down her glass of elderflower *pressé*

and gave her husband a look of wry amusement. 'I made myself available on an escort agency website and Theo took against it.'

Goodness, thought Georgie. That she hadn't known.

Theo arched an eyebrow, although a faint smile played at his mouth. 'Indeed,' he said, his dark gaze taking in Finn and Georgie. 'How about you?'

'Georgie picked Finn up in a bar,' Carla said with a wide grin.

'I wouldn't put it quite like that,' Georgie muttered, feeling herself blush.

'Why not?' said Finn, the glance he slid her holding a wicked glint. 'You did.'

'I don't remember you putting up much of a protest.'

'I put up no protest at all.'

'The sparks flying off the two of them could have set fire to a forest,' Carla said, taking a sip of champagne. 'I went up to them to see if Georgie was OK and had to back off for fear of getting singed.'

Oh? 'I don't remember you doing that.'

'I'm not surprised. The fire alarm could have gone off with sprinklers and everything and you'd have been oblivious.'

'And how do you two know each other?' asked Kate, indicating her and Carla.

'Our parents lived on the same commune for a while when we were teenagers,' said Georgie, remembering how excited she'd been at hearing the news of the latest arrivals.

'We clicked instantly,' said Carla. 'Took a few walks together on the wild side. Even after my family moved on we stayed in touch.'

'She's my best friend,' said Georgie.

'Back at you,' said Carla.

'Thank you,' said a suddenly serious Finn to Carla, who, to Georgie's astonishment, blushed.

'You're very welcome.'

'I'll make coffee, shall I?' said Georgie before either of the too-sharp-for-their-own-good Knoxs could voice the curiosity that was filling their expressions.

'I'll help,' said Carla.

Feeling oddly peculiar, Georgie practically ran into the kitchen, with Carla hot on her heels.

'God, Finn really is divine,' said her friend, faux fanning herself with a hand while Georgie turned on the boiling water tap and filled a cafétière. 'All that intensity and focus on you. Blazing. The vibes are extraordinary. Watching you two together *and* Kate and Theo almost makes me want to give up singledom.'

'Finn and I aren't like that, as you know perfectly well,' said Georgie, her chest nevertheless tightening.

'Then what are you like?'

'I'm not entirely sure.'

But she had the suspicion that she knew exactly what she might want it to be like, and she stuck a lid on it because there was absolutely no point chasing rainbows.

And it was a good thing she did too, because it meant that at breakfast a couple of days after the dinner party when Finn made his unexpected announcement she was able to handle it. Josh was squashing a piece of banana between his fingers as he tried to cram it into his mouth. Finn was devouring a croissant and looking so dishevelled and sexy from her early-morning ministrations that Georgie, who was sipping coffee, felt her heart turn over, as it was increasingly wont to do whenever she looked at him.

'I have to go to Paris next weekend,' he said, jolting her out of her reverie and causing the mouthful of coffee she'd just taken to go down the wrong way. 'The Bellevue is finally opening. There's a launch party.'

She coughed and spluttered and banged her chest.

'Are you all right?' he asked with a faint frown of concern.

'Yes,' she said, thumping her chest one last time. 'Fine.'

She was just surprised, that was all. The Bellevue was finished? Well, that was excellent news. She knew a bit from him about how long the works had been going on and how stressful they'd been. She had no reason to feel stung by the fact that Finn had never mentioned the imminent launch of the hotel or the party, a party that must have been planned for weeks, if not months. Or by the lack of an invi-

tation. He owed her nothing. The debt went entirely
the other way. She'd be of no benefit to him at such
an event anyway.

'When are you going?'

'Saturday.'

In six days. Gutting. Her period was due imminently, which would put a temporary halt to orgasms—
for her at least—a halt that would now apparently last
longer than she'd hoped. But she'd handle it. It wasn't
as if she wouldn't survive without the pleasure he
evoked in her. In fact, the delay would make his return all the sweeter.

'That's a shame,' she said, deciding to attribute
the disappointment she nevertheless felt to PMT.

'Why?'

'Because I'll miss…'

You.

Well. She certainly wasn't going to tell him that.
She'd sound pathetic. Besides, she was already too
vulnerable when it came to him. He held all the
cards. She held none. So she pulled herself together
and lowered her voice, even though Josh was way
too young to understand, and finished '…what we've
been doing.'

His blue eyes gleamed. 'You don't have to.'

She looked at him quizzically. What did he have
in mind? Phone sex? That was something they hadn't
tried yet. Could be fun. 'What do you mean?'

'Come with me.'

Her heart skipped a beat and then began to race. 'Really?'

'Why not? Think of it as a belated mini honeymoon.'

Hmm. She'd be better off *not* thinking that actually, since, whatever they were doing, it wasn't romance and she'd be wise not to forget it. 'For how long?'

'A couple of days, maybe three. The party's on the Saturday night and I have some business on the Monday and Tuesday. We'd be back by Tuesday evening at the latest.'

'What about Josh?'

'He can stay here with Mrs Gardiner.'

As usual Finn had all the answers and he made it sound not only easy but also unbelievably tempting. Three days on her own with him in Paris, strolling through the parks and sitting in divine restaurants that had white tablecloths, sparkling crystal and soft, flickering candles…

Or perhaps not, since he'd probably be in meetings most of the time, but whatever. She could see it now—the party, the luxury and the almost-sex that would have an added frisson, given that it was Paris—and to her shame she wanted it all quite desperately.

But could she really do it? Wouldn't it be the height of selfishness to leave behind her tiny son to go off gallivanting around one of the most romantic cities in the world in search of pleasure, oblivion and her old self?

Well, maybe it would and maybe many would judge her for that, but maybe she ought to give herself a break. Didn't she deserve some fun? And how badly would her absence actually affect Josh? She'd only be away for three days max. Would he even notice? And if he did, would it scar him for life? She didn't think so. She had the utmost faith in Mrs Gardiner, which was ironic when she thought about how suspicious of the whole idea of having a nanny she'd been initially, and there was always the phone. It wasn't exactly difficult to get back from Paris, should for some reason she need to.

'Well?' Finn queried with an arch of an eyebrow that sent thrills of excitement skidding along her veins and a lovely warmth spreading through her body.

'Oui, d'accord,' she said, feeling the beginnings of a wide, silly smile spread across her face despite her best efforts to contain it. 'I'd love to.'

At ten o'clock on the following Saturday evening—French time—Georgie was floating on the most incredible high.

She and Finn had arrived in Paris earlier, having caught the train in London and travelled first class. A car had picked them up at the station and had then smoothly whisked them to the latest addition to the Calvert Collection portfolio.

When they'd pulled up outside the Hotel Bellevue on the Rue du Faubourg Saint-Honoré she'd had trouble keeping her jaw from hitting the floor. The pale, sand-coloured stone of the six-storey building gleamed in the afternoon sun. Each room had a black wrought-iron balcony from which spilled rich red flowers. Some had their red and white striped blinds down, some had their doors open to let in the warm spring breeze. Above the revolving glass and gold front door was a fine black awning, and either side of it stood a tub containing a perfectly clipped ball of a laurel tree. The doorman who tipped his black top hat to them as they approached was wearing a dark coat decorated with gold braid and polished brass. Inside, everything was soft whites and elegant *eau-de-nil*, marble floors and sparkling crystal. Beyond the reception desk, through a pair of huge patio doors, Georgie had seen a terrace where tables with bright white parasols had been placed around an area of emerald-green grass bordered with low, neat hedging.

'What do you think?' Finn had asked as they'd gone up in the lift to their suite.

'Breathtakingly stunning.'

'I couldn't agree more,' he'd replied, giving her a direct look that sent heat and desire stealing through her.

The honeymoon suite, which had been put at their disposal, was equally as beautiful with its calming off-white and taupe décor and gorgeous antique furniture. Disappointingly, Finn had disappeared pretty much immediately to go off and do things that, as owner of the hotel, he had to do. But Georgie had managed to occupy herself by exploring the vast suite and terrace, before kicking off her shoes and flopping onto the enormous bed to call Mrs Gardiner for quite possibly the twentieth time.

It hadn't been easy leaving Josh. It had actually been rather more of a wrench than she'd expected. For one dithering moment, just before she'd walked out of the penthouse back in London, she'd genuinely considered going downstairs to where Finn was waiting and telling him to go ahead without her. But Mrs Gardiner had shooed her off, practically locking the door behind her, and so she'd slunk off, torn between wanting to go and guilt at leaving.

That guilt, which had accompanied her throughout the journey to Paris, hadn't fully gone away but she'd been assured during every call she'd subsequently made that her son seemed to be taking their absence in his stride, and finally she'd been able to relax and enjoy the party.

And what a party it was. Five hundred guests, who'd earlier been divided into small groups and given an exclusive tour, now mingled in the ballroom. Members of the waiting staff wove through the journalists, upmarket travel company owners and anyone else lucky enough to have received a coveted invitation, offering up exquisite signature cocktails and the tiniest, most delicious canapés Georgie had ever tasted. She'd laughed and chatted all evening, remembering how much she'd once loved socialising and going giddy with the realisation that it was all coming back to her.

Having Finn at her side helped. His proximity was as reassuring as it was intoxicating. He looked so incredibly handsome this evening in his impeccably tailored navy suit that matched his eyes and a pale blue shirt. His imposing height and the impressive breadth of his shoulders stood him apart from everyone else, and then there was the aura of confidence and power that surrounded him and sent shivers of anticipation rippling through her.

Georgie had only really ever seen Finn the father or Finn the deliverer of outstanding orgasms. She'd never experienced this side of him, the utterly compelling, totally in command, billionaire tycoon. It was dazzling being with him, knowing he was hers, and she was no more immune to his effect than any of the other couple of hundred or so women present this evening.

However, it wasn't the luxury of her surroundings or the endless supply of champagne or even Finn's presence beside her that was causing Georgie's state of heightened excitement. Nor was it the memory of him raising the privacy partition in the car as they'd made their way from the station to the hotel, then sliding his hand up her skirt and making her come silently and hard within minutes, which kept slipping into her head and making her blush. It wasn't even

the euphoric relief at knowing she was truly better
and could therefore stop taking her medication, a
plan she'd implemented this morning.

No.

What was responsible for the dizzying delight
whipping through her was the unexpected yet shattering conclusion she'd come to while having her
hair and make-up done this afternoon in the hotel's
very exclusive salon.

To get there she'd had to pass the hotel's *pharma-
cie*, which was as elegantly designed as the rest of
the building. As she'd settled back to have her hair
washed, she'd found herself idly wondering what sort
of pharmaceutical things a guest might need while
staying in such a hotel but may not have. A forgotten toothbrush perhaps. A plaster or an aspirin. Or
something they might possibly need unexpectedly,
such as a tampon or, if they were very lucky, a condom. This naturally had got her to thinking about
sex, with Finn, how much she longed to do it and
what a crying shame it was that they couldn't.

And then it had struck her like a breath-stealing
blow to the chest that maybe they could. Her period
had finished yesterday—no unexpected need for a
tampon—and her cycle was long. So the chances
of getting pregnant at this stage of it were remote.
Really remote. And therefore if she and Finn were
extra-careful, she'd thought, her head spinning and
her heart thumping while the stylist lathered her up,
what was stopping them from having full-on sex to-

night? What was stopping them from making up for lost time and having full-on sex *the entire weekend*?

As far as she could tell, absolutely nothing. It would be virtually risk-free. Certainly risk-free enough for her to consider it an excellent idea. The only potential obstacle was Finn, but surely he wouldn't object. While unravelling her in the car he'd murmured that he'd found the last week impossibly frustrating, despite her extreme and self-less generosity on that front, so presumably he'd be as thrilled with her proposal as she was.

And so, once she was all styled and made up and fairly bubbling over with excitement and anticipation, Georgie had gone back to the pharmacy to acquire supplies for what she hoped would be at least forty-eight hours of mind-blowing sex, give or take a meeting or two, and returned to her room to get dressed as if floating on air.

For the duration of the party she'd hugged her plan to herself, but it wasn't for much longer. In an hour or so the party would surely begin to wind down and they'd be done, and then she and Finn would head upstairs and with any luck start burning up his one thousand thread-count sheets properly.

And, quite frankly, she couldn't wait.

CHAPTER NINE

THERE WAS SOMETHING different about Georgie tonight,
Finn thought, watching through narrowed eyes as she
chatted and laughed with a small group of guests. And
it wasn't just the way she looked, although that was
pretty magnificent. The dress she had on was strap-
less and tight, knee-length and of a forest-green velvety sort of fabric, the kind of dress he wanted to peel
off her with his teeth. Nor was it the relaxed ease with
which she interacted with people, which reminded
him of the vibrant, sexy woman he'd originally met.

Over the last couple of weeks, that Georgie, the
one he recognised, had showed increased signs of returning, and he was glad for her sake. And also his,
if he was being honest. They might not be having
full sex—slightly frustrating although completely
understandable—but what they did get up to blew
his mind every time. She was so responsive. So en-
thusiastic. A fascinating and inventive distraction,
and just what he'd needed, in fact. Again. Because,
what with work and Josh and her, he'd barely had

time to think about the progress his investigation agency wasn't making. Nor did he have the head space to continue to mentally rage at Jim and Alice.

The tension that had been gripping him for what felt like decades had begun to lessen and life had become marginally easier in other respects too. While many of the circumstances surrounding his adoption remained painfully confusing, some of the chaos seemed to be settling. He was no longer short with his colleagues and subordinates. He scowled less and his behaviour had become less unpredictable. Only yesterday he'd made a snap decision without even having to think about it, and he was one hundred per cent certain that this was all down to the release he found with Georgie.

Tonight, however, frustratingly, that tension was back. Georgie might look unbelievably beautiful and achingly hot but she kept smiling to herself and drifting off into her own little world, which he found deeply unsettling. He couldn't work out what might have put that sparkle of mischief in her eyes. It couldn't have been the interlude in the car when he hadn't been able to resist touching her. Hours had passed since then. So what was it? He didn't know and he hated it.

But he wouldn't remain in the dark for much longer, he assured himself, his jaw tight. He'd had enough of trying to second guess what Georgie may or may not be planning. All evening he'd been in work mode, ruthlessly focused on the launch, but now the party was coming to an end and he was getting answers.

Taking her elbow and muttering their excuses, he drew her away from the throng and manoeuvred her behind one thick, towering pillar, into the shadows and out of the sight of prying eyes. He backed her up against it, pressed himself close, and she didn't seem to mind.

'What are you up to?' he murmured, planting one hand on the pillar beside her head while wondering where on her body to put the other.

She arched an eyebrow in a way that sent darts of desire shooting through him and smiled up at him coyly. 'What makes you think I'm up to anything?'

'You have a look about you.'

'What kind of a look?'

'As if you're keeping a secret.'

'Maybe I am.'

'I don't like secrets,' he muttered, deciding that high on the curve of her waist with access to the lower side of her breast would be a good place for his hand. He ran his thumb over the soft swell there and the pulse at the base of her neck fluttered.

'You'll like this one,' she said, her voice husky and her eyes darkening.

'What is it?'

'You'll see.' Her gaze dropped to his mouth and he heard her breath catch. 'Are we done here?'

'Nearly.'

'Because I think we should go upstairs. Now.'

'Why?'

'I've recently thought of something else we can try. Something new.'

His pulse thudded heavily and heat infused every inch of him. Something else? Wasn't what they'd already done enough? Was she trying to kill him? 'Like what?' he asked, his body hardening unbearably.

Without taking her eyes off his, she opened her bag, took something out and pressed it into his hand. He glanced down and saw a condom packet in his palm and his heart lurched. 'What's this?'

'Do you really need me to explain?'

Yes, as a matter of fact. 'I thought sex was off the table.'

'It was. But I've reconsidered. I realised this afternoon that it's all about the timing.'

'Which is now?'

She gave a nod. 'It is. And it will be for a couple of days.'

A couple of days? Halle-bloody-lujah. 'Are you sure?'

'Very much so.'

'Then we're going to need a lot more than one.'

'I bought out the pharmacy.'

She was truly unbelievable. 'You know what?' he muttered, practically passing out with the strength of the need now drumming through him. 'I think we're done here.'

To Finn's intense frustration, however, leaving the party took a while. As he strode towards the exit, just about resisting the temptation to drag Georgie along behind him and instead maintaining a civilised although determined speed, people kept coming up to him wanting to chat. Infuriatingly, no one seemed to be deterred either by the electricity he knew was rolling off him or the curtness of his replies. How he managed to refrain from telling everyone to move the hell out of his way so he could get upstairs and ravish the woman at his side he had no idea. The five minutes during which they had to stop and pose for a series of press photographs were quite possibly the longest of his life.

By the time they made it into the lift Finn's jaw was tight and he ached all over with the effort of restraint. Once inside, Georgie took up a position on one mirrored side of the car and he leaned against the opposite wall. Any closer and he might not be able to wait for privacy. He didn't even trust himself to speak, just kept his hand in his pocket, touching the condom, as if not doing so might make it a figment of his imagination. But he didn't take his eyes off her and she didn't stop looking at him, their gazes and their bodies communicating in a way that rendered words unnecessary.

Time passed agonisingly slowly, the space between them filling with tension and vibrating with need, but eventually the lift arrived at their floor. The minute the doors whooshed open, Finn grabbed Georgie's hand and strode towards their room. As soon as he got her inside he had her up against the door and in his arms, their mouths meeting in a hot clash of teeth and tongues that went on and on until his head emptied of everything but her and the clawing need to be inside her.

He ran his hands down her body, moulding them to her shape while she tugged furiously at his shirt. At the feel of her hands on the skin of his back he shuddered and for a moment wanted to pause and revel in her touch, but he wasn't to be distracted. Nothing was going to stop him from ridding of clothes the parts of her he wanted naked.

When he reached her mid-thigh and the fabric of her dress had some give he bunched it in his fists and shoved it up. With a soft, encouraging moan that turned him to granite she edged her legs apart and pushed her hips forwards. He skimmed his hand over the delicate lace of her knickers and she gasped, and when he slipped his fingers beneath the thin waistband her breathing became shallow, her breasts heaving against the restrictive bodice of her dress.

'You're so hot,' he muttered. 'So wet.'

'Stop talking,' she panted.

'No foreplay?'

'Haven't we had enough of that already?'

'More than enough.'

'Then hurry. I'm not sure how much longer I can wait and I *really* want you inside me when I come.'

The desperation he could hear in her voice stoked his desire like a can of petrol being tossed on a bonfire, and the flames raged within him. Shaking slightly, he eased away to yank his trousers and shorts off and roll the condom on while she pushed her knickers down and kicked them to one side. And then he was back in front of her, wrapping his hands around the backs of her thighs and lifting her up.

Their gazes locked as he thrust up and she pushed down, and he saw something hot and unidentifiable flare in the depths of her eyes before she closed them with a soft, ragged groan. Her head thudded against the door as she dropped it back and he couldn't help moving.

Driven on by an urgency and total lack of control he'd never felt before, Finn buried his head in her neck and pulled out of her and then thrust back in, as deep as he could go. He did it again and again, harder and faster, until she was clinging on to his shoulders, her legs tight around his waist, her breath coming in short, sharp pants as she muttered little cries of, 'Oh, God, yes.'

And then suddenly he could feel his orgasm rush towards him with the speed and force of a tsunami and he was too far gone to hold back. Everything inside him tightened, the pressure coiling in his groin so intense that it almost hurt. And when, with a cry, Georgie shattered, trembling in his arms and convulsing around him, he thrust one last time, hard and deep, and erupted as the pleasure hit and spun through him like a starburst.

How long he spent slumped against her in the quiet darkness, his heart thundering in time with hers, he had no idea. After what could well have been the most intense experience of his life, he wasn't capable of thought, much less reason. All he could do was drop his forehead to hers, his breathing harsh and his control in pieces, and whisper, 'You are incredible.'

The following morning when she woke, Georgie stretched and grinned like the cat who'd got the cream, or a woman whose body had been put to thoroughly good use.

Muscles deep inside her ached. She felt all soft and languid and buzzy. Last night had been brilliant. She hadn't realised how frustrating not having full sex had been, but it had clearly been very frustrating indeed, because with the flourishing of that condom she'd unleashed a beast in both of them that had kept going until the early hours of the morning, when they'd both collapsed into a sated, sleepy tangle of sheets. Hard and fast, soft and sensuous, on the bed, in the shower, they'd done it all...

But it wasn't just the mind-blowing sex that had made the night so amazing. It was the realisation she'd just come to that, after months of darkness, there was finally light. Everything was falling into place and, to her giddy relief and delight, the shadows were fading and it felt as if *she* was back.

And, while she didn't know about being incredible, she certainly felt invincible right now, which was in no small part down to the man stretched out beside her, who was sliding a hand down her body and doing a very good job of making her forget everything but him and her and the way he made her physically feel.

Or, rather, attempting to.

Because she wasn't quite so addled with desire that she'd forget about her son.

'I should call Mrs G and see how Josh is,' she murmured, determinedly ignoring the heat beginning to wind through her and reluctantly trying to ease away from him.

'He'll be fine,' Finn muttered against the sensitive skin of her neck that he was nuzzling as he clamped his hands on her hips to hold her still and then rolled over to pin her to the bed. 'I, on the other hand, am not,' he said, his eyes dark with need as he looked down into hers. 'I'm in pain.'

'You're insatiable.'

'That would make two of us, then.'

'A good mother would prioritise her son over sex.'

'You are a good mother.'

'You have to be kidding,' she said, staring up at him in disbelief. 'I've been a terrible mother.'

'Rubbish.'

'Have you forgotten how Josh and I came into your life?'

'You were ill.'

'Doesn't matter.'

Clearly realising that sex wasn't happening, although to his credit he didn't emit so much as a whisper of a resigned sigh, Finn lifted himself off her and lay on his side, propping himself up on his elbow beside her instead.

'Of course it does,' he said, with such certainty that she was almost convinced. 'How's he doing?'

She thought about her happy little boy and the way his tiny, chubby arms lifted up and reached for her when she walked into the room. About how, when she lifted him up, he actually snuggled into her. Josh's well-being couldn't *all* be down to Finn and Mrs Gardiner, could it?

'OK, so maybe I'm not so bad *now*,' she said as a different kind of warmth stole through her, 'but before...'

'Remember your bedsit?'

A picture of peeling paint and threadbare carpet flashed into her head and at the back of her throat she thought she could taste a trace of damp. 'I'd rather not,' she muttered with a shudder, pulling the sheet up to dispel the flurry of goosebumps.

'You weren't going to let me take Josh without you.'

'Well, no, but—'

'Trust me. You're doing fine. And you're around,' he added. 'Which is a plus.'

A shadow flitted across the lean lines of his face and her heart twanged in her chest. 'How did you cope without your mother?'

'I have no idea.'

'But you did.'

'Of course.'

Oh, to have his confidence, she thought wistfully. To not be in doubt about anything or anyone. She'd never met anyone so sure of himself and it was hard not to envy him. 'I was so jealous of you, you know,' she said, shooting him a quick smile.

'When?' he asked with a faint frown.

'Those first few days after we came to stay. When I walked into your kitchen the morning after we arrived and found you feeding Josh so adeptly. There was a time when I couldn't work out which bottle to use or how to mix formula. And then later, being with him, playing with him... You just automatically seemed to know what you were doing and I resented that.'

'Believe me, I didn't.'

'Really?'

'I've never had such a steep learning curve.'

Oh. 'Weirdly, that's good to know. It's easy to assume everyone else has it sorted while you feel like you're floundering, and I floundered more than most for what felt like the longest time.'

'What happened once you got to hospital, Georgie?'

A chill ran through her and she shivered. 'You don't want to know.'

'I do.'

Hmm, that was all very well, but what purpose would it serve either of them? She could see no advantage in rehashing the past. Much of it, blessedly, she couldn't even remember. And, while sharing might have been recommended as therapy, as far as she could see she was doing perfectly well without it. 'Why?'

'I want to know everything about you.'

Oh.

Well.

That was different, then, she thought, her heart slowly turning over as she scoured his eyes, looking for signs of flippancy and finding none. That was shifting this...whatever this was...to another level. And as her heart melted and her resistance evaporated, quite suddenly she wanted to tell him. She wanted him to tell him everything. She didn't want anything to remain between them. He could handle it. He'd handled everything so far with rock-solid strength and complete equanimity, and she rather thought that, even if they hadn't been legally joined, he'd stick it out. She'd trusted him with her body. Surely she could trust him with her secrets.

'It's not pretty,' she warned, nevertheless scarcely able to believe she was going to open the door for him on what had been for her the darkest of times.

'I won't judge.'

'If you did, you'd find me guilty.'

'None of it was your fault.'

'I know that, but that doesn't lessen it.' She swallowed hard to ease the tightness in her throat and took a deep breath. 'I never mentioned how I ended up in hospital in the first place, did I?'

'No.'

'While I was staying with Carla and everything started to fall apart, not only did I begin to behave erratically and have delusions, but I also found myself beginning to really resent Josh. I started to believe that his arrival had ruined everything and...' She paused, momentarily unable to continue, hating herself for what she was about to reveal but reminding herself that it had been a symptom of her illness. 'I didn't want him,' she finished shakily. 'I fantasised about how much easier things would be without him. I became obsessed with leaving him somewhere like outside the hospital and just walking away. One night I even got as far as the bus stop.'

'What happened?'

'Carla showed up and when I told her I was going to the hospital said she'd take me herself. Only when we arrived she had me sectioned.'

'That must have been distressing,' he said, his voice gruff.

'It was. I sort of knew that it was the right thing to be doing but I also hated her for it. The diagnosis that followed was a double-edged sword. On the one hand it was a relief to know there was an explanation for what I was doing and thinking and feeling, but on the other it was a struggle to make sense of it all.' She shook her head and frowned. 'I was supposed to be so *together*. Something like that was never supposed to happen to me. And then it got worse.'

'How?' he asked, his gaze darkening with a concern that heated the chill in her blood and eased the pain of her memories.

'I naively assumed that when it began, the treatment would instantly sort everything out and I'd be better. But it didn't. I was all over the place. For days I'd feel full of energy and be buzzing, convinced that I was doing fantastically. I clearly remember a week or so when my thoughts zipped along, hopping from one to another at incredible speed, and it was so exhilarating to be able to think so fast and so brilliantly. But then I'd suddenly crash to unbelievable lows. I had the most unimaginably horrible hallucinations.'

'About what?'

'Death,' she said. 'My death mainly. I kept having visions of a bunch of doctors and nurses decked out in scrubs and face masks approaching my bed in order to lift me off and put me into the coffin that sat beside it.'

'My God,' he murmured, visibly blanching.

'I did warn you it wasn't pretty,' she said, watching his jaw tighten and his Adam's apple bob as he fought for...well...something. 'The periods in between were filled with the many anxieties I had over Josh. Because of the medication I was on I couldn't breastfeed him. I couldn't interact with him most of the time and I became obsessively worried about how that was going to affect him. Like how he wasn't going to achieve his milestones and things because I wasn't capable of teaching him anything. How badly

I was letting him down. I was also terrified I was going to in some way harm him. Or myself.'

'But that never happened.'

'No.'

'It never would have happened.'

'I have to think not,' she said, determined to believe it. 'Eventually the medication kicked in and suppressed the mania but even that wasn't easy to deal with because it put me in a fog of nothingness which was almost as horrible as what had gone on before. At least then I had the ups.' She fell back against the pillows and gave a sigh of regret and sorrow. 'Looking back, I don't recognise any part of myself. I have no idea who I was. I totally lost me and that makes me sad because I'll never be the person I was before again, and I rather liked her. She was fun and fearless. I'm not even sure who I am now.'

'Josh knows who you are,' he said with quiet conviction.

'That's what the doctors told me. It's taken a while to believe it myself. And to believe that I will be, that I *am*, OK.'

'Are you?'

'I think so,' she said, casting him a small smile. 'But I've been here before. A relapse isn't out of the question. And I worry about getting depression. I've been warned that women who've had post-partum psychosis can end up with bipolar disorder.'

'If any of that happens, I'll be there to catch you. I'll keep you safe.'

He would, wouldn't he? 'Thank you.'

'I should be the one thanking you,' he said gruffly. 'But in all honesty I really don't know what to say.'

'Then why don't you kiss me instead?'

'That I can do.'

He reached out and wrapped a hand around the back of her neck as she moved towards him, and captured her mouth in a soft, soul-stealing kiss that slowly swept away the memories and the anguish and replaced them with a rush of heat and want.

'I'm sorry,' he murmured when they broke for breath.

'What for?'

'Not being there for you.'

'You couldn't have known.'

'The morning after the night we met, just before you left, I was going to suggest we exchange numbers.'

Her eyes widened. 'Were you?'

'I thought about asking you to dinner.'

'Did you? Why?'

'I liked you.'

'It was just sex.'

'No, it wasn't.'

She had to agree, and when she fleetingly thought about what could have been if only she'd had his number her heart squeezed with regret. 'Hindsight is pointless,' she said quietly. 'That me doesn't exist anymore.'

'Yes, she does.'

'She's battered and bruised.'

'She's brave and resilient and stronger than anyone I've ever met.'

God, someone should bottle him. 'I bet you say
that to all the girls.'

'You'd be surprised,' he murmured. 'And in any
case, there hasn't been anyone else since I first met
you a year and a half ago.'

For a moment she just stared at him. 'Are you
serious?'

'Why would I lie?'

A good point. 'Why not?'

'It's been a turbulent time.'

'Your father's illness?'

He hesitated and sympathy tugged at her heart.

'You don't have to talk about it if you don't want
to.'

'I would if I could,' he said, looking utterly, hope-
lessly tortured.

'But you can't so you shan't?'

'Something like that.'

'Too raw?'

He nodded and his eyes filled with bleakness.
'Shattering. In so many ways.'

Overwhelmed with the need to comfort him,
to ease his torment in any way she could, Georgie
shifted and rolled him onto his back, sliding her hand
down the hard planes of his body and watching as
the distress in his expression slowly disappeared.

'What happened to needing to know that Josh is OK?' he said, his voice thick with growing desire.

'We'll definitely call,' she said, giving him a slow smile. 'But later.'

It was quite a bit later when they finally made that call. Shortly afterwards, with great reluctance, Finn dragged himself out of bed and headed off for a meeting with the hotel management, which he had a feeling was going to be a challenge, when all he could think of was Georgie and how she continued to blow his mind.

She might not know who she was, but he did, and he was in awe. He'd never met anyone so insanely tough yet so unbelievably soft. So doggedly determined yet at times so achingly vulnerable. So generous and giving and fearless. Not of the struggles she'd had—those merited every bit of fear she'd felt—but of facing up to them. The way she was able to work through hugely difficult, personal, emotional topics and talk about them was staggering.

How did she *do* that? he wondered as he stepped into the lift and hit the ground floor button. Where did she find the strength to acknowledge her problems and confront them, her shoulders back and head high? He'd never figured out how to achieve any of that. Give him a complex strategic issue and he was all over it. Impossible deals and intransigent planning departments, no problem. A massive upheaval to his personal life, however, with all the tumultuous emotions that came with it, and he fell apart. After everything Georgie had told him about her experiences in hospital, he couldn't even talk about how he felt about Jim's death. He didn't know where to start.

Maybe he ought to ask her for tips. Maybe he ought to open up to her. A little. Because he might as well admit it, he thought, striding through Reception and walking into the meeting room, where a dozen of his staff shot to their feet, it wasn't just sex that had made his life less tense and stressful and somehow better over the last couple of weeks. It was her.

CHAPTER TEN

GEORGIE WHILED AWAY the hours Finn was out mostly by wafting around the suite and reflecting on her Parisian adventure so far, starting with the sex, which had surpassed her wildest expectations, and she'd had a fair few. The night they'd met had been scorching, but now... Well, now, in addition to the red-hot physical chemistry, there was knowing and feeling and, dare she say it, *liking*.

What would have happened if he *had* taken her number that morning? she wondered as she lathered up in the shower and tingled at the memory of Finn's hands on her body. Would they have dated? Would he have somehow noticed what she'd failed to? Could her pregnancy have been as it should have been? It was a pointless exercise if ever there was one, but that didn't stop her imagination playing out the various scenarios or her heart squeezing in response.

Conversely, what if she *hadn't* found him the evening she'd gone looking for him? She liked to think that she'd have muddled through somehow and that she and Josh would have been all right, but life was so much richer, so much brighter for having Finn in it.

Reliving the harrowing details of her stay in hospital had been agonisingly difficult, but ultimately she was glad she'd told him everything. She had no secrets left now and nothing more to hide, and, while she'd taken a massive risk and made herself incredibly vulnerable, she had no doubt that he'd take care of what she'd given him. Not only was he the sexiest man she'd ever met, he was also the most patient and the most understanding.

And then there were the glimpses of his soul that she caught through the tiny cracks that appeared in his armour from time to time. Beneath his brusque and aloof exterior lay a seething mass of emotion, she was sure. The issues he clearly had surrounding the death of his father made her heart wrench every time she recalled how desolate and devastated he'd looked, lying there next to her.

He was everything she could possibly ask for in a co-parent or a lover yet the things she found most attractive about him had nothing to do with Josh or his devastating looks and wicked bedroom skills and everything about who he fundamentally was. He took his responsibilities seriously. His support was steadfast. She had no doubt she would always be able to depend on him.

Little wonder, then, that she was beginning to fall for him.

And, as if all that wasn't enough to make her heart melt like butter over heat, Finn was now feeding her. When he'd returned from his meeting he'd announced that he was taking her out to lunch and told her to hop to it.

It was a glorious spring day so they'd walked, taking in the gardens and the parks and lingering in the Jardin des Tuileries, before being seated on the terrace of the fanciest restaurant she'd ever been to. While a string quartet nearby played something light and uplifting Finn tucked into a plate of seabass and she tried not to devour her delicious seared tuna too greedily.

The weekend was turning out to be as wonderful and romantic as Georgie had imagined, maybe even more so, and she was so overwhelmed by it that she thought she'd best stick to business before she did something unwise like tell him how she was beginning to feel about him.

'So, was the launch considered to be a success?' she asked, putting her fork down on her empty plate and taking a sip of crisp chilled Chablis in an effort to appear cool and collected.

'Yes.'

'Is anything you do *not* a success?'

He flashed her a quick smile that set off fireworks in the pit of her stomach. 'Rarely.'

'And again, I envy you,' she said with a sigh.

'Why?'

'It feels like a long time since anything I did was successful.'

'Not from where I'm sitting,' he said, giving a nod of thanks to the waiter who cleared their table, then sitting back and eyeing her thoughtfully. 'You know, we're very similar, you and I.'

She felt her eyebrows shoot up. Seriously? Finn was a put-together billionaire who knew exactly who he was and where he was going. She was still a bit of a mess who knew next to nothing about anything. She could see no similarity whatsoever. 'Are we?' she said sceptically. 'How?'

'We're both survivors.'

'I suppose,' she said, although she still didn't really know enough about him to judge.

'But that's not all. We're both determined. Both ambitious. We've both come a long way and done it with little outside support.'

Hmm. 'Well, I might have been all that once upon a time,' she conceded, wondering whether that might be why she felt such a strong sense of recognition whenever she looked at him. 'But I'm not sure about now.'

'You will be again.'

'Not in the field of law,' she said, nevertheless warmed by his belief in her. 'My career in that is pretty much over, I suspect. I was sectioned. I haven't looked into it but it wouldn't surprise me if that didn't disqualify me from practising. And I doubt I'd get a glowing reference from my last company anyway.'

'Want me to take them on?'

'Why not?' she said with a grin.

'I mean it.'

Her grin faltered and her heart gave a great thump. 'Would you do that?'

'All you have to do is say the word and they're history.'

As if she needed a reminder of his power and influence or another reason to fall a little bit more in love with him. 'Thank you, but no.'

'Sure?'

'Yes.'

'Shame.'

'I'll figure something out workwise,' she said, forcing herself to focus on something other than how giddy she felt at having someone on her side for possibly the first time in her life, at being part of a team. 'Maybe I'll retrain and do something to help people who are going through what I did. I had amazing care. I'd like to give something back. Maybe I could fundraise or something.'

'Let me know what I can do to help.'

He already had, more than he could possibly know. 'I will,' she said with a smile.

His gaze dropped to her mouth then, his eyes darkening in a way that never failed to render her hot and breathless. 'Let's have dessert back at the hotel,' he said, and called for the bill.

Quite some time later, as Georgie lay sprawled across the bed, unable to move for lazy lethargy, it occurred to her that the thing that had been bubbling away inside her all day, filling her with light and hope, was happiness. She was happy. Actually happy. Her confidence and self-esteem were soaring and it felt as though her demons were finally in retreat, which only went to show how very good for her Finn was.

She'd had the best day, and now, as she listened to the sound of the shower and contemplated joining him in it, she couldn't help wondering if there was anything stopping them from turning this relationship that had started for the benefit of Josh into one that also benefited them. Because not only was she happy, but Finn too seemed remarkably content with the way things were. He was certainly less stressed and more relaxed than he'd been a month or so ago.

They appeared to be on the same wavelength and there was lust and there was trust and possibly even the beginnings of love, so who knew? Their relationship could go anywhere, and she cautiously examined the heart-thumping idea that the tight, stable, supportive family unit she'd always longed for might actually be within her grasp for the first time in her life.

Closing her eyes, she tried envisaging it, and it wasn't that hard because her common sense was no match for the allure of that which she craved deep inside. Within minutes she had herself and Finn and Josh living in a gorgeous house in the country filled with laughter and lust and love in a place where it was perpetual summer and the birds didn't stop singing.

It was a heady, if utterly unreal, bubble and one

that kept expanding preposterously until it abruptly burst when Finn's phone started buzzing its way across the bedside table. The phone fell to the floor before she could reach it, but she leaned down to pick it up anyway, and as she did so, out of the corner of her eye, she caught sight of the caller.

Osborne Investigations.

The name sparked something in the dusty recesses of her memory.

What was it?

Hmm…

Oh, yes.

The night he'd scooped her and Josh up and whisked them to his hotel. The night she'd been left with no option but to tell him where she'd been and what she'd been doing because if she hadn't he'd have had an investigating agency on to it so fast it would make her head spin.

That was it.

But what could Finn possibly need investigating? she wondered, replacing his phone on the bedside table and lying back against the pillows. Was it something to do with work? A person? A company? Or something else entirely? It was none of her business, of course, yet she couldn't help but be curious. She was curious about everything to do with him.

'Why do you have an investigation agency working for you?' she asked when he emerged from the bathroom in a cloud of steam and a fluffy white towel wrapped around his hips, a sight she didn't think she'd ever tire of.

He visibly tensed, and all the little hairs at the back of her neck stood up in response to the conclusion that she was on to something interesting. 'Why do you ask?'

'Your phone vibrated and then fell on the floor, so I picked it up. Their name was on the screen.'

He went even stiller and seemed to pale. 'Did you answer it?'

'Of course not.'

'When did they ring?'

'About a minute ago.'

'Right.' He tossed the towel onto the bed and, to her disappointment, since it clearly meant that some more of that lovely, headboard-banging sex was temporarily off the agenda, spun away to don a pair of jeans and a shirt.

'Well?' she prompted.

'Excuse me,' he muttered distractedly as he strode to the bedside table and grabbed his phone. 'I need to return that call.'

With the last twenty-four hot, intense and strangely perturbing hours instantly wiped from his mind, Finn stalked out of the bedroom, across the hall, and into the sitting room. He closed the door behind him with deliberate control, his gut churning and his pulse racing. Alexandra Osborne called him once a week, same time, same day, regardless of whether

she'd made progress, and Sunday evening at six—
or five p.m. back home—was neither that day nor
that time.

Beginning to pace up and down, he located the
missed call and returned it, and when she answered
said, 'What do you have for me?'

'You might want to sit down,' she replied without preamble.

He drew to an abrupt halt and dropped into the
nearest available chair. 'Go ahead.'

'Early last week one of the leads we've been working on finally came good.'

'In what way?'

'It's been established that your adoptive parents
visited Argentina six months after you were born.
They went on their own and returned with you.'

The world skidded to a standstill and his heart
gave a great lurch. Argentina? What the hell?

'My contact managed to trace their movements
while they were there,' Alex continued while Finn
grappled for calm and forced himself to focus, 'and
placed them in La Posada.'

'Which is what?'

'A small, abandoned village near the border with
Bolivia. It consists mainly of a derelict orphanage
and a handful of ruined houses. While most of it was
looted years ago, the office of the orphanage had
barely been touched, quite probably because the filing cabinets had been bolted to the walls. In amongst

the papers they contained he found a number of birth certificates. We believe one of them to be yours.'

His lungs tightened. A punch of adrenaline kicked him in the chest and his pulse raced. 'How can you be sure?'

'The recorded date of birth is a match.'

'Does it have the names of the parents?'

'Yes. Juan Rodriguez and Maria Gonzalez. I'll email you a copy of everything we have. I apologise for it taking so long. The trail has been extremely well buried. We're still working on why that would be the case.' Alex paused, while Finn reeled, then said, 'There's something else.'

'What?'

'Are you still sitting down?'

'Yes.'

'There were two other birth certificates in the same file. Both boys. All of you born at around the same time on the same day.'

It took a second or two for the implication of what she was saying to sink in, but when it did the ground beneath his feet tilted violently. His vision blurred and he could hardly breathe. He felt as if he was about to pass out. 'I have brothers?'

'It would appear so. The evidence would suggest you're triplets.'

'Where are they? Are they alive?'

'Impossible to know at this stage.'

'Find them,' he said, his voice thick and his throat

clogging. 'Whatever you have to do, however much you have to pay, find them.'

'We will.'

Finn ended the call and as the phone slipped out of his hand and fell to the floor, the calm front he'd presented to Alex shattered. Every bit of him started shaking. His heart was beating too fast. His stomach was roiling. He was going to throw up.

Blindly, he got to his feet and made it to the terrace doors, which he threw open, and gulped in some much needed air while the information he'd just been given went round and round in his thoughts.

He'd been born in South America. He'd spent time in an orphanage. He had parents, brothers, was one of a set of triplets. Identical? Non-identical? What had happened to the other two? Where were they and why had they been separated?

The ping of an incoming message on his phone pierced the fog swirling around in his head and he stumbled back to where he'd been sitting. With trembling fingers he bent down to pick the device up and then collapsed into the chair before his legs gave way. Somehow he managed to unlock it. Somehow he found the right app, tapped the email and, his heart thundering so fast and hard it hurt, opened the attachment.

It contained three birth certificates plus translations. All identical, save the times of birth and the names. Mateo. Diego. Juan. His parents, his brothers, his family.

But which was his? Who was he and where were the others? Above all, *why*? Why the adoption? Why the separation? And who'd known? Had Jim and Alice been aware he was one of three? Surely not. Surely they couldn't have been so cruel as to keep that from him. Yet no one had ever mentioned Argentina. He even had a hotel there. In Buenos Aires. Jim had been at the opening six years ago and he'd never said a thing.

Having scoured the details and committed them to memory, Finn dropped the phone again, then rubbed his hands across his face and leaned forwards, his elbows resting on his knees, his head buried in his hands. How the hell was he going to deal with this? He'd assumed that with information would come clarity, but he was wrong. That assumption had been based on the most simple of explanations, yet the news Alex had just delivered threw up an explanation that was anything but simple.

Instead of being answered and filed away for cool, calm analysis, the questions were multiplying, ricocheting around his head faster and more chaotically and he couldn't sort any of them out. It was all too huge, too overwhelming.

As was the pain now beginning to slice through him as the shock-induced numbness faded. Thirty-one years he'd lost. Thirty-one years that he could potentially have known his siblings, his brothers. He could have had an entire other life. Would it have been better? Worse? It didn't matter. He'd been denied the choice because of Jim and Alice's silence, and the sense of betrayal that he assumed had abated now flayed him all over again, ripping open old wounds and stabbing at them afresh.

He'd thought he had it all under control, but he didn't. He had nothing under control. The pain powering through him was like a living thing, writhing around in his belly and thundering along his veins, leaving every inch of him raw and exposed and bleeding.

'Are you all right?'

At the sound of Georgie's voice, filled with concern, coming from far, far away, Finn froze. He hadn't heard the door open. He hadn't noticed the shadows lengthening across the floor. She couldn't see him like this, he thought frantically, a cold sweat breaking out all over his skin—weak, vulnerable and suffering, a man on the brink of collapse. He couldn't let her help. He couldn't allow her to push and prod as she was wont to do. It would drive him over the edge.

'Get out,' he said, his voice hoarse and cracked.

'What's happened?' she said, walking into the room and dropping to her knees beside the chair in which he was sitting, crowding his space and his thoughts, too close, too dangerous.

'I said, get out.'

'I know. But you're white as a sheet and shaking. I'm worried about you.'

'I'm fine.'

'Talk to me.'

'It has nothing to do with you,' he said sharply, desperately, seeing her flinch, which only added to his torment.

'Try.'

His strength was failing. His control was unravelling. He didn't have much time. 'No.'

'Yes.'

'All right,' he said harshly, his resistance crumbling beneath the need to get her out of his space before he completely lost it. 'How's this? Last November I discovered that I was adopted at the age of six months and that my entire life has been a lie. Fifteen minutes ago I learned that not only was I born in Argentina and left in an orphanage, but that I also have two brothers. We're triplets. As you may be able to understand, it's quite a lot to take in. I need some time and space to process it. So I'd appreciate it if you would respect that and leave me the hell alone.'

Wow.

Just wow.

For the briefest of moments all Georgie could do was stare at Finn as the frustration and torment rolled off him in waves and engulfed her, the shock of what he'd told her and how brutally he'd delivered it rendering her immobile. She could barely process it. He'd been adopted? He'd just found out he had a family he'd known nothing about? No wonder he was in such a spin.

When she'd seen the man she was in love with hunched over like that, clearly hurting, clearly in pain, her heart had twisted, and even though she hadn't known what was troubling him, she'd just felt a clamouring urge to race over and give him a hug. All she wanted to do was help. Genuinely.

But he didn't want it, she realised, the breath catching in her throat as her chest tightened. He didn't want comfort. He didn't want anything from her, as was clear not only from his words but also from the way he was jerking to his feet, turning away from her and stalking over to the window, a blunt, brutal dismissal that sliced her in two.

To think she'd been worried about him, she thought, her eyes stinging and hurt scything through her as she pushed herself to her feet and took a shaky step back. That all the time she'd spent showering and dressing while the minutes ticked slowly by she'd been wondering whether he was all right. What a waste of time and effort that had been.

He didn't want her and he certainly didn't need her. He probably never had. He was wholly self-contained. And as for the idea that they might be embarking on something resembling a proper relationship, what had she been *thinking*?

There may be lust but there was certainly no trust. Not on his side anyway. He must have been carrying the burden of his adoption for months, and the discovery of it, the uncertainty surrounding his identity, must have been cataclysmic. And he hadn't said a word. She'd told him virtually everything there was to know about her, warts and all, and he'd revealed practically nothing.

Every time he'd asked her something about herself she'd spouted like a fountain. She'd told him things, this morning in particular, that she'd never told anyone, things that she'd only just begun to acknowledge. Yet when the tables were turned and she dared to ask him anything even *remotely* personal he deflected it. She knew next to nothing about his upbringing or his parents or how he felt about any of it. How had she let that happen?

And why had he never told her that he was adopted? He'd told her that he didn't like secrets, but he'd been harbouring a massive one of his own, and on top of everything else that made him a hypocrite. So who else knew? Was she the only one who didn't? Why hadn't he wanted to talk about it with her? What was wrong with her? Was it the state of her mental health? Was that why he'd told her he wanted to know everything about her when they'd been talking this morning? She'd seen his interest as a sign their relationship was shifting to another, more intimate level but perhaps he'd just been looking out for Josh by trying to find out how stable she really was?

They had no relationship and no connection, she realised as she stalked into the bedroom, blinking rapidly to ease the prickling in her eyes, and she'd been a fool to even begin to think otherwise. Everything she'd stupidly imagined they'd shared was entirely one-sided. Even this weekend, which had meant so much to her, would now be nothing more than a permanently tarnished memory.

She'd been falling for an illusion, a man who didn't exist, a man she'd conjured up out of her own imagination because that was what she needed. She'd been delusional, which wasn't a word she used lightly, and worse, naive. What would someone like Finn with his gorgeous looks and confidence and billions in the bank ever see in a woman like her anyway? How could her judgement still be so off?

Well, no more, she thought grimly, grabbing her suitcase and depositing it on the bed. Enough of the imbalance. Enough of being the pathetic, soppy drip she turned into around him. If she didn't want to end up being even more hurt, perhaps even irreparably so, she could afford neither.

Nor was she having her recently rediscovered confidence and self-esteem knocked by Finn and his stick-his-head-in-the-sand attitude. She had to protect herself, although how she was going to do that now that they were civilly partnered and therefore stuck with each other and living in close proximity she had no idea. But she'd think of something. She'd have to.

In the meantime there was no way she was hanging around like a punchbag for all the emotions he must be feeling and clearly couldn't handle. She was packing up and going back to London. Back to her son, who, unlike Finn, *did* need her. And then Finn would have all the space and time to think that he wanted.

CHAPTER ELEVEN

FINN STOOD AT the window and stared blankly onto the streets of Paris stretching out far below, the silence telling him that Georgie had finally done what he'd needed her to do and in the nick of time. Treachery, hurt and sadness had wound their tendrils along every vein and around every cell, and he felt shattered, broken, as though he was being pummelled to within an inch of his life.

He had to calm down, he told himself desperately, forcing himself to take a deep, shuddering breath and loosen his white-knuckled fists. He had to stop. For the sake of his blood pressure and the woman he'd sent away, who was no doubt cursing him with every breath she took. He couldn't go on like this, snapping and snarling in a way he thought he'd long since buried. He'd hated that man. He wouldn't allow himself to regress again.

As he battled to control the pandemonium churning him up inside, he thought too how he hated the way he'd responded to Georgie's offer of help. How

savagely he'd lashed out at her. At the memory of
the way in which he'd spoken to her, he inwardly
cringed. She'd done nothing to deserve such treatment. All she'd wanted was to help.

And maybe, despite his assertions to the contrary,
he needed it. Because he didn't hold much hope of
sorting the turmoil out on his own. He didn't exactly
have a great track record on that front. He'd bottled up how he'd felt about his mother's death. He'd
pushed aside his father's diagnosis initially with alcohol and sex and, subsequently, work. He'd responded
to the discovery of his adoption by being unpleasantly short and rude to anyone who had the misfortune of finding themselves in his vicinity.

What he hadn't done was talk about it. Any of it.
To anyone. He didn't do talking. He never had done.
His father had been the stoical, stiff-upper-lip type,
unable to show emotion. Even when Finn's mother
had died, he'd hidden his grief behind a wall of im-
penetrability. As a result, when it came to feelings,
Finn had always been self-reliant, a master of inter-
nalisation, choosing to box up what he felt so as not
to have to deal with the inevitable messy fallout.

Only this morning—God, was it only this morning?—he'd considered perhaps asking Georgie for
tips, and if ever there was an occasion to do so, this
was it. Who better to talk to? She knew what it was
like to stumble around blindly, looking for answers.
She knew him. And, more to the point, for some

unfathomable reason he *wanted* her to know. They were a team. In this thing, whatever it was, together.

He was under no illusion that it would be easy. It would probably be hell on earth, even assuming that Georgie was receptive to the idea, which was doubtful, given how he'd dismissed her. But it was worth a shot. He had to do *something* that made sense. And at the very least he owed her an apology.

Finally finding a path through the chaos, Finn spun round and strode out of the sitting room and into the bedroom, only to come to an abrupt halt at the sight of Georgie packing a suitcase.

'What are you doing?' he said, his brows snapping together in a deep frown.

She didn't look at him, just carried on folding the stunning green dress she'd worn last night and which he'd peeled off her what felt like a lifetime ago.

'What does it look like?' she said, her voice utterly devoid of the warmth and concern with which she'd asked him what was wrong back there in the sitting room.

'You're packing.'

'Yes.'

'Why?'

'You wanted space. You wanted time. I plan to give you both.'

What? 'I meant I needed a couple of minutes,' he said. 'Ten. Maybe fifteen. I didn't mean for you to leave.'

'Well, there seems little point in hanging around.'

At the realisation that she actually meant it he felt a sharp stab of something to the chest, and for a moment he thought, well, of course she was. Leaving was what people who he cared about or who were supposed to care about him did, after all. But he shoved it aside in order to focus because this was one occasion at least in which he *did* have the power to take control. 'Don't go.'

'Give me one good reason not to.'

'You were right. I think I probably should talk to someone.'

She flung her hairbrush into the case, then whirled round to scoop up her make-up that was scattered on the dressing table. 'So find a therapist,' she said, dumping it in there too.

'But you're here.'

'Right.'

'Please. I'm sorry for lashing out,' he said, his jaw clenching as he recalled how he'd spoken to her. 'I didn't handle things well.'

'It's fine.'

'It isn't.'

She shrugged. 'You'd had a shock.'

That was an understatement. 'Nevertheless, it's no excuse,' he said gruffly. 'I really am sorry.'

'Apology accepted. Now, if you wouldn't mind…'

'Please, Georgie.'

She must have heard the note of torment in his voice because she stopped what she was doing, *finally*, and gave a great sigh. 'OK, fine,' she said, abruptly sitting on the bed and looking at him, her eyes wary and her expression cool. 'God knows you've had to listen to me prattle on enough.' *Prattle?* he thought with a frown. She did *not* prattle. 'So if you want to talk I'll listen.'

With a rush of relief, Finn stalked into the room and leaned against the edge of the dressing table she'd just cleared. He rubbed his hands over his face and then shoved them into the pockets of his jeans. He cleared his throat and braced himself.

'So it turns out that I find it hard to process big things,' he began, inwardly wincing at how pathetic he sounded. 'Especially big *emotional* things. I have a tendency to lock things down.'

'That's understandable. Although probably not very healthy.'

'No.' It wasn't healthy at all. God only knew the damage he'd caused his nervous system recently. It also smacked of hypocrisy because it had just occurred to him that by withholding the truth from her and obfuscating he'd been behaving like Jim and Alice, which did not sit well.

'Have you always done it?'

He gave a short nod. 'Ever since my mother—Alice—died.'

'That's a long time.'

'Yes.' Too long, with hindsight. 'I bottled up how I felt about that for years. I was only ten. I didn't know what the hell was going on. Jim—my father—

or, rather, my adopted father—did the best he could but he wasn't one for emoting either.'

Her eyebrows lifted. 'You didn't talk to anyone? A counsellor? A teacher?'

He shook his head. 'No one. Not until the lid of the pressure cooker flew off when I was a teenager.'

'What happened then?'

'Nothing all that dramatic. I got into a couple of fights when I was sixteen. Spent a night in jail for being drunk and disorderly.'

'And then you had therapy?'

'Of a kind. The officer in charge that night asked what I was thought I was doing and it all came out. She gave me some good advice. The incident turned out to be a huge wake-up call. However, it turns out that internalising things is a hard habit to break.'

'We all have our ways of coping.'

Yes, well, unlike hers, his weren't working out so well. 'Jim's diagnosis was something else I didn't talk about,' he said, forcing himself to keep going because she needed to know everything in order to be able to help.

'Did no one ask?'

'Not many knew. I told the people who did that everything was fine.'

'So how did you find out you were adopted?'

'I was going through Jim's papers after he died. The certificate was in a box that had been stored in the attic of his house.'

'That must have been devastating.'

'It was. I was in the middle of a full-blown identity crisis when you turned up with the news about
Josh.'

'No wonder you were so insistent on rescuing
him. He's your only flesh and blood.'

'As far as I know.'

She frowned and gave a faint nod. 'Right.'

Unable to bear the intensity of her scrutiny or
suppress the restlessness whipping around inside
him any longer, Finn pushed himself off the dressing table. 'It's been a disorientating time,' he said,
shoving his hands through his hair as he began to
pace. 'I feel as if I've been manipulated. As though
everything about me has to be redefined and rene-
gotiated. I'm thirty-one. It's been tough trying to
work out how much of my life has been real and
how much a lie. I can't figure out why Jim never said
anything, especially after Alice died, and it's been
driving me mad.'

Georgie gave a loud sigh of what sounded like exasperation. 'Oh, for the love of God, will you *please*
stop calling them that?' she said heatedly.

Stunned at her tone, wondering where the hell
the sympathy he'd been expecting was, Finn came
to an abrupt halt and whipped round to stare at her.
'What?'

Her colour was high and her eyes were blazing
and the need that suddenly streaked through him
nearly knocked him off his feet. 'Look, Finn, I get
that you feel let down and betrayed. And, believe

me, I know what it's like to have your whole world turned upside down and your identity stripped away. But Jim and Alice were, to all intents and purposes, your parents.'

He ruthlessly quashed the desire and frowned at her, denial reeling through him. 'I fail to see how.'

'Biology doesn't automatically grant parental rights,' she said bluntly. 'Nor does it guarantee the ability to parent successfully. Look at mine. They're hardly an advert for parents of the year. They never gave a toss about me, not properly, and they still don't. Carla's looked out for me far more than they ever did. She's the reason I was able to find you all those weeks ago. If she hadn't made me send her a photo of you along with your name the night we met, things could have turned out very differently. You had two people who loved and cared for you. And, yes, then, tragically, only one, but nevertheless you had someone on your side for *years*, someone who by your own admission never failed to support and champion you when it mattered most. You honestly don't know how lucky you were.'

'What if my mother's death wasn't an accident?' The question shot out of his mouth before he could stop it and he froze, every muscle in his body as taut as a bow string.

'What do you mean?' she asked carefully and he suddenly found himself on a knife edge.

He could easily deflect the question, he knew, but what would be the point of that? He needed her perspective and her insight into things he couldn't make head or tail of, and that meant unlocking the doors on his greatest concerns and flinging them open, so he took a deep breath and said, 'What if she killed herself deliberately because of me, because of what I was or wasn't?'

He hated the catch he could hear in his voice, but he didn't regret the question because her face softened and, ah, there was the sympathy he'd been in need of. 'Do you really believe that?'

'I don't know.'

'What do you remember of her?'

He scrolled back twenty years, searching for memories that were faded and hazy but nevertheless still there. 'She smelled of roses,' he said eventually. 'She taught me poker and played football with me. Every Saturday she'd bake brownies.'

'She sounds lovely,' Georgie said, a trace of wistfulness flitting across her face.

'She was.'

'Did she make you eat your vegetables?'

'Yes.'

'Make you do your homework and go to bed on time?'

'Yes.'

'Were you ever sent to your room or grounded?'

'Frequently.'

'Then she loved you,' she said with quiet conviction. 'Very much. Take it from someone who knows what it feels like not to matter. They must have wanted you very much too, to go all the way to Argentina to fetch you. And they must have had their reasons for keeping it from you.'

'I guess I'll never know,' he said, his throat oddly tight.

'Unless your investigation agency digs something up.'

'Maybe not even then.'

'So much in life we just have to accept.'

'As I'm discovering.'

'Me too.'

With a strangely sad sort of smile she pushed herself off the bed and returned her attention to the suitcase, and as he watched her pull the top down and zip it up it hit him like a blow to the chest that, despite everything he'd just revealed, nothing had changed.

'You're still planning to leave?' he asked, the blade of rejection slicing through him like a knife.

'I have to get back to Josh.' She shot him a quick glance, full of something he was too stung, too busy reeling, to identify. 'Unless there's any other reason for me to stay?'

'No, nothing,' he said, coolly, calling himself a fool for wanting her to stay, for thinking that he was good enough for her, for believing that they were in this together. 'Go. Please. Don't let me stop you.'

All she'd wanted was for him to say that he wanted her to stay, thought Georgie numbly as she stepped off the train at St Pancras and, dragging her wheelie case behind her, went in search of a taxi. That they were a team. A tightly knit unit. That she mattered to him as much as he mattered to her, despite her best efforts to deny it.

But he'd let her go with such ease, and that hurt unbelievably badly. So much for thinking that she could somehow avoid more pain, that she could protect herself. Or that she was only beginning to fall for him. She already had. There could be little doubt about it. She had to be head over heels in love with him for his indifferent dismissal to cause this much agony.

But however much it hurt, the pain wouldn't last because that love hadn't been real. Finn wasn't the man she'd thought him to be. She'd given him attributes—loyalty, honesty, integrity—that he didn't have, and really she had no one to blame but herself. She was the one who'd placed him on a pedestal so high and wobbly that it was inevitable he should fall off it. She was the one who'd misread every look and every word, reading things into his actions that simply hadn't been there. This whole mess was entirely her fault.

The train journey from Paris had lasted two and a half hours and every minute of it she'd spent analysing their relationship, such as it was. And she could see now that she'd been a fool. Finn had never wanted her. Not really. All he wanted was Josh. She came as part of the package and was handy for sex, but that was about it.

She knew this to be true because right from the start she'd been the one in the driving seat. In the bar the night they'd first met she'd been the one to approach him, and then the one to proposition him by telling him she wanted to leave, with him. He hadn't chosen her that night. She'd chosen him.

And so it had been ever since.

She'd given him no option but to take up the role of father and provide his support. What else could he have done in the circumstances? How could she have forgotten the reluctance with which he'd taken her in along with Josh? How she'd made him spend his evenings with her and then virtually forced him into going to bed with her by following him into his room the night he'd told her to put on a dressing gown and whipping her top off? Ditto when she'd pressed the condom into his hand at the party last night and told him she wanted sex. He hadn't even planned to take her to Paris. The invitation had been last-minute and he'd only asked her because of what they'd been getting up to after dark.

And then take this evening, when he'd finally opened up to her about how he felt about his parents and the revelations surrounding his adoption. He'd only done that because she was there. Because she was convenient. He hadn't particularly wanted to talk to *her*.

He'd volunteered nothing willingly, she could see now. He obviously didn't see her as an equal in this relationship. Maybe not in anything. They weren't partners in any sense of the word. They were nothing. She was nothing. And so, frankly, what was the point in them continuing with this ridiculous charade?

CHAPTER TWELVE

FINN SPENT THE torturous hours following Georgie's departure railing at himself while ploughing through half a bottle of Scotch. He'd been a fool for telling her everything. He'd made himself insanely vulnerable and unacceptably weak. He'd invested too much in the power of her response, and, unlike any other he'd ever made, that investment had badly backfired. The hurt and disappointment that roared through him when he recalled how carelessly she'd left him were precisely why he didn't share. How could he have forgotten that? At what point had he recklessly decided to ignore what he knew to be true—that other people's behaviour was incalculable and that the only person he could rely on was himself? What had he been thinking?

All in all, he was glad she'd gone. He had a hectic schedule over the next couple of days and he needed to focus. He did not need extra stress and he did not need Georgie. He was perfectly capable of working through everything going on in his head on his own. It might take some time, but he was going to let it play out and eventually he'd get there. He had to obliterate the ridiculous feelings of rejection and abandonment, and regroup.

However, with increasing frequency, he found himself revisiting their conversation, assessing what Georgie had said and stripping the words of emotion. Grudgingly, he came to the conclusion that she'd had a point. Possibly even more than one. Because the truth was that, however hard he looked, however much money he threw at the investigation, he may never get the answers he sought.

So what was he going to do? He couldn't spend the rest of his life being bitter and resentful. He had to accept that he'd become the man he was now because of Jim and Alice, who *had* been his parents in all ways that counted. The memories he had of his mother were warm and happy. The photos they'd taken of him had filled dozens of albums. His father had not once let him down while alive. He'd been an unfailing tower of strength. Only in death had he turned out to have feet of clay. But as neither of them was around to defend or explain their actions and decisions, what had gone before was beyond Finn's control.

How he went forward, however, *was* within his control. Whatever the reasons for his adoption and the subsequent secrecy surrounding it, he had to forgive his parents, his father in particular. He could understand now a paternal determination to protect a

child to the exclusion of all else. To not let anything
upset the status quo. Whatever else he might think,
he had to understand that none of it was anything
to do with him and believe it. His parents had done
their best and they'd been good people, and Georgie
was right: he had been lucky. It was all right to regret
that his father had never got to meet Josh and it was
all right to resume the grieving process that had been
interrupted with the discovery of that certificate.

He had to let it go and focus on the family he did
have instead of chasing relentlessly after wisps of
the one he may or may not have elsewhere. He had
so much to appreciate. So much to value.

Especially Georgie.

Who, despite her apparent rejection, despite his
attempts to put her out of his mind, he was missing
more than he could have ever imagined. He'd got
used to having her around, in his home and in his
bed, and he felt her absence like a physical loss. It
was more than just the phenomenal sex he missed.
He missed her wit and her smile, her wisdom, the
way she challenged him and made him face up to
things he'd rather ignore, and the conversations that
had relaxed and deepened with time. Their relationship might have started out as one of convenience
for the sake of Josh but it wasn't any longer. They
knew every inch of each other's bodies. And minds.
He'd trusted her with his secrets and she'd trusted
him with hers, her honesty so raw that it had torn at

his soul and filled him with even more burning regret that his support had come so late.

Finn had never been in love before. He'd never even so much as thought about it, so he had nothing with which to compare the feelings that were swirling around inside him, feelings that were so intense, so powerful they couldn't be locked away even if he tried. Nevertheless he was now pretty sure that the way his heart leapt whenever she walked into the room, the unrelenting need, the respect and admiration he had for her, and the hammering desire to protect her and grow old with her met the definition of it. So too did the happiness and sense of rightness that spread through him whenever she entered his head, which was virtually all the time. And when he thought about the shimmering warmth with which he occasionally caught her looking at him and the way her eyes sparkled when she was with him he was equally sure that she felt the same way about him.

Or at least she had done.

Until he'd behaved like an idiot and let her go. Even if he hadn't realised at the time quite why he needed her, he should have come up with a reason for her to stay. As she'd asked. A request, which, now he thought about it, now he could clearly recall how she'd put it, had been made with the answer she wanted in mind. Of course, it was entirely possible that she *had* simply wanted to get back to Josh. But equally, what if she'd wanted something else entirely? What if he'd allowed his insecurities to dominate and had overreacted? What if she hadn't been rejecting *him*, but the abominable way he'd behaved? More importantly, what might have happened if he hadn't let her go?

As Finn strode out of the hotel on Tuesday afternoon and climbed into the car he thought with grim determination that there was only one way to find out whether or not he'd ruined things with Georgie for good. And, since he was now through with boxing up emotion and ignoring it, however difficult, he was going to take it.

Finn had texted her earlier to say that he was on his way home and had given her an ETA, but Georgie, who was sitting cross-legged on the sofa and staring into space, couldn't summon up the energy to care. The last couple of days hadn't been easy. In fact, apart from the time she spent with Josh, they'd been miserable. She felt so cold, so tired. What with all the thinking she'd been doing about her and Finn, she hadn't been sleeping too well, and watching out for Josh, who'd started crawling and was constantly getting to places he shouldn't, was exhausting. This morning she'd barely managed to haul herself out of bed when her son had called for her for the fifth time in as many hours.

Contrary to her expectations, the disappointment and sadness she felt at knowing that the man she'd fallen in love with didn't exist hadn't faded. Everything had worsened and then amalgamated and now thrashed around in the pit of her stomach, giving her no respite. The delirious happiness she'd once thought she felt had been nothing but an illusion. The realisation that the secure, loving family unit she craved was as distant a possibility as it ever had been was devastating.

Nothing she did alleviated the gloom. She'd tried writing about how she felt in her journal but the last two days' pages were blank. She didn't know where to begin. Going out and getting some fresh air seemed like a huge effort, so she hadn't bothered. Even venturing onto the terrace presented a mammoth challenge. She certainly hadn't had the energy to pack up with Josh and leave, as she'd originally planned. And in any case, where would she have gone? She could hardly move into a different hotel room, and Carla would ask too many questions that Georgie wouldn't be able to answer. Besides, she and Finn needed to unpick this disaster of an arrangement and sooner rather than later.

She fed Josh and changed him and played with him, but she felt oddly disengaged, as if she was simply going through the motions. And, while a tiny part of her recognised that how she was feeling wasn't normal and was concerned by it, the greatest part of her was too drained to pay any attention. Finn would be back soon anyway, and when he was he could take over, so she could crawl into bed and stay there for a month, at which point maybe they could then talk. In fact, she thought dully as the sound of the front door opening reached her, here he was now.

She felt the air shift, and glanced up from the journal that was sitting open and empty in her lap to find Finn standing in the doorway and emanating a weird sort of taut determination, his face set and his eyes dark.

'Hi,' he said, removing his jacket and rolling the sleeves of his shirt up with an efficient competency that not so long ago would have had her quivering with desire but now left her distressingly unmoved.

'Hi.'

'How have you been?'

Freezing, actually. But spring could be like that. Maybe she ought to have turned the heating on. 'Fine.'

'Why are you sitting in the dark?' He stalked over to a lamp in the corner and switched it on.

'I didn't realise it was so late,' she said, blinking at the sudden light.

'How's Josh?'

'He's fine. He's asleep.' Finally. 'He started crawling yesterday.'

'Did he? I'm sorry I missed that.'

'He's fast,' she said, attempting a weak smile. 'I envy his energy.'

Finn sat down on the ottoman, leaning forwards and resting his elbows on his knees, and peered at her, his eyes narrowing slightly. 'Are you all right?' he asked. 'You look tired.'

'Josh has another tooth coming through. It's been keeping us both up at night.'

'Where's Mrs Gardiner?'

'I gave her a couple of days off.'

His dark brows snapped together. 'Why?'

'It was her granddaughter's birthday. She lives in Wales. Mrs G was keen to go.' And she'd been keen to have her go because even conversation had started being hard work.

'When is she back?'

'I'm not sure.'

'I'll give her a call later.'

'How were your meetings?'

'Fine,' he said, his gaze locking with hers and not letting it go. 'But I don't want to talk about my meetings.'

Of course he didn't. He didn't want to talk to her about anything. Why would he?

'I want to talk about us.'

Oh, the irony. 'There is no us,' she said, her chest nevertheless squeezing.

He went very still, something she couldn't even begin to identify flickering in the depths of his eyes. 'Do you mean that?'

'Yes.'

'Why?'

'Because you clearly don't trust me.'

His eyebrows shot up. 'What?'

'You don't trust me.'

'Why would you think that?'

She closed the journal with a snap, a sudden hot rush of emotion obliterating the numbness and firing her deadened nerve-endings. 'I told you everything about me, Finn. Everything. Yet every time I asked you anything about your parents or anything even vaguely personal you brushed me aside. You told me nothing. Until you absolutely had no choice.'

'What are you talking about?'

'Your adoption. That huge thing that you didn't think to share with me.'

He stared at her, a tiny muscle in his jaw pulsating. 'I couldn't,' he said gruffly. 'I could barely make sense of it myself. I certainly couldn't have talked about it any sooner than I did. With you or anyone.'

'No one else knows?'

'You're the only person I've told. The only person I *wanted* to know, I've recently realised. You unlocked me in that respect. You made me re-evaluate the past and see things from a different perspective. I don't regret any of that. I do, however, regret how that conversation ended. I'm sorry. I let decades-old hang-ups get the better of me. I was an idiot for letting you leave.'

'If you'd told me that I mattered to you and that we were in this together I'd have stayed.'

A flicker of warmth and something that looked like hope leapt in the depths of his eyes. 'You *do* matter to me and we *are* in this together.'

'Because of Josh.'

His gaze intensified and heated. 'Not entirely.'

No, she thought acidly. It wouldn't do to forget the sex side of things, would it? Or to be careless and ignore the need to protect herself. 'Yes, well, I have regrets too.'

'What do you regret?'

'Everything,' she said with deliberate bluntness. 'Our entire relationship is completely wrong.'

He paled. 'In what way?'

'In every way,' she said. 'Would you have chosen to be with me if it wasn't for Josh?'

'That's a wholly unfair question,' he said, his jaw tightening as a flash of wariness flitted across his face. 'Not to mention impossible to answer.'

Which meant no. And only went to prove her point. 'Right from the beginning I've forced you into doing things you can't possibly have wanted to do.'

'Such as?'

'Being a father. Accommodating me and Josh, me in particular. Giving up your evenings. Taking me to bed. The dinner with friends I made you have. Then Paris. The sex. The talking. You name it, I've made you do it.'

He looked at her as though she'd come from another planet. 'That's ridiculous.'

'Is it?'

'Are you serious?'

'Deadly.'

'I have never done anything even remotely reluctantly in my entire life,' he said, his steady gaze fixed to hers. 'If I want to do something, I do it.

If I don't, I don't. If I'd known about Josh sooner I'd have been right there with you every step of the way. The night you came into my room and took off your top I wanted you so badly I was at the end of my tether anyway. I wanted you from the first moment I saw you again. Why do you think I spent so much time out of the apartment when you and Josh first moved in?'

'Work?'

'Not work,' he said darkly. 'I spent every evening in the fitness suite trying to obliterate the need, much good that it did me. If you hadn't come to me that night I would have gone to you. You were just quicker, that's all.' He gave his head a quick shake and then rubbed his hands over his face. 'I didn't deliberately delay us having dinner with friends, although I will admit to wanting you to myself for a while longer. And I didn't need to take you with me to Paris. I've never taken anyone to Paris. Or anywhere else, for that matter. I didn't even need to be there myself. I don't usually. I prefer to stay in the background and let my extremely efficient PR company take care of that side of things.'

She swallowed hard, torn between wanting to believe him and not wanting to believe him. 'So why did you?'

He looked at her for a moment, as if the question had taken him by surprise. 'I wanted to show you my hotel,' he said with a faint smile. 'I wanted to show you off.'

'Not for the sex?'

'We weren't having it then. But I admit there may have been an element of that too. It had been a while.'

'Why didn't you call me?'

'When?'

'At any point over the last forty-eight hours. It occurred to me that you might be busy thinking about your other family.'

'I wasn't. I spent the hours I wasn't in meetings processing the grief for my father that was interrupted when I found that certificate. And then thinking about what you said, how right you were and trying to figure it all out in my head. Would you have answered if I had called?'

'Possibly not,' she had to admit.

He leaned forwards and peered at her closely, confusion swirling in the depths of his eyes, a deep frown creasing his forehead. 'What's going on, Georgie? Where is all this coming from?'

Wasn't it obvious? It was all coming from him. From their situation. From his lack of trust and her crushing disappointment that he wasn't the man she'd desperately wanted him to be. From the realisation that they had no relationship outside parenting Josh and never would. From his shattering of her heart and the subsequent fracturing of her dreams.

Or was it?

Finn was still staring at her, his gaze clear and unwavering, as if he was trying to see into her soul, his presence about the only solid thing she could fix on. And through the fog of nothingness in her head, there was a spark of…something.

Light.

Clarity.

A seed of doubt planted itself in her head, its roots spreading fast and wide. That tiny voice of concern grew louder. And as fragments of what Finn had been saying spun through her thoughts, solidifying, gaining credence, gaining volume, those doubts exploded and she went icy cold.

Oh, God.

What if all this had come not from him but from *her*? From her insecurities, from her illness? What if this was the setback, possibly even the depression, she'd been fearing?

As she frantically analysed everything that had happened over the last couple of days, the way she'd been feeling, the suspiciousness, the hopelessness and the sadness, her heart began to race and a cold sweat broke out all over her skin.

She was right in the middle of it, she realised with a sickening jolt. One tug of the rug from beneath her feet, one toss of the sea and she'd tumbled into a return of the paranoia, a deadening lack of energy, of libido, and icy numbness.

That was all it had taken.

She wasn't better, she thought as a shaft of agony and despair cut through her and she began to tremble all over. She wasn't anywhere near better. She may never be. And it was crucifying.

'I'm sorry, I can't do this,' she said, her throat tight and her eyes stinging.

'Can't do what?'

'Whatever it is you think we're doing.'

His dark gaze didn't leave hers, but it did nothing to calm the distress suddenly whirling around inside her. 'I think we're building a relationship,' he said. 'A real relationship.'

'We aren't,' she said hoarsely. Even if he *was* the man she'd thought he was—and God, she didn't know which version to believe any more—they couldn't be. She wasn't capable of it. She wasn't strong enough. She didn't know if she ever would be. 'We never have been.'

'I disagree. Our civil partnership stopped being a pragmatic arrangement weeks ago. If it ever was in the first place.' He stopped and took a deep breath. 'I love you, Georgie.'

As the words hit her brain a bolt of panic shot through her, denial screaming at her. 'No.'

'Yes,' he said, his eyes suddenly blazing with a heat that only emphasised how cold and confused she felt. 'I am head over heels in love with you.'

How could he be when even she didn't know who she was anymore? 'You don't know me.'

'I do. I know exactly who you are. And I think you love me too.'

That was what she'd thought once too but now she didn't know what to think. 'I don't know you.'

'You know me better than anyone.'

'Even if I could believe that, even if you're right, I can't be what you want,' she said, her voice breaking. How could she possibly lumber him with her when she was like this? How fair on him would it be if she had a setback every time he did or said something unexpected? How long would it be before they were both walking on eggshells, communicating only about their son?

'Yes, you can. You already are.'

'Do you want more children?'

'Not if you don't.'

'I don't believe you.'

'OK, maybe I would like Josh to have siblings,' he said. 'Maybe I would like to be part of a bigger family. But there's surrogacy. Or, dare I say it, adoption?'

He'd already thought that far ahead? 'I'm sorry,' she said, growing cold with fear and desperation. 'I can't handle this right now. It's all too much.'

'Either way, Georgie, I'm not letting you go. I told you I'd keep you safe and I meant it. Whatever is going on we'll deal with it together.'

'No. We can't.'

'We can.'

'You don't understand.'

'I'm trying to.'

'It's impossible.'

'Nothing is impossible.'

This is, she thought, sadness and confusion pouring through her. *This is.*

'I need to go.'

He recoiled as if she'd slapped him. 'Where?'

'I don't know,' she said, scrambling to her feet and taking a shaky step back. 'Somewhere else.'

'Don't fight me,' he said, his voice cracking as he rose too. 'Fight *for* me. Like I'm trying to fight for you. For us.'

'I told you before, there is no us.'

'You don't mean that.'

'I do.'

'I've never begged for anything,' he said, his voice low and rough, 'but I'm begging you. If you won't stay for me, at least stay for our son.'

Why? What was the point? What good could she possibly be to anyone while still so ill? 'He'll be far better off with you than me.'

'He needs *you*. *I* need you. I love you.' He raked his hands through his hair, his eyes wild with confusion and desperation. 'Georgie, you matter so much to me. The night we met I felt we had a connection that went far beyond chemistry. It was like something in me instinctively recognised something in you. And it's only grown since then. Everything about you fascinates me. The way you twist your hair and chew on your pen. The way you are with our son, your patience and your gentleness. You're the strongest, most incredible person I've ever met. You confront your fears and deal with them and you've made me do that too. You let me get away with nothing. You're beautiful and clever and funny and the woman I love. I've never felt like this about anyone ever. I don't want to be without you, Georgie. I can't.'

'I'm sorry,' she said, her eyes stinging and her throat tight as she stumbled back in the direction of the door.

'Don't do this. Please.'

'I have to.'

He moved towards her and put his hands on her shoulders, his expression fierce. 'You don't.'

'I do,' she cried, wrenching away.

'Where will you go?'

'I'll let you know.'

'It's late.'

'I'll be fine.'

'I won't let you do this, Georgie. I won't let you leave. Not this time.'

'This time,' she said, turning and heading for the door before the tears could spill over, 'you don't have any choice.'

CHAPTER THIRTEEN

As the door closing rang in his ears, Finn stood there rooted to the spot, reeling as torment and bewilderment spun through him.

What the hell had just happened?

He'd returned home, all fired up with ferocious determination and the hammering need to put things right, the rings he'd bought her in Paris burning a hole in his pocket. He didn't know what he'd expected to find on his arrival. He hadn't given it much thought. However, if he had, Georgie sitting on the sofa in the dark, pale and drawn, would not have been it. The sight of her had knocked him for six. Concern had slammed into him. But nothing had stunned him as much as the conversation that had then ensued.

He felt as if he'd stepped into an alternative universe, one in which there were no rules and nothing made sense. Did she really believe everything she'd said? he wondered, his head spinning and his gut churning. That they had no relationship and never would? How could she, after everything they'd been through together?

Yet that was how it seemed. The more he'd tried to convince her that they did have something, that he loved her, the more she'd backed off. It had been like trying to hold on to water and somehow, unintentionally and agonisingly, he'd made things worse.

Georgie was not in a good way—she'd walked out on *their son*—and his entire body began to ache with the knowledge that perhaps he couldn't help her. Perhaps he'd never be able to help her. Her despair, her desperation and the tears that she'd struggled to contain cut through him like a knife. He'd thought he could bind her to him with a civil partnership, but no ties were strong enough to overcome this. Nor was how he felt about her, because he'd tried everything. He'd tried reasoning with her and then pleaded with her and it had made no difference. He didn't know how to fix this. Never had he felt so powerless. It was agony. It was terrifying.

But there was one thing he did know. When she'd told him he didn't have a choice she'd been wrong. Dead wrong. It was pretty much the only thing he did have right now, and, despite not having a clue about anything, he was making it because he was *not* losing her again.

Georgie fled down the hall, the tears that she'd been wretchedly holding back spilling over and streaking down her cheeks. With every step she took the knife slicing her heart to pieces struck harder and faster, the pain flowing through her veins unbearable.

Why was this happening to her? she thought with a desperate sniff. Why was life, her illness, so cruel? What had she ever done to deserve any of it? Why couldn't she be happy? Why couldn't she be normal?

Reaching the lift, she pressed the button with one trembling finger, but the lift seemed to be as broken as she was because nothing happened, no matter how much she jabbed away at it. And she really needed it to work because she had to escape. She had to find somewhere to hole up and lick her wounds, wounds that were raw and deep and indelible.

But what if there was no escape? a little voice inside her head cried. What if no matter how far she ran, how hard she tried, this was always going to be her reality? What if she was destined to be dogged by what had happened for the rest of her life, never happy, never normal? She couldn't run for ever. She didn't want to be that person, constantly in fear of the present and the future, continually up and down, vulnerable and helpless. She *wasn't* that person. She wouldn't be. She had to face up to it.

Starting now.

What was she doing? she asked herself urgently, taking a step back from the lift, away from the edge. Where was she planning on heading? Was she *really* going to walk away from Josh? From Finn? Who claimed to love her? Who maybe *did* love her?

In the still quiet of the hall, the only sound in her ears the hammering of her heart, Georgie thought about the calm, steadfast way he'd countered all her accusations. About his strength and resilience in the face of her increasing panic. About everything he'd said and done over the last few months. If she accepted that she'd been in the grip of paranoia and doubt caused by her illness then she also had to accept that his version of events was the right one.

And God, she wanted it to be. She had to take a chance on them. She *wanted* to take a chance on them. Because she loved him back. He *was* the man she'd imagined him to be. She hadn't got that wrong. The happiness she'd felt hadn't been an illusion. Nor had any of the feelings she had before she'd left Paris. Everything had been real. Her hopes and dreams still lay within her grasp if only she was brave enough to grab them.

She would take control of this thing winding its wicked tendrils around her thoughts and emotions, she promised herself as she blew her nose and set her jaw. Come hell or high water, she *would* beat it. She'd seek help and go back on the medication. She should never have stopped taking it in the first place. What had she been thinking when she'd even been warned of the dangers of doing exactly that? She was going to fight for herself. And fight for Finn, for them, just as he'd asked her to.

With determination powering through her, Georgie spun on her heel and retraced her steps, only to slam to a halt a moment later at the sight of Finn striding down the hall towards her.

'This is not happening,' he said with a fierceness on his handsome face that heated all the places that had been so cold lately. 'You are not leaving me. You are not leaving Josh. I love you and you don't get to run away. I won't allow it. I know it's complicated but we'll figure it out. Together.'

'Yes,' she said simply, the emotion pummelling her on the inside practically wiping out her knees. There was much, *much* more that she wanted to say but her throat was so tight and the emotion so thick that she couldn't. All she could do was throw her arms around his neck and pull his head down to hers and kiss him with everything she was feeling.

With a harsh groan Finn whipped one arm around her waist and the other around her shoulders, pulling her tightly against him as he kissed her back with equal heat and need and desperation.

'God, Georgie,' he muttered when he eventually lifted his head, his breath ragged, his heart pounding against hers.

'I'm so sorry,' she said, hearing the catch in her voice and swallowing hard. 'I had a relapse and panicked. I convinced myself that you weren't who I thought you were. I've been so confused. So lost.'

'So have I,' he said passionately. 'But we belong together. We belong to each other.'

'I don't want to live without Josh. Or you. I love you.'

He rested his forehead against hers and she could feel him shaking with emotion. 'I think I fell in love with you the moment you walked up to me in my club and asked me if you could join me. You were dazzling.'

'I'm not that person any longer.'

'You're all that and more.'

'I still need help.'

'We'll get it,' he said, stroking his thumbs over her cheeks to smooth away the tracks of her tears and the remnants of her fears. 'I will always be there for you, Georgie, whatever happens.'

'And I'll always be there for you.'

He kissed her again, this time more gently, more deeply, and by the time he lifted his head, the sense of peace and hope and joy that had been beginning to spin through her filled her to the brim, overwhelming her all over again.

'Don't cry,' he said, kissing away the tears. 'It'll be all right.'

'Will it?'

'Of course,' he said gruffly. 'I bought you these,' he added, digging his hand briefly into his pocket and then sliding a plain gold band and then a stunning diamond solitaire onto the third finger of her left hand. 'In Paris.'

'They're beautiful,' she said, her throat tightening and her heart swelling as she placed her hand over his heart and looked at them.

'You're beautiful.'

'I'm a mess.'

'You're mine.'

'Your lift is broken,' she said with a watery sniff.

'I had it stopped.'

'You had it stopped?'

'I couldn't risk losing you again,' he said, his eyes darkening with emotion, his hold on her strong and secure.

'You won't.'

'Promise?'

She nodded. 'I promise.'

EPILOGUE

Ospedale San Giovanni,
Venice

PROPPED UP IN bed in the dark, quiet private hospital room where his shattered body was gradually healing, Federico Rossi stared one last time at the image on the screen, a photo of a couple at the recent launch of the seven-star Hotel Bellevue in Paris—at one Finn Calvert in particular, a man who was the spitting image of himself but without the scars and the broken nose—and slowly, thoughtfully, closed the lid of his laptop.

* * * * *

Invitation From The Venetian Billionaire

MILLS & BOON

DEDICATION

For Katie

For the brainstorming and the chats over coffees, walks and wine

CHAPTER ONE

'Say cheese!'

Somewhat inexpertly holding her brand-new godson, Carla Blake looked at the camera and concentrated on not dropping the eleven-month-old that belonged to her best friend, Georgie, and Georgie's husband, Finn. They'd only been posing for a couple of minutes, yet already her arms ached in an effort to contain the squirming child. The strain of maintaining her smile was taking its toll on her facial muscles and her head throbbed.

Not that she wasn't happy for Georgie and Finn, or indeed to be here. She couldn't be happier. She was delighted to have been asked to be Josh's godmother, and, with everything that her best friend had been through recently, Georgie deserved every one of the bright grins wreathing her face. Finn was divine—gorgeous, supportive, utterly in love with his wife—and as for their son, who was the spitting image of his father, dark of hair, blue of eye and rosy of cheek, well, he was simply adorable.

Nor was she jealous. As picture perfect as today's

christening had been so far, Carla did *not* want what Georgie had. She couldn't think of anything worse than swapping the bright lights and high-octane buzz of the city for a sprawling pile in the middle of nowhere, however beautiful.

In no conceivable way would a baby fit with her career, and she certainly didn't want a husband or partner. She didn't even want a boyfriend. Casual flings? Absolutely. Anything long term? Definitely not. She didn't have the time, and her freedom and her independence were too important to her to ever compromise.

In fact, the mere thought of putting the welfare of her emotions into the hands of a man sent chills shooting up and down her spine. Besides, she wouldn't know how to actually have a romantic relationship even if she *did* want one. Not a proper, healthy, adult one, at any rate.

No, the tension gripping her body and the pounding inside her skull were purely down to stress and exhaustion. Twenty-four hours ago she'd been in Hong Kong, massaging the ego and manipulating the mind of a truculent CEO who'd spent far too long point-blank refusing to accept that the only response to the massive data protection breach the company had just experienced was an apology to every single customer and a generous goodwill gesture to those directly affected.

Once he'd eventually seen sense and the way forward had *finally* been signed off, Carla had dashed to the airport, making her flight with minutes to spare. Having landed and cleared Customs early this morning, she'd swung by her flat to shower and change and had then driven the ninety minutes it took to reach the chocolate box Oxfordshire village Finn and Georgie had recently moved to.

She'd bust a gut to get here on time but she didn't mind one little bit because she and Georgie were more than best friends. The moment they'd met on the commune where Georgie had been living, and to which Carla and her parents moved, they'd each recognised a kindred spirit in the other and from then on they'd shared everything. Together they'd navigated the challenges of adolescence and a parenting style that bordered on neglect. Through the bleakest of times they'd provided each other with badly needed support.

However, jet lag was catching up with her now and the adrenalin that had been keeping her going was flagging. Her usual party mojo had disappeared without trace. Conversation was proving an unfamiliar slog and the heat was stifling.

But it wouldn't be long before she could go home and crash out. And once there, *then* she'd be able to worry about possible burnout and ponder the wisdom of requesting some leave. In the meantime she would simply pull herself together and carry on smiling because today was all about Georgie and her family, and nothing—least of all, *she*—was going to ruin it.

The photographer finally gave her the thumbs-up, and as he turned away to check the pictures he'd taken Carla set Josh on the grass. While he toddled off in the direction of the gazebo where lunch was being set up, she straightened and shook out her arms, and tried not to grimace when her muscles twinged.

'My godson is as wriggly as an eel,' she said to Georgie, who'd been standing a few metres away but now stepped forward.

'He took his first solo steps a week ago,' said Georgie with a fond smile while her gaze tracked her son's progress. 'Now he just wants to practise. All the time.'

Carla watched as Josh toppled like a ninepin then got up without a whimper and resumed his journey, her amusement turning to admiration. 'His determination is impressive.'

'He takes after his father.'

'How is Finn?'

Georgie's grin faded and a small frown creased her forehead. 'Climbing the walls while trying to pretend everything's fine.'

'Still no news?'

Late last year Finn had learned he'd been adopted as a six-month-old, and had poured considerable resources into investigating his roots. Back in March he'd discovered that he'd been born in Argentina and was one of a set of triplets, but as far as Carla was aware that was all anyone knew.

Georgie sighed. 'None.'

'It must be so frustrating.'

'It is. Finn says it doesn't matter, that he's let it go because he has us now, and I think he genuinely wants to believe that, but he isn't as good at pretending as he thinks. It's eating him up.'

And because it was eating Finn up, it was eating Georgie up too, Carla knew, and she hated knowing her best friend was hurting. If only she could somehow *fix* it. 'What's being done?'

'The investigation agency is still trying to track down his brothers but the trail's gone cold.'

'Is there some way I can help? Some kind of PR campaign, maybe?'

'I don't think so,' said Georgie with a shake of her head. 'But thank you. And thank you for coming today. I know what an effort it must have been.'

'There's truly nowhere I'd rather be,' said Carla, meaning it despite the stress of the last twenty-four hours. 'It couldn't be more perfect. Josh is a very lucky little boy. Besides, you know how much I love a good party.'

And this certainly was a good party, mojo or no mojo. Not a cloud blemished the great swathe of cobalt-blue sky. The honey-coloured stone of the house gleamed in the mid-June sunshine, the glass panes of the huge sash windows glinting with warm light. The vast expanse of lawn stretched out from the terrace like an emerald carpet, bordered by hedges that had been immaculately clipped, their edges and angles a sharp contrast to the softly swishing leaves of the towering trees behind. Champagne and sparkling fruit juice flowed, mopped up by exquisitely delicate canapés, and all-round chat and laughter resounded.

'I'd better go and see to lunch,' said Georgie in response to a signal from the caterer who'd emerged from beneath the gazebo. 'Will you be all right?'

'I'll be fine,' said Carla with a reassuring smile, very glad she didn't want any of this for herself, for if she had she'd have been consumed with envy. 'Go.'

As Georgie turned to leave, Carla scanned the

throng, her gaze bobbing from one elegant guest to another, when it suddenly snagged on something in the distance.

A figure stood in the shadows beyond the hedge, leaning against a tree, his arms folded across his chest, his face obscured by the dappled shade. Something about the way he was standing and watching, sort of *skulking*, triggered Carla's instinct for recognising trouble. Every sense she had switched to high alert and the tiny hairs at the back of her neck shot up.

'Wait,' she said, putting a hand on Georgie's arm to stop her just as she was about to head off.

'What?'

'Is everyone who's meant to be here, here?'

'Yes.'

'Are you expecting anyone else?'

'No.'

'Then who's that?'

Georgie looked in the direction she indicated and frowned. 'I have no idea. But I swear he wasn't there a moment ago.'

'Want me to go and check it out?'

'Are you sure?'

'Of course.' Rooting out potential problems and neutralising threats was what she did for a living, and a speedy assessment of the situation deemed any risk negligible.

'Thank you,' said Georgie with a grateful smile.

'No problem.'

'Yell if you need back-up.'

'I will.'

* * *

He'd been spotted.

From his position beneath the wide-spreading branches of the tree he'd been leaning against for the last couple of minutes, Federico Rossi clocked the exact moment the blonde noticed him. One minute she'd been chatting animatedly to her friend, the next her sweeping gaze had landed on him and she'd frozen. Long glances in his direction from both women had followed, a quick exchange of words then a nod, and now she was striding towards him, her progress impressively unhindered by her sky-high heels.

Her long limbs were loose and her hips swayed as she crossed the lawn. The top half of her red sleeveless dress moulded to her shape, but from her waist to her knees the fine fabric flowed around her thighs and drew his attention to her legs. There was nothing particularly revealing about what she was wearing but her curves were spectacular and the fluid confidence with which she moved was mesmerising.

Rico wasn't here in search of female company. He'd come solely to meet one Finn Calvert and to find out if his suspicions about who he was were correct, to ascertain the facts, and absolutely nothing else. Nevertheless, it was a relief to know that he could still appreciate an attractive woman when he saw one. Three months ago, in the immediate aftermath of the accident that had fractured his back, shattered his pelvis and broken his femur, it had been doubtful that he'd walk again, let alone regain his ability to respond quite so viscerally to a woman.

However, through sheer force of will, determination and the resilience with which he'd survived the streets of mainland Venice, which had eventually become his home following the sudden death of his parents when he was ten, he'd defied all medical expectations, and viscerally was how he was responding now.

Because as she continued to approach and he continued to watch, her face came better into focus and he saw that she was more than merely attractive. She was stunning. Sunlight bounced off choppy blonde hair that surrounded a heart-shaped face. Even at this distance he could see that her eyes, fixed unwaveringly on him, were light, possibly green, and fringed with thick dark lashes.

He couldn't have looked away even if he'd wanted to. All his attention was focused on the desire that was beginning to stir and fizz in the pit of his stomach, sending darts of heat speeding along his veins, igniting the sparks of awareness and accelerating his pulse. A dose of adrenaline shot through him and his muscles tightened as if bracing themselves for the most thrilling of attacks. And, despite the fact that her mouth was currently set in a firm, uncompromising line, he was filled with the hot, hard urge to draw her back into the shadows with him, pin her up against the tree and find out what she tasted like.

Parking that unexpectedly fierce response for later analysis and getting a swift grip on his control, since now was neither the time nor the place to find out how fully he'd recovered in that department, Rico unfolded his arms and pushed his sunglasses onto the top of his head. He thrust his hands into the pockets of his jeans to cover the inevitable effect she was having on him and levered himself off the tree trunk. He stepped forwards, out of the shadows and into the sunlight, stifling a wince as the muscles of his right leg spasmed, and at that exact same moment, a couple of feet in front of him, the woman came to an abrupt halt.

Every inch of her stilled. For the longest moment she just stared at him, as if frozen in shock. Then she raked her shimmering green gaze over him from head to toe and back up again, her eyes widening, her face paling and her mouth dropping open on a soft gasp.

'Oh, dear God,' she breathed in a way that momentarily fractured his control and filled his head with scorching images of her tangled in his sheets and moaning his name despite his intention to ignore her allure.

'Not quite,' he drawled, ruthlessly obliterating the images and focusing.

'Who *are* you?'

'Federico Rossi. My friends call me Rico.' Well, they would if he had any.

'Where did you come from?'

Originally, who knew? Who cared? He didn't. 'Venice.'

'How did you get in?'

'With unexpected ease,' he said, remembering how he'd sailed through the gates and up the drive. 'Someone left the gates open.'

'For the coming and going of staff.'

'Finn should take his security more seriously.'

'I'll let him know.' She gave her head a quick shake

in an apparent effort to pull herself together. 'I can't quite believe it,' she said, nevertheless still sounding slightly stunned and appealingly breathy. 'What are you doing here?'

Well, now, *there* was a question. On the most superficial of levels Rico was here to find out if what he suspected was true. On every other level, however, he had no idea, which was confusing as hell. All he knew was that ever since he'd come across that photo in the financial press he'd been perusing while laid up in hospital, drifting in and out of pain, his broken bones recently pinned and splinted, he hadn't had a moment's peace.

Initially, he'd dismissed the electrifying jolt that had rocked through him on first seeing the face that could almost have been his staring out at him from his laptop. He'd ignored too the strange, unsettling notion that a missing piece of him had suddenly slotted into place.

Nothing was missing from his life, he'd reassured himself while willing his heart rate to slow down and his head to clear. He had everything he could ever wish for. He neither needed nor wanted to know who this man who looked so like him might be.

However, with the interminable passing of the days that turned into weeks, the sensation swelled until it was gnawing at his gut day and night, refusing to stay unacknowledged and relentlessly taunting him with the unwelcome suggestion that here might possibly be a blood relative, whether he wanted one or not.

Eventually he hadn't been able to stand it any longer. The growing pressure to do something about it had borne down on him with increasing intensity until he'd had no choice but to give in to the instinct he hadn't yet had cause to mistrust, and take action.

An internet search of Finn Calvert had turned up nothing in the way of personal details, so he'd hired an investigation agency, which, last week, had. The seismic revelation that Finn's date of birth matched his own, leading to the conclusion that they might be more than just blood relatives, they might be brothers and quite possibly twins at that, had shaken him to the core. He still hadn't fully recovered from the shock and he certainly hadn't had the head space or time to contemplate the implications.

Not that he was telling this woman any of that. He'd sound ridiculous. He didn't have a quick answer that made any sense, so instead, with a slight smile and half a step towards her, he went for one that did.

'Right now,' he murmured, out of habit letting his gaze drift over her and noticing with interest the sudden tell-tale leap of the pulse at the base of her neck and the rush of colour that hit her pale cheeks, 'I'm admiring the scenery.'

For the briefest of moments her eyes dropped to his mouth, a flash of heat sparking in their depths. He thought he caught the tiniest hitch of her breath and sensed her moving minutely in his direction, briefly dizzying him with her scent, and it hit him like a punch to the gut that instead of suppressing the nuclear reaction going on inside him he ought to be encouraging it. Because, while he didn't fully understand the strange, primitive instinct that had compelled him to come here, to this house and its owner, he well understood desire.

He'd gone without sex for the last twelve painful weeks, and he'd missed the fierce buzz of attraction, the sizzling heat of electrifying chemistry and the blessed oblivion that inevitably followed. Here was a potential opportunity to rectify that. He hadn't planned to stay overnight in the country, intending instead to return home to Venice once he was done, but he was adaptable. He'd change his plans and invite the goddess before him to dinner in London. And afterwards, if she was amenable, he'd take her back to the penthouse apartment he owned there, tumble her into bed and prove to anyone who cared to know just how well he'd recovered from the BASE jumping accident that had nearly killed him. It would be a satisfying and enjoyable way of getting through the hours, if nothing else.

The swiftness with which she appeared to be rallying, jerking back with a quick, tiny frown, was disappointing but no great obstacle. Her captivating gaze might have turned cool, her breathing steadying and the pretty blush on her cheeks receding, but he knew what he'd seen. He knew what he'd heard. And he was going to capitalise on it.

'I meant, why the tree?' she said with impressive composure, as if she hadn't even noticed the chemistry let alone responded to it, which perversely made him only more determined to get her to agree to a date.

'What?'

'Why are you out here by a tree? What was wrong with the front door?'

Ah.

He'd had his driver park the car in front of the house

at the end of a line of half a dozen others. Realising there had to be a party going on, since the investigation he'd commissioned had thrown up no suggestion that Finn was particularly into fast cars, he'd decided to assess the situation first instead of barging in. He'd walked round the side of the house, skirting the tall, wide hedge, unnoticed and surprisingly unchallenged, before identifying this tree as the best spot from which to observe the man he'd come to see, and taken up a position in the shadows, a place he was very familiar with and very comfortable in. 'Gate-crashing a party's not my style.'

Her eyebrows lifted. 'But skulking is?'

'Skulking?' It wasn't a word he'd heard before.

'Lurking. Loitering. Hiding.'

'I prefer to think of it as…observing from a distance,' he said, dismissing the flicker of apprehension that came when he realised with hindsight that perhaps he *should* have hidden, because now he'd been caught there was no backing out. No leaving without anyone being the wiser. No coming back another, quieter time. Or not at all. It was too late for regrets. He'd set these events in motion. He'd see them through. And in the meantime he'd distract himself by pursuing the beautiful woman before him.

'You're here to meet Finn.'

'I am,' he said, giving her a practised smile and feeling a surge of satisfaction when her gaze once again dipped to his mouth for a second as if she just couldn't help herself.

'Your brother.'

'Quite possibly.'

'Then you'd better come with me.'

CHAPTER TWO

WHILE CARLA HAD been making her way over, buzzing with a surge of adrenaline that wiped out her weariness and put a bounce in her step, a number of options with regard to the identity and purpose of the stranger lurking in the shadows had spun through her mind.

He was a curious neighbour, maybe. A paparazzo with pound signs in his eyes. Or something a tad more sinister, perhaps. Finn was a billionaire who owed a string of hotels, restaurants and nightclubs. Some kind of personal attack wasn't out of the question. Josh was tiny and precious and the threat of a kidnapping was real.

Never in a million years would she have guessed the truth. It was almost unbelievable. But not quite, because that this individual, this Federico Rossi, was one of Finn's long-lost brothers was undeniable.

He *had* to be.

They were identical.

Well, almost identical.

They might share eye and hair colour and possess the same imposing breadth of shoulders and towering height, but Finn didn't have the scar that featured on this man's face. His nose had never been broken and no accent tinged his English. Finn too lacked the deep tan, and sharp angles and hard lines in the bone structure department. Other than all that, though, the likeness was uncanny.

So why the man falling in beside her as she turned and set off on a discreet route back to the house should have triggered such an unexpected and intense reaction inside her when all she felt for Finn was a vague sort of fondness, Carla had no idea.

Was it the lazy confidence? The deep, gravelly, insanely sexy voice? The air of danger and the accompanying notion that, despite the laid-back exterior, Federico Rossi was a man who did and took what he wanted when he wanted and to hell with the consequences?

Whatever it was, once she'd got over her shock at his obvious identity, she'd experienced a jolt of an entirely different kind. He'd smiled at her, a slow, smouldering, stomach-melting smile, and a rush of heat had stormed through her, igniting her nerve endings and setting fire to her blood. His intense navy gaze had roamed all over her, and in its wake tiny explosions had detonated beneath her skin. By the time he'd finished his leisurely yet thorough perusal of her entire body, desire had been pounding through her and for one brief, mad moment she'd wanted to press herself up against him and seal her mouth to his.

But then some tiny nugget of self-preservation, recognising what was going on as attraction of the most lethal and inadvisable kind, to be neither entertained nor underestimated, had burst into her consciousness and she'd taken a sharp step back from the brink of madness while wondering what on earth she'd been thinking.

Everything about this man, every instinct she had, urged her to proceed with utmost caution, and that was exactly what she was going to do because she got the feeling that *he* wasn't to be entertained or underestimated either.

When it came to the opposite sex she never allowed her emotions to run riot and dictate her actions. She'd done so once before, as an affection-starved teenager who thought she'd found love where she absolutely hadn't, and that was enough. If Rico Rossi could threaten the iron-clad control she kept on her feelings with just a smile, he could be beyond dangerous, and she had zero interest in prodding the beast.

She did, however, have an interest in keeping him away from Finn and Georgie's guests, who by now were presumably having lunch but couldn't fail to be curious should he march straight into the party, the spitting image of their host, only dressed in faded blue jeans and a black polo shirt instead of a suit. So she'd deposit him in the study and then go in search of Finn to impart the surprising yet excellent news that one of his brothers had turned up, and from that moment on she need have nothing to do with him directly ever again.

'So you know my name,' he said, shortening his stride to match hers, a move that put him so close she caught a trace of his scent—male, spicy, dizzyingly intoxicating—

so close she could reach out and touch him should she wish to do so, which she very definitely did not. 'What's yours?'

'Carla Blake.'

'Carla,' he echoed, rolling the 'r' around his mouth in a way that sent an involuntary shiver rippling down her spine.

'That's right,' she said with a brisk nod, deciding to inhale through her mouth and keep her eyes ahead to lessen his impact on her senses while upping her pace so that they might reach their destination that little bit quicker.

'And this party?'

'A christening. Your nephew's, probably. I'm a god-parent. Georgie is my best friend. She's Josh's mother and, I'd hazard a guess, your sister-in-law.'

'A family occasion,' he muttered in a way that suggested he wasn't entirely comfortable with the idea, which was no concern of hers.

'Yes.'

'It's a beautiful day for it.'

'Indeed it is.'

'It's a beautiful day for many things.'

'Such as?'

'Making new acquaintances.'

'Your brother and his family?'

'I actually meant you, *tesoro*.'

In response to the slight deepening of his voice and the hint of silky seduction that accompanied his words, Carla's stomach tightened while heat flooded her veins.

Was he flirting with her?

Feeling strangely trembly inside, she glanced over

at him to find him looking back at her, the intensity of the heat she saw in his glittering gaze nearly knocking her off her heels.

'I have plenty of acquaintances,' she said, a lot more breathlessly than she'd have preferred.

'Any like me?'

Attractive enough to turn her into a puddle of insensibility and lay siege to her control? In possession of a smile that commanded her attention against her will and rendered her all hot and quivery? Thankfully, no. 'One or two.'

The expression on his face now suggested he didn't believe her and that knowing arrogance—even if he *was* spot-on with that assumption—was enough to blast the sense back into her.

Enough was enough, she told herself sternly as she led him towards an arch in the hedge. The reaction going on inside her was ridiculous. She didn't *do* flustered. Ever. She was cool in a crisis. She was the eye of the storm. She was *not* a pulsating mass of desire, completely at the mercy of her hormones, no matter how great the provocation.

'What are you doing when the party's over?' he asked, standing aside to let her pass through the arch ahead of him.

'Going home and crashing out,' she replied, taking great care not to let any part of her body touch any part of his on her way.

Rico ducked his head and followed her through onto the stretch of gravel that led to the house. 'That doesn't sound like much fun.'

'Perhaps not.'

'I can think of far more entertaining things to be getting up to.'

As if on cue, before she could even *think* to prevent it, her head filled with images of Rico grabbing her arm right now, drawing her into the shadows, pulling her into a tight embrace and lowering his head to give her a mind-blowing kiss while she pressed eagerly against him.

'I don't doubt it,' she said tightly, grinding her teeth in frustration as the gravel crunched beneath her feet and her body temperature rocketed. 'Nevertheless, it's what I'm doing.'

'How about dinner?'

'Toast,' she said bluntly. 'I may go wild and smash an avocado to have with it.'

'I meant you having it with me.'

'I know you did.'

'Well?'

She shook her head decisively and set her sights on the door in the side wall of the house. 'I think not.'

'Another evening, then.'

'No.'

'Are you married?'

'No.'

'Boyfriend?'

'No.'

'Girlfriend?'

'Not my thing.'

'Then why not?'

She gave the door a shove to open it and marched in. 'Do I have to have a reason?'

'Don't you?' he said, sounding genuinely curious and at the same time impossibly conceited.

Well, no, of course she didn't *have* to, although obviously she *did*. Rico's invitation to dinner might be shockingly and appallingly tempting, despite her attempts to convince herself otherwise, but she knew first-hand the risk confident, self-assured men like him posed. How all-consuming and seductive they could be. She knew what it was like to succumb to the power and charm until you no longer knew what was right and what was wrong. To lose your identity along with your inhibitions. To be persuaded to make unwise choices and to believe that you were happy about making them.

She had no intention of making the same mistake twice. She was more than content with the steady, careful, safe life she'd created for herself. She would allow nothing to upset it. Never again would she be rendered powerless, vulnerable and helpless by a man. Never again would she be manipulated into willingly giving up her freedom and her independence, things she hadn't had the maturity then to value.

'Does anyone ever turn you down?' she asked, having no intention of telling him any of that and determinedly suppressing the memories of the distant but nevertheless frightening and confusing year she'd been groomed.

'No,' he said, closing the door behind him and easily keeping up with her as she strode through the house. 'But that's irrelevant and I'm not into games. You find me as attractive as I find you, *bellissima*. Dinner could prove interesting.'

His compliment made her shudder, as compliments from men—so often used with the expectation of something in return—always did, but she suppressed that too and focused. Dinner could prove disastrous and it wasn't going to happen. She would never be up for the sort of fun Rico offered, no matter how tantalisingly packaged. 'Find someone else to seduce.'

'I don't want to seduce anyone else. I want to seduce you.'

'I'd have thought you'd have other things on your mind at the moment.' Like, say, a new-found brother.

'I excel at multitasking.'

This time, thank God, she *did* manage to stifle the images of exactly how he might excel at multitasking that instantly tried to muscle their way into her head. 'My answer is still, and always will be, no.'

Without missing a step, he reached into the back pocket of his jeans and pulled out his wallet. He extracted a card and handed it to her. 'Here's my number just in case you change your mind.'

'I won't,' she said, taking it to dispose of it later, since there wasn't a bin to hand.

'You wound me.'

'You'll recover.' She stopped at the study, opened the door and stood back. 'Here we are,' she said, practically drowning with relief at finally being able to escape the dangerously sensuous web he was spinning around her with the intensity of his focus and the persistence of his pursuit. 'Wait in there. I'll go and find Finn. Once he's got over his shock, he's going to be thrilled you've turned up. He's been looking for you for months. Family is *everything* to him. This is going to be life-changing. So don't you dare go anywhere.'

As he listened to the sharp tap of Carla's heels marching across the polished oak floorboards of the hall, loud at first but fading with every step she took away from him, Rico had no doubt that he would indeed recover from her declination of his invitation to dinner.

Whatever it was that was slashing through him would ease soon enough. Pique, most probably, since generally he barely had to make any effort at all when after a date. It certainly couldn't be disappointment that he wouldn't be getting to know the stunningly beautiful, incredibly sexy Carla Blake better. He didn't do disappointment. Or regret. Or any kind of emotion, for that matter. It was of no concern to him why she'd chosen to ignore the chemistry they shared, even though she hadn't denied that she found him as attractive as he did her when he'd mentioned it.

Besides, she wasn't *that* intriguing. Stunning, yes, but their conversation, while mildly entertaining, had hardly been scintillating. He knew plenty of women who would be only too happy to while away the hours with him without engaging in any kind of conversation at all.

So it wouldn't take long for the sting of her rejection to fade, or the impact of her on his senses. Or the curve of her mouth that made him ache to know what she tasted like…the magnetic pull of her heat and her scent…the prickly obstinacy that fired his blood in a way it hadn't ever burned before…

In fact, it already *was* dissipating, and now, as he stood alone in the cool quiet of the study, taking in his surroundings while in the distance he could hear the faint clink of cutlery against crockery, the pop of a cork and the hum of chatter, with the pleasant diversion of Carla gone, his earlier unease returned tenfold.

Everywhere he looked he saw photos. On the desk, on the shelves, on the walls. Of the man who could be his double bar the scar and the broken nose, sometimes wrapped around a beautiful brunette, sometimes with a small child, mostly with both. In all of them, everyone was either smiling or laughing, clearly relaxed and happy, a tightly knit trio of emotions, history and belonging, and the closer and longer he looked, the greater the roll of his stomach and the chillier the shivers that ran down his spine.

He had no concept of such things. Living on the streets as an adolescent for four years had taught him that emotions rendered a man weak and vulnerable. They led to manipulation and exploitation, not intimacy and connection. As he understood, relationships involved attachment and commitment, compromise and understanding, none of which he'd ever experienced. They were for other people, not him, which was why Carla's reference to further potential relatives, the nephew and the sister-in-law, not to mention the nature of the occasion today, a *family* occasion, had unexpectedly knocked him for six.

He and this brother of his might look similar, but it

was becoming increasingly apparent that DNA was the only thing they had in common. Judging by the photographs before him they certainly didn't share a temperament. Finn's eyes lacked the hard cynicism Rico knew lurked in the depths of his own, and the fine lines fanning out from the corner of them suggested Finn knew how to laugh and mean it. His brother wasn't a loner who preferred the shadows to the limelight. He had family. Friends. A life full of laughter and joy.

They'd evidently had very different experiences of growing up, quite apart from geography. Finn's relaxed, content exterior clearly didn't hide a great, gaping void where his soul should be. He couldn't have spent his formative years fighting for survival, sleeping with one eye open and scavenging for food in order to stave off the kind of hunger that made you hallucinate. And had Finn ever found himself part of a gang as a kid, searching for somewhere to belong, somewhere where he counted, only to be forced to do things he didn't want to do and badly let down by people in whom he'd impulsively and unwisely put his trust? It didn't seem likely.

It had been a mistake to make this trip here, Rico thought darkly, a frown creasing his forehead as he shoved his hands in his pockets and stalked over to the window in an attempt to escape the photos and the inexplicable resentment and jealousy he could feel brewing at the injustice of his and Finn's very different upbringings. A mistake to allow himself to be recklessly driven by an intuition he didn't understand to such an extent that he'd rashly dismissed the advice of his doctors to stay put and had ordered his plane that he had on permanent standby at the airport in Venice to be readied instead.

He'd acted on instinct and hadn't given a moment's thought to the ramifications. But, with hindsight, he should have because Carla's parting comment that Finn had been searching for him for months and that he'd be thrilled to have found him made his scalp prickle and his stomach churn. He wasn't interested in a sentimental reunion or a prolonged catch-up on the last thirty-one years, in back-slapping hugs and the swapping of life stories. The mere thought of engaging in a *You like chess? So do I! You're a billionaire? So am I!* kind of conversation punched the air from his lungs and drained the blood from his brain.

He didn't need anyone, least of all a sibling he'd known nothing about his entire life. He never had. Family might mean everything to Finn but Rico didn't know what it meant, full stop. Not now. He'd spent most of his life alone and he was used to it that way. He was dependent on no one and had no one dependent on him. The only person he trusted was himself and should he ever be let down now he had only himself to blame.

He didn't belong here, in a beautiful home among beautiful people who led beautiful lives that didn't deserve to be sullied by his darkness. He didn't belong anywhere. He never would. So he had nothing to gain from actually meeting Finn. Carla had already confirmed the suspicion he'd come to investigate for himself. He'd done what he'd felt compelled to do. He didn't need to hang around any longer to find out more and feel the embers of resentment and jealousy flaring into a hot, fiery burn that would scorch and destroy what little good was left in him.

In fact, if he took control of events and left right now, he could be in the air in half an hour. He'd be home by dark. And once there, he could set about resuming the life he'd led before the accident and forget that today had ever happened.

'What do you mean, he's gone?'

At the table beneath the gazebo, now cleared of lunch and instead spread with everything needed for the provision of coffee and tea, Carla stared at Georgie open-mouthed, the party and the guests milling about outside all but forgotten.

'Exactly that,' Georgie replied quietly, her face filled with confusion and worry. 'Federico Rossi is nowhere to be seen. Finn's just spent twenty minutes scouring the house and the grounds. He couldn't find him anywhere.'

Noting that her hand was trembling slightly, Carla carefully put down her coffee cup. 'I put him in the study and asked him to wait,' she said, a chill of apprehension and dismay running down her spine. 'He couldn't have just *left*.'

'I think he must have done.'

'No note?'

'No nothing,' said Georgie with a shake of her head. 'Did he give *any* indication he might leg it?'

Carla racked her brains, the conversation they'd had spinning through her head and filling her with shame, since it should have been about Finn but instead had been all about her. 'No.'

'So why did he go?'

'I have no idea.'

'I wish he'd never come here in the first place,' Georgie muttered, her expression hardening. 'To dangle a carrot of hope like that and then whip it away… Why would anyone do that? How could he be so cruel? Why wasn't he interested in getting to know Finn? Or me and Josh? What's wrong with us? I'd sort of already slotted him into our lives if that makes sense—a relative, a *real* relative, who could maybe join us for Christmas and birthdays and things—and it was going to be so great.' She gave a big sigh. 'I'm such an idiot.'

Georgie was the *last* person in this scenario who was an idiot, thought Carla, her heart beginning to thump as the truth dawned on her. *She* was the one who'd been an idiot. And not only that, but also a shockingly and appallingly self-centred one.

Under any other circumstance she'd have considered every possible consequence of leaving Rico alone in Finn's study. She'd have weighed up what she'd learned about him, however little, and assessed the risks. Doing precisely that was part of her job, a job she'd had for the best part of a decade and supposedly excelled at.

But she hadn't. She'd fled without a moment's thought because she'd been too desperate to escape his overwhelming effect on her to think straight. For the first time in years, despite her recognition of the danger he presented, she'd let her emotions get the better of her and dictate her actions, and as a result she'd ruined everything.

What if her parting comments had been the trigger? What if Rico had been spooked by her insistence about the importance of family and her claim about how pleased Finn would be to meet him? She'd noticed his discomfort at the idea of a family occasion. If she hadn't been so derailed by her need to get away from him she'd have been more considered with her words.

'I should have locked him in,' she said, the weight of guilt and self-reproach crushing her like a rock on her chest. 'I'm so sorry.'

'It's not your fault,' said Georgie darkly. 'It's *his*.'

'How's Finn?'

'Completely gutted.'

'That's understandable,' said Carla, feeling sick at the realisation of how thoughtless and self-absorbed she'd been and how badly she'd let her friends down.

'Maybe he just needs more time.'

'It's possible.'

'And what else can we do but wait and see if he gets back in touch at some point?' said Georgie with a helpless shrug that cut Carla to the quick. 'It's not as if he left any contact details. All we can do is give Alex what we have and let her get on with it.'

Yes, they could indeed do that. With a new name to add to the mix, no doubt Alex Osborne of Osborne Investigations, hired by Finn to track down his biological family, would be able to unearth no end of information. But she'd only be able to find the facts. Carla could probably do better than that.

Because Georgie was wrong.

Rico had left his number.

He'd handed her his card, which she'd intended to

toss into the bin where it belonged but had put in her bag instead.

Why, she had no idea, but that didn't matter. All that mattered was that she had a way of contacting him, which was excellent because she wasn't having any of this. She wasn't having Finn and, by extension, Georgie devastated by anyone. Georgie's pain was her pain, and her best friend meant far too much to her to let it lie. She owed Georgie quite possibly her *life*.

Carla had been only fifteen when she'd fallen into the clutches of a man twice her age, who'd spotted an opportunity to prey on a naïve, vulnerable teenager and taken it. Starved of attention and affection by her parents, desperate to have proof that her love for them was returned and not getting it, she'd willingly been swallowed up by his flattering interest and the close emotional bond he'd deliberately and maliciously created. She hadn't questioned his requests to send him increasingly explicit pictures. She hadn't noticed she was becoming more and more isolated. When he'd finally persuaded her to run away with him she'd thought herself so sophisticated, so mature, so in love. She'd been so excited and such a fool. If it hadn't been for Georgie, who hadn't given up on her even when she'd been truly horrible, who'd eventually managed to come to her rescue, things could have turned out very differently.

Carla still didn't trust compliments and emotional intimacy. She still found it hard not to instinctively question men's interest in her and her ability to judge what was healthy when it came to relationships and what wasn't, which was why she tended to steer well clear of them, opting for short, casual flings instead. But at least, thanks to her best friend, she'd regained her self-confidence and self-esteem. At least she knew that what had happened hadn't been her fault and believed it.

Her abuser's previous victim hadn't been so fortunate. After the trial that saw him locked away for five years it had been revealed that Carla wasn't the only girl he'd preyed on. His first victim had been groomed in the same way, only she hadn't escaped. When she'd become too old for him and he'd left her, she'd been so messed up she'd taken an overdose and died.

Without Georgie, that could easily have been Carla's fate, so there was *nothing* she wouldn't do for her. They might not share any DNA, but they were sisters in every way that counted. In fact, they were closer than many of the pairs of actual siblings she knew.

So, whatever her personal feelings about Rico Rossi, Carla could help. She wanted to. And not only that. She needed to fix the mistakes she'd made today. Rico had invited her out for dinner and she'd accept. She'd use the occasion to try and change his mind about meeting his brother. Failing that, she'd mine him for information that she could then pass back to Finn in the hope it might give him at least some comfort. It wasn't a brilliant plan, but it was a start.

She could ignore the effect he had on her, she told herself, determination setting her jaw as it all came together in her head. Now she'd had some breathing space she could see that she'd overreacted earlier. He posed no threat. He was just a man. A devastatingly attractive one, sure, but she was immune to that. She had no interest in the hypnotic blue of his eyes and the way they seemed to look right into her, and she'd certainly soon forget how well his body filled out his clothes and the easy confidence with which he moved.

She was no longer an innocent teenager yearning for adventure and love, wild, gullible and ripe for the picking. She was older, savvier, stronger, and well able to withstand any attempt at seduction Rico might be foolish enough to make, especially if she reinforced the control she wielded over her emotions so that it was unbreakable. She was tenacious and focused when it came to a goal and, at the end of the day, it was only dinner.

'I might have an idea,' she said to Georgie, the need to put things right for the people she cared so much about now burning like a living flame inside her. 'Leave it with me.'

CHAPTER THREE

HIS PLANE HAVING just taken off from the small private airfield that was located conveniently close to Finn's house, Rico was travelling at a speed of three hundred kilometres per hour, staring out of the window, a glass of neat whisky in his hand, his relief at having made a lucky escape soaring with every metre they climbed.

Carla had called his aborted meeting with Finn life-changing, but he didn't need his life changed, he told himself grimly, knocking back half his drink and welcoming the heat of the alcohol that hit his stomach. He was perfectly happy with it the way it was. Or at least, the way it *had* been before the accident that had not only broken his body but also, he could recognise now, short-circuited his brain.

What on earth had he been *doing* these last few weeks? Yes, he'd had time on his hands and little to occupy his brain, given that he'd spent much of it dosed up on morphine and therefore in no fit state to work the markets, but to cede all control to an intuition he didn't even understand? He had to have been nuts.

He should have got a firmer grip on the curiosity

that had burgeoned inside him on coming across that photo. He should have forgotten he'd seen it in the first place. He should certainly never have allowed any of it to dominate his thoughts to such an extent that it sent him off on a course of action that he barely understood.

Well, it all stopped now. He needed to return to being the man he'd been for the last fifteen years, who lived life on the edge and to whom nothing and no one had mattered since the moment he'd escaped the gang he'd joined, his dreams destroyed and his soul stolen, and he'd realised he was better off on his own. He needed that familiarity, that certainty, that defini-tion of who he was. He didn't like the confusion and the doubt that had been crippling him lately.

His lingering preoccupation with Carla, with whom he'd irrefutably crashed and burned, had to stop too. De-spite handing her his card, he wasn't expecting to hear from her, so he had no reason whatsoever to dwell on what might have happened had she accepted his invita-tion. No reason to continue contemplating her stunning green eyes and lush, kissable mouth. She wasn't the first woman he'd wanted, and she certainly wouldn't be the last. She was hardly irreplaceable. In fact, when he got home he'd set about doing precisely that.

The beep of his phone cut through his turbulent thoughts, and he switched his attention from the wide expanse of cloudless azure sky to the device on the table in front of him. He didn't recognise the UK number and on any other occasion would have let it go to voicemail, but today, now, he was more than happy to be disturbed.

With any luck, it would be someone from the

London-based brokerage firm he used with something business-related. Details of a unique and complex opportunity in an emerging market, perhaps. A forex swaption recommendation. An unexpected profit warning. As long as it was something that made him money and required significant focus, he wasn't fussy.

'*Pronto.*'

'Rico? Hi. It's Carla Blake. We met earlier.'

At the sound of the voice in his ear—very much *not* the head of research at the London-based brokerage firm—every inch of him tensed and his pulse gave a great kick. Her words slid through him like silk, winding round his insides and igniting the sparks of the desire he hadn't managed to fully extinguish. He could visualise her mouth and feel her hair tickling his skin. It was as if she were actually there, beside him, leaning in close and making his groin tighten and ache, and all his efforts to put her from his mind evaporated.

'How could I possibly forget?' he said, sitting back in his seat and forcing himself to get a grip on his reaction to her and relax.

'I was hoping that might be the case.'

'Why?'

'I'd like to take you up on the offer of dinner.'

The jolt of pleasure that rocked through him at that took him by surprise. 'I see,' he said, deciding to attribute it to satisfaction that she hadn't been able to resist him after all.

'If the invitation still stands, that is.'

He ought to tell her it didn't. He'd intended to wipe today from his head—every single second of it—and pursuing Carla with her connection to the brother he wanted nothing to do with would not be conducive to a return to his former shackle-free, nihilistic life.

But he didn't like rejection. He didn't like failure. He wasn't used to either. And the fact remained, he did still want her. Badly. Plus there was the intriguing volte face. Why had she changed her mind when only at lunchtime she'd been so adamant in her refusal? Had she finally decided to accept the chemistry they shared and act on it? The potential for a night of scorching, mind-blowing sex wasn't something he was going to ignore. Reclaiming the upper hand and taking back control of their interaction wouldn't hurt either.

'It still stands,' he said, anticipation at the thought of seeing her again and everything that might entail now thrumming through him and setting his nerve endings on fire.

'Excellent.'

'Why the change of heart?'

'I'll tell you when I see you.'

'I can hardly wait.'

'Where should I meet you?'

'La Piccola Osteria.'

'Hmm. I don't think I know it,' she said, and he could hear the frown in her tone. 'What's the address?'

'Calle dell'Olio. Venice.'

There was a stunned silence, and then a breathy, *'Venice?'*

'I'm on my way home.'

'Already?'

'One of the many advantages of having a private

plane,' he said, shifting in his seat to ease the ache and tension in his groin that her soft gasps had generated. 'So if you want to have dinner with me, *tesoro*, you'll need to come to Venice. Tonight. After which my invitation expires. It's your call.'

On the other end of the line, Carla stood in the cool hall of Finn and Georgie's home, every cell of her body abuzz. The effect of Rico's deep, masculine tones in her ear had been unexpectedly electrifying, sending shivers rippling up and down her spine while heating her blood, but that was nothing compared to the shock that was reeling through her now.

So much for the blithe assumption of an easy acceptance of his earlier invitation, she thought, her heart hammering wildly while her head spun. This was an entirely different prospect.

Dinner in Venice?

Tonight?

It was impossible. She'd never make it. She was knackered. The last thing she needed was another dash to another airport for another flight. The whole idea of haring halfway across a continent with next to no planning to meet a man she barely knew smacked of recklessness, something she abhorred and had taken great care to avoid after what had happened to her when she was young. She'd have to be mad to even consider it, as Georgie would no doubt tell her if she knew what Rico had just proposed.

On the other hand, when would there be another opportunity to at least try and fix the mistakes she'd made? If she didn't accept his challenge, how would she be able to change his mind or keep the lines of communication open?

She couldn't wimp out now. She had to give it a shot. The situation could hardly get worse and she could catch up on sleep any time. In fact, she might even request the next week off. And yes, she loathed the idea of giving in to any man's demands, but ultimately whether or not she went to Venice would be *her* decision. Rico wasn't forcing her to do anything. No one was. She was in total control of her choices, which was crucially important to her, and that was where she'd stay. And even if she weren't, for her best friend she'd make that sacrifice.

The fluttering in her stomach and the racing of her pulse had nothing to do with nerves. Or excitement. Or anticipation. Everything going on inside her was purely down to the crushing weight of responsibility she felt. Finn was worried that Rico could vanish into the ether for good and, because it was her fault he'd left in the first place, it was up to her to prevent that whatever it took.

'What time?'

At half-past ten Italian time, thirty minutes after she and Rico had been due to meet, Carla grabbed her suitcase and stepped off the water taxi she'd caught at the airport.

She was still barely able to believe she'd actually made it, she thought dazedly, heading for the restaurant he'd named. None of this felt real. Not the racing from Oxfordshire to her flat to the airport. Not the packed two-hour flight for which she'd been on standby and which she'd caught by the skin of her teeth. Not even the buzzing energy and the anticipation and excitement that were crashing around inside her.

The energy was a relief, but she had no business feeling excited about anything, least of all seeing Rico again. Wary? Definitely. Determined to find out why he'd run and then complete her mission? Absolutely. Anything else? Out of the question. Because this wasn't a date. Or a minibreak in a romantic city she'd never visited before. This was going to be a conversation, a retrieval of information, possibly a negotiation, nothing more, which she simply could not forget.

With her suitcase stowed in the cloakroom, Carla took a deep, steadying breath and followed the waiter out onto the terrace, channelling cool, calm control and reminding herself of the goal with every step, but no amount of preparation could have braced her for the impact of seeing Rico again.

He was lounging at a table in a far, shadowy corner of the terrace, impossibly handsome and insanely sexy in the candlelight, and when his gaze collided with hers it was as if the world suddenly skidded to a halt. Her surroundings disappeared, the twinkling fairy lights winding over and around the pergola, the clink of cutlery, the chatter of the clientele and the dashing around of the waiters gone in a heartbeat. All she could hear was the thundering of her blood in her head. All she could feel was the heavy drum of desire. All she could do was weave between tables covered with red cloths and flickering candles, as if tied to the end of a rope he was slowly hauling in.

She tried to convince herself that the flipping of her stomach was down to hunger or stress or relief that he hadn't given up on her and gone home, but she had the unsettling feeling that it was entirely down to the darkly compelling man now slowly unfolding himself and getting to his feet without taking his eyes off her for even a second.

When she reached his table, he leaned forwards, dizzying her with his spicy, masculine scent, and for one ground-tilting, heart-stopping moment she thought he was going to put his hand on her arm and drop a kiss on her cheek. In a daze, she went hot, her heart gave a great crash against her ribs and her gaze automatically went to his lips. How would they feel on her skin? Hard or soft? Would they make her burn or shiver or both?

But with a quick frown and a minute clench of his jaw he straightened at the last minute, and the searing disappointment that spun through her nearly knocked her off her feet. Her response contained none of the relief she should have felt at the fact that he hadn't kissed her, and the realisation hit her like a bucket of icy water.

God, she had to be careful here. She was miles out of her comfort zone and on his territory. It would be so easy to lose control and herself in the highly inconvenient and deeply unwanted desire she felt for him. One slip and everything she'd worked so hard to achieve could be destroyed. One slip and she'd have more than a mistake to rectify.

She *had* to focus on why she was here and keep it at

the forefront of her mind at all times. She *had* to get a grip on her reaction to him and remain composed, no matter how powerful the attraction, which surely had to lessen with familiarity.

'*Buonasera,*' she said, her voice thankfully bearing no hint of the struggle going on inside her.

'You're late,' he said with a smile so easy it made her wonder if she'd imagined his discomposure a moment ago.

'The traffic was terrible.'

'The canals can get busy at this time on a Saturday night. How was your journey?'

'Tight,' she said with a thank-you to the waiter who whipped out the chair opposite him so she could sit down. 'As you knew it would be when you told me it was Venice or nothing.'

Rico lowered himself into his own seat and sat back, the smile curving his mouth deepening. 'Yet here you are.'

'Here I am,' she agreed, hanging her bag on the back of her chair before making herself comfortable and then fixing him with an arch look. 'As are you, which is a surprise.'

'Why would you say that?'

'You don't do waiting, do you?'

He frowned for a moment, as if he had no idea to what she was referring, and then the frown disappeared and the smile returned. 'I decided to make an exception for you.'

'I'm flattered.'

'Drink?'

God, yes. 'That would be lovely.'

'What would you like?'

'Whisky, *per favore*. Could you make it a double?'

'*Certo.*'

'*Grazie.*'

With a minute lift of his head, Rico summoned the waiter while contemplating bypassing the request for two double whiskies and simply ordering the bottle.

God knew he could do with the fortification. He was still reeling from Carla's appearance at the door of his favourite restaurant. He'd been sitting at his usual table, frowning at his watch and feeling oddly on edge, when his skin had started prickling and his pulse had leapt, a crackle of electricity suddenly charging the air around him. He'd glanced up and there she'd been, standing at the edge of the terrace, scanning the diners for him.

She'd changed from the red dress she'd been wearing earlier into tight white jeans and a silky-looking pink top over which she wore a dark jacket, but the effect she'd had on him was just as intense as it had been when he'd met her beneath the tree. The bolt of desire that had punched him in the gut was equally as powerful. The whoosh of air from his lungs had been none the less acute.

Time had slowed right down as she'd walked towards him, her gaze not leaving his for even a millisecond, and he'd been so mesmerised that instinct had taken over. Out of habit he'd got to his feet and he'd been this close to kissing her cheek when a great neon light had started flashing in his head, an intense sense of self-preservation pulling him back at the last minute.

For one thing, if he touched her he might not be able to stop, and for another, it hadn't looked as if any sort of physical contact would be welcome. Carla's expression as she'd approached him had been severe, her gaze unwaveringly cool and her mouth once again a firm, uncompromising line, which was…unexpected.

Disappointingly, she neither sounded nor looked like someone keen on exploring the searing attraction that had arced between them, but the night was young, by Italian standards, and, at the very least, the last three months had taught him patience.

Nevertheless he was going to need his wits about him if he was going to maintain control while convincing her that taking ownership of the attraction they shared and acting on it was a good idea, which was why he decided against ordering the bottle.

When their drinks arrived a few moments later, he watched Carla pick hers up, tip back half of it and sigh with appreciation.

'Long day?' he asked, noting the faint smudges of tiredness beneath her eyes and briefly thinking about all the other ways in which he'd make her sigh once she'd come round to his way of thinking.

'Long week,' she corrected. 'I was in Hong Kong until ten o'clock last night their time.'

'Work?'

'Yes. I went straight from the airport to my flat to the christening, then did the whole journey in reverse, only ending up here instead of there.'

'And now *I'm* flattered.'

She set her glass down and arched her eyebrow. 'I wouldn't be.'

'What made you reassess my invitation?' he said, rolling his own glass between his fingers, her spiky attitude once again only intensifying his interest. 'I was under the impression that it would be a cold day in hell before you would have dinner with me.'

Her gaze dropped to his fingers for one oddly heart-stopping moment before slowly lifting back to his. 'Toast and smashed avocado lost its appeal.'

'Really?'

'No,' she said drily. 'Of course not. Your visit was brief but devastating. You departed in a hurry and left chaos in your wake. I'd like to rectify that.'

'Why?'

'Finn is upset and Georgie's my best friend. If he's upset, she's upset, and that upsets me.'

'Enough to accept an impromptu invitation to dinner in Venice?' He couldn't even begin to imagine a relationship that deep.

'Evidently so.'

'That's some loyalty,' he said, although who was he to judge when he'd done a similar thing, compelled by an intuition he didn't even understand?

'It goes both ways.'

Not always. In his experience, loyalty was a fickle, one-sided thing that could destroy and traumatise. Life, he'd come to discover, went a lot more smoothly if you expected nothing from anyone and no one expected anything from you. Not that now was the moment to be thinking about the gang he'd joined as a youth and the mistaken belief he'd found a place to belong and a bunch of people who'd turn into family.

'So you're here to change my mind about meeting Finn,' he said, ruthlessly suppressing the harrowing memories before they could force their way into his head and focusing on Carla instead.

'Yes.'

'And there was me thinking you were interested in my charm, my wit and my devastatingly good looks.'

'I'm afraid not.'

'What a waste of a journey,' he said, ignoring the tiny dent to his ego, since he had no doubt he'd be able to change her mind. He'd caught the flicker of heat in her shimmering green gaze when she'd looked at his hand a moment ago. He'd heard the barely-there hitch of her breath. Just as when they'd been talking by the tree earlier today, she wasn't as uninterested in him as she was trying to make out.

'Not at all,' she said pleasantly. 'If I can't change your mind, I will find out as much as I can about you and report back.'

'Good luck with that.'

'Oh, I won't need luck,' she said with a smile that didn't quite reach her eyes. 'I do a similar thing on a daily basis for work.'

'I'm not one of your clients.'

'You looked me up?'

He gave a brief nod. 'I did. After leaving school at eighteen you went straight into an internship at the top PR firm in London at the time. Six years with them then you moved to your current company. You specialise in corporate damage limitation and crisis management. Your clients span the globe. Your reputation is stellar.'

'You've done your research.'

'I can't be manipulated.' Not any more.

'Everyone can be manipulated,' she said with a slight lift of her chin. 'The trick is subtlety. To make them unaware of it. I'm very good at my job.'

'So I understand,' he said easily, knowing that no one would ever be good enough to prise out *his* secrets.

'But I wouldn't take you on as a client anyway,' she said with a shrug and a sip of her drink.

'Why not?'

'In my line of work transparency is key and you're too…' she thought for a moment '…shady.'

His eyebrows lifted. 'Shady?'

'You're not the only one who decided to do some research, Rico. There's virtually no information about you online and that's strange. Normally there's something—however minor—about everyone. But apart from the one article I found that briefly described you as one of Italy's most successful but least-known hedge fund managers, your digital footprint is practically non-existent.'

Yes, well, he took care to stay out of the public eye. He didn't want anyone poking around his less than salubrious background. He'd better check out that article and have it removed. 'I value my privacy.'

'What do you have to hide? I wonder.'

What *didn't* he have to hide? Nothing he'd done as an adult had broken the law, but some of the things he'd done between the ages of twelve and sixteen as a member of the gang had. Those things were intensely personal and had caused him excruciating pain, disillusionment and shame before he'd cut off all emotion by shutting himself down. He had no intention of ever unlocking *that* door, so the last thing he wanted was Carla's curiosity aroused.

'What would you like to know?' he said expansively, feigning the transparency she was apparently so keen on in an attempt to detract her from rooting around in his psyche any further. 'Ask me anything. To you, I'm an open book.'

The look she gave him was sceptical. 'I doubt that very much.'

'Try me.'

'All right,' she said with a nod. 'Why did you turn up at Finn's house today?'

Rico inwardly tensed and fought the urge to respond to the jolt of discomfort that slammed through him. Was this her idea of subtlety? It wasn't his. But, given her reputation, perhaps he should have expected a direct hit.

'To confirm a suspicion,' he replied as casually as if she'd asked him what his favourite colour was.

'Yet you didn't stick around to do so.'

'I didn't need to. You did it for me the second we met.' The image of her standing in front of him, her green eyes wide, the pulse at the base of her neck fluttering, shot into his head and predictably sent all his blood to his groin. 'I don't think I've ever seen shock quite like it.'

'You were unexpected.'

'Evidently.'

'How did you find out about him?'

'I saw a photo of him in the press,' he said, remembering the earth-shattering moment he'd wondered firstly exactly how much morphine was in his system and secondly how the hell a picture of himself had made it into the papers. 'At the launch of his hotel in Paris.'

Carla sat back and frowned, lost in thought for a moment. 'That was taken back in March.'

He gave a brief nod. 'Correct.'

'What took you so long?'

'I've been recovering from an accident.'

'What kind of accident?'

'A bad one,' he said, lifting his glass to his mouth and knocking back a third of its contents. 'A BASE jump in the Alps went wrong.'

'A BASE jump?'

'It stands for buildings, antennae, spans and earth. Four categories of fixed objects you can jump off. Spans are bridges and earth includes mountains. Mont Blanc on this occasion. I landed badly.'

'Ouch.'

'Esattamente,' he agreed, although 'ouch' was something of an understatement. Having crashed into a tree and plummeted to the ground, he'd lain on the rocky terrain battered and broken, the physical pain unlike anything he'd felt before.

'I haven't been fit to travel,' he added, putting the accident from his mind, since it was in the past and he'd be done with it just as soon as the aches and twinges disappeared.

'Until today.'

Not even today, in all honesty. But the Finn-lined walls of his house in the Venice lagoon had been closing in on him and he hadn't been able to stand the not knowing any longer. 'That's right.'

'So, having spent three months recovering from an accident that must have been pretty severe if it did that much damage, you travelled to Finn's house with the intention of meeting him and then you left, without actually having done so.'

'Yes.'

She tilted her head and her gaze turned probing. 'A bit strange, after going to all that effort, don't you think?'

'Not at all,' he said, feeling a flicker of unease spring to life in his gut. 'Simply a change of plan.'

'Aren't you at all curious about him?'

Yes, very, was the answer that immediately came to mind before he shoved it back in the cupboard in his head where it belonged. 'No.'

'He's a good man.'

'I don't doubt it.'

'So why aren't you interested?'

'I don't really have the time.'

'Even if that was true, you should make time for family.'

'Do you make time for yours?'

'We're not talking about mine,' she countered swiftly, and he could practically see the barriers flying up.

'I'll take that as a no.'

'You can take it any way you like,' she said with a defensiveness that suggested he'd hit the nail on the head.

'Interesting.'

'Not in the slightest.' She leaned forward and regarded him shrewdly. 'And you know what? I don't believe you. I don't believe you'd have made such an arduous journey the minute you could just to confirm a suspicion. If that was all you wanted to do you could have called. Or even emailed.'

'I employ a driver and own a plane,' he said in a deliberate attempt to draw her attention away from her more disconcerting observations while the discomfort inside him grew. 'It wasn't that arduous.'

'What happened between me leaving you in Finn's study and you deciding to simply walk out? Was it something I said?'

It was what she'd said and the photos, the occasion and the relatives. The sudden, stomach-curdling feeling that if he stuck around his life might irrevocably change, and quite possibly for the worse. That was what had happened. But Rico didn't want to rehash the events of earlier. He didn't even want to have to think about them. And he'd had enough of this interrogation.

He'd changed his mind about Carla's suitability as a lover, he thought darkly, ignoring the stab of disappointment that struck him in the gut and focusing on the rapid beat of his pulse and fine cold sweat now coating him instead. When he'd first laid eyes on her, he hadn't given much thought to her personality. He'd been too blown away by her looks and then too focused on distracting himself to properly acknowledge the dry, clever bite to her words.

However, now there was no denying that she was far more perceptive and tenacious than he'd anticipated, and that was way more dangerous than it was intriguing. She had the potential to see too much. Demand too much. And she'd use every weapon in her no doubt considerable arsenal to get it. No matter how intensely he set about seducing her, she wouldn't let up with the questions. If he showed any sign of succumbing to a moment of weakness she'd slip beneath his guard and have him revealing every secret he held, which simply could not happen.

However much he wanted her, he'd never put himself in a position that would leave him defenceless and exposed and vulnerable to attack. He hated the thought of being manipulated and, even worse, being unaware of it. It had happened once before, when he'd been young and desperate and an easily exploitable target, and he had no intention of allowing it to happen again.

So he'd feed her and deposit her at her hotel, bidding her goodnight instead of following her up as had been his original plan, and that really would put an end to today.

'It's getting late,' he muttered as he picked up and scoured a menu that he knew off by heart. 'We should order.'

CHAPTER FOUR

Hah...

Carla sat back, not falling for the relaxed demeanour or the dazzling yet practised smiles for a moment. Rico was hiding something. She knew it. His tells were tiny and no doubt invisible to anyone whose job wasn't all about perception and seeking out the truth behind the facade, but she'd caught the odd moment of tension that gripped his big, lean frame and the occasional flare of wariness in the depths of his eyes.

She hadn't missed the way he'd brushed off his accident as if it had been nothing more than a mild inconvenience when it had to have been anything but. Or how when she'd suggested he ought to make time for family he'd neatly turned it back on her. And the fact that he'd left unanswered her question about exactly what had made him leave Finn's study had not gone unnoticed.

He was no more an open book than she was and she may not understand *why*, but she did recognise *what* he was doing. Deflection and dissembling and carefully curating responses were tactics she deployed herself. She shared nothing of significance with the few men she dated. No details of her past, no hopes and dreams for the future and certainly no emotion. With information came power. With emotion came vulnerability, and the idea of giving a man that kind of control over her made her stomach roll. Could it be that Rico was protecting himself too?

It was none of her concern. What *was* of concern was that she badly needed to know what hidden depths lay beneath the charming exterior and the dry words, and it looked as though his armour might be harder to penetrate than she'd assumed.

But that didn't mean she was going to give up. Oh, no. If she concentrated on what was at stake tonight—Finn and Georgie and their happiness—she would get what she wanted. She usually did in the end. She hadn't been lying when she'd told Rico she believed it was all about manipulation. She knew first-hand how powerful a tactic that could be and how easy it was to shape and mould people's beliefs and behaviours, and she wasn't unaware of the irony of having made a career out of it.

However, turning a negative into a positive had been a major factor in getting over what had happened to her. She didn't feel any pangs of guilt about what she did. Controlling the narrative was key, and all the weapons she had at her disposal to achieve this were entirely compatible with the openness, honesty and transparency that were so important to her.

But manipulation probably wasn't going to work here, she reflected, picking up a menu of her own as her stomach gave a rumble and just about managing to decipher it, since pasta was pasta in almost any language.

Rico was too sharp, too wary. So maybe she ought to switch tactics. She'd gone for the jugular, hoping to catch him off guard, but perhaps some of that subtlety she'd espoused a moment ago would be more successful.

As soon as they'd ordered, she'd start with some innocent questions. About his English, perhaps. Where he learned it and how it had got so good. About where he'd been raised and how he'd become involved in hedge funds. Surely he'd have no objection to providing that kind of basic information.

In the event, however, she didn't get a chance to find out. Their order was taken and the food arrived with impressive efficiency, and that was pretty much it for conversation. If Rico had been lacking in expansive answers before, he turned positively tight-lipped now. Her questions met with monosyllabic responses that dwindled into mutters, and eventually she gave up in frustrated exasperation.

She'd never seen anyone so wholly focused on their food. Each bite seemed uniquely important, a moment to be relished and protected. His head-down, methodical approach to eating was intriguing. He was utterly absorbed in the process. He didn't even notice when someone who'd clearly overdone the chianti bumped into her chair.

Although, to be fair, she barely did either.

For one thing her *spaghetti alla puttanesca* was exquisite, an all-encompassing experience of sublimely balanced flavours that exploded her taste buds and made her want to groan in pleasure. For another, with conversation non-existent, she'd found herself giving in to the temptation she'd been fighting all evening and studying him instead.

Up until now she'd had to keep her wits about her and her mind off his many attractions, but now, unobserved, she could indulge her senses. Just a little and just for a moment, because he really was unbelievably gorgeous. Beneath the white cotton of the shirt he'd changed into at some point his shoulders were wide and strong enough to carry the weight of the world. When she looked at his hands, she could envisage them on her body, sliding over her hot, bare skin and making her tremble with need. Her own hands itched with the urge to ruffle his thick, dark hair and she had to tighten her grip on her fork.

She badly wanted to know how he'd got the scar that cut a pale, jagged line at his temple and how he'd acquired the bump in his nose, the imperfections which only made him sexier. His easy, practised smile, which never quite made it to his eyes, and which she suspected was designed to both fool and conceal, was nevertheless still blinding enough to do strange things to her stomach, no matter how much she tried to resist.

For several heady minutes while they ate in silence, Carla's entire world, her focus and her attention, was reduced to the magnetising, enigmatic man sitting opposite her, so it was little wonder she'd been caught by surprise when that fellow diner had knocked into her chair.

Little wonder too that she jumped and blinked when Rico's voice cut across her surprisingly lurid thoughts.

'Are you done?'

'What?' she managed, her voice strangely husky. 'Oh. Yes.'

'Would you like anything else?'

'No, thank you,' she said, mustering up a smile of her own and fighting back a blush at having been caught staring. 'That was amazing. I'm stuffed.'

'Then I'll get the bill.'

What? The bill? That was unexpected. He'd all but promised her a seduction. She'd been braced for it and equally prepared to use it as leverage. If she was being honest, she'd been looking forward to it. To the challenge, naturally. Instead, Rico was catching the eye of a waiter and calling him over with a quick scribble in the air, clearly keen to be rid of her.

'Really?' she said, unable to prevent the frown she could feel creasing her forehead.

'It's late.'

True, but still. 'So that's it?'

'What else were you expecting?'

Good question. She was exhausted. She wasn't here on a date. She should be glad that the chemistry between them had evaporated and he no longer wanted her in that way. It mattered not one jot *why* he'd changed his mind. She wasn't interested in that in the slightest. Yet she was nowhere near achieving her mission. She'd barely even started. 'You said dinner could prove interesting.'

'I was wrong.'

'I disagree.'

'Too bad.'

Okay. So that was a bit rude, but he both sounded and looked resolute and she never begged for anything these days. Adaptability and flexibility were key in her line of work and she had both in spades. She also had his number. Her flight was scheduled for tomorrow evening, so she had all day to bombard him with phone calls until he realised that he felt the way about the Finn situation she wanted him to. Now that she'd established contact she wasn't going to give it up without a fight. Finn and Georgie deserved more than that, and coming all this way was not going to have been for nothing.

'I see,' she said, pulling herself together and aiming for breezy. 'Well, then. Thank you for dinner.'

'You're welcome,' he said, his expression dark and unfathomable. 'I'll see you to your hotel.'

So she could be subjected to further insult along the way? She didn't think so. 'There's no need.'

'I'd like to.'

'Why?'

'You're a tourist and an easy target.'

'I may not have been to Venice,' she said a tad archly, 'but I have travelled extensively, often alone. I am perfectly capable of getting myself to a hotel in a strange city.'

'Humour me. Where are you staying?'

'The first hotel that came up with any availability.'

'Which is?'

'I don't remember the name,' she had to admit, never more regretting that she didn't have the answer to hand. 'Unsurprisingly, when I was making plans this afternoon everything was a bit of a rush. The details are on my phone. There wasn't a lot to choose from. Most places seemed to be fully booked.'

'It's high season.'

'So I gathered.'

While Rico paid the waiter, who then started whisking away their empty plates, Carla twisted to unhook her bag from the back of her chair. Her lovely, expensive designer bag that contained her passport, her cards, her cash, her keys and her phone—virtually her entire life.

Her bag that was no longer there.

It wasn't under her chair, she realised, her blood running cold, her heart pounding and the food in her stomach turning to lead. It wasn't beneath the table. It wasn't anywhere.

'What's the matter?' asked Rico, who sounded as if he were six feet below the surface of a distant canal.

'My bag,' she said dazedly as her head began to buzz. 'It's gone.'

Once Rico settled on a course of action, nothing swayed him from it, and this evening was no different. He'd decided against seducing Carla and from that moment on he just wanted supper over and done with. Her effect on him was too hard to ignore and he was tired of fighting it.

With every mouthful he'd taken, the usually delicious food tasting strangely of nothing, he'd been aware of her eyes on him, burning right through the layers of clothing and searing his skin. He was so attuned to her frequency he'd even caught the tiny variations in her breathing while she'd been studying him, which was as extraordinary as it was baffling when he'd never before experienced such awareness. But at least he'd had the consolation of soon being able to escape.

Not so now.

Fate clearly had other ideas for this evening.

'What do you mean, gone?' he asked, the unease that had faded with every passing second now slamming back into him with a vengeance.

'Exactly that,' she said, her face white, the green eyes that met his wide and troubled. 'My passport, my keys, my money, my phone. Everything. Practically my whole life. Gone.'

'How?' he said sharply. 'When?'

'I don't know.' She ran her hands through her hair, a deep frown creasing her forehead. 'But someone bumped into my chair earlier, while we were eating. I thought they were drunk. It could have happened then.'

Rico inwardly tensed, stunned disbelief ricocheting through him as the impact of her words registered. Someone had knocked into her? How the hell had he not noticed that? He, who'd once lived on the streets and still slept with one eye open. Who had razor-sharp instincts and missed nothing. He shouldn't have allowed himself to be distracted by her focus on him, *dannazione*. He shouldn't have been so determined to get through the evening as quickly as possible, to the extent that nothing else mattered.

'Do you remember what they looked like?' he asked, not liking one little bit the apparent dulling of the wits he'd relied on from the age of twelve.

'Not really. I barely caught a glimpse of him. Or her.'

'No CCTV out here.'

'No… Damn…' She took a deep breath and grimaced. 'Look, I really hate having to ask, but could I use your phone? I need to find somewhere else to stay.'

The reality of her situation—and his—hit him then and his jaw tightened minutely. The only hotels available were no doubt less than salubrious and who knew how long it would take to find a vacancy? He knew what it was like to spend the night on the streets, cold and alone and afraid, and he wouldn't wish it on anyone. Venice was labyrinthine and not all of it was pretty enough to end up on a postcard.

He couldn't abandon her, no matter how much he might wish to. Carla was here because of the challenge *he'd* issued and she was stuck because he'd allowed himself to be distracted and had lowered his guard. There was only one solution, and it didn't appeal in the slightest, but this was the price he had to pay for both his impulsivity and his carelessness.

'You'd better come home with me.'

Carla went very still, her gaze jerking to his, the horror he saw there and on her face suggesting she was as keen on the idea as he was. 'Oh, no, I really don't think that's necessary.'

'You'll be perfectly safe.'

She shook her head, her blonde hair shimmering beneath the twinkling lights distracting him for a moment. 'That's not it.'

'Then what is it?'

'I don't much like being dependent on anyone,' she said with a slight jut of her chin.

No, well, he could identify with that. 'I don't much

like having anyone dependent on me, but we don't have a choice.'

She stiffened and something flashed in the depths of her eyes. 'I *always* have a choice.'

'As I said, it's high season. Everywhere decent will be full. There are areas of Venice you do not want to find yourself in, however briefly. It's nearly midnight and you must be wiped out. I know I am.' The exertions of today were taking their toll and his muscles were beginning to ache, so perhaps it was just as well he'd decided against seducing her, not that that was remotely relevant right now. 'But you're right. It *is* your choice. Here.'

Fishing his phone out of his jacket pocket, he put it on the table and pushed it towards her. For several long moments Carla just stared at it warily, as if it might be about to bite, and then she sighed and nudged it back towards him, her shoulders falling as she gave a brief nod.

'All right,' she said, looking impossibly weary and dejected, the smile she was trying to muster up weak. 'Thank you.'

'Things will look better in the morning,' he said, not having a clue why he felt the need to reassure her but for some reason really disliking the way the fight had drained from her.

'Of course they will.'

'Do you have a suitcase?'

'In the cloakroom.'

'Andiamo.'

While from the centre of his boat Rico navigated the canals that were a lot less busy than they'd been earlier,

Carla sat at the back and used his phone to cancel her bank cards and her passport. Her phone had face recognition but she cancelled that too, just in case.

She was too preoccupied to take any notice of the tall, dark buildings as they slid quietly past, thinning out until they were far behind them. She wasn't in the mood to luxuriate in the inky depths of the night that enveloped her as they crossed the lagoon and the cool, fresh breeze that caressed her face, or admire Rico's skill and ease at the tiller of a vintage boat that was all beautiful varnished wood and sleek lines. She lacked the energy and enthusiasm to request a tour of his home, which she was sure would be huge and airy, based on the little of it she did see. She certainly didn't have time to contemplate the implications of having her most important material possessions stolen, practically from beneath her nose.

That, thanks to jet lag, came at three am.

Upon disembarkation at the jetty to which he'd tied the boat, Rico had grabbed her overnight bag and then alighted. He'd held out his hand to help her off, releasing her as soon as she'd done so, and headed up a path with an instruction to follow him tossed over his shoulder. Too battered by shock and weariness and the sizzling effect of his brief yet electrifying touch to do anything else, Carla had complied.

Once inside the house, he'd led her through a dimly lit but spacious hall, up a set of wide stone stairs and shown her to a guest suite that was probably the size of her entire flat. He'd then bade her a curt goodnight before turning on his heel and disappearing. She'd instantly flopped onto the bed and crashed out almost the minute her head hit the pillow.

Now, two hours later, she was wide awake, hot and sweaty, the sheets twisted around her from all the tossing and turning she'd been doing in a futile attempt to get back to sleep.

With a sigh of frustration, Carla disentangled herself and got up. She crossed the room, opened the doors that gave onto one of two balconies and stepped out into the darkness in the hope that cool night air might blast away the thumping of her head and quell the sick feeling that had started in the restaurant and had now spread into every cell of her body.

But the breeze that carried a welcome freshness and a hint of salt was no panacea for the churning of her stomach. The distant cries of seagulls couldn't drown out the rapid drum of her heartbeat. No distantly beautiful view of perhaps the world's most romantic city could sugar-coat the reality of her situation.

She was stranded, her plans derailed and her certainty about what she'd been doing shaken, her freedom and independence snatched away along with everything else. She was trapped, firstly by her arrogant assumption that the plan which seemed like such a good idea at lunchtime would work and secondly by her own stupidity.

How could she have let it happen? she wondered, swallowing down the wave of nausea rolling up her throat as she gazed across the lagoon at the odd sparkling light of the city far away. She knew how important her phone and her passport were and she knew the risks associated with leaving a handbag hanging on the back of a chair in a public space. As she'd so blithely and loftily told him, she'd travelled a lot.

Yet she'd been so thrown by Rico's effect on her, she'd failed to deploy her common sense. She hadn't given the security of her things a moment's thought at any point during dinner. She'd been reckless and un-thinking and, worst of all, breathtakingly stupid, and as a result she was now entirely at the mercy of a man once again.

This time, the situation might be wholly her fault and not at all like the one in which she'd found herself as a teenager, but the emotions were all too familiar—the helplessness and the confusion, the vulnerability and the stripping away of her agency and her identity.

It had taken her months to rid herself of the chill that was rippling through her now, the self-doubt she could feel beginning to creep in and the tightness in her chest. She didn't like feeling this way when it wasn't who she was any more, and she hated even more the disturbing memories it invoked of a time when she'd been so naïve, so foolish.

Nor did she like being here, wherever here actually was, but Rico had been right—there hadn't been an al-ternative. It had occurred to her as she'd sat there staring at his phone, and burning up with regret and anger that she hadn't taken better care of hers, that she couldn't strike out on her own. She had no money and no ID. No hotel would take her in, even if she *had* managed to locate the details of the one she'd booked. She'd had to accept his offer, however nasty the taste it left in her mouth, however sick it made her feel.

But her enforced dependence on him wouldn't be for long, she assured herself, determinedly pushing the feelings and the memories away and pulling herself together. In the morning—well, later on, seeing as how it was already morning—she'd file a police report and investigate getting a new passport. She'd look at moving her flight and contact Georgie to ask her to get her locks changed, just to be on the safe side. She'd email her boss and let her know she wouldn't be in on Monday. Once she'd figured out how to get hold of some money she'd buy a phone and a few more clothes and then she'd find herself a hotel to stay in. Despite it being high season, surely the city would be less busy during the week than at the weekend.

She might be stranded but she would *not* be a victim, she told herself firmly as she gave her upper arms a quick rub before turning and heading back inside. Not again. *Never* again. She had resources. Somehow she would get herself out of this mess.

She needn't be troubled by her host. He'd hardly know she was here. She had plenty of things to be getting on with and presumably he did too. In the unlikely event their paths did cross, however, she'd be on her guard. She'd be polite but distant and think of some other way to encourage contact with Finn. She had no intention of giving up. Just because this plan had backfired badly didn't mean another would.

The one thing she definitely *wouldn't* be doing, she thought, climbing into bed and punching her pillow into shape, was indulging the attraction she felt for Rico, which just wouldn't seem to go away. She'd made that mistake with him once already and look what had become of it. Whatever else happened, she would *not* be making it again.

CHAPTER FIVE

IT WAS NEARING lunchtime when Carla finally emerged, not that Rico, who was in the kitchen throwing together something to eat, had been watching the clock.

In fact, he'd spent most of the morning ploughing up and down the pool in an effort to soothe and exercise his aching muscles. Despite taking painkillers that had knocked him out pretty much instantly, he hadn't slept well. For most of the night he'd thrashed about, his dreams filled with disjointed montages of his life on the streets as an adolescent, triggered by his continuing incredulity that he hadn't noticed the theft of Carla's handbag, the kind of dreams—or nightmares—that he hadn't had for years.

He wasn't in the best of moods and his acute awareness of his unexpected house guest wasn't helping. He didn't have people to stay. He didn't have people in his life full stop. He didn't want them and he certainly didn't need them. He might have thought he had once upon a time, and he might have thought he'd found the loyalty and family and sense of belonging he craved in the gang he'd joined when he was twelve, but he hadn't.

The moment those hopes and expectations had been crushed was the moment he'd realised that he was on his own, and that the only person he could truly count on was himself.

All he needed to survive now was his isolation and his solitude, and he went to great lengths to protect them. It was the main reason he lived on an island in the lagoon instead of the *sestieri*. The fewer neighbours the better. He didn't want people nosing about in his business. Even his housekeeper, who came three times a week, went home at the end of each day she was there. Should he feel the need to entertain, he did so in the city.

This particular property of his might extend to fifty hectares, but Carla being in even a tiny part of it felt like a violation of his space, a further threat to his peace of mind, which was already in some turmoil. Her constant but unwelcome presence in his thoughts was frustrating. As if his dreams about his youth hadn't been disturbing enough on their own, up she'd popped in a number of them, teasing him with the spikiness that he found perversely attractive and tempting him to behave in a way that might be worth suffering a few aches and pains for.

Everything about the whole situation that he now found himself in was immensely irritating, and the realisation he'd come to mid-swim an hour ago made it additionally so. One unforeseen consequence of his reluctant chivalry was that if he wanted Carla gone, and gone fast, which he did, he'd have to be the one to facilitate it. Overnight, the private nature of his island, which he'd always considered a definite positive, had become a serious negative. She had things to do that could only be done in the city and he'd have to take her, which, he was forced to acknowledge with a grind of his teeth, was perhaps another example of acting in haste and repenting at leisure.

But he badly wanted his life back to the trouble-free, easy way it had been before he'd met Carla, before he'd seen the photo of Finn, before even the accident, and if that meant accompanying her every step of the way as she set about reclaiming what had been taken from her, to make sure she actually had the wherewithal to leave, then so be it.

He could resist the temptation she posed, he assured himself grimly, aware of a sudden shift in the air and bracing himself before turning to find her standing in the doorway, wearing a yellow sundress and flip-flops, looking like sunshine, her hair wet from the shower he would not be imagining her in ever. He could retain his grip on his control and shut down his response to her. If he ruthlessly stuck to the plan and deployed his usual devil-may-care approach to life, the one that had been strangely absent during the last twenty-four hours, everything would be fine.

'Good afternoon,' he said, fixing a lazy smile to his face and sounding pleasingly unmoved by her appearance.

'I didn't mean to disturb you.'

Far too late for that. 'You aren't. Come in.'

'I had no idea of the time,' she said, sliding her gaze to the clock on the wall above his head and giving a faint grimace as she stepped forward. 'I'm still recovering from my trip to Hong Kong, jet lag is a bitch.'

'Coffee?'

'That would be great, thank you.'

She came to a stop on the other side of the vast kitchen island unit and hopped up onto a stool. Resolutely not noticing how the movement tightened her dress around her chest, Rico turned his attention to taking a pot off the stove and poured the contents into a tiny espresso mug, which he then handed to her across the expanse of marble.

'Milk? Sugar?'

'No, thanks.' She took a sip and closed her eyes, while he watched her smile in satisfaction and for a moment forgot his name. 'Oh, that *is* good,' she said, which instantly had him imagining her breathing that exact same thing into his ear as he held her tight and moved inside her.

'Help yourself to brunch,' he muttered, with a quick cough to clear the hint of hoarseness from his voice and the unacceptably vivid image from his head.

'You cooked?'

'I can.' And well. Once upon a time, he'd sworn he would never go hungry again and he hadn't. 'However, today I merely assembled.'

Getting a ruthless grip on the imagination that had never troubled him before, Rico turned to the section of counter top where he'd been working and set about transferring plates of prosciutto and salami, mozzarella and Gorgonzola, and bowls of artichoke hearts, sun-dried tomatoes and olives to the island. With ciabatta and focaccia, in hindsight, it was rather a lot for two people but, 'I didn't know what you'd like.'

'I like it all,' she said with an apologetic wince as her stomach rumbled loudly. 'It looks delicious.'

She looked delicious, was the thought that shot into his head before he could stop it, and he wanted to devour her. 'Take a plate.'

'Thank you.' She did as he'd suggested and began filling it, only to pause a moment later. 'You know...' she said, then stopped.

'What?'

'Nothing.' She gave her head a quick shake, as if to clear it, and said instead, 'Thank you for putting me up last night.'

'You're welcome.'

'I'll be out of your hair just as soon as I can.'

The sooner the better, because what if, contrary to his expectations, he couldn't keep a lid on the attraction that instead of fading only seemed to be getting worse? What if he succumbed and lowered his defences and she went in for the kill? It didn't bear thinking about. 'I will help.'

'I can manage,' she said, flashing him a smile of her own, one that didn't quite reach her eyes and gave him the impression it was about as genuine as his.

'I don't doubt it.'

'So that's settled, then.'

If only. 'Not quite.'

Her green gaze narrowed slightly. 'How so?'

'Do you have any idea where you actually are?' he asked, thinking obviously not, judging by the faint frown that appeared on her forehead.

'Enlighten me.'

'Isola Santa Margherita.'

'Which is?'

'My island.'

She lowered the spoon she'd been using to her plate and stared at him. 'Your island.'

'Corretto.'

'Neighbours?'

'No.'

'Access to the city?'

'Boat.'

For a moment a shadow passed across her face and he thought he saw a shudder ripple through her but both were gone before he could be sure.

'There are taxis, I presume?'

He gave a brief nod and reminded himself that he needed to know as much about shadows or shudders as he did about smiles that weren't genuine, which was nothing. 'There are, but they're expensive and you have to book ahead. I and my boat, however, are free and entirely at your disposal.'

'Oh, I'm sure you must have lots to be getting on with,' she said, replacing the spoon in the bowl of olives and picking up a napkin.

'As a matter of fact, I don't. I'm supposed to be taking things easy.'

'Then you don't need to be ferrying me around.'

'It would be my pleasure,' he said with an easy coolness that matched hers. 'I'll take you anywhere you need to be.'

Quite frankly, Carla thought as she watched Rico embark on piling food onto his plate, she needed to be anywhere other than here, on a private island, cut off from the city, from people, from help. Anywhere other than having brunch with the man who'd presented her with a smorgasbord of deliciousness that had momentarily tempted her to divulge tales of the horrendous food she'd had to eat while growing up on a commune, which could well have wound up becoming a conversation about her instead of him and potentially led down a path she'd really rather not tread.

If only she hadn't hung about in the doorway to the kitchen, transfixed by the sight of him and rooted to the spot, but had instead got a grip and made herself scarce. If only she hadn't stood there, staring at his back, watching the muscles of his arms bunch and flex as he did whatever he was doing, struggling for breath and going weak at the knees while her temperature soared.

An effect of her still malfunctioning body clock? Probably not, but it was the excuse she'd decided upon and she was sticking to it. She was contemplating using it too as an explanation for actually considering accepting his suggestion to act as her taxi, despite her deep-seated desire to take care of herself.

Not that she really needed one.

If she applied clarity and reason to her thinking she'd see that this situation was nothing like the one it had reminded her of in the early hours of this morning. There was no malicious intent behind Rico's offer of help. No attempt to control her actions or her thoughts. No demand for anything in return. The island might be cut off but she wasn't. No one was stopping her from going anywhere.

She'd be better off focusing on the reality of today and not the memories of a decade ago, she told herself, adding a spoonful of artichoke hearts to her plate. Yes, she didn't want to be indebted to him and yes, it was bad enough that he'd had to rescue her in the first place, but surely the quicker she sorted everything out, the quicker she'd be home. With his means of transport and knowledge of the city, neither of which she had, Rico would definitely speed things up. She only understood enough Italian to be able to order off a menu. He'd be able to slice through the bureaucracy in a way that she simply couldn't.

Maybe she ought to learn to accept help without feeling as if she was somehow failing by not being able to handle things on her own. Just because she was capable didn't mean she had to be all the time. Maybe, occasionally, it would be a good idea to let someone else take the reins, on a practical level at any rate.

And, perhaps, he'd lend her some cash?

Carla had been financially independent for years, ever since she'd realised that having her own money and plenty of it would give her choice and freedom. She paid her credit card off in full every month. The only money she borrowed was for her mortgage. But even if she asked Georgie to send her some, with no ID she wouldn't be able to pick it up. Without her phone she couldn't access her digital wallet. However strong her motivations, however excellent her intentions, she had to be practical.

'OK, well, first of all,' she said, taking a great leap in her personal development by choosing to look forward not back, 'I need to go to the police station and report the theft of my things.'

'We can leave as soon as you're ready to go.'

'I also need to get a phone.'

'I thought you might,' he said, one corner of his mouth kicking up in a way that did sizzling things to her stomach which she could really do without. 'So I had this delivered this morning.' The model he slid in her direction she knew to be the latest of its kind and worth over a thousand euros. 'It's yours if you want it.'

See? she told herself while struggling to get a grip on the heat that was threatening to turn her into a puddle of lust. He wasn't trying to cut her off. Quite the opposite, in fact. 'On loan?'

'If you wish.'

'I insist.' She took a deep breath, then said, 'And on the subject of loans... I was wondering...'

'How much do you need?'

With a wince, she told him and he nodded. 'Not a problem.'

'I'll pay you back as soon as I can.'

'No hurry.'

There was every hurry, she thought as she popped an olive in her mouth and watched intrigued as Rico turned his attention to his own plate and began working through it with the same degree of focus he'd had last night. Because she might not disturb him any longer, but Rico, with his dark looks, cool confidence and decisiveness, certainly disturbed her. He was so attractive and so hard to resist on any number of levels. She had to take care not to let this practical help of his slide into something more dangerous where her emotions became involved and she became infatuated with him. The sooner she removed herself from his magnetising orbit and returned home, to her job, her friends, her *life*, the better.

But when it came to the actual police station visit itself, Carla was unexpectedly rather glad of his presence. As they approached and then pulled up at the jetty immediately in front of the entrance to the building, she welcomed the distraction provided by his proximity and solidity and didn't even bother to resist the temptation to keep glancing over and drinking in how very good he looked in shorts that revealed the lower half of a pair of very sexy legs, a T-shirt that moulded to his muscles, and mirrored sunglasses.

The only other time she'd been anywhere near such an establishment was immediately after she'd been rescued from the seedy east London hotel she'd ended up in when she'd run away to be with the man she'd thought she'd loved. The occasion had been invasive and embarrassing and horrible, she remembered, her pulse beginning to race and her stomach churning as they alighted, and, just in front of the arch through which she and Rico had to proceed, her step faltered.

'Are you all right?' he asked, concern flickering in his gaze as he looked down at her.

She took a deep breath and fixed a smile to her face. 'I'm fine,' she said, aiming for breezy but not quite hitting it. 'Just not a huge fan of police stations. So let's get this over and done with, shall we?'

She went ahead of him, and stepped out of the bright

sunlight and into the dark, busy station, and it wasn't the same, obviously, but the uniforms and the noise and the musty, damp smell acted like a trigger, and recollections of being interviewed and inspected, stripped and swabbed, suddenly slammed into her head.

In an instant she was awash with memories of the confusion and discomfort she'd felt at the intrusion, along with the fury and outrage and resentment at what had been done to her by those who'd ripped her away from her one true love. She remembered how it had all been brought up again at her abuser's trial, by which time she'd broken free of his malevolent influence and could see what had happened for the horror it really was, which had converted the resentment and fury into the shame and guilt that still faintly lingered even now, a decade later.

And today it was all too much. She was hot and she was tired. Her defences were weakened by the robbery and jet lag. She didn't want to be reminded of her abuser and what he'd done to her and how she'd facilitated it. Yet now it was all she could think of. The naïvety and the neediness she'd felt. The hundreds of emails they'd exchanged that contained an angst-ridden outpouring of her concerns, her worries, her hopes, her dreams. The intimate photos she'd sent and the innermost thoughts she'd shared.

The memories and the emotions whirled round her head faster and faster, as if she were on some kaleidoscopic, out-of-control merry-go-round. Her heart thundered as if trying to break her ribs. Her lungs tightened, her dress clinging to her body clammily. She couldn't breathe. Her head was swimming. Her limbs were turning to liquid. She felt as if she was about to throw up.

God, she wasn't going to faint, was she?

No. She couldn't be. She wasn't the type. She was strong and capable and a survivor. Yet her knees felt weirdly weak. Sweat was trickling down her back and her blood was pounding in her ears. She was hot, so very hot, and her vision was now blurring at the edges and her head was going all prickly.

The last thing she was aware of before her legs gave way was a strong arm whipping round her waist, a hard wall of muscle into which she collided, and then there was nothing but darkness.

Rico had experienced many, *many* things in his thirty-one years on the planet but having someone pass out on him was not one of them.

Thank God he'd caught Carla before she fell. Given the direction in which she'd listed, she'd most likely have hit her head on the corner of the very solid-looking table to her right and that might well have put her in hospital. Instead, she'd collapsed into the relative safety of his arms.

Ignoring the screaming protest of his body, he scooped her up in all her dead weight glory and barked out a series of orders that resulted in chairs being swiftly assembled into a row.

Now was not the time to notice how soft she felt gathered up against him or how delicious she smelled. Nor was it the time to dwell on how well he knew this building, how often he'd spent the night here in these cells, having been caught earning money and later 'running errands' on the *sestieri*, a cocky and mouthy youth on the surface, a lost and petrified child beneath. Now was the time to lay her down to get her blood flowing in the right direction and procure the paperwork.

With what wasn't his most elegant of moves Rico set Carla down, pausing only to slide the strap of her dress that had fallen down up over her shoulder and absolutely not indulging in the temptation to linger.

Dio, the things he'd done, he thought darkly as he straightened and stalked over to the desk, the small crowd in front of it taking one look at the scar at his temple and the bump in his nose and parting like the waves. Willingly at first when he'd been desperate to prove himself and fit in but then increasingly less willingly when he'd gained the respect of his bosses and been asked to take on a bigger role and more responsibility, although by that point he'd been in so deep he hadn't been able to see a way out.

He hadn't been anywhere near this place in years. Not since that last time, when, at the age of sixteen, he'd been charged with crimes relating to money laundering. But it might as well have been yesterday. He could still recall how terrified he'd been despite the bravado. How slowly the hours had passed while he waited for his bosses to come and bail him out. How sick with devastation and disillusionment he'd felt when he'd realised no one was coming, that the loyalty he'd given them would not be repaid, and how unbelievably naïve and stupid he'd been to put his trust in people who'd dealt only in exploitation and had never known a code of honour.

But that was ancient history, he reminded himself with a clench of the jaw. On leaving the courtroom that day he'd slammed the door shut on everything that had happened to him between the death of his parents and turning his life around, and it no longer had the ability to affect him. Nothing on any level other than the purely physical did these days.

By the time he returned to Carla, forms in hand, she'd recovered and was sitting up, looking slightly dishevelled, slightly stunned, yet oddly, mystifyingly… adorable.

'What happened?' she asked, her question cutting through his bewilderment, since he'd never found anything adorable, oddly or otherwise, while the huskiness of her voice sent a jolt of awareness through him.

'You passed out.'

She stared at him. 'Seriously?'

'Yes,' he said curtly in an effort to pull himself together. 'You went out like a light.'

'Who *does* that these days?'

'You do, evidently. How are you feeling?'

'A bit odd,' she said, after thinking about it for a moment, and then added with a grimace, 'A lot mortified.'

'Should I call the paramedics?' he asked, the fact that he was asking a question instead of issuing an order and expecting it to be obeyed a further source of irritation. But if there was one thing he was beginning to realise about Carla, it was that she preferred to make her own decisions and didn't respond well to being told what to do, however well intentioned.

'No. I'm fine.'

He looked at her, caught the paleness of her face and the turmoil in the shimmering depths of her eyes, and frowned. 'You really don't like police stations, do you?'

'No,' she said with a faint shudder.

'Why not?'

She tensed. 'Does anyone?'

Well, he certainly didn't, which would have given them something in common had he ever been remotely interested in seeking such a thing with anyone. 'What made you faint?'

'The heat,' she said, and he might have believed her if she hadn't bitten her lip and shifted her gaze from his.

'It's not that hot.'

'Jet lag and lack of sleep on top of a stressful week and even more stressful weekend, then,' she said with a scowl. 'How would I know?'

Of course she knew. She wasn't the type to stumble. Or collapse. Besides, he'd felt the tension vibrating off her. He'd caught the turmoil in her expression the second before she'd fallen into his arms. But actually it didn't matter what he did or didn't believe. It was none of his business. He didn't need details. He was just here to facilitate her departure and get his life back. 'Do you need any help with the forms?'

'No, thank you.'

In the ten minutes it took her to fill in the details, Rico distracted himself by going through the seventy-five emails that had come in since they'd left the house, deleting or replying with single-minded focus and ruthless efficiency.

One unexpected disadvantage of working on his

own with only back office support was that during the fortnight he'd spent in hospital being put back together while dosed up on morphine he'd been unable to operate his phone, let alone engage with the highly complex financial instruments he used to manage his funds. As a result he'd lost millions, which he was still in the process of recuperating.

The markets might be closed today but decisions still had to be made. Strategies had to be clarified. Requests had to be considered and, in the case of the email from one Alex Osborne of Osborne Investigations, who was apparently looking into his and Finn's biological family and was after details about him that he had either no intention of sharing or else didn't know, ignored.

Responding to or even engaging with the investigator, however briefly, would not help him in his quest to return his life to normal. It was bad enough that Finn kept popping into his head, triggered by Carla's revelation last night at dinner about how upset his brother had been by Rico's departure from his house.

The nonsensical guilt that came with these appearances was not something he appreciated. He doubted he could shed any light on anything anyway. He certainly didn't need to open the email that had come directly from this new-found brother of his. He wasn't interested in anything he might have to say. He wasn't interested in family full stop, and that was where this ended.

'That's it,' said Carla briskly, snapping him out of his dark, rumbling thoughts. 'I'm done.'

She stood up and swayed and Rico was on his feet in an instant.

'Steady,' he said, instinctively putting one hand on her shoulder, which he realised was a mistake the minute he did it. She tensed beneath his touch and her breath caught. Her gaze jerked to his, a flash of heat lighting the emerald-green depths of her eyes, which exploded a reciprocal burst of desire inside him before she shook his hand off at the exact same moment he snatched it away.

'Sit down,' he said curtly, resisting the urge to curl his hand into a fist to squeeze out the burn. 'I'll take them.'

For once she didn't protest but did as he suggested with alacrity, and by the time he returned with the report his hand had just about stopped tingling and the memory of the feel of her soft, smooth skin beneath his palm had just about gone.

'Want to get out of here?' he asked, looking down at her and noting with relief that she now displayed no hint of her reaction to his touch.

'Very much so,' she said coolly, clearly having decided, like him, to take the denial approach.

'Are you going to pass out again?'

'No.'

'Well, I don't know about you,' he muttered as they stepped outside out of darkness and into the light, 'but I could do with a drink.'

CHAPTER SIX

WHILE RICO ORDERED a couple of beers and pastries from
the terrace of a cafe that had apparently been serving
drinks from the same spot since 1750, Carla investigated
the ways in which she might replace her stolen passport. It wasn't as complicated as she'd feared, helped
by the fact that once upon a time she'd uploaded copies
of her birth certificate, driving licence and passport to
the cloud. Nevertheless, it still took far longer than it
should have, in no small part because her thoughts kept
drifting off and circling around what had just happened.

First of all, she couldn't believe she'd actually fainted
like that. She'd never fainted before, ever. And to do so
now, in front of a strong, controlled, insanely sexy man
like Rico, well, embarrassing didn't begin to cover it.
Nor did disappointment. She hated that the memories
of a time she thought she'd dealt with had flooded back
with such ease and such vividness.

Secondly, there was all the *contact* that had taken
place. She could still feel the steel band of Rico's arm
around her waist and the warm wall of hard muscle
against which she'd been clasped moments before she

lost consciousness. Her shoulder still burned with the imprint of his hand from when she'd stood up too fast and he'd steadied her. The high-voltage charge of electricity continued to zap through her blood and the flash of desire in his eyes was singed into her memory.

Most shocking of all was the realisation that Rico wasn't as immune to her as she'd assumed, that the attraction on his side hadn't gone and up until that moment he'd simply just been very good at hiding it.

Well, whatever.

None of it made a scrap of difference to how she proceeded, Carla told herself sternly as she clicked on the submit button and a moment later received a confirmation email. In a couple of days she'd be gone and this little blip in her otherwise well-ordered, smoothly running life would be over.

'So I've ordered an emergency travel document,' she said, mightily relieved to have gained at least a modicum of control of the situation. 'It'll be ready at the British Consulate in Milan on Wednesday.'

'Wednesday?'

At the hint of censure in Rico's voice she glanced up at him to find him frowning, the expression on his face dark and disapproving, which was odd, since the machinations of bureaucracy were hardly anything to do with her. 'It takes two working days, minimum.'

'Give me a minute.'

He put down his bottle of beer, took out his phone and a minute later was rattling away in Italian. Carla listened, trying not to stare at his mouth, which was difficult when it was such a beautiful mouth producing such a beautiful language in deep, rich, spine-tingling tones, and idly pondered taking lessons. Not that she was planning to return any time soon, of course, and it wasn't as if she wanted a memento of her time here, but—

'Your new passport will be ready tomorrow.'

Jolted out of her musings, she wrenched her gaze from his mouth to his eyes. An actual passport? Tomorrow? Oh. Right. Well. That was good. 'How did you do that?'

'I'm owed a favour.'

By the British Consulate? Who was he? And why was she feeling ever so slightly piqued that he was as keen to see her leave as she was to go? That made no sense. She ought to be delighted they were on the same page, even if it did truncate the amount of time she had to achieve her goal.

'Are you owed enough of a favour to have it couriered here?' she asked, deciding to attribute that particular anomaly to jet lag, along with everything else.

'Unfortunately not. You need to pick it up in person.'

So checking out trains was another thing she was going to have to do as well as changing her flight to Tuesday morning and booking a hotel.

'Never mind,' she said, thinking that at least she wouldn't have to wash out her underwear any longer than was necessary. She'd only packed for an overnight stay and she hadn't been looking forward to having to put on damp knickers. 'Thank you, anyway.'

'You can continue to stay with me until you leave. I'll take you to Milan in the morning.'

What? No. No way.

'And before you object,' he added when she automatically opened her mouth to do exactly that, 'it is not an inconvenience. I am aware that you are extremely capable and can handle this on your own. I know you're no damsel in distress and I have no intention of telling you what to do, or preventing you from doing anything you want to do, if you insist upon it. It's simply an efficient use of resources and makes the most sense. That is all.'

Hmm. Carla didn't know about that. In her opinion, staying with Rico would mean approximately thirty-six more hours of trying to keep a lid on the attraction that instead of dissipating seemed to be growing in intensity. It would mean spending time with him, which would result in the kind of stress and discomfort that did not appeal. It would mean further reliance on someone who wasn't her, and worse, on a *man*.

On the other hand, it *would* provide an opportunity to restart her temporarily derailed mission to change his mind about meeting Finn. Earlier, she'd opened an email from Georgie, in which her best friend had asked how she was getting on and whether she'd made any progress. The deluge of guilt and shame she'd felt at the realisation that she'd allowed her own issues to take over had prevented her from replying. She didn't want to have to admit that she hadn't made very much progress at all. She didn't want to have to confess to all the reasons why.

Now was the chance to get back on track and rectify that. If she accepted his proposal and installed herself in his house, Rico would be a captive audience. She'd give him no option but to talk. She might not have much time, but in the course of her career she'd achieved a lot more with less, and here, failure was not an option. This time, nothing was going to get in her way. Her focus would remain unshakeable.

She'd put her plan into action the minute they returned to his island. He wouldn't know what had hit him. She'd start with his house and go from there. You could tell a lot about a person from the place they called home. And then she'd move on to everything else she wanted to know, such as why he'd really walked out of Finn's study yesterday lunchtime and what exactly he had against police stations. She'd noticed the tension that had radiated off him when she'd been filling in the forms. It hinted at dark secrets she badly wanted to uncover. For the job she was here to do, naturally.

Why he obviously now had no intention of acting on the attraction he still felt for her was not something she needed to know, any more than why he affected her so fiercely. The mission was her number one priority. It was the only thing that mattered now, so she'd be a fool and a coward not to accept his offer, not to mention an appalling best friend, and she hoped she was no longer any of those things.

'Thank you,' she said with a nod, ignoring the flutter of misgiving that nevertheless flickered deep inside her. 'That would be great.'

What Rico was doing inviting Carla to stay, to invade his space and shatter his privacy, he had no idea. He'd caught the flare of triumphant satisfaction in her eyes while she'd been considering what best to do. He knew what she was going to attempt. Hadn't he recognised her tenacity and her resourcefulness and decided to have nothing to do with her precisely because she might slip beneath his guard? By taking her back to his home, by exposing himself to the barrage of prying questions that was undoubtedly coming his way, wasn't he potentially not just lowering his guard but also quite possibly tossing it aside altogether?

Rico had been taking risks from the moment he'd woken up to the harsh realities of life at the age of sixteen and discovered he cared about absolutely nothing. He had no responsibilities, was accountable to no one, and therefore had zero to lose. So why shouldn't he pursue the thrill his reckless actions gave him, especially when they unfailingly turned out well?

Telling Carla she could continue to stay with him, however, was reckless beyond belief, a risk too great even for him to take. He knew that. It destabilised the status quo. It threatened the very essence of who he was. So why had his instincts, the ones he'd never yet had cause to doubt, prodded him to do it? Why did inviting Carla into his space, regardless of what she might do with it, feel so right?

Steering the boat towards the jetty, Rico eased off on the throttle and tossed a buoy over the side. The boat bumped gently against the wood, jarring the thoughts knocking around his head, and he threw a loop of rope over the mooring post.

Perhaps he was overthinking this, he thought grimly as Carla grabbed the replacement bag she'd bought and hopped off before he could even think about offering her a hand, which was a relief. Where was the danger really? If she started bombarding him with questions about himself and reasons why he should establish proper contact with his brother he'd be ready. If she decided to get personal, he could choose what to reveal and what to keep secret. He'd been doing it for years. And as for the scorching desire he felt for her, his will power was strong and she'd be gone soon enough.

Shaking off the unease and focusing on the eminently sensible way he was going to handle the next thirty-six hours, Rico stepped off the boat and set off up the cypress tree-lined path that led to the house.

'What made you choose to live here instead of the city?' she asked, falling in beside him.

'It's cool in the heat of the summer,' he replied, and it was partly the truth. She didn't need to know about his craving for space, clean air and greenery after calling the dirty urban streets home for too long. 'There's plenty of room for the pool. Plus you can't land a helicopter in the city.'

'I can see how that would be inconvenient.'

'You'll see just how convenient it is tomorrow when I take you to Milan.'

'We're going by helicopter?'

'Fastest way to get there.'

'Speed is good.'

Not always. He could think of plenty of occasions when slow was better. But now wasn't one of them, so he upped his pace, as uncomfortably aware of Carla hot on his heels as he was of the sharp complaint of his muscles.

'We'll leave at eight.'

'I'll change my flight to Tuesday morning,' she said with a slight breathlessness that he ruthlessly ignored. 'Just in case there's any delay tomorrow.'

'I'll take you to the airport.'

'That would be appreciated.'

'It's no problem at all.'

They continued in silence for a moment and then she said, 'So if I'm going to be staying here for a little while longer, would you show me around? I wouldn't want to get lost and wind up somewhere I shouldn't.'

'Now?'

'Unless you have somewhere else to be. The standard tour will do.'

'There is no standard tour,' he said, faintly disturbed about the thought of her nosing around his home even though it was too late for regrets.

'The premium one, then.'

'There's never been a tour of any kind.'

'Don't tell me I'm your first house guest.'

'All right, I won't,' he said, coming to a stop at the front door and glancing at her as he pushed his sunglasses onto his head then fished his keys from the pocket of his shorts.

Her eyes widened as she reached the obvious conclusion. 'Am I?'

'As I told you, I value my privacy.'

'My lips will remain sealed.'

As if on cue, his gaze dropped to her mouth and the world seemed to stop, keys, tours, privacy forgotten and in their place nothing but a drumming need that drowned out everything but the two of them.

He wanted to step forward, plant his hands on her shoulders and press her up against the warm, solid oak of the door. He wanted to lower his head to hers and cover her mouth with his and kiss her until neither of them could think straight.

He could almost feel her arms around his neck, her fingers tangling in his hair. He could imagine all too clearly her arching her back to plaster herself against him and the soft, sighing gasps she might emit.

She was standing so close he wouldn't even have to make much of a move. One step and he could yield to the hot, powerful desire surging through him. One step and she'd be in his arms and kissing him back because he just knew the same thing was running through her mind. She'd gone very still and her smile was fading. She was as transfixed by his mouth as he was by hers and a flush was appearing on her cheeks.

She wanted him as much as he wanted her, only this time, he realised while his body hardened and throbbed, she wasn't rejecting it. This time she wasn't pulling back. This time she was actually leaning towards him, her eyes darkening with desire that he badly wanted to stoke.

But to act on the attraction that still burned between them could expose him to her perceptiveness and un-canny insight and there was no way in hell he was going to allow that to happen. Besides, he had a plan for how to handle her—a sensible one, which was remarkable for a man who thrived on recklessness—and he had every intention of sticking to it.

The house, he reminded himself, taking a mental step back from the brink of insanity and clearing both his throat and his head. That was what she'd asked him about. The house.

Swiftly putting some distance between them, he turned to unlock the door. 'The villa was originally built by a seventeenth-century industrialist as a summer retreat,' he said, striding out of the dazzling, reason-wrecking heat and into the cool, calm interior.

'What?'

He glanced over his shoulder, the slight huskiness to her voice grating over his nerve-endings, and he noticed that she was looking a little flustered, which was only fair when she'd had a similarly devastating effect on him. 'You asked about the house.'

'Right,' she said, giving herself a quick shake and following him in, composure unfortunately restored. 'Yes. So how long have you lived here?'

'Since the renovations were completed five years ago.'

'And before that?'

'Milan.'

'What were you doing there?'

Grafting, mainly. Working sixteen-hour days and moving quickly up the ranks. Making the most of the opportunity he'd been given to shed his past and turn his life around. 'Building my career.'

'Do you live here permanently?' she asked as he led her through the huge drawing room, the snug, the study and the dining room that could host supper for twenty, looking at the space through a visitor's eyes and wondering what she thought, even though her opinion really didn't matter. With his wealth he could have bought any number of lavish palaces, but he didn't need opulence. He just needed space and light and comfort.

'I have places elsewhere,' he said. 'But this is my home.'

'It's beautiful,' she said, stopping at the base of a set of wide stone steps that went up and round, while he wondered what to do with the strange kick of pleasure he felt at the approval he'd told himself he didn't want. 'Light and airy but very, *very* minimalist.'

'Thank you.'

'It wasn't necessarily a compliment.'

'Oh?'

'Where are all your things?'

He frowned, disquiet zigzagging through him. 'What things?'

'Photos, knick-knacks, trinkets, mementos. You know, the stuff and clutter a person generally accumulates as they go through life.'

'I don't have any.'

Her eyebrows lifted and she stared at him in astonishment. 'None?'

'I prefer to look forward, not back.'

'So you hang on to *nothing*?'

'I don't see the point.'

'I guess it saves on the dusting.'

It saved on the navel-gazing. It prevented the stirring up of memories of times he'd long since blocked out, and unwanted, unnecessary emotional ties. It facilitated a life free of burden and responsibility. But he'd been right in his initial assessment of her. She *did* see far too much. Which meant he had to be exceptionally careful about what else he allowed her access to.

'What's up there?'

'My bedroom suite.'

For a moment, his words hung between them, charging the sudden silence with crackling static, while their gazes locked as if held by some invisible unbreakable thread, and then, with a swallow and a shaky laugh, she said, 'I probably don't need to see that.'

'No,' he agreed with an evenness that belied the fierce heat suddenly whipping around inside him, making him harden and ache. 'You don't.'

And there was no 'probably' about it. It was bad enough that she could roam around the communal areas of the house. Bad enough that he could envisage her walking up the stairs ahead of him, looking over her shoulder with heat and desire in her mesmerising green gaze and then gliding into his room, shedding her clothes and pulling him down with her onto his bed. Under no circumstances was she checking out his suite just in case she 'got lost and wound up somewhere she shouldn't'.

Instead, having hauled his body back under control, he took her up another set of stairs at the opposite side of the hall that led to the guest rooms, all four of them, one of which was temporarily hers, which again, did not need to be seen by either of them, and then back down, through a set of French windows and into the garden.

'The gym is a recent addition,' he said, stalking towards the studio and opening the door onto a vast room furnished with state-of-the-art equipment, where he'd spent much time slowly regaining his strength.

'Installed after your accident?'

'Yes.'

'You said a BASE jump went wrong.'

'That's right.'

'What led to the bad landing?' she asked, weaving between the machines, inspecting them with interest as she went.

Annoyingly unable to take his eyes off her, Rico leaned against the wall and jammed his hands in his pockets. 'The jump itself was fine,' he said, remembering the thunder of nerves and anticipation as he'd stepped off the top of a snow-capped mountain that rose up two thousand metres above sea level and begun soaring through jagged cliffs, high on speed and adrenaline and invincibility. 'But, coming in to land, a gust of wind caught my wingsuit and blew me off course. I over-adjusted and slammed into a tree, and from there I crashed to the ground.'

The disbelief had almost been as great as the pain, he recalled, still unable to fully credit what had happened. He'd been BASE jumping for years, thriving on the exhilaration, taking ever-increasing risks in this as with everything he did, because why not?

The few accidents he'd had had been expected and minor. Until this one, which had seen him airlifted to hospital in Courmayeur, where he'd endured hours of complex surgery, followed by a stint at a clinic back

home in Venice and then a gruelling physiotherapy pro-
gramme that technically he was still supposed to be in
the middle of.

'A rookie mistake?'

'I have a thousand skydives and two hundred BASE
jumps under my belt,' he said. 'It's simply one of the
most dangerous sports you can do and on this occasion
I was unlucky.'

The look she threw him was disconcertingly shrewd.
'Is the danger the attraction?'

'Yes.'

'You're a risk-taker.'

'I am. Are you?'

She gave her head a shake. 'Quite the opposite. I like
things planned, organised and well thought through. I
like control.'

'Yet you work in crisis management and damage
limitation, where the unexpected is the norm.'

'True,' she admitted, 'but the unexpectedness is expected. Will you go back to doing it?'

'BASE jumping? No,' he said, realising, once his
brain had caught up with his mouth, that it was true.
Which was odd. Because why would he want to give it
up? Yes, he'd been injured, but he'd been injured before,
albeit not quite so severely, and been back in the sad-
dle as soon as he could. What was different about this
time? And why was his chest tight and his pulse fast?

'What will you do instead?'

'I don't know,' he admitted uneasily, apparently unable to answer anything right now.

'Doesn't it get a bit lonely, rattling around here on your own?'

'No.'

'You should get a pet.'

The thought of it sent a shudder through him. 'I don't think so.'

'Why not?'

Because he needed attachments like a hole in the head. Because he preferred to move through life alone and apart, and that precluded animals. 'I don't want one.'

'Why not?'

'What business is it of yours?'

'I'm seeing a theme.'

'What kind of a theme?' he asked, a strange sense of apprehension beginning to trickle though him.

'No neighbours, no pets, no clutter, no attachments of any kind. You don't just live on an island, Rico, you *are* an island. So was that why you left Finn's study?' she asked with a tilt of her head. 'Did the thought of potential attachment spook you?'

'Not at all,' he said easily, although how close she was to the truth was making him sweat. 'I merely remembered I had somewhere else to be.'

'Here?'

'Precisely. And now, if you'll excuse me, I'm going for a swim.'

CHAPTER SEVEN

AS IF A swim was going to succeed in putting her off, thought Carla, watching Rico stalk out of the gym as if he had wolves snapping at his heels.

She'd been right in her belief that one could discover a lot from exploring another person's house. In Rico's case, she'd indirectly learned that exiting a conversation when it touched a nerve was what he did, and it revealed more than she suspected he was aware of. It gave her points to note and avenues to pursue, such as why he moved through life like a ghost, living in such isolation, even if the isolation was splendid, as indeed it was.

The walls throughout his house were a soft off-white, the floors made up of great slabs of travertine covered with huge, ancient earth-toned rugs. Fine voile hung at the open windows and fluttered in the breeze. The furniture that was wood gleamed, while the sofas and chairs looked sumptuous and inviting.

But the stark absence of personal effects intrigued her. Even the kitchen, which was filled with shiny gadgetry and utensils that obviously weren't simply for show, bordered on the clinical. And as for his study, a room in which presumably he spent much of his time, well, she'd never seen such order. His desk was bare apart from three massive monitors and a telephone, and not a file was out of place on the floor-to-ceiling shelves that lined one wall.

Did Rico have a place elsewhere crammed to the rafters with all his things? If he didn't, and this was him, was there really nothing and no one in his past that he wanted to hang on to, to remember? How sad and lonely his life must be with no family and no friends, she thought, feeling a tug on her heartstrings even though how he lived was no concern of hers.

But if he needed breathing space, she was more than happy to let him have it. She knew when to push and when to retreat. How to plant the seed of suggestion and wait for it to take root. Not that she had a lot of time to get anything to take root, but it gave her a bit of breathing space too, which she badly needed after what had happened at his front door when he'd gone very still, his mesmerising blue eyes darkening to indigo and his expression unfathomable as he looked at her with heart-thumping intensity.

She'd had the crazy notion that he'd been contemplating kissing her and even more crazily, for one split second, she'd actually hoped he would, instinctively softening and leaning in and preparing herself for fireworks until he'd suddenly drawn back, leaving her feeling mortified and rattled.

This feeling of being constantly unsettled and on edge was unacceptable, she told herself for the thousandth time as she made her way to her room to send

Georgie an email giving her a temporary number and an update, and to arrange some annual leave for next week. As was the longing to know what Rico's bedroom looked like, and not just because perhaps *that* was where he stashed all his things. She did not need to know anything about his bedroom or how exciting it would be to kiss him.

The only interest she had in his attitude to risk was that it was another thing to investigate and report back to Finn. An analysis of how different it was to hers was not required, any more than was the kick of appreciation she'd felt in the pit of her stomach when she'd realised that he recognised her ability and need to take care of herself.

She would not be sidling across her room to the balcony that overlooked the terraces to check out the splash she'd just heard that indicated a gorgeous man might now be in the pool, scything slickly through the water while wearing virtually nothing. She would not be contemplating how deliciously tanned his skin might be, how powerfully he might move or whether the well-honed definition of his muscles was limited to his arms.

Time was marching on and she had a job to do, and she would concentrate one hundred per cent on that.

Rico tended to do much of his strategising while pounding up and down his pool, and the swim he'd just taken was no exception. As the rhythmic strokes cleared his head of the tangle of unanswerable questions Carla had stirred up, and his body of the excruciating tension that had been gripping him, he'd had something of an epiphany. Not about the shift in his attitude towards BASE jumping—that was still clear as mud—but about how to handle Carla and her continued attempts to prise information out of him.

One excellent way of putting a stop to it, it had occurred him as he'd flip turned and switched from crawl to butterfly, would be to divert the focus of conversation from him to her instead. He had no interest in finding anything out about her, of course, but if she was talking about herself she wouldn't be able to interrogate him. She'd be too busy picking and choosing her own answers, the way she had at dinner last night and the police station earlier.

He might be out of practice when it came to conversation, while she was anything but, but how challenging could it be to turn her questions back on her? How hard would it be to drum up some of his own that might just wrong-foot her the way hers did him?

It was an approach that would require focus and caution, he thought with a stab of satisfaction and relief at finally having come up with a way of taking back the upper hand, but it would get him through the hours until she left, certainly through the supper he was about to start preparing, and it was a solid one.

Determined to concentrate on the job she'd come to do and not get distracted once again by the subject of her investigations, Carla walked into the kitchen and didn't even break stride at the unexpectedly sexy sight of a big, handsome man standing at the island and pouring boiling water over a couple of tomatoes in a bowl.

'How was your swim?' she said, noting when he

glanced up at her that there was a gleam to his eye that she'd never seen before, which was both shiveringly unsettling and unnecessarily intriguing.

'Refreshing,' he said with the easy-going smile that she'd learned concealed so much. 'Wine?'

'Thank you.'

He poured her a glass of something pale and cold and—she took a sip—utterly delicious. 'Is there anything I can do to help?'

'You can get the clams from the fridge.'

Reminding herself to focus, which was hard when she could feel his eyes burning into her back, Carla put down her glass and walked over to the appliance he'd indicated and opened the door.

'Wow,' she said, staring at the shelves that were crammed with more food than she'd ever seen in one place outside a supermarket. 'You have one very well-stocked fridge.'

'I like to eat.'

Yet there wasn't a spare ounce on him. She'd felt him when she'd fainted into his arms. Nothing but warm, solid muscle… 'So I've noticed,' she said, hauling her recalcitrant thoughts back on track with more effort than she'd have liked.

'Oh?'

'Last night,' she said, locating the box of clams and taking it out. 'At the restaurant. You ate as though you were afraid that if you put your fork down for even a second someone would whip your plate away.'

'The food there is good and I'd missed lunch.'

Hmm. 'It seemed like more than that. And you did it again at brunch today.'

'Do you cook?'

'I never learned.'

'Why not?'

'Work's always been crazily busy,' she said, as an image of her fridge, which generally contained milk, ready meals and not a lot else, slid through her mind. 'I've been putting in fourteen-hour days for years. That doesn't leave a lot of time for haute cuisine.'

'What were you doing in Hong Kong?'

'Dealing with a crisis and a CEO who didn't believe there was one.'

'I imagine you eventually persuaded him to see things your way.'

'Of course,' she said with a quick grin that drew his gaze to her mouth and for the briefest of moments stopped time.

'You really enjoy what you do, don't you?'

'Very much.'

'Why?'

'I like solving problems and fixing things. I also love a challenge,' she said with a pointed look in his direction, which was rather wasted, since he'd switched his attention to peeling a clove of garlic. 'Do *you* like what *you* do?'

'Yes.'

'How did you get into fund management?'

'I have a talent for numbers and a drive to make money,' he said, then added, 'You should be careful you don't burn out.'

What was it to him? she wondered, as bewildered by his concern as she was by the rogue flood of warmth she felt in response to it. Why did he care whether she burned out or not? And hadn't they been talking about him in the first place?

Ah.

She saw what he was doing, she thought as the warmth fled and strangely cold realisation struck. He was trying to manipulate the conversation. Well, that was fine. At least she'd recognised it. And now she had, she could use it. This whole exercise was supposed to be about her extracting information from him, not vice versa, but perhaps things would move more efficiently if she went along with his plan. She need give away nothing of significance. She hadn't so far and now she was on her guard, she wouldn't. There'd be no more warmth stealing through her at anything he might say and there'd be no more grins, quick or otherwise.

'And that's why I've taken next week off,' she said, taking a sip of her drink and noting a fraction more acidity than she had before.

'What are you going to do?'

'I have no idea. Sleep probably. I haven't had a break in months. I suppose I could learn to cook. I might even take up Italian. And, talking of languages, how come your English is so good?'

'It's the language of business and I have an ear for it.'

His reply was too quick and too smooth, and undoubtedly only partly the truth. 'You understand nuance and inference and your accent is almost flawless. That's quite an ear.'

'*Grazie,*' he said, taking a knife to the garlic and slicing it with impressive deftness.

'Where were you raised?'

'Mestre. Across the lagoon, on the mainland. You?'

'On a series of communes in various corners of the UK.'

'Not much opportunity for haute cuisine there, I imagine,' he said with a smile that bounced off her defences.

'None whatsoever. We mainly survived on lentils and vegetables.'

'Siblings?'

'No.'

'Parents?'

'Yes.'

'Do they still live on a commune?'

'Yes.'

'Are you certain?'

'Why wouldn't I be?'

'You don't make time for them.'

Why would he think such a thing? she wondered for a moment before recalling their conversation last night in the restaurant. 'I never said that.'

'You didn't need to.'

'All right,' she admitted, faintly thrown by the fact that he'd remembered such a tiny detail too. 'I don't see them all that often. It's complicated. Are yours still on the mainland?'

'Mine died in a car crash when I was ten.'

A silence fell at that, and despite her attempts to remain coolly aloof Carla couldn't help but be affected.

God, how awful, she thought, her chest squeezing and her stomach tightening. How tragic. He'd been so young. How did something like that affect the boy and then the man? How had it changed him? She couldn't imagine being so wholly on her own. After what had happened to her, her parents had felt so guilty and regretful that they'd gone from borderline negligent to smothering, and yes, their relationship was strained because of it but at least they were around.

'I'm so sorry,' she said with woeful inadequacy.

He gave a shrug. 'It was a long time ago.'

'Finn lost his mother at the age of ten, too.'

'And what were *you* doing at the age of ten, Carla?' he countered, neatly avoiding the point.

Trying to get her parents' attention, mostly, she thought, remembering how she'd constantly played up at the various schools she'd attended. Figuring out how to persuade them to stay in one place long enough for her to make friends. 'I don't know,' she said, shifting on her stool to ease the stab of age-old pain and disappointment. 'Listening to music and hanging out with the other kids on the communes, I guess.'

The look he gave her was disconcertingly shrewd. 'Why do I get the feeling that isn't all?'

'I truly can't imagine,' she said before deciding to engage in a bit of conversational whiplash of her own. 'Did you know you were adopted?'

'It was never a secret. There was some effort to locate my birth parents after the death of my adoptive ones.'

'But they weren't found.'

'No.'

'Weren't you ever interested in carrying on the search?'

'No.'

'Why not?'

'I discovered I preferred being on my own.'

'You aren't any more.'

He didn't respond to that, just slid the garlic from the board into the sizzling oil in the pan, and then gave it a toss, which made her think it could be time to shake things up on the conversational front too. She had to at least *try* and make him see reason about the family he could have now.

'Did you know you were born in Argentina?' she asked, dismissing the guilty feeling she might nevertheless be crossing a line because for Georgie and Finn there never would be a line.

'No.'

'Then you can't know that there are three of you.'

'What do you mean?'

'You're one of three. There's you and Finn and one other. You're triplets. All boys.'

The only indication that what she'd said had had any impact at all was a tiny pause in his stirring of the garlic. 'Who's the third?' he asked after a beat of thundering silence.

'No one knows.'

'He hasn't been found?'

'Not yet. You may be able to help.'

'I couldn't even if I wanted to.'

'Which you don't.'

'No.'

'Why not?'

'I'm not interested.'

But Rico was lying. He'd resumed his methodical stirring of the garlic but she could tell by the tension gripping his body and the muscle ticking in his jaw. He *was* interested and it gave her the encouragement to persist. 'What did you think when you first saw Finn's photo?'

'I was surprised.'

'That's it?' she said. 'No lightning bolt of recognition? No sense of… I don't know…everything suddenly falling into place or something?'

'Absolutely not.'

'Well, *something* drove you to seek him out in his own home,' she said, beginning to feel a bit riled at the way he was deliberately blocking her at every possible point yet determined not to give up. 'So I think you're not only lying to me, but also to yourself.'

'You don't know me well enough to make that kind of judgement,' he said, the even tone of his words not quite disguising the warning note she could hear, telling her to retreat this minute.

'You're generous with your time and your resources,' she countered, ignoring it. 'You like police stations as little as I do. You back off when conversation gets too close. You're a risk-taker and a thrill-seeker and you have an unusual relationship with food. And lastly, you're attracted to me yet you don't want to be, which is odd when only yesterday lunchtime you were asking me out.'

'A mistake.'

'Evidently.'

'And the only reason I've been helping you is to ensure you leave Venice just as soon as is humanly possible.'

Okay. Well. 'What I *do* know,' she said, absolutely refusing to take offence at those last two points of his, since she didn't care what he thought of her, 'is that no man is an island, not even you, Rico. Everyone needs someone and you have the very best of a someone. You have a brother. I can't understand why you wouldn't be moving heaven and earth to make up for lost time.'

'And I can't understand why you're so desperate for me to meet Finn,' he said bluntly. 'You came to *Venice*, Carla. What is your interest in this?'

'I told you,' she said, refusing to be intimidated by the darkening of his expression. 'Georgie is like family to me.'

'Why?'

'We've been through a lot together.'

'Such as?'

She wasn't ready to tell him. She'd never be ready to tell him. 'We're not talking about me.'

His eyes glittered. 'I think we should start.'

'There's no point.'

'There's every point. Why don't you see your parents, Carla?'

'Why don't you like police stations?' she shot back.

His jaw tightened. 'Why do you work so hard? What are you running from?'

'Why have you decided to shut yourself off from everyone and everything? What are *you* running from?'

'Nothing.'

'I don't believe you.'

'That's not my problem.'

'So what *is* your problem?' she asked, her blood heating to a simmer.

'You are.'

'Then you should have let me stay in a hotel.'

'I know.'

'Why didn't you?'

'I don't know,' he said roughly. 'Maybe I didn't want you to come to any harm by fainting again and falling into a canal. Maybe I wanted to uncover your secrets the way you're so determined to hunt down mine. Maybe for some inexplicable reason I felt responsible for you.'

For a moment a flame of pleasure flickered into life inside her but she swiftly extinguished it because none of that could be true. If it was it would mean she was somehow beginning to matter to him, which couldn't be the case when he was detachment personified. And the very idea of him being responsible for her was ridiculous. 'Distracting me won't work.'

'Then what will?' he said, putting down the spoon and stalking round to her side of the island, his eyes glittering and his shoulders rigid. 'What *will* it take to stop you talking?'

She could think of something. She could think of lots of things, all of them accelerating her pulse and heating the simmer to a boil. He could give her a smile—a real one—that would drain the blood from her head and suck the breath from her lungs. He could pulverise her thoughts with a touch and stop her mouth with a kiss, and he would barely have to even try.

'Agreement to go and see Finn,' she said a bit breath-lessly, struggling to block out the images of him doing all of that.

'That's not going to happen.'

'Answers, then.'

'You're getting them,' he said softly, taking one step closer to her, trapping her against the island and loom-ing over her in a way that should have felt threatening and should have triggered a need to escape but was in-stead having the opposite effect.

'Not the ones I want.'

'So what *do* you want, Carla?'

Something she really shouldn't but was finding it in-creasingly hard to resist, she thought, burning up in re-sponse to his size and proximity. Because Rico might be a threat to her self-control and an attack on her defences, but right here, right now, with her thoughts spinning and her body on fire, she couldn't quite remember why.

All she knew was that she wanted him and he wanted her. Heat flared in the inky blue depths of his glitter-ing eyes. She could feel the tightly leashed power and tension tightening his body. Her heart thundered. Her breath hitched. The intensity with which he was look-ing at her was stealing her wits and stoking the desire whipping around inside her and she didn't even care.

'You know what I want,' she said, giving him the op-tion to interpret her words in one of two ways, trying to tell herself she was still talking about Rico meeting

Finn but actually meaning she wanted *him*, and practically erupting with excitement when he got it.

Whether it was the way she'd jutted her chin up in silent challenge or whether he was equally at the mercy of the attraction that flared between them and could no longer deny, she neither knew nor cared. He took her in his arms and with a muffled curse brought his mouth down on hers and all that mattered then was kissing him back as fiercely as he was kissing her.

With a moan she wrapped her arms around his neck and wound her fingers through his hair, which was as thick and soft as she'd imagined, and pressed herself so close that there was barely an inch of her that wasn't touching him. The heat and skill of his mouth, his lips, his tongue sent shock waves of desire shooting through her, fogging her brain and focusing all her attention on him and what he was doing to her.

She moaned again and he tightened his hold on her, deepening the kiss as he put his hands on her waist and lifted her onto the island as if she weighed nothing. She instinctively opened her legs and he stepped between them, and she could feel the thick, hard length of his erection pressing against the spot that was aching and desperate.

She tilted her hips to increase the pressure and writhed against him, needing him closer, inside her, while his hands were in her hair, on her back, large and warm against her body, holding her in place, scorching through the thin fabric of her dress.

With a harsh groan he moved his mouth to her neck, to the sensitive spot beneath her ear, and a hand to her breast, which instantly tingled and tightened and made her wish there was no material in the way either on her or him.

Suddenly desperate to discover what she'd denied herself by not checking him out in the pool earlier, she tugged at his T-shirt, he reared back and pulled it over his head, and there was his chest in all its naked glory. Tanned. Muscled.

And scarred.

A small brown circle lay just above his heart and another on his opposite shoulder. A thin white mark cut a jagged line through the smattering of fine dark hair at the bottom of his ribcage.

But before she had time to even think about what they could be or what they might mean, he'd leaned forwards and bent his head for another scorching kiss and all she could focus on was the desire hammering around inside her. The heat that was igniting her blood and making her burn.

And that wasn't the only thing that was burning.

Through the swirling fog of desire and the intoxicating scent of him, came the trace of smoke. Acrid smoke. That unless they'd set fire to the island came from the stove.

With Herculean effort and a rush of alarm, Carla broke away, breathing hard, and put her hands on the rock-solid wall of his chest.

'The garlic,' she managed hoarsely. 'It's burning.'

'Dio,' he muttered after a moment in which he looked as dazed as she felt.

Raking his hands through his hair and giving himself

a quick shake, Rico stepped back, taking the heat and the madness with him, and went off to investigate the damage, which gave Carla an all too clear view of herself in the mirror that hung over the fireplace. Her hair was a mess, her cheeks bright red and her lips swollen. Her heavy, tingling breasts strained against the bodice of her dress and her legs were spread wide.

Who was this woman in the mirror with the desire-soaked eyes and the heaving chest? Where had that unexpectedly fierce and wanton response come from? She didn't recognise herself. If they hadn't been interrupted she and Rico wouldn't have stopped, and it was suddenly terrifying because this wasn't who she was. She didn't act on instinct and throw caution to the wind with no thought for the consequences. She never allowed herself to be dazzled to distraction by a handsome face and a great body. She took great care to avoid any situation in which the kind of lust that could lay waste to her judgement might arise.

So what had she been thinking? How could she risk destroying the wall around her emotions and the control she'd worked so hard to achieve? Was she insane? More pressingly, how could she and Rico possibly sit down to dinner after *that*? It would be excruciating.

'You know what?' she said, slipping off the island and pulling her dress down with still trembling hands. 'On second thoughts, I'm not really hungry. And I should probably go and make some calls,' she added, unable to look at him as she backed away just as fast as

her unsteady legs could carry her. 'So, ah, thanks for
your help today and I guess I'll see you in the morning. Goodnight.'

CHAPTER EIGHT

IT WAS GOOD that Carla had fled when she had, Rico thought darkly as he shoved the *linguine alle vongole* he'd finished off making—minus the burnt garlic—into the fridge, his appetite, for food at least, gone. Her sense of self-preservation was clearly as strong as his, even if it had kicked in late.

His, on the other hand, hadn't kicked in at all. He'd taken one look at her, at the challenge and heat in her gaze, and he'd known exactly what she wanted. Too tightly wound and befuddled by need to recall at that precise moment why getting involved with her was a bad idea, he'd succumbed to the temptation to give it to her.

The kiss had been wild and hot, far more explosive than anything he'd imagined. The minute their mouths had met desire had erupted inside him, powering along his veins and channelling all his blood to his groin. The longer the kiss had gone on, the hotter and harder he'd become, and if she hadn't stopped him he'd have leaned her back, pushed her dress up and taken her right there and then. The entire kitchen could have been on fire and he wouldn't have noticed.

What the hell had he been thinking? he wondered, still dazed by the intensity of the encounter, as he switched the lights off and crossed the hall to his flight of stairs with barely a glance in the direction of hers. Where had his control gone? And why on earth had he approached her in the first place? Everything had been fine until he'd stalked round to her side of the island and foolishly positioned himself within reaching distance of her in a move designed to scare her off but which had spectacularly backfired.

Well, maybe not that fine, he mentally amended, striding into his room, tossing the T-shirt she'd pulled off him into the laundry bin and shuddering at the memory of how warm and soft her hands had felt on his naked skin.

Despite his outward cool, he'd been on shaky ground ever since they'd met. On her arrival in Venice cracks had begun to appear when he'd realised how tempting she was but how dangerous she could be. And when she'd stood there in the gym and questioned him about the accident, those cracks had opened up into great, jagged fissures.

He didn't like the burgeoning possibility that his accident could have affected him emotionally as well as physically. The idea that he had somehow been fundamentally altered by what had happened was troubling. Yet, there was no denying that he'd experienced more doubt, bewilderment and wariness in the last three months than he had in the last two decades, and who was he if he wasn't the man who was supremely confident in what he did, who'd always thrived on risk and recklessness and to hell with the consequences?

Nor did he appreciate the stirring up of his past. He hated thinking about the senseless death of his parents at the hand of a recklessly overtaking driver who'd ripped him from everything he'd ever known. Family. Home. Love. And he *never* allowed himself to wonder how his life might have turned out had they lived.

He didn't wish to revisit any of those memories in any great detail, or contemplate his regret at having repeatedly run away from his foster carer in search of what he'd thought would be a better life, with a need to take control. He certainly wasn't ready to welcome back the maelstrom of feelings he'd had at the time, which had become so overwhelming, so unbearable, that he'd shut them down. He doubted he ever would be, and that was all right with him.

What *wasn't* all right was allowing Carla to have pushed that far in the first place. He should have put a stop to it sooner, when he could have done so with a cooler head. Despite having had virtually no experience of that kind of conversation, he should have pressed her for more instead of allowing her to fight back. But even though he hadn't, he should have been one hundred per cent ready for whatever she chose to throw at him.

However, he'd failed at that too.

He didn't know why he'd been so rocked to learn that he'd been born in Argentina and was one of three. As he'd told her, he'd always known he was adopted, so it shouldn't make any difference where he'd been born.

Nor should it matter how many siblings he potentially had. He wasn't interested in one, let alone two.

So why did the letter that his parents had left with a law firm in Milan, which he'd been told about at the age of eighteen and ruthlessly ignored, suddenly now seem significant?

On learning of its existence he'd instructed the solicitor to do whatever he liked with it, since its contents held zero appeal. He'd already been on his way to making his first fortune. Every gamble he'd taken had paid off and everything he'd touched had turned to gold. He'd been living the hedonistic life his new-found wealth afforded him and he absolutely had not needed a reminder of his past, of the crucifying rejection and abandonment he'd felt in the aftermath of his parents' death, the gaping hole they'd left, and how vulnerable and gullible he'd once been.

Now, as he unbuckled his belt and shucked off his shorts, he wondered what had become of it. Had the solicitor done as he'd instructed and destroyed it? What had it contained? Could it have held information about the circumstances of his birth? He couldn't seriously be contemplating trying to track it down, could he?

The crushing pressure of now questioning everything he'd always considered a certainty was pushing him to the end of his tether and fraying his control. All day he'd been on edge, and it was largely down to Carla, who he wanted with a fierceness that blew him away. Who dazzled him and robbed him of reason and possibly now knew more about him than he'd realised he'd revealed. Who was just as tenacious and dangerous as he'd suspected and had to be kept at arm's length by whatever means possible.

Tuesday morning, he thought grimly, stepping into the shower and turning it on to cold, couldn't come fast enough.

With her body clock finally back on track Carla should have slept beautifully. She should have woken up firing on all cylinders, feeling strong and invincible and raring to go.

Unfortunately, however, the kiss in the kitchen the night before had put paid to any rest she'd been hoping for. The heat…the passion…the wanton yet terrifying lack of control… If she hadn't been jolted back to reality by the burning garlic she and Rico would have had hot, wild sex right then and there, and that was something she just couldn't seem to stop imagining.

The sizzling memory of it and the myriad questions she had about the scars on his chest, not to mention the intense emotion that had blazed in his eyes, which she'd never seen before in him but which confirmed her suspicion that still waters ran deep, had kept her tossing and turning in bed for hours. Exhaustion had finally won out in the early hours, and as a result she woke up feeling gritty and on edge, her nerves frayed by desire she just couldn't shake no matter how hard she tried.

And now they were going to be spending most of the day together.

Petrified of bumping into Rico over breakfast and having to make horrendously awkward chat, Carla waited for the all clear before darting into the kitchen and grabbing a pastry from the fridge while keeping her gaze firmly away from the scene of the crime.

On the dot of eight she arrived at the helipad that was situated a couple of hundred metres from the house. Rico was already there, mirrored sunglasses concealing his eyes, his expression unreadable, the headset he had on thankfully precluding conversation.

Apparently as disinclined to acknowledge what had happened last night as she was, he barely glanced at her as she climbed aboard. He merely handed her a headset of her own and coolly indicated that she should buckle herself in before returning his attention to the dozens of dials and switches in front of him.

Moments later, the engine fired and the rotors started turning, and then they were up and away, soaring above the lagoon, leaving Isola Santa Margherita far behind and heading for the mainland, hurtling through the air in such a tiny contraption at such a great speed that her stomach was in her throat, while she clung on to her seat, her knuckles white.

To her relief, Rico's concentration on what he was doing, combined with the noise of the helicopter, prevented any further communication. But as the journey continued, the urban sprawl giving way to a patchwork of fields dotted with villages, Lake Garda in the distance and the foothills of the Italian Alps beyond, and her nerves began to ease, she became increasingly aware of him.

The space was naturally confined and he filled it. His masculine scent surrounded her, making her head swim and her mouth water. Every inch of him was within touching distance. His thigh was unsettlingly close to hers. If she moved even a millimetre to the left, her shoulder would brush against his. Focusing on *not* doing that, when they kept being buffeted about by the wind, was taking every drop of strength she possessed, as was keeping her eyes off him.

It was so hard not to stare at his profile and linger on the scar and the slight bump in his nose which gave him the hint of badness that she found so attractive. So hard not to look at his fingers wrapped around the stick that he was using to fly this thing and not remember them in her hair and on her skin. She'd always had a penchant for competence, and it was even harder not to melt into a puddle of lust at just how skilled he was at the controls.

But not impossible.

Because of far greater importance than any of that was the clock counting down her time in Italy, which was ticking louder and louder with every passing second. Patience while waiting for seeds of suggestion to take root was all very well but in this situation she needed to get a move on.

Last night's attempts to lull Rico into a false sense of security hadn't exactly worked, so quid pro quo was how she was going to proceed, she decided, blocking out the infuriatingly unsettling effect his proximity was having on her and focusing. A back and forth of information that she'd start and force him to follow.

This time, *she* was going to control the conversation and she might have to dig deeper than she'd have ideally liked, but by carefully revealing to him layers of herself no one else apart from Georgie had ever seen she'd show him he had nothing to fear. She certainly didn't. She had no doubt that Rico wouldn't respond in an emotional sense to whatever she told him. Her revelations would bounce right off the steel-plated armour he surrounded himself with. He didn't let anyone close and she saw no reason he'd ever decide to make an exception for her. Apart from the sensational chemistry they shared, which this morning he was ignoring in the same way she was trying to but with a greater degree of success, he simply didn't have a sufficient level of interest to bother. Or any, in fact. Which was totally fine with her.

There was no point in waiting until another monosyllabic meal, she told herself, mentally unlocking the past and bracing herself for the reality of laying it out in front of this man. If she really was going to do this— and for the sake of her best friend she absolutely was— she had to strike while the iron was hot. And that meant implementing her plan as soon as they landed.

Generally Rico got a massive kick out of flying his helicopter, but as he landed the machine at Linate Airport and switched off the engine he thought he'd never been so glad to see the back of it.

The trip to Milan had been nothing short of torture. He'd been agonisingly aware of Carla sitting beside him, close enough to touch, close enough to pull onto his lap and kiss the living daylights out of again, so damn affecting that he might as well not have bothered with the numerous cold showers he'd taken throughout the very long night.

The tension in his muscles was excruciating. His jaw was so tight it was on the point of shattering. The restraint he was having to exercise, a novel concept he had no intention of repeating ever again once she'd gone, was intolerable.

Why was it so hard to control his response to her? he wondered darkly as he jumped down and then strode around the front to help her alight too. Was this yet another effect of his accident? Another weakening of the defences he'd always considered impregnable?

Whatever it was, he didn't like it, any more than he liked the strength of his desire for her. He'd experienced need before, many times, but the intensity and the wildness with which he wanted *her* was new. What was it about her that was different? Why did she and she alone affect him in this way?

Releasing her hand as soon as she was on solid ground as if it were on fire, Rico turned on his heel and made for the car that was waiting for them on the tarmac. With a nod to Marco, his chauffeur in Milan, who was opening the door for Carla, he climbed in and slammed the door shut. Once she was in too it hit him that, since the car was as spacious as the helicopter, the journey to the consulate was going to be equally torturous. Possibly even more so, since now he didn't have the distraction of flying, which was why he *had* to stop thinking about both the incredibly passionate way she'd responded to him last night and the astonishingly good feel of her beneath his hands.

'So,' she said, making herself comfortable before taking off her sunglasses and turning to face him, something about the set of her jaw and the determined look in her eye raising the hairs on the back of his neck. 'Milan.'

'What about it?' he said, aiming for the cool nonchalance that so often eluded him when she was in his vicinity, and, for once, just about nailing it.

'It's where you started on your journey to fund management world domination.'

'I wouldn't put it quite like that.'

'Then how would you put it?' she asked. 'The article I read described you as mysteriously elusive, but a man with the Midas touch, which I guess would explain the island, the private jet and the helicopter.'

'The jet and the helicopter do save time,' he said, reflecting that the description of him was apt, although none of his success had been by design. He'd had no ambition to make a fortune when he'd been given a chance to escape a life of crime and despair. He'd had no plans at all and nothing to lose, so he'd taken risks with little care for the consequences. In a fairer world he'd have squandered everything several times over, but his world had had other ideas and rewarded every reckless move he'd made, as if making amends for everything he'd once had and lost.

'And what do you do with the time you save?'

'I manage to keep myself entertained.'

'I'm sure you do,' she said smoothly. 'So tell me what led you into it.'

Not a chance. 'Only if you tell me first what took you into crisis management,' he countered with a wide, easy grin, confident that she'd back right off since when it came to personal information she dodged and feinted as much as he did.

'All right.'

What? As the word exploded between them like some kind of bomb, every cell of his body froze and his stomach roiled. Damn. 'I was joking.'

'I wasn't,' she said calmly and he realised with a stab of alarm and a jolt of panic that she really wasn't. 'And I'm going to hold you to it.'

'No need.'

'There's every need.'

'Why don't you tell me about your favourite band instead?' he said, never more regretting the fact that they were speeding along a motorway and therefore unable to screech to a stop so he could get the hell out.

'The main reason I went into crisis management,' she said, clearly deciding to give that absurd question the consideration it deserved, which was none, 'was to put something bad that happened to me to good use.'

At that, Rico snapped his head round and went very still, his heart giving a great thud. And even though the very *last* thing he wanted to be having was this conversation, even though he knew he ought to respond with something flippant designed to shut her down and maintain the distance, instead he found himself saying, 'Something bad?'

'When I was fifteen, I was groomed.'

What the hell? What did that even mean? 'What happened?'

'As I told you, my parents are hippies and I was

raised on various communes. They were too busy smoking weed and chanting to pay me any attention, so I went in search of it myself. One afternoon I was hanging out in an internet cafe and I got chatting online to someone I thought was a boy my age.'

'But he wasn't,' he said as sickening realisation began to dawn.

'No,' she said with a slow shake of her head. 'He very definitely wasn't. But he was clever and patient. He asked me all about myself and I told him everything. He took the ammunition I gave him and used it on me quite calculatingly. He knew exactly which buttons to push and how to shower me with the affection and love I craved so desperately. And he knew that when he withdrew it I'd beg him to give it back, which I did.'

Bastardo.

'Within weeks I was addicted to his messages and started skipping school early to get to the cafe. He sent me a phone so we could actually talk and I used it to send him the photos he asked for. When he came clean and told me he was thirty to my fifteen I didn't care. I was in far too deep by that point. It was our secret and it was thrilling and I was obsessed. Before long I stopped hanging out with my friends or talking to anyone but him, really. Georgie tried, but he gave me some great excuses to use and my parents weren't paying any attention to what was going on anyway. When he suggested we meet, I didn't hesitate for a single second. I packed a bag, took the money he'd also sent me and was off.'

'Where did you go?' he asked, his head spinning so

fast he was barely able to comprehend what she was telling him.

'I met him in a hotel in east London.'

'Separate rooms?'

'One room. Double bed.'

His jaw clenched so hard it was on the point of shattering. 'And you were fifteen.'

'Yes.'

And he thought he knew the depths of depravity people could sink to. He'd been wrong.

'We spent three days there,' she continued, clearly oblivious to the rage beginning to crash though him. 'The plan was to run away to France but I didn't have a passport, so it was then Scotland, but before that could happen the police turned up.'

'How did they find you?'

'I couldn't resist sending Georgie a photo of the hotel, even though by that point I wasn't letting her speak to me. I thought I was so grown up,' she said with a tiny frown, as if she thought she was somehow to blame, which was staggeringly wrong. 'I was showing off. She called the police. I owe her big time. I still can't believe she didn't cut me off completely. I was vile.'

'It wasn't your fault.'

'No, I know that,' she said that with a nod that, thank God, suggested she not only knew it but also believed it. 'None of it was my fault. It was all *his*.'

'What happened to him?'

'He went to jail, came out, did it again, and went back. As far as I know he's still inside.'

'He'd better stay there,' he muttered, thinking it was

for his safety because if he ever got his hands on the *figlio di puttana* he wouldn't be responsible for the outcome.

'He will. For a while, at least,' she said, frowning faintly before rallying. 'So, back to the original question, that's why I went into crisis management. I know how powerful manipulation can be. I know its effects and the way in which it can be used to change people's behaviours and make them believe whatever you want them to believe. It felt like a good fit. I realise it might sound strange, but channelling what happened to me into a successful career has been cathartic. So there we go,' she finished with a quick smile that frankly defied belief. 'That's me. It's your turn now.'

She sat back, regarding him expectantly, while inside he reeled. His turn? He could barely think straight. How could she be so composed when he wanted to hit something for the first time in years?

And how the hell could he not reciprocate after all that? How could he not answer her questions when she'd answered his with such frankness and honesty? He didn't want to simply brush aside what she'd told him, as if it meant nothing. It didn't. Not to her.

He'd never told a living soul what he'd been through, but how much of a risk would it really be to share with her some of it the way she had with him? In one sense at least, her experiences hadn't been all that dissimilar to his. They'd both been used, manipulated and exploited for the benefit of others. She had to know some of the disillusionment he'd once felt, the shattering of hopes and dreams and the determination to never allow it to happen again. Any revelation he chose to make would therefore be safe with her. He had nothing to fear. He hoped.

'What do you want to know?' he said, and the look of relief that filled her expression, as if she'd fully expected him to refuse to stick to his side of the bargain despite everything she'd told him, was like a blow to the gut. He might have many flaws, but a lack of integrity wasn't one of them nowadays.

'What made you go into fund management?'

'I was given an opportunity and took it,' he said, silently vowing to at least try to be as open and honest as she'd been in an effort not to disappoint her.

'When?'

'When I was sixteen.'

Her eyebrows lifted. 'That's young.'

To some, perhaps. But not to him. He'd lived two brutal lifetimes by that age. 'I started off at an investment bank working as a clerk. In a year I'd acquired the qualifications necessary to trade on La Borsa.'

'The Italian stock exchange?'

'*Corretto*. It's here in Milan. I told you I was good with numbers. Well, I was also good at spotting opportunities no one else could see. I took risks and they paid off. I made my first million at eighteen. When I was twenty-four, I left to set up my own fund. I had no trouble picking up clients. I now have six billion euros under management.'

'All on your own?'

'With the exception of some back office support, yes.'

'That's quite an achievement.'

'As is yours.'

'We're not quite in the same league,' she said with a wry grin—a real one—that lit her eyes and stole his breath, before it disappointingly disappeared and her expression sobered. 'So where were you for the six years between your parents' death and starting work at this investment bank?'

He tensed, every fibre of his being demanding that he shut up, but he wasn't going to. He'd agreed to this and he didn't go back on his word these days, no matter how great the temptation. 'Initially I went into foster care,' he said, forcing himself to relax while telling himself it would be fine.

'You had no other relatives?'

If only. 'No. I lived with four different families in two years. Every time I thought I was settled I got moved on like an unwanted parcel. Eventually I decided that *I'd* be in charge of where I lived. I ran away. Frequently. At first I was caught and returned, but after a while they simply stopped looking.'

She stared at him, her eyes wide and filling with an emotion he couldn't begin to identify. 'Just like that?'

'Pretty much. I was very good at hiding.'

'What did you do?'

'I lived on the streets for a while, sleeping in doorways by night and scavenging for food by day. But then it started getting colder. One night I broke into an empty building, only to discover that it wasn't an empty building. It turned out to be the headquarters of I Picaresqui, which was then one of the most notorious street gangs in Veneto. They thought I might be a spy for the police.'

'Oh, my God. What happened?'

'You saw the scars,' he said, remembering the way the fire had scorched his skin, the panic and the terror that had scythed through him.

A flush bloomed on her cheeks for a moment. 'The two on your upper chest looked like cigarette burns,' she said, her voice strangely husky and tight.

'They are.'

'And the others?' she asked, her gaze lifting to the scar at his temple and the bump in his nose.

'A fight with a rival gang member over territory a year or two later.'

Her eyes jerked back to his, the shock he saw in them sending a dart of what felt like shame shooting through him. 'You *joined* them?'

'*Si,*' he said, stamping it out since he didn't need judgement. From anyone, least of all her. He'd judged himself plenty.

'Why?'

'It felt like a good idea at the time.'

'What sort of things did you have to do?'

'I started off by fleecing unsuspecting tourists,' he said, sticking to the facts and the facts alone. 'Pickpocketing and coin tricks were my speciality, but anything really that made money quickly. You asked me why my English was so good.'

'I remember.'

'It *is* the language of business and I *do* have an ear for it, but I also spent a lot of time watching films and reading books in order to be able to scam tourists better.'

'I bet you were good at it.'

'I was. Very.'

'And then?'

'Once I'd earned the respect of the leaders, I moved into the accounting side of the business.'

There was no need to tell her some of the other more brutal things, more shameful things he'd had to do to prove himself loyal—the fighting, the righting of perceived wrongs, the collecting of debts. Or about the complex tangle of feelings he'd once had about it all.

'Did you ever get caught?'

'I spent more nights in the cells than I care to remember.'

'No wonder you have a thing about police stations,' she said, which proved once again how sharp she was. 'You were tense,' she said in response to the quizzical look he gave her. 'I noticed.'

'You fainted.'

'It brought back painful memories for me too,' she said, her eyes clouding for a moment, and he had to fight back an urge to demand more. He didn't need more. He'd never need more.

'So how did you get out?' she asked, yanking his thoughts back on track. 'How on earth did you go from being part of a gang to working at an investment bank in Milan?'

'I was arrested on money-laundering charges and hauled in front of a judge. I confessed to nothing, but during the course of the trial my skill with money and numbers kept cropping up. It was never clear quite what the judge saw in me, but one morning she told me she had a contact here and gave me a choice. Jail or a job.

I chose the latter and now I exploit the markets, which when I think about it is as ironic as you manipulating perception for your job. What?' he finished with a frown, not liking the strange look that was appearing on her face one little bit.

'We're kindred spirits,' she said with a softness that he hoped to God wasn't pity. 'Who knew?'

'We're nothing of the kind,' he muttered with a sharp shudder as he glanced at the building in front of which they were pulling up and thought he'd never been so grateful to arrive at a destination. 'What we *are*, is here.'

CHAPTER NINE

THE BUSINESS OF procuring her new passport prevented any further conversation beyond the practical, but that didn't stop Carla's head spinning with everything that Rico had told her in the car.

When she'd finished telling her tale, which oddly hadn't been as difficult as she'd feared, and prompted him to reveal his, she'd never *dreamt* it could be as upsetting as it had been.

The things he'd been through... The loss of his parents... The shunting between foster families and finding himself on the streets... And then the horrors of the gang he'd joined that she couldn't even *begin* to imagine...

He'd been so young. He'd suffered so much. He'd been abandoned and then left to fend for himself. He'd been tortured, by the sounds of things, and she was sure that wasn't all of it. How could her heart not have twisted and ached for him? How could she not have burned up with the injustice of it? She could barely bring herself to think about the brutality he must have experienced. And yet he'd been so cool, so unfazed as he'd recounted the desperate nature of his childhood, as if he were talking about someone else entirely.

How had he achieved that level of acceptance? she wondered, her eyes still stinging faintly and her throat still tight as they were ushered into an office without Rico even having to give his name. Had shutting himself down been the only way to handle the impact of his experiences? Was that why he'd chosen to cut himself off from others both geographically and emotionally?

It was astonishing he was as together as he was, in all honesty. Unlike her, it didn't sound as if he'd had any support, at least in the emotional sense. Unlike her, he'd had to make sense of everything entirely on his own. Yet, somehow, *like* her, he'd come through it and used it to make a success of his life. His determination and resilience matched her own. As did the lengths he went to in order to protect himself.

So where else might the similarities lie? she couldn't help wondering, even though it had no bearing on anything. They'd both lacked a proper home with roots. They both had an insanely strong work ethic and a reluctance to share personal information. Apart from unbelievable chemistry, what else might they have in common?

She didn't get the opportunity to probe further and find out. The consul himself—whose wife apparently ran a charity supporting homeless kids, which Rico generously supported, hence the owed favour—appeared within moments and ten minutes later, having obtained her passport, she and Rico were heading for the exit.

But when she suggested taking a tour of the city with

the aim of continuing their earlier conversation under the guise of seeing the sights, he claimed he needed to get back to work. Her subsequent invitation to lunch was refused, and when she told him she knew how he felt about skipping meals he merely muttered something about grabbing a sandwich at the airport.

The guard he'd momentarily dropped for her had shot back up, she realised in the car on the way back to his helicopter—a journey spent in an uncomfortably prickly silence—and it was more disappointing than she could have imagined, because she sensed there was so much more to him and his story.

Never mind the fact that she'd revealed nothing of the effects her experience had had on her. She wanted to know more about how *his* had affected *him*. Not for Finn, who'd be fine with the facts, but for herself. Now she'd had a glimpse of the intriguing man beneath the surface, she wanted to smash through his defences and find out everything.

And not just on that front.

His continued indifference to her after what had happened last night was another source of increasing bewilderment and distress, even though she really ought not to be thinking about it at all. Why wasn't he suffering from her proximity the way she was from his? was the shameful thought that kept running through her head. Why, when he'd mentioned the occasion she'd seen the scars on his chest, had he remained so unmoved, while she'd instantly caught fire? How could he continue to act as if nothing had happened?

Maybe he really had wiped it from his mind. Per-

haps what she'd assumed to be denial was, in actual
fact, a complete lack of interest. Perhaps she'd in some
way disappointed him. And yet she hadn't imagined
the heat and fierceness of their kiss, or his loss of control that had gone with it. The swirling intensity of his
eyes, blazing into hers, was seared onto her memory.

And she might as well admit she wanted more of
it all.

In the absence of conversation, the desire she'd managed to get under some sort of control while they'd been
talking was flooding back, drumming through her with
increasing potency with every passing moment, and
by the time they were back in the helicopter and once
again flying over the land below she couldn't help feeling that perhaps she'd been a bit pathetic by fleeing his
kitchen like that.

Since when did she run away from anything these
days? Why hadn't she stayed and handled the hot situation with the cool she was capable of? She'd dealt
with far worse. So what had she been so afraid of? How
awful would it have been if she hadn't been distracted
by the burning garlic and things had reached their natural conclusion?

She had nothing to fear from Rico or the fierce passion he aroused in her. They weren't *really* kindred
spirits, despite her overly dramatic proclamation, which
had been made in a rare moment of emotional weakness, and it wasn't as if she was actually contemplating
a relationship with the man. The last thing she wanted
was commitment, or any kind of emotional intimacy,
for that matter, when emotions involving the opposite

sex were so dangerous, but he clearly wasn't all that keen on attachment either.

So surely there was nothing stopping her having one night with him, she told herself, going a bit giddy at the very thought of it. She was leaving in the morning. She could embrace and explore the desire she felt for him without the fear of being manipulated or sucked in any deeper, and she could depart with no looking back and no regrets. Who knew when she'd next get the chance?

She wanted him, quite desperately, and, while whether he still wanted her was another matter, one thing was certain—she would never know if she didn't ask.

Now they were back, Rico needed to remove himself from Carla's vicinity before he made a move from which there would be no return.

Two moves, actually.

First off, it appeared that revealing the barest details of his life to date had acted as something of a trigger and he'd found himself wanting to tell her not only everything but also how he felt about it all, which was wholly unacceptable and made absolutely no sense.

Why would he *ever* want to do that? he'd asked himself while she'd been signing the forms and taking possession of the travel document that was so important to her. To create that kind of connection he'd have to be mad, and even he couldn't be so reckless as to risk that kind of insanity.

Nevertheless, despite his best efforts to put it from his mind he'd been so unsettled by their conversation in the car he'd automatically answered her question about the favour owed him by the consul, and at that point he'd realised he'd be better off not talking at all.

Which brought him to move number two, namely the increasingly difficult to resist desire hammering away inside him that in the absence of conversation had swollen to unbearable proportions.

He hated the fact that it was so hard to control. He couldn't shake the disturbing feeling that one tiny loosening of his grip on it would unravel him completely. He didn't want to want Carla—she'd been bang on about that—any more than he wanted to keep dwelling on what she'd told him about being so sickeningly abused. He didn't want to wonder how she'd felt about it then or how she felt about it now, or what long-lasting effects it might have had. He wasn't jealous of the support she'd had in the shape of a best friend. The stab of shame that he'd felt when he'd caught the appalled shock in her eyes at his confession he'd actually joined the gang, as if he'd somehow let her down, had been wholly unnecessary. He had no need to apologise for anything. There was no point in regretting anything he'd done and it didn't matter one jot if he disappointed her. Why did he care about proving to her his integrity? They weren't kindred spirits. They couldn't be.

The crushing pressure of everything battering at his head and body was too much to bear and he didn't know how much longer he'd be able to hold it together. So he was going to hole up in his study until six o'clock in the morning, repairing the dent in his fortune and those of his clients while cobbling together some sort of control over everything he was suffering, and to hell with whether that made him a lily-livered coward and a terrible host. Carla could fend for herself. He'd had enough.

'Rico, wait.'

Nope. Not happening. She was probably going to thank him and he didn't think he could take her gratitude when he wanted something else entirely from her yet shouldn't and couldn't have. But apparently she was not to be deterred because his progress back to the house wasn't as fast as he'd have liked it to be and within seconds she'd caught up with him.

'Stop,' she said, panting slightly in a distracting way and planting a hand on his bare forearm, which singed his skin and rooted him to the spot.

'What is it?' he snapped, too frayed to even attempt to make a stab at cool, easy-going levity.

'I have a question. About last night.'

That was worse than any thank-you. 'There's nothing to discuss,' he muttered, shaking her off and resuming his march to the house.

'I think there is.'

'In what way?'

'What would have happened if the garlic hadn't burned?'

What the hell? 'What do you think would have happened?' he said, the memories of their kiss burning through him and having their inevitable effect.

'I think we wouldn't have stopped. I think we'd have had sex right there on your kitchen island.'

His pulse began to gallop, the images smashing into his head, desire breaking through the flimsy dam he'd

constructed and coursing through him in a great rush
of molten heat. He wanted to deny it, but it was impossible. 'Well, then. There you go. Is that it?'

'I hope not.'

His brows snapped together and he wheeled round
to face her. 'What do you mean by that?'

She took a deep breath and looked him square in the
eye. 'I want to finish what we started.'

He tensed, fighting with every inch of his control
the clamouring urge to grab hold of her and do exactly
that. 'That is not a good idea.'

'Why not?'

Yes, quite. Why not? 'It's complicated,' he muttered,
shoving his hands in the pockets of his shorts, any pretence of equanimity long gone.

'It needn't be.'

Nevertheless, it was. For a whole host of reasons.
He didn't know who he was these days. He understood
none of the things he'd done recently. And then there
was his unwise interest in the woman standing in front
of him and his curiosity about all the things they had in
common and those they very much did not. His heart
banged against his ribcage while his head throbbed with
the intensity of the pressure pushing in on him from all
sides. 'I'm injured.'

'I'd take care.'

But what if he didn't? What if he let his guard down
even more than he already had? What if she somehow
tripped him up and before he knew it had him telling
her everything? Or worse, wound up wanting more than
he could ever give?

'It would just be one afternoon and one night, Rico,' she said, as if able to read his mind. 'My flight is booked for the morning and that's not going to change. There's no room in my life for a relationship. Seriously. You'd be perfectly safe from me.'

Safe? Really? He'd never met anyone quite so threatening.

But, *Dio*, her words rang in his ears like a siren call, tempting him across the calm waters of reason towards the treacherous rocks of hedonistic ecstasy.

One afternoon. One night. Free of strings. Free of complications. Drenched in pleasure. He hadn't felt this alert, this alive in months. And as for his ability to perform... Pain? What pain? The only ache he had right now was deep in his pelvis. He wanted her as badly as she'd just admitted she wanted him, and really, would it be so bad? How dangerous could she possibly be? He'd never allowed a woman to expect more than what he was able to offer and he wasn't about to start now. And wouldn't actually acting on the desire make it lessen, or even obliterate it altogether?

As the reasons for objecting ran out and the last of his resistance crumbled, Rico reached for her, pulled her against him and slammed his mouth down on hers.

Oh, thank God for that.

For the longest of moments, Carla had really thought Rico was going to stick to his guns in refusing her request and she'd been all ready to back down, since a no was, after all, a no, even a humiliating one. But to her relief he'd obviously had a change of heart because the next thing she knew she was in his arms and he was kissing her as if his life depended on it.

She softened and melted into him instantly, parting her lips and moaning his name as they came together in a clash of teeth and tongues and a tangle of hands. She wound her arms around his neck and pressed herself close, and at the feel of him, so big and solid against her, shivers shot down her spine.

To actually be able to touch him after a morning spent resisting the urge to do exactly that was utterly intoxicating and she couldn't get enough. She ran her hands over his shoulders and down his arms and he shuddered and groaned into her mouth. His muscles tensed with every caress and she could feel his granite-hard erection pressed against her.

With one hand he angled her head and deepened the kiss, and her breasts tightened and tingled, her nipples stiffening with the need to be touched. With the other he pulled her hips more tightly to him, sending shocks of electricity spiralling through her.

When he pulled back, breathing raggedly, he looked as if he was in as much of a fog as she was. The blue of his eyes had darkened to the deepest navy, the desperate hunger she could see in them reflecting the frantic need she knew her own contained. Before he could have time to even *think* about the wisdom of what he was doing she breathed huskily, 'Complete the tour and show me your room,' and thankfully he didn't need to be told twice.

Taking her hand, he strode into the house and across the hall. At the bottom of his stairs he stopped, his eyes blazing and a muscle pounding in his jaw, and said, 'Go on ahead.' In response to the quizzical look she gave him, he merely added, 'I had a fantasy about exactly this scenario only yesterday afternoon.'

'What was I doing?' she said, her pulse thudding heavily at the dizzying realisation that he'd imagined this, just as she had.

'Simply walking up the stairs.'

'I think I can do better than that.'

She turned and began slowly climbing the stairs, swinging her hips and running her fingers over the banister as she went. Halfway up, she paused to look over her shoulder and give him a wicked grin, and the intensity with which he was watching her knocked the breath from her lungs. At the top, she crooked her finger at him, and within seconds he'd taken the steps two at a time.

'How was that?' she breathed as he led her into his bedroom with indecent haste.

'Better than I could possibly have imagined.'

He had her back in his arms in a flash and in between hot, frantic kisses she tugged on his T-shirt while he shoved her top up, only releasing her so that they could free themselves of items that neither had any need for. Jeans and shorts and shoes immediately followed and then he was backing her towards the bed and tumbling her onto the mattress.

For a moment, as she lay sprawled on the sheets catching her breath, he just stood there staring at her as if he'd never seen a nearly naked woman before, and while every cell of her body quivered in response to the heat of his gaze she took the opportunity to do the same.

Everywhere she looked she saw hard muscle and tanned skin, his broad chest and powerful thighs sprinkled with a smattering of rough, dark hair. In the region of his hips and pelvis were scars which, in contrast to those on his chest, were livid and recent, presumably a result of the surgery he'd had to have. But she couldn't have asked him about them even if she'd wanted to. All her attention was drawn to the enormous erection that lay beneath the fabric of his black shorts and made her pulse race and her mouth water.

As stunning as the view was, though, the desperation throbbing inside her was becoming intolerable.

'What are you waiting for?' she said with a seductiveness that was surprising even to her ears.

'You're too perfect.'

If only he knew, she thought, the gruffness of his voice tugging at something deep inside her. She might not have too many lumps and bumps on the outside, but the fears and doubts she had on the inside more than made up for it. 'Believe me, I am far from perfect. But I am burning up with desire for you. I need you. Now, Rico.'

He must have heard the desperation in her voice because in an instant he'd joined her on the bed. He lowered himself on top of her, pressing her down with his delicious weight, his hardness a heady contrast to her softness. With a rough groan he brought his head down to hers and captured her mouth with a mind-blowing kiss, and she wound her legs around his hips and her arms around his neck until she was enveloped by his scent and warmth and her head cleared of everything but him.

After a moment that seemed to stretch for hours he rolled onto his back, taking her with him, which had her straddling him and rubbing herself against his erection, her breaths coming in short, ragged pants while he undid the clasp of her bra. She shrugged it off, her blood thick and hot, her pulse thundering, and a moment later he flipped her back over.

'Nifty,' she gasped.

'A miracle, quite frankly,' he murmured. 'A couple of days ago a move like that would have had me reaching for the painkillers.'

She grinned and then he cupped her breast, his palm fitting to her perfectly, and her smile gave way to a sigh as sensation skated through her body. She arched her back and he trailed kisses down her throat, across the slope of her chest and took her hard nipple in his mouth. She moaned his name and grabbed his hair, and when he moved his other hand down her body, his fingers slipping beneath the waistband of her knickers and then into her tight, slick heat, she gasped.

He transferred his attention to her other breast while he rubbed her clitoris with his thumb, his fingers moving inside her, and all coherent thought fled. When he shifted and moved and added to her torment by putting his mouth to the spot where his fingers and thumb were creating such devastation she nearly leapt off the bed.

'Enough,' she panted after a few minutes of agonisingly exquisite torment.

'No.'

'Yes. I want you inside me when I come. Don't make me beg.'

'It has a certain appeal.'

'Don't.'

He gave her a hot, hard kiss, which dazzled her senses, and then he reared up, reached over and rummaged around in the drawer of his nightstand. Ogling his back, she heard the crinkle of a foil packet, the harsh hiss of breath, and then he came back to her, sliding her knickers down and off. She opened her legs wide and he settled between them, and as he crushed his mouth to hers he thrust into her with one long, hard stroke and the pleasure was so exquisite she nearly came right there and then.

Lodged deep inside her, he stilled, but she didn't need time to adjust to him so she dug her fingers into the taut muscles of his buttocks to pull him in further and gave her hips a quick twist, which seemed to do the trick.

With a harsh groan he pulled out of her and then back in, and did it again and again, setting a rhythm that started off slow, drugging her with desire, but became harder and faster within seconds until her breath was coming in increasingly short, sharp pants. Her entire body was on fire and she could feel the tension coiling deep inside her, swelling and tightening, and just when she thought she couldn't stand it any longer he kissed her hard, and suddenly she was flying apart, ecstasy exploding inside her like fireworks. With a great rough groan Rico thrust into her one last time, as deep as he could, and exploded, pulsating into her over and over again.

'I thought you were supposed to be injured,' she said once she'd regained enough breath to speak.

'I believe I've made a miraculous recovery,' he said, sounding as dazed as she was.

'So it would seem,' she said, feeling him twitch and harden inside her. 'Which is a shame.'

'Is it?' he murmured, one dark eyebrow raised. 'Why?'

'I was going to offer to kiss you better.'

'Well, you know, I'm not *completely* healed,' he said with a slow, devastating smile.

'Where do you hurt?'

'Everywhere.'

CHAPTER TEN

THE ALARM THAT went off on the phone Rico had lent to Carla shattered the early-morning peace and jolted him out of the deepest sleep he'd had in years, which on the one hand was surprising when he usually slept fitfully, but on the other wasn't, given that night had been making way for dawn by the time they had finally crashed out.

He'd never had a night like it, he thought, giving his eyes a quick rub and his body a stretch that made his muscles twinge. He didn't think he'd ever forget the sight of Carla sidling up his stairs—his fantasy brought to life, only better—and then lying sprawled on his bed, a goddess of his very own in all her nearly naked perfection. Nor would he ever forget the scent and taste of her, spicy and sweet, or the wildness of her response.

For the briefest of moments it had struck him that he shouldn't be sullying her perfection with all his flaws and the murky history of the things he'd done, but then she'd revealed how much she'd wanted him and his mind had gone blank. The minute he'd put his hands and mouth on her that had been that for rational thought.

He'd been swamped with heat and desire and sensation and had had no sense of time.

Eventually, driven by hunger of an entirely different kind, he'd brought up the linguine from the night before, which they'd devoured before going for a late-night dip in the pool that had been less of a swim than a hot, wet tangle of limbs that had resulted in a lot of water being sloshed over the side.

He'd lost count of the number of orgasms he'd given and received. Even though he said it himself, for someone who'd recently had the kind of accident that required surgery and rehabilitation, his stamina had been impressive. But then, he'd had a powerful incentive. He'd forgotten how much he enjoyed the sharp sensations that came with sex and the sweet oblivion that followed. How intensely he felt, how sensationally he came alive.

Not that he'd ever had sex like this. He'd never met anyone like Carla, who so easily matched his voracious demands and wasn't afraid to make some of her own. He'd never experienced pleasure so great it blew the top of his head off.

It was a shame she was leaving. He wouldn't mind some more, because instead of going away, as he'd idiotically assumed it would, his need for her had only got stronger. But she *was* leaving. And that was that.

Unless it wasn't…

Maybe she didn't have to go just yet, he thought, his pulse suddenly pounding, every muscle in his body tensing at the realisation that perhaps he could have more. Maybe she could stick around for a little while longer. Hadn't she told him she'd arranged a week's leave? Hadn't she said she had no real plans? What if he asked her to stay? Not for ever, never that, but certainly until she had to return home to work.

If she said no, that would be that. After her revelations about her youth, there was no way in hell he'd try and manipulate her into changing her mind. He'd accept her decision with good grace, see her off and set about restarting his interrupted plan to get back to the life he'd had prior to his accident.

But he badly hoped she'd say yes, because he wasn't ready to let her go.

With the echo of the alarm still ringing in her ears, Carla shifted and yawned, achingly aware of the devastatingly talented man lying beside her, who'd taken her to heaven and back several times over the course of yesterday afternoon and last night. She opened her eyes to find him propped up on an elbow, watching her with an expression that was as unfathomable as it was intense, and gave him an unstoppable smile.

'Buon giorno,' he said, his sleep-roughened voice sending shivers rippling through her and bringing with it a hot flurry of scorchingly vivid memories of everything they'd done together.

'I don't know about that,' she murmured, feeling herself flush and stamping down hard on the regret that they wouldn't be doing any of it again. 'It's horrendously early. But I should start packing. My flight leaves in less than two hours.'

'Stay.'

At the huskily uttered word—not quite a suggestion, not quite a demand—Carla went very still. 'What?'

'Stay.'

Was he joking? He didn't look as if he was. He looked more serious than she'd ever seen him. So could she be dreaming? Nope. She was awake. *Wide* awake now.

What was he doing?

Perhaps the novelty of sex after three long months without it—to which he'd confessed while heating up the linguine—had addled his brain. Or perhaps it was the lack of sleep. He'd gone out like a light the minute his head hit the pillows he'd retrieved off the floor after they'd taken a long, hot shower to wash the chlorine from the pool off each other. She'd taken a while longer, partly because he'd spread himself across the vast bed as if trying to occupy as much space as possible, which had left her perilously close to the edge, and partly because he was not a peaceful sleeper. He twitched and shifted as if the slightest noise might have him sitting bolt upright—a hang-up from his life on the streets?—and it had made her conscious of her breathing, which had kept her awake for a while.

'I thought we agreed this was a one-night thing only,' she said carefully, willing her strangely galloping pulse to slow down.

'I've changed my mind.'

'Why?'

'You're on leave and I want more.'

Well, so did she, if she was being honest, because she'd never experienced the fiery passion he aroused in her, but extending her stay was out of the question.

She had things to do back home. She wasn't sure quite what yet, but the minute she landed she'd be compiling an extensive to-do list.

And despite the head-wrecking pleasure she'd experienced recently she hadn't forgotten the whole justification for deciding to sleep with him in the first place. She needed to leave to protect herself. Rico was far too compelling and fascinating and she couldn't risk developing an interest in him that went beyond the physical. If that happened she'd slide into seriously dangerous territory where her emotions became involved and the very essence of who she was would be at risk.

On the other hand, where was she ever going to get sex like this again? She might as well admit that she was already addicted to the way he made her feel. By sticking to the plan and waltzing off with a breezy smile and a casual wave, might she not be cutting her nose off to spite her face?

She had no doubt that it would be far safer to walk away and continue to live her perfectly fine life, which had no soaring highs but no plummeting lows either, but was that really how she saw the rest of her existence? Didn't that somehow smack of opting out? Didn't it imply that she was still affected by what had happened to her when she was young?

What if she actually took a risk for a change? So what if they talked? Where was the danger in that? She was struggling to continue to deny the curiosity burning up inside her. She was desperate to get to know the man beneath the surface, and it wasn't as if she was going to lose control or anything. While Rico's interest in her was flattering, it was hardly something she would let go to her head, and with his detachment she had no need to worry about the dangers of getting emotionally involved. He'd never allow it. Her defences would remain in place. She'd keep herself safe. And it hadn't escaped her that she still hadn't managed to convince him to meet Finn.

Here was a chance to kill several birds with one stone, she thought, a faint stab of guilt piercing the fiery desire that was unfurling in the pit of her stomach and stealing into every part of her. She might never have the opportunity again.

'All right.'

Twenty-four hours later, with the thundering of his heart receding and his breath evening out, Rico stared up at the ceiling of his bedroom, which was still spinning, and congratulated himself once again on the brilliance of his decision to ask Carla to stay. The moment she'd agreed—which had filled him with greater relief than he could ever have imagined the suggestion warranted—he'd rolled her beneath him, and, with the exception of the phone call he'd made half an hour later, they'd barely made it out of his bed since. He was feeling fitter and more energised than he had in ages and he couldn't think of anyone with whom he'd rather make up for the abstinence of the last three months.

'So what are we going to do today?' she murmured huskily, stretching languidly beside him.

'I have an idea,' he said as unbelievably his body began to stir yet again.

She batted him with a pillow. 'I know *I'm* on leave,' she said with a quick grin that for some reason struck him square in the chest like a dart, 'but don't you have to work? What will happen to your billions under management if they're not being managed?'

'But they are.'

'Who by?'

'I hired someone.'

She sat up, to his immense disappointment clutching the sheet to her chest. 'Wow,' she said, staring at him, all tousled and rosy cheeked, which was a very good look on her, and, even better, a look put there by him.

'It makes sense,' he said, not quite sure why the news should provoke quite such surprise.

'I know. But…well…wow. When?'

'Yesterday morning.'

'The phone call?'

'That's right.'

'Who?'

'My nearest competitor. He jumped at the chance to come and work for me and he's extremely keen and exceptionally able. So I'm utterly at your disposal for as long as you want me.'

'Don't worry,' she said lightly. 'I still only want you until Saturday.'

'Of course,' he said smoothly, ignoring the strangely bitter taste the thought of her departure left in his mouth.

She stared at him for a moment longer, the expression in her eyes unreadable, and then gave her beautiful shoulders a quick shrug. 'Well, we can't keep on doing nothing but having sex.'

'Can't we?'

'I've never been to Venice before. I'd like to see some sights.'

'Plenty to look at here,' he drawled, pulling down the sheet that was draped across him.

'Stop it,' she said with a smile. 'I'm serious. I vaguely recall a plan to learn Italian. I have a hankering to try some proper tiramisu. And even though I haven't had much use for them lately I'm also going to need to buy some new clothes.'

'Va bene,' he said, reflecting that, since he'd given his housekeeper the week off, they probably did need to pick up some supplies. 'If I really can't tempt you back into bed, we will visit the city. Give me an hour to make some arrangements.'

By the time they sat down to lunch in a divine cafe that appeared in no guidebook but apparently served the best tiramisu in the city, Rico had taken Carla on a private tour of the Doge's Palace and had St Mark's Basilica and the Bell Tower closed to the public so that they might explore them in peace and solitude. They'd had an argument about whether biscotti were better on their own or dipped in *vin santo* and a discussion about up to exactly what time it was acceptable to order a cappuccino. The entire morning had been an incredible experience and, for Carla at least, very much needed.

Not for a second had she regretted agreeing to stay with him for a few more days. She'd had no doubts about changing her flight to Saturday morning, which would give her the rest of the weekend back home to prepare for the week ahead and proved that she was still using her head, not her heart, to make decisions. She wouldn't have thought it possible, but instead of lessening in passion and heat, the sex had been only getting better.

But she'd woken up this morning needing a change of scenery. The hours since the moment he'd caved in to the desire he had for her had been incredibly intense, increasingly light on chat and heavy on action. And while she hadn't exactly felt trapped, she'd definitely felt a need for space and a break.

'So you're an exceptionally good tour guide,' she said, taking a sip of her chianti and thinking of the deluge of information he'd presented her with, dates and facts that indicated an encyclopaedic knowledge of the city.

'I've had plenty of practice,' he answered, his eyes shielded by his mirrored shades. 'I know these streets and canals and everything within them like the back of my hand.'

Her head immediately swam with everything he'd told her about his youth, but she pushed it aside because it was far too beautiful a day for an analysis of his distressing past.

'Well, if this person you've hired proves too good and you become surplus to requirements,' she said, thinking instead about how taken aback she'd been by the news that he, who'd always operated totally alone, had taken on the responsibility of an employee, 'at least you know you have an alternative employment option.'

'I won't. I'm excellent at what I do and I need to do it.'

'You're very driven.'

'As are you.'

'Why do you think that is?'

'Probably because if you keep moving forwards at great pace, it's harder for the past to catch up with you.'

'This is true,' she said, tilting her head while she gave it some consideration and came to the conclusion that he could be right. 'Although I'm totally over mine, of course,' she added, thinking of the return of her confidence and self-esteem and the way she'd eventually had sex again, even though it had taken another four years before she'd been brave enough to take the plunge.

'Are you?'

She nodded. 'Endless conversations with Georgie and the therapy my parents arranged worked wonders. You ought to try it.'

His dark eyebrows lifted. 'You had therapy?'

'A lot of it. And counselling. For at least a year. They felt terribly guilty. '

'And so they should.'

'Well, yes,' she admitted, remembering being in plays at school that no one came to and coming top in tests that no one praised her for. 'But they weren't to blame any more than I was. Shortly after I was rescued, they started talking about moving off the commune and adopting a more conventional lifestyle, but I persuaded them out of it. They'd got a bit smothering by that point and I just wanted it behind me.'

'Is that why you don't see much of them?'

'That and distance,' she said with a nod. 'They're now halfway up a hill in Wales.'

'I can see why Georgie means so much to you, even if I don't get it.'

'What don't you get?'

'The depth of your relationship.' He took a sip of his beer and she really wished he'd take off his sunglasses.

'How deep do your relationships go?'

'I don't have any.'

Just as she suspected, she thought, and her heart squeezed at the realisation of how lonely he must be. 'That's a shame.'

'It's never bothered me,' he said with a casual shrug that made her suddenly wonder if she was wrong. Maybe he wasn't lonely at all. Maybe he was perfectly content with his life the way it was. Maybe that was why he had no interest in meeting Finn.

'Well, Georgie and I are closer than sisters,' she said, not entirely sure what to make of that, 'and I owe her a debt I'll never be able to repay.'

'Is that why you accepted my invitation to dinner?'

'Partly,' she said. 'I also needed to assuage my guilt.'

'Your guilt?'

'I allowed you to leave that day. That shouldn't have happened. I should never have left you alone. I made a mistake I'd never normally have made.'

'Then why did you?'

'You threw me off balance.'

'Did I?'

'You must have known you did.'

'You are a master of concealment.'

'Takes one to know one. And, talking of relation-ships and that afternoon,' she said with a deep breath, not willing to consider the idea that he might genuinely be fine on his own and that her mission might fail, 'have you had any thoughts about meeting Finn?'

'No.'

'Because I really think you should, Rico, and not just because he wants it but because it would be so good for you too.'

'It's none of your business.'

'Well, no, but—'

'Are you trying to ruin the day?'

The smile he gave her was faint, but she could hear a chilly bite to his words. Her throat went dry and her stomach clenched. 'Of course not,' she said, the wine in her system turning to acid.

'Then stop.'

Having got through the rest of lunch with mercifully little conversation, Rico left Carla in the hands of the top personal shopper at the top department store he'd rung earlier, and took himself off to the Capella di Santa Maria, not because he was remotely religious but because he'd always found comfort in the shady coolness of the small but perfectly formed building, and since it wasn't on the tourist trail, which meant it had never been a location for any of his adolescent scams or thiev-ery, it dredged up no memories.

Was there *any* hope of finding comfort now?

With everything crashing around inside him, it didn't seem likely. He couldn't seem to stop thinking about the support Carla had had in the aftermath of her experience. That kind of help hadn't been made available to him at any point between his parents' death and the moment he'd torn free from gang life. And when he'd been older and it could have become an option, he'd had that part of his life locked away so long he hadn't known where the key even was.

But what if he *had* had access to help? was the thought now ricocheting around his head as he shoved open the heavy oak door and went in. What if he had been able to talk it through with someone who wouldn't have judged but could have helped him make sense of it all? How differently might his life have turned out? Could he have had friends? Could he have had what Finn had? A wife, a child, a family?

And why the hell was he even thinking about it? His instruction to Carla to quit pushing Finn on him could just as easily have been directed at himself, because for some infuriating reason it was becoming harder to put him from his mind too. He didn't *want* what Finn had. Regrets were pointless. Hindsight was something only fools indulged in. Envy, the kind that had sliced through him when Carla had been talking about how fortunate she'd been to have a friend like Georgie, served no purpose whatsoever.

And yet, it struck him suddenly, perhaps he *did* have the chance to talk about it now. With Carla. She was always encouraging him to reveal his secrets and pushing him for answers. What if he trusted her with his past and gave them to her?

No.

That was one reckless move even he couldn't make. He couldn't afford to make connections and allow emotions to invade his life. He didn't want to ever suffer the pain of rejection and abandonment again, or experience the devastation when everything went wrong. The way he'd chosen to live his life, free from exploitation, free from fear, *alone*, was fine.

But what if it wasn't? What if it could be better?

The insidious thoughts slunk into his head and dug in their claws, and his heart began to thump. What if Carla had had a point about no man being an island, even him? He was finding it impossibly difficult to maintain his facade with her, but maybe he ought to simply stop trying. Maybe he ought to let her see the dark, empty man beneath the easy-going surface. She'd been through it. She'd understand. She'd be the last person to judge. And then perhaps he'd be able to ease up on the constant drive for more and find some kind of peace.

All he had to do, he thought, nevertheless sweating at the mere concept of it, was take that risk.

By the time they'd finished dinner and everything had been cleared away Carla, staring out over the lagoon from the terrace upon which they'd eaten, was unable to stand the tension radiating off Rico any longer.

From the moment they'd left the city, she laden with bags, he carrying a ten-kilo box of groceries as if it weighed nothing, he'd been on edge and distant, as if somewhere else entirely, and it had twisted her stomach into knots.

What was behind it? she'd asked herself all evening, the knots tightening. It couldn't be the amount she'd spent on clothes because she was paying him back, for everything. So was he concerned she was going to continue to try and persuade him to meet his brother again?

Well, he had nothing to fear on that front. She'd gone over it endlessly while trying on outfits, and it had struck her suddenly that she could be flogging a dead horse here, that he might never feel about Finn the way she wanted him to, and perhaps she ought to stop.

And while her heart broke for him, and for Georgie and Finn, if she was being brutally honest, it *was* none of her business. It was between Rico and Finn. Or not. But either way, however great the debt she owed Georgie, she had to let it go, because who was she to tell Rico what to think or what to do? Her family wasn't exactly functional, and what made her an expert on relationships anyway?

She'd blithely told him that she was over what had happened to her, but she'd realised that was a lie. If she was truly over it she wouldn't fear commitment. She wouldn't fear getting swallowed up and losing her identity and her independence. By now she'd have had at least one proper relationship. She might even be married. So she was a big fat fraud and it was time to stop.

Taking a deep breath, Carla slid her gaze from the dark waters of the lagoon and turned to him.

'I'm sorry,' she said quietly, her heart pounding when he met her gaze, his eyes and expression unfathomable.

'What for?'

'Well, firstly for getting my bag stolen and upturning your life this last week. I can tell how hard it's been for you. And secondly, for trying to get you to see the whole Finn thing differently. You've made it very clear that you don't want to discuss it and I haven't respected that. I've been overstepping. Hugely. With the best of intentions, but still. So I apologise.'

For a moment there was silence and then he gave her the faintest of smiles. 'Don't go giving up on me now, Carla.'

Something in his voice lifted the tiny hairs at the back of her neck and she went very still. 'What do you mean?'

'I was hoping to talk to you.'

'What about?'

'My youth.'

Her heart thudded against her ribs. 'Why?'

'You suggested therapy.'

'I'm no psychologist.'

'But you understand and I trust you and I'd like your insight. Please.'

The thumping of her pulse intensified and she went hot with apprehension. He was shedding his detachment. He'd decided to put his trust in her. This was the kind of emotional intimacy she'd always striven to avoid. She couldn't get involved. Yet she already was, she had to acknowledge. She had been from the moment she'd started pushing him to open up and answer her questions. And for him to even think about asking for her insight—although what made him think she'd have any she had no idea—must have cost him greatly.

How could she possibly refuse him? Maybe she *could* help him. Maybe, however unwise it might turn out to be, she even wanted to. 'I'll fetch more wine.'

CHAPTER ELEVEN

No AMOUNT OF alcohol was going to make this easier, thought Rico, his heart beating a thunderous tattoo at the realisation that there was no going back from this. But at least it was dark.

'I'm not entirely sure where to start,' he said thickly, once Carla had filled their glasses and set the bottle down on the table.

'Why don't you tell me about your parents?'

Shifting on his seat to ease the discomfort, he forced his mind back to the people he barely remembered. 'My mother was a dentist, my father was an estate agent. From what I can recall, which isn't a lot, we were a small, normal, middle class family.'

'Were you loved?'

He allowed a tiny seam of memory to open up, a hazy blur of hugs and kisses, and felt a ribbon of warmth wind through him. 'Yes.'

'You said they died in a car crash. What happened?'

'I was at school,' he muttered, rubbing his chest as if that might erase the sharp stab of pain. 'A car overtaking on a bend went straight into them. They were killed instantly.'

'And the driver?'

'Him too.'

'So you didn't even get justice.'

Her statement lodged deep and then detonated. 'No,' he said, realising with a start that he'd never thought about in that way even though it was an obvious explanation for the intense anger he'd felt at the time. 'I got no closure at all. I had no time to process the shock or the grief before I was taken into care. It was like I'd been hurled off a moving ship and into a heaving, churning sea.'

'I can't begin to imagine,' she said softly, her voice catching.

'I was so lost and so alone. I'd been ripped apart from everything I'd ever known and tossed into a whole new world. A new school, new faces, a new home. Except none of the places I lived in were home. There was nothing wrong with them, it was just that I quickly learned that wherever I was sent was only ever going to be temporary and so to make attachments would be pointless. I realised I belonged nowhere and I ran away to find something better.' He gave a bitter laugh and shook his head. 'If only I'd known... *Dio*, the fear...the hunger...'

'So the gang became your family.'

'That was what I'd hoped,' he said, for a moment losing himself in the sympathy he could see in her gaze and feeling the ribbon of warmth begin to unfurl and spread. 'I was so excited about it. I genuinely thought

I'd found a place to belong, but I was swiftly disabused of that too.'

'In what way?'

'There was no loyalty,' he said, his chest tightening as the memory of the shock, bewilderment and finally devastation flashed into his head. 'No code of honour. I was just useful and light-fingered and suited their purposes. And then when I was arrested and therefore no longer of any use they were nowhere to be seen, which is why I took the job.'

'That must have been devastating to discover,' she said softly, her eyes clouding in the candlelight.

'It was. I put my trust in the wrong people and I allowed myself to be exploited. But by the time I realised what was going on I was in too deep to get out.'

'You said you were responsible for the accounting,' she said, her eyes fixed to his.

'I was good with figures. They didn't care that I was only fifteen. They put me in charge of cleaning the money and collecting the debts. I was handy with my fists and big for my age. One time I nearly put a man in hospital. I carry the shame and guilt of every dirty, terrible thing I did to this day.'

'You were so young.'

'But old enough to know right from wrong.'

'None of it was your fault.'

'Wasn't it?'

'No,' she said vehemently, sitting up and leaning forwards, the sudden burn in her eyes scything through the numb chill he'd lived with for so long. 'Your parents' death was a tragedy, and there was nothing anyone could have done about that, but you were let down by a whole host of people who should have done more. You were what, eleven, twelve, when you started running away?'

'About that.'

'They should have tried harder. Someone should have fought for you. You should not have been allowed to slip through the net.'

Maybe she was right, he thought, the tension gripping his body easing a fraction. He'd been little more than a child. He'd been dealt an impossibly tough hand and he'd had no idea how to play it.

'And as for your later actions,' she continued in the same fierce tone, 'I suspect you've been trying to atone for them ever since.'

'What makes you say that?'

'The donation to the consul's wife's charity for homeless children. What other charities do you support, Rico?'

Plenty. Anonymously where possible and always at a distance. 'A few.'

'I thought so. I bet you've done an immense amount of good over the years.'

'It will never be enough.'

'You have to forgive yourself.'

'That's easier said than done.'

'But not impossible. If I can, you can.'

He frowned. 'I thought you said you knew you weren't to blame.'

'That was after the therapy,' she said. 'Initially, I blamed everyone for what happened to me but the person responsible. I was livid at having been discovered. I'd considered myself so sophisticated, so much more interesting and mature than everyone else. I accused Georgie of being jealous and my parents of not wanting me to be happy. When the scales finally fell from my eyes, thanks to the therapy, I felt like the biggest fool in the world. I hated that he'd had the power to do that to me and that I'd been so easy to manipulate. I swore that I would never allow it to happen again, and it hasn't. So I know all about shame and guilt and grubbiness.'

'You're beautiful.'

'In this old thing?'

'You are the most beautiful woman I've ever met.' And the strongest. Whereas he felt utterly weak and drained. The ground beneath his feet was unstable and he suddenly felt strangely adrift, which was why he turned his attention to something he could hold on to, something he did understand. 'Let's go to bed.'

Rico did an excellent job of attempting to wear Carla out, but while he slumbered away on the bed, of which he now seemed to hog less and upon which he now barely twitched, sleep eluded her.

While she sat on the balcony watching the sparkle of moonlight on the water, their conversation ran through her head as if on a never-ending loop, the details of which she didn't think she'd ever forget.

Her throat closed and her eyes prickled just to think about it. Her heart was in tatters for the boy he'd been, for all the children all over the world who one way or another slipped through the net. She couldn't imagine the loneliness he must have felt. The terror and the confusion and the hunger, the fear of which he still clearly carried with him. And all the while struggling to come to terms with the death of his parents.

His detachment and desire to move through life on his own made so much sense now. No wonder he kept himself apart and relied on no one but himself. No wonder he didn't form attachments when he'd experienced the destruction they could bring. She could totally understand why he didn't want to look back and why he had no mementos of the past he'd spent a long time trying to forget. He'd been exploited and abused, manipulated and badly let down. Who'd want to remember that?

How on earth had he had the strength to survive? she wondered, her chest tightening as she tried and failed to imagine the horror and brutality he'd been a part of. She'd always thought that she'd had a rough time of growing up, but compared to his experiences, hers had been a walk in the park. She'd had people looking out for her, even if she hadn't appreciated it at the time. Rico had undergone hell and, with the exception of the judge who'd given him a way out, had had no one on his side, no one fighting his corner.

He'd learned how to hide it, and hide it well, but once upon a time he'd been as vulnerable as her and just as easy to prey upon. He knew as well as she did what it was like to be manipulated and exploited. Was that why she had the feeling that he instinctively got her? Was that why when he called her beautiful she didn't inwardly cringe as usual but deep down purred instead? Compliments, which could be flimsy, easily given and weren't to be trusted, had always made her uncomfortable, but when they came from Rico—was she really the most beautiful woman he'd ever met?—they made her melt.

In fact, she thought, something in her chest shifting and settling, everything about him made her melt. His strength. His resilience. His innate if reluctant chivalry and the way he'd taken care of her after her bag had been stolen, even though she'd resisted with every bone in her body.

Even if he couldn't figure out what the judge had seen in him, she could. She saw a frightened, grieving child who'd found himself in a situation of indescribable torment. She saw an indomitable will to survive by any means necessary, and the inherent good that had made him the incredible man he was today.

'What are you doing out here?'

His deep, rumbling voice broke into her swirling thoughts and she turned to see him standing in the doorway wearing nothing but a white towel wrapped around his waist.

Feeling strangely giddy, her heart thumping unusually fast, Carla got to her feet and undid the belt of her robe. She didn't want to talk. She didn't want to dwell on the way the foundations of her existence seemed to be shifting. She just wanted to feel. So she put a hand on his chest and gave him a little push and they tangoed back until he was lying on the bed and she was straddling him, his towel having been discarded en route.

Without a word she leaned down, put her hands on his head and sealed her mouth to his. She kissed him hard and long, her pulse pounding and desire throbbing deep inside her. He clamped one big, strong hand on her hip and the other at the back of her neck, his palms like a brand on her heated skin.

Tearing her mouth from his, her chest heaving and her breath coming in pants, she dotted a trail of tiny kisses down the column of his throat, the hard-muscled expanse of his chest, her heart thumping as she took extra care with his scars, and then lower, over the ridges of his abdomen, shimmying down his body until she reached his long, hard erection, steel encased in velvet.

She could feel the tremors gripping his large frame and when she wrapped her fingers round the base of him and her lips around the tip the groan that tore from his mouth sent reciprocal shivers shooting up and down her spine. She took him deeper into her mouth and his hands moved to her head, threading through her hair, holding her when he needed her, guiding her yet giving her the freedom to use her hands, her mouth and her tongue to drive him to the point where his hips were jerking and his breathing was harsh, his control clearly unravelling.

And then he was lifting her off him and rolling her over, applying a condom and sliding into her with one long, hard, smooth thrust, lodging deep inside her, and staring into her eyes as if trying to see into her soul.

She clung on to him, her gaze locked with his as he began to move, slowly, steadily, driving into her, pushing her higher and higher each time, making her shatter once, white lights flashing in her head, and then again, and again, before with a great groan he buried himself hard and deep and poured into her.

She was wrung out physically and emotionally and her last drowsy thought before she finally fell asleep was, *I could stay here with him for ever.*

At the helm of his boat, with Carla sitting in the stern, Rico was feeling lighter than he had in years yet at the same time oddly uneasy, as if the world had been broken up and put back together with the pieces in the wrong place.

Something had shifted inside him last night, he thought, the frown that he felt he'd been wearing all morning deepening as he increased the throttle and they sped off in the direction of the island of Murano. With her insight and understanding Carla had sliced through his long-held doubts and shone a light on his darkest fears. She'd somehow given him permission to let go of the shame and the guilt he'd carried around for so long—even if he didn't think he could let it go just yet—and he had the strange sensation that tiny droplets of light might slowly be beginning to drip into the great well of nothingness inside him.

But he'd sensed something change in her too and that was the source of his discomfort. The shimmering emotion he'd seen in her gaze when he'd found her on the balcony, before she'd subsequently blown his mind, wasn't something he'd needed to witness. He didn't want her pity or her sympathy. He didn't want anything more with her than what he already had.

But it was what *she* might want that was his concern. He'd assumed she was on board with the temporary nature of their arrangement, but what if for some reason what they had now became not enough for her? What if she wound up wanting more? Under no circumstances could he allow that to happen. He'd never be able to give her more, no matter how much talking they did. He'd been on his own for so long it simply wasn't in him. But he would never want to hurt Carla, so he had to prevent such a situation arising at all costs and nip things in the bud before they got out of control.

And not only for her benefit, he forced himself to acknowledge.

Yesterday while he'd been showing her the sights he'd started to see his city through her eyes and it had been illuminating. He'd noticed less of the grey and the grime and more of the glitter and shine. Colours had seemed strangely brighter, sounds sharper, smells more intense. Even the heat, which he was well used to and had not changed, felt fiercer.

This shifting of the sands over unstable ground couldn't continue. A stronger-willed man would send Carla home now, and retreat to rebuild his walls, but he wasn't a stronger-willed man. He was a man who wanted her in his bed for as long as they had left. He just had to keep reminding himself that great sex was all it was.

The island of Murano, famed for its glass and a stone's throw from Venice, was amazing. Far less busy than its much bigger neighbour, it had colourful low-rise houses, wide, tranquil canals and a laid-back vibe that made Carla want to stop and linger along the walkways so she might have time to take it all in.

Vibrant glass sculptures stood in piazzas, glinting and sparkling in the midday sun. Rico had taken her to a workshop off the beaten track where she'd spent a good half an hour watching a glassblower creating a vase. She'd even picked up a bauble of her own.

The only minor awkward moment came when, while strolling down a walkway beside him, she'd suddenly been overwhelmed by the romance of it all, giddy with the effect this man had on her, and had reached for his hand, only to feel him jerk it away when her fingers brushed his.

'After all this,' said Carla, hiding her mortification behind a bright smile and determinedly reminding herself that she didn't, ever, do romance and, more importantly, neither did he. 'London's going to feel very pedestrian.'

'But it's your home.'

'It is and it's great,' she said, thinking that she really *did* love it with all its energy and buzz and variety, and she really *was* looking forward to getting back to it. 'But this is beautiful and Venice is stunning. Everywhere you turn there's another incredible piece of architecture and it's such… I don't know…an *effervescent* city.'

'And unfortunately,' he said drily, 'sinking.'

'So I've read. Why's that happening?'

'Early settlers drained the lagoon, dug canals and shored up banks by piling tree trunks into the silt. They laid great wooden platforms on top of the piles and stone on top of that and started building from there. But increased traffic in the canals—not to mention the cruise ships—has started churning up the water and the silt and the trunks are being exposed to oxygen that's making them rot. There's a campaign to ban everything but gondolas and small boats and it has my full backing.'

She knew how Venice felt, she thought dreamily, wondering for a moment what it would be like to be fought for like that. She too had been fine for years and then stirred up and exposed. She too had the sensation she was slowly sinking into deeper waters than felt safe, only in her case there was no one there to save her.

'You care,' she said, focusing on the topic of conversation and not the sliver of worry that slid through her at the thought that even though she'd done her best to prevent it she might be getting involved.

'It's complicated.'

'It's your home.'

'It was also my prison.'

'It's shaped the man you are and it's in your blood. I can't imagine you living anywhere else.'

'Neither can I. Can you imagine living anywhere other than London?'

Yes. She could imagine living here. With him. All too easily. But, despite what she'd thought last night, addled with emotions, this wasn't for forever. 'No,' she said, because it was the only answer she could give and anything else was simply not possible. 'As you pointed out, it's my home. I can't wait to get back.'

'Tomorrow's your last day,' he said, his eyes fixed on hers but curiously devoid of anything. 'What would you like to do?'

'I think I'd like to learn to pilot a gondola,' she said, struggling to ignore the tightening of her chest at the thought of leaving, determined instead to make the most of what little time she had left.

'Your wish is my command.'

But if only her wish *was* his command, thought Carla wistfully the next day, perching on the padded bench seat as Rico steered the *batela* through the busy and choppy canals and out into the relative calm of a more placid section of the lagoon. Because she was beginning to wish she hadn't been quite so sensible in booking a flight for tomorrow morning. She didn't need a whole day and a half to prepare to go back to work. She'd only been on leave for a week. What *had* she been thinking?

'I thought I was going to be learning to pilot a gondola,' she said, looking up at him, so breathtakingly gorgeous her heart turned over.

'Patience,' he said with the arch of one dark eyebrow. 'A gondola is a very technical boat. Tourists start on these.'

'And is that what I am? A tourist?'

'What else would you be?'

It was a question to which she didn't have an answer, even after an hour's tuition that took two, since shortly after it had begun there'd been a rocky moment during which she'd needed close contact support and her concentration had fled.

She was none the wiser when he handed her the oar and murmured, 'Your turn now,' or when she arched an eyebrow, gave him a wide grin from her position at the front of the boat and asked, 'Do you trust me?'

It was only when he replied, 'You already know I

do,' with a smile so blinding, so real, that it lit up his face and stole her breath, which weakened her knees, robbed her of her balance and promptly toppled her headlong into the lagoon, that she realised she was head over heels in love with him.

Rico had dived straight in after her. By the time he'd hauled himself back onto the boat and then pulled her up too, the coastguard had arrived. An hour later, with the paperwork completed and tetanus shots administered, they'd been delivered back to his island, where they'd got out of their wet things and taken a scalding shower.

Carla had been unusually quiet for the rest of the evening. No doubt, she was still in shock. He knew he was. He didn't think he'd ever forget the moment she'd fallen into the water. Time had slowed right down, but the sheer terror that had ripped through him, wilder than any tide, had been swift and immense. She'd gone under for the briefest of seconds, but to him it had felt like a lifetime. He hadn't thought twice about diving in to rescue her. The only thought screaming through his head was that he couldn't lose her.

And that was equally terrifying.

She wasn't his to lose. Or keep. She never would be. She was leaving in the morning and going home. He was going to wave her off with no regrets, and reclaim the life he'd led before the accident had blown it apart. That was the plan and it was a good one, a necessary one.

Nevertheless, when he held her in his arms in bed that night he did so a little more tightly. He found himself noting every sound she uttered, every move she made, and storing them somewhere safe. And when he moved inside her, he realised he was trembling.

'Are you all right?' she asked softly, once the sweat had cooled on their skin and their harsh, heavy breathing had faded.

'I'm fine,' he said, but he wasn't. He didn't know what was wrong with him. All he knew was that he wasn't fine at all.

CHAPTER TWELVE

ON THE MORNING of her departure, while Rico was in the shower Carla was methodically folding and putting clothes into the suitcase she'd had to buy to accommodate her recent purchases. But if anyone had asked her to itemise those clothes, she'd have merely blinked in bewilderment.

The drenching she'd had yesterday afternoon had been an almighty shock but not nearly as great as the one that had led to it. Ever since, she'd been able to think of nothing but the stunning realisation she was in love with Rico.

Which couldn't possibly be.

She'd known him for less than a week. She didn't know what love was. Not this kind of love. She loved Georgie, of course, and even her parents, despite all their flaws, but this was entirely different. This was... well, she didn't know what this was.

And yet all these feelings, which had been rushing around inside her for a while but now flooded her like a tsunami, had to mean something. Why else would her heart tighten every time she thought of what he'd been through? Why else would she overflow with admiration and respect at what he'd achieved? He was the only person she wanted to talk to. The only person alive she wanted to tell everything to and find out everything about. He'd become her world. He'd even saved her from sinking.

So much for steering clear of emotional intimacy, she thought, her pulse pounding and her head spinning as she distractedly packed. She'd been creating it and encouraging it since the moment she'd met him.

And had that been such a bad thing?

No.

Quite the opposite in fact.

He'd shown her that ceding emotional ground didn't have to lead to vulnerability and weakness. It could actually lead to empowerment and healing instead. He'd shown her what a proper relationship could look like, free from manipulation and fear. How it could be a give and take of ideas and opinions, an exchange of thoughts and experiences, hopes and dreams, and not a loss of identity. He'd given her space. He'd given her choice. If this was love, then she adored him, and when she focused on the happiness beginning to spread through her like sunshine, it was glorious.

When she thought of what Georgie had it didn't fill her with horror, it filled her with envy. When she thought of combining a family with a career she realised it was a challenge she'd be thrilled to embrace.

Could she dare to hope that Rico had reached a similar conclusion and now felt the same way? she wondered, her throat dry and heart thudding wildly as he took her cases downstairs and loaded up the boat.

Like her he'd said little since her dip in the lagoon, but somehow she sensed that, like her, he'd changed. He'd dropped his facade and shown her the whole of the man beneath. He'd opened up to her. He'd told her things she didn't think he'd told anyone ever before. He'd trusted her with his past and his soul. Despite his reluctance, he'd let her into his sanctuary, into his life. That had to have meant something.

And then, the tenderness with which he'd made love to her last night… That had definitely been new, as was the glittering warmth with which she'd caught him looking at her on several occasions over the last couple of days.

There was so much to this amazing, complex, beautiful man, she thought dizzily as they sped across the lagoon towards the airport, the exhilarating rush of wind blowing through her body and whipping up a storm inside her. So much more that she longed to know. She wanted to talk with him, make love with him and fight his corner, today, tomorrow, for ever.

So what happened now? Time was running out. All too soon the airport hove into view and then he was slowing the engine of the boat and tossing a loop of rope over a mooring post.

Did she dare hope he might, like her, want more? Might he ask her to stay the rest of the weekend? What would she do if he did? What would she do if he didn't? Was she brave enough to take the initiative herself? Was she ready to take the greatest risk of her life?

Oh, this was *awful*.

Having deposited her bags on the jetty, Rico helped her off the boat and pushed his sunglasses up onto his head. 'Well, here we are,' he said, his voice giving away absolutely nothing.

'Do you mind if I send your phone back in a day or two?' she said, her stomach churning with nerves while her heart hammered frantically. 'It has my boarding pass on it.'

'Keep it as long as you need.'

'I'll put it in the post as soon as I get home and I'll transfer the money I owe you.'

'Fine.'

He looked as if he was going to take a step back and her throat went tight.

'I bought you something,' she said in a rush, swallowing hard as she dug around in her new handbag for the gift she'd seen and impulsively bought for him the day before yesterday. 'A gift. A kitsch gift, admittedly, and one that was technically bought with your money, but still, here.'

She handed it to him, her fingers brushing against his, which made her heart leap for a moment and then plunge when he frowned.

'What is it?'

'A fridge magnet. I picked it up in Murano.' She'd seen it and been amused by it and had a vivid vision of it actually on the door of his fridge, the only personal possession on show in his house.

He stared at the scene of his city, complete with canal, bridge and gondola, depicted in appallingly rendered relief above a bright red 'Venezia', as if he'd never seen such a horrendous thing in his life and had no idea what to do with it, which instantly made her regret her decision to give it to him.

'*Grazie,*' he muttered, eventually slipping it into his pocket, since clearly there was nowhere else for it to go.

'It's I who should be thanking you,' she said, wishing fervently she'd never bought it in the first place and covering her embarrassment with a shaky smile. 'It's been quite a week.'

'It has indeed.'

For a moment he just looked at her while she willed him to ask her to stay, but he remained resolutely silent, so she took a deep breath and before her courage could desert her said, 'I wondered if maybe you'd like to meet for dinner in London, next time you're there.'

He froze. For the briefest of seconds she thought she caught a glimpse of pleasure light the depths of his eyes, but it was gone in a flash and there instead was the cool indifference she'd thought long gone. 'I'm not planning on a trip any time soon,' he said, with a return to the drawl she hated.

'Maybe I'll find myself back in Venice some time,' she said doggedly. 'Maybe I'll look you up instead.'

'You'd be wasting your time. There'd be nothing waiting for you here.'

The flatness of his tone struck her square in the chest, knocking the breath from her lungs, and she reeled. Where had the man she'd fallen in love with gone? Where was the smile and the warmth?

'Are you sure?' she said, her voice cracking a little in response to the ice she could feel forming inside him.

'Quite sure.'

His expression was unreadable and his eyes were devoid of every emotion in existence, but his meaning couldn't be any clearer. For whatever reason, he didn't want her the way she wanted him and it was agony.

'Right. No. Of course not. Sorry,' she said, a thousand tiny darts stabbing at her chest.

'We agreed a week.'

'I know.'

'I'm sorry I can't give you what you want, Carla.'

Couldn't? Or wouldn't? She wasn't going to ask. There was only so much humiliation she could bear. 'It's fine,' she said, dredging up a smile from who knew where because she was not going to fall apart in front of him, however much it cost her. 'It's not your fault I fell in love with you.' The almost imperceptible widening of his eyes was the only indication he'd heard what she'd said. Other than that he remained silent, his face expressionless. 'None of this is your fault,' she continued. It was hers. All hers. She was the one who'd read too much into everything and come to conclusions that didn't exist. However much it broke her heart, he might never be ready to embrace everything she and life had to offer and there was nothing she could do about it. 'I just have one last request,' she said shakily, determined that *some* good should come of this.

'Name it.'

'I know I can't force you to see things my way about getting to know Finn, but you've been looking for a family, Rico, and you have one. A great one. Please say you'll at least think about meeting him. At least give me that.'

For the longest of moments he didn't say anything—was he really going to make her beg, after everything?—but then he gave a short nod. *'Va bene,'* he said. 'I can give you that. I'll think about it.'

'Thank you.'

And with her heart in bits, her body aching with sadness and disappointment, the warmth of the day and the sunshine beating down on her a bitter contrast to the chill seeping into her bones and the darkness now enveloping her like a heavy black cloud, Carla turned on her heel and walked away.

With every step she took the strength leached from her limbs, but despite the stinging of her eyes and the sobs building in her chest she held it together through Check-in. She made her way through Security and Passport Control without giving in to the pain clawing at her stomach and shredding her heart.

It was only once she was on the plane and in the air and Rico hadn't made a dramatic appearance to declare his love for her and beg her to stay—as she'd secretly, *stupidly*, been hoping—that her defences exploded and she crumbled.

How could she have got it so wrong? she thought desperately, tears leaking out of her eyes and rolling down her cheeks as she stared out of the window, her heart breaking at the realisation that with every second she was leaving him behind. She'd been so sure. He'd taken on an employee in order to spend more time with her. He'd sought her counsel and shared intimate details of his past. He—a man who had spent so long on his own—had let her into his world.

But she *hadn't* got it wrong, she told herself, nudging her sunglasses out of the way so she could wipe her eyes with a tissue as she went over the conversation for the hundredth time. He'd been tempted to say yes to dinner. He'd wanted to embrace everything she'd offered. She'd felt it. So why the resistance? Why didn't he want to fight for her the way she wanted to fight for him? Why was his attachment to the past more important than a future with her? Why wasn't she enough? Why wouldn't he allow himself to love her?

She'd taken the biggest gamble of her life, she realised, the pain slicing through her and splitting her wide open unlike any she'd felt before, and she'd lost. What was she going to do?

Rico spent the first day following Carla's departure once again thanking God at having had such a lucky escape. He'd been right to recognise the danger of her wanting more. He'd been right to reject her offer of dinner in London.

But as the relief faded the guilt set in. That she'd fallen in love with him was his fault. He should have put a stop to it sooner. He should have resisted her allure. He should never have opened up to her. He should never have let her into his life in the first place.

The rampant remorse sent him to his gym, where he tried to sweat out the image of how devastated she'd looked when he'd said there was nothing left for her here, which seemed to be permanently etched into his memory. He'd hurt her further when she'd declared she was in love with him and he hadn't said a word, he realised grimly as he rowed a stretch of the Arno on the ergometer, his muscles screaming with every stroke. He'd done more than that. He'd crushed her. But who the hell fell in love in a week?

If only he could remove her from his head as decisively as he'd removed her from his home. He didn't want her hanging around in there with her smiles and her warmth. It shouldn't have even been hard to do. It wasn't as if she'd left anything behind apart from that *maledetto* fridge magnet that was hideous and served no purpose and which he should have tossed in the bin instead of slapping it on the door of his fridge and then doing his best to ignore it. He'd never wanted reminders of the past, he was all about looking forward, and he'd never understood why people grew so attached to things.

Carla definitely fell into the category of 'the past' yet annoyingly, *frustratingly*, his house was full of her. Everywhere he looked he could see her, especially in his bedroom, and the images that bombarded him were as vivid as they were unsettling. The villa felt strangely empty without her and when he wasn't on the treadmill, running up and down virtual hills and pounding along virtual paths through virtual valleys and villages, he prowled around it, oddly restless and unpleasantly on edge. Being alone had never bothered him before. It was irritating and frustrating that it did now. He didn't even have much work to distract him, since the fund manager he'd hired was so keen to impress.

Unable to stand it any longer, Rico went to Milan to visit a client. The fact that the city was also home to the law firm where his parents had lodged their letter to him all those years ago was not a coincidence.

Because when he wasn't remonstrating with himself about how badly he'd handled Carla and regretting the promise guilt had forced him to make, he found he couldn't stop thinking about these brothers of his, the family he might have out there. Long before he'd met her and lost his mind, Finn at least had been lurking in the depths of his conscience, unwelcome and unacknowledged but nevertheless there.

Rico remembered all too clearly how he'd felt when he'd first seen the picture of his brother in the press, the sense of something missing slipping into place. Carla had been right about that, and although it pained him to admit it he was beginning to wonder if she might have been right about other things. Such as the importance and the significance of family. The basic human need for connection. He'd always operated alone and relied solely on himself—he'd even found having to put himself in the hands of medical experts in the aftermath of his accident frustrating and annoying—but perhaps that was what he'd subconsciously been seeking while taking ever-increasing risks and continually pushing himself to do and be more. Maybe that was what he'd always wanted but had been too wary of being exploited and used again to actually reach out and grab. And so perhaps it wasn't the accident on its own that had affected him, but seeing the photo of Finn in conjunction with it.

Rico had never been bothered by the idea of his own mortality, but it looked as if he was now. He didn't want to die alone in some mountain range. He didn't want to die full stop. His nihilistic approach to life no longer appealed. He didn't want to just fill the days with things that would merely pass the time. Risks now needed to be calculated and recklessness curtailed. He wanted to *live*.

And if everything now running through his head was quite possibly true, then wouldn't it be a good idea to establish contact with Finn? Couldn't he do with allowing someone else into his life and vice versa? How would he know if the gaping void where his soul should be could be filled if he didn't give it a chance?

At least if Finn had been searching for him for months, the likelihood of being rejected by him was low. His brother's email, which had been lurking in his inbox, repeatedly snagging his attention until he'd had no option but to open it and which had contained an invitation to visit at any time, had certainly been encouraging.

Actually meeting his brother needn't open the can of worms he'd feared, he told himself repeatedly. And even if it did, what made him automatically assume he wouldn't be able to handle it? Wasn't it a bit cowardly to keep hiding himself away under the pretext of being better off alone? Was *anyone* better off wholly alone and cut off?

Well, he was about to find out.

Exactly two weeks after he'd first made the trip here,

Rico found himself once more at Finn Calvert's door. Not skulking beneath a tree, but actually on the doorstep, on another Saturday afternoon in June.

For a moment he stood there, stock still, his heart thumping so hard and fast it reverberated in his ears, his every muscle tight with tension, anticipation and trepidation. Despite his efforts to downplay the significance of what was about to happen, it was huge. With every passing second his brother and a life irrevocably changed came that bit closer. If he wanted to, this was his last chance to walk away. But he didn't. He was done with the life he used to lead. He and Finn had an appointment and this time he was going to keep it.

And it would be fine, Rico assured himself, taking a deep breath and stiffening his spine as he banged the huge brass knocker twice against the door. This brother of his dominated the hospitality industry and one didn't get to a position like that by being sentimental. There wouldn't be an overload of emotion. No one needed that. And in the unlikely event a heart-to-heart *did* appear to be in the offing, if things moved too fast all he had to do was deflect it and slow them down.

The seconds ticked interminably by, and then came the sound of footsteps, just about audible above the thunder of his pulse. The latch lifted and the door swung open and there, on the other side of the threshold, stood his brother. His *identical* brother, physically at least, bar a few superficial differences. He'd been right about that. Expecting it, even, given how long he'd spent looking at the photo over the last couple of days.

What he hadn't been expecting, however, was the

sense of recognition that suddenly slammed into him, smashing through his exterior and striking at his marrow, crushing the air from his lungs and leeching the strength from his knees.

Staring into his brother's eyes was like looking in on himself. The urge to stride over and give him a hug roared up through him, along with the sudden extraordinary concern that Finn might not like him, none of which made any sense, when he hadn't hugged anyone in over twenty years and it didn't matter what Finn thought of him.

'Federico Rossi,' he said, getting a grip of the emotions running riot inside him and holding out a hand to forestall any attempt at something closer from the man who was staring back at him with a gaze containing just as much shock and curiosity that his own had to have. 'Rico.'

'Finn Calvert,' his brother said, taking it. 'Come in.'

'*Grazie,*' he replied, glancing down at the familiar fingers gripping his with similar strength for a moment before forcing himself to let go.

'You have no idea how pleased I am to meet you,' said Finn, breaking into an enviably easy, genuine smile as he stood back to allow Rico to pass. 'I've been looking for you for months. I thought Carla was mad when she told us she was going to Venice to get you to change your mind, but I can't deny I'm glad it worked.'

His heart lurched at the mention of her name, but he swiftly contained it and got a grip. 'How much did she tell you about me?'

'Not a lot. A few basic facts. She said she hadn't got very far.'

She'd got very far indeed. Too far. At which point he'd pushed her away. Which had been absolutely the right thing to do. He had no business wondering how she'd been, he reminded himself, biting back the question on the tip of his tongue. No business knowing he didn't deserve her loyalty but being inexplicably pleased he had it anyway.

'But she did mention that we were identical.'

'Not quite,' Rico replied, snapping himself out of it and forcing himself to focus.

'No. How did you get the scars?'

'A misspent youth.'

'I look forward to hearing all about it,' Finn said, opening the door to the study that only a fortnight ago had put the fear of God into Rico, and heading on in. 'I had one of those briefly. Drink?'

'Sure.'

'Take a seat.'

'Thank you.'

Selecting one of the two wing-backed armchairs in front of the fireplace, Rico sat down and glanced around. Strange to think that this room with all its photos had once had him running for the hills, while today he could take it all in with relative equanimity, even if the sight of so much clutter was making him inwardly wince. Even stranger to think that where once he'd had no interest in his brother, now he could barely contain the curiosity ripping through him. The force with which

questions were ricocheting around his head, multiplying
with every second, was making his pulse race.

'How do you feel about milk?' said Finn, bending
down at the sideboard and opening a cupboard.

'It makes me want to throw up,' Rico said, willing
everything inside him to calm down so he could process it.

'Me too. We'd better stick to Scotch.'

'Fine with me.'

Finn took a moment to fix the drinks, then handed
Rico a generously filled glass and sat in the chair opposite. 'So what made you change your mind about
meeting me? You disappeared pretty quickly the last
time you were here.'

'I wasn't prepared.'

'But you are now?'

'Not entirely.'

For a moment his brother just looked at him in
shrewd understanding. 'I can appreciate that. When
I discovered I was adopted—and that I had siblings I
knew nothing about—it turned my world upside down.'

'In what way?'

'In pretty much every way. Everything I thought I
knew had been a lie. Or that was what I believed, at
least.'

'You don't now?'

'Thanks to Georgie, no.'

Another woman with undue influence, although Finn
didn't seem particularly bothered by it. Judging by the
smile playing at his mouth and the softening of his ex-

pression, he didn't mind at all. And perhaps his brother's life had been as gilded as he'd assumed.

'I came because of this.' Reaching into the top pocket on the inside of his jacket, Rico withdrew the letter he'd picked up from the solicitors only yesterday. As if having his thoughts dominated by Carla and Finn wasn't frustrating enough, he hadn't been able to stop thinking about that either, wondering now what it might contain, whether it might somehow be useful. He'd had to find out if it still existed before he drove himself mad. To both his astonishment and that of the archivist, it had been found in a file in a box in the basement.

'What is it?'

'A letter left for me by my adoptive parents to be read at the age of eighteen.'

'And did you read it?'

'Not then. I have now.'

'What does it say?'

Rico didn't have to look at it to remind himself of its contents. He knew every word off by heart. It was a letter penned by his mother and filled with love. She'd written about how much she and his father loved him and always would, but if he ever wanted to look for his birth parents, they'd understand and he should start here. He had broken down when he'd read it. The anger, grief and regret that he'd never had a chance to process had slammed into him and he'd sunk to the floor, racked with so much torment and pain that it had taken hours to blow itself out.

'It gives the name of the agency my parents used to adopt me,' he said gruffly.

'Would you mind if I gave that information to the investigator I have working on the case?'

'Not at all.'

'Thank you.'

'No problem.'

'And how would you feel about doing a joint interview?'

'What kind of an interview?'

'The kind that might go viral and be seen by our elusive third brother.'

It would mean stepping out of the shadows, Rico thought with a faint frown as he rubbed his chest and briefly wondered at the absence of the cold sweat he might have expected at the idea. It would mean a rejection of the past and embracing the future.

But perhaps that was all right.

He'd once thought his life didn't need changing, but he could see now that it most definitely did. His life before Carla had blown into it like a whirlwind had been terrible. A cold, empty desert, devoid of colour and light and warmth. For the week he'd shared it with her, it had been brighter and shinier and better.

She'd shown him what it could be like to let someone in. When he thought about the void he'd lived with for so long, he couldn't find it. She'd filled it with promise and hope. She'd helped put him back together. She'd risen to his defence. She'd never once been anything other than honest and upfront with him. She'd given him her love and her loyalty, even after everything she'd been through, and what had he done?

Still determined to believe that he could only survive if he remained alone, he'd sent her away.

What he'd lost hit him then with the force of a battering ram, slamming into the mile-high walls he'd spent years constructing and reducing them to rubble and dust.

Carla, with her unassailable belief in family and friends, was everything he'd never known he wanted, he realised, his head pounding with the realisations now raining down on him. Everything he'd been subconsciously seeking his entire life while convincing himself that he wasn't lonely and he didn't need anyone. She was strong and brave and tough. And, *Dio*, the loyalty she so fiercely believed in... He'd been on the receiving end of that and it had been stunning.

He'd had the chance to build a future with someone who understood him and who he understood. After years of searching he'd finally found a place to belong and develop new foundations upon which, with her, he could have built a life, something brilliant and strong.

How could he have been such a fool?

Well, he was done with allowing his preoccupation with the past to influence his present. He'd let it dictate his thoughts, his behaviour and his actions for too long. Carla had shown him a glimpse of what his life could be if he took a risk and spent it with her.

And taking the risk was exactly what he was going to do, because as he looked briefly around Finn's study he realised that he wanted the photos. He wanted what Finn had. All of it. And he wanted it with Carla. Seven days ago he'd wondered who the hell fell in love in a week. Well, apparently, he thought, giving free rein to the emotions that had been clamouring for acknowledgement for days and letting them buffet him, that would be him.

'Fix up the interview,' he said, his heart banging so hard against his ribs he feared one might crack. 'It's a good idea.'

'It was Carla's.'

Of course it was. All the good ideas were hers.

'Would you mind if we continued this conversation another time?' he said, leaping to his feet as if the chair were on fire. 'There's somewhere I have to be.'

CHAPTER THIRTEEN

CARLA SAT AT the table on her tiny roof terrace, the glass of rosé before her untouched and the rays of the setting sun doing little to warm the chill she felt deep inside her that just wouldn't shift.

When was it going to stop? she wondered with a sniff. When was the pain going to go away?

She'd done her best to keep herself busy over the last seven days. Unable to face work when she was liable to burst into tears without warning, she'd requested another week's leave. She'd gone to Wales to talk to her parents because in the midst of her agony it had struck her that she'd never told them she didn't hold them responsible for what had happened to her and she'd needed to rectify that. There'd been conversation and hugs and even more tears and she'd invited them to come and stay any time before leaving, feeling as if a great weight had lifted from her shoulders.

If only the same could be said for the weight in her heart.

She'd tried so hard to talk herself out of her feelings for Rico. She'd been one hundred per cent mistaken in her conviction he did feel something for her, she'd told herself resolutely. She'd had no indication that what they'd shared had been anything other than casual. He'd considered her a tourist, someone who by definition was transient. For all she knew, he shared his past with all his lovers. She might be the only one he'd ever invited to stay on his island but that had just been circumstance. She hadn't been special and she'd been a fool to think otherwise.

But even if she had been special, none of it had been real. For the brief period they'd been together, they'd existed in a bubble. Neither of them had been living their real life. He was based in Venice, while she lived here in London. He was a billionaire, while she was most definitely not. He owned funds and islands, private jets and helicopters and who knew what else? She owned a one-bedroom top-floor flat in Zone 3 and a six-year-old second-hand car.

What she thought she'd been doing giving him that fridge magnet she had no idea. He'd looked at it as if he'd never seen such an awful thing in his life. Clearly the sun had got to her because what on earth would a worldly billionaire with scars and an edge want with a fridge magnet? He, the man who didn't do trinkets of any kind, let alone seriously tasteless ones, was hardly going to have had a revelation about something *she'd* given him. No doubt it had gone in the bin the minute she'd left.

In fact, she'd had a lucky escape, she'd just about managed to convince herself. If things had carried on in the same vein, with that intensity, how long would it have been before she found herself so wrapped up in him she didn't want to be anywhere else? Before her identity and her independence completely disappeared? Before she became wholly reliant on him for her happiness and well-being and everything else? And see how she'd feared putting her emotions into the hands of a man? Well, she'd been right to.

She was *glad* he hadn't asked her to stay, and even gladder he'd been honest, even if it had been brutal. He'd saved her from a world of torment. Except he hadn't, because she was in torment now, and she didn't believe any of the stuff she'd been trying to tell herself anyway.

But the pain would subside eventually, she told herself wretchedly, as yet another wave of sadness washed over her, pricking her eyes and tightening her throat. She'd get over him and this endless misery. She'd got over far worse. The excruciating longing she felt when she thought about everything Georgie had would fade with time. Of course it would. She had work. She had friends. And now family. She wasn't alone.

On Monday she'd send his phone back. She had to rid herself of her ridiculous obsession with scrolling through all the photos of him she'd taken. It wasn't healthy. The amount of wine she'd consumed over the last week wasn't particularly healthy either. And as for the *linguine alla vongole* she ordered night after night from her local Italian restaurant, well, that had to stop too.

Tonight's delivery, she vowed, despondently getting to her feet in response to the buzzer and heading into the kitchen to let her favourite delivery guy in, would be the last. Because what choice did she have but to move on, however much it broke her heart?

But when she opened the door and found Rico standing there, actually there on her doorstep, holding her bag of food and looking so handsome he took her breath away, she realised she could no more move on than she could fly to the moon. She was rooted to the spot, her heart suddenly thundering and her head spinning.

'May I come in?'

His voice was gruff, and he looked as tired as she felt, and she desperately wanted to take him in her arms and smooth the exhaustion away because God, she'd missed him so much. But she didn't know why he was here, and he'd hurt her badly, so instead she lifted her chin and straightened her spine. She had to be so careful around this man.

'Sure.' She stood aside to let him in, and closed her eyes against the effect of his scent on her.

'Here,' he said, handing her the bag of food once she'd closed the door and turned back to him. 'Supper?'

'Yes,' she said, taking it from him and dumping it in the kitchen before heading onto the terrace, where at least there was air. And rosé. 'Wine?' she asked him, indicating the bottle with a wave of her hand before sitting down.

'No, thank you,' he said, folding himself into the only other chair on her balcony and fixing his gaze on her, at which point she realised that her eyes and nose were probably red and her cheeks had to be horribly blotchy, but it was too late to worry about that. He was too big for her balcony, really. Not to mention wildly out of place, with his gorgeous Italian looks and the edge that she found so attractive, while she looked a wreck. She'd been right about their lives being worlds apart. His house had a view of Venice. Hers had a view of a car park.

'So what are you doing here, Rico?' she said, unable to stand the scrutiny and the tension any longer. 'I thought you weren't planning a trip to London.'

'I went to see Finn this afternoon.'

Oh. Well. That was good. 'I'm glad.'

'It was time.'

What else might it be time for? Her? No. She was through with trying to figure out what he was thinking. 'Are you going to see him again?'

'I'm hoping to, yes.'

That was probably why he'd come. To give her an update about something he knew she cared deeply about. 'Then I guess our paths are bound to cross in the future,' she said, the smile she fixed to her face the hardest thing she'd had to do in weeks. 'But it needn't be embarrassing. You don't need to worry that I'll be making a fool of myself again. It'll be like nothing ever happened.'

He gave a harsh laugh and shoved his hands through his hair. 'Believe me, *tesoro*, that is *not* something I'm worried about.'

'Then what *are* you worried about?'

'That I might have screwed things up with you for good.'

Her heart hammered and time seemed to slow right down. 'What do you mean?'

'I'm in love with you, Carla.'

She went very still as his words hit her brain. 'What?' she breathed.

'I love you.'

'Since when?'

'Since the moment I met you, I suspect,' he said with the faintest of smiles that faded when he added, 'I only realised it, however, two hours and thirty minutes ago. I'm sorry it took me so long to figure it out.'

'But you sent me away,' she said, desperately wanting to believe him but so very wary at the same time.

'I know.'

'You hurt me.'

'I'm so sorry. Every time I think about what I said, it kills me.'

'Why did you?'

'I've been alone a long time,' he said, holding her gaze steadily and making no attempt to dodge or deflect the question. 'It's a hard habit to break. I didn't recognise what was happening to me.' He inhaled deeply. 'The thing is, *amore mio*, when I arrived in Milan to start work, I shut myself down and put it all behind me. It was the only way I could move forward. I closed off my emotions and kept myself apart. Nothing mattered. I took risks because I had nothing to lose. I've lived like that for years. And it was fine. And then I had the accident and saw the photo of Finn and it wasn't quite so fine, although I had no idea why. You asked me why I showed up at his house. Well, I genuinely had no idea. I'd acted purely on instinct. You showed me why, Carla,' he said, leaning forwards and enveloping her with his heat and the scent she loved so much. 'And because of you I don't want to be alone any more. You were right all along. Something has been missing from my life and I know what it is now. I've been looking for a place to belong and someone to belong with ever since my parents died, and I've finally found it. With you. We *are* kindred spirits, Carla. You were right about that too. We belong together. I love you and I'm sorry beyond words that I hurt you. I asked you once before not to give up on me. And I know I don't deserve it but I'm asking you again. Please don't. I don't think I could stand losing you again.'

He stopped and looked at her, everything in his heart there for her to see in his expression. His eyes were dark and intense and the love and absolute certainty she saw in their depths shattered the fragile barrier she'd hastily erected around her heart. And suddenly she was awash with all the emotions she hadn't dared to dream.

This was what love was, she thought dizzily, revelling in the swelling of her heart and the overwhelming happiness that was now rushing through her. This. Trust and belonging and healing and the promise of forever.

'You won't,' she said, her throat tight with emotion.

'Really?'

'I never gave up on you, Rico,' she said, rising from her seat and moving towards him at the same time as he reached out and pulled her astride him, 'and I never will.' He let out a shuddering breath and dropped his head to her chest. 'I love you,' she said against his hair. 'You've shown me the life I want to live. And that life is with you. Although how we'd make it work when you live in Venice and I live in London I have no idea.'

'I can work from anywhere,' he said, lifting his head and shifting her closer. 'I have an apartment here.'

'But Venice is your home.'

'My home is wherever you are,' he said softly, taking her hand and placing it over his wildly thundering heart. 'Show me your world, Carla. It's so much brighter than mine. You've given me back hope. You've given me a future. Look.' Easing back slightly, he took his phone out of his jacket pocket and she noted that his hand was shaking a little too. After a moment he held the device up to her and she gasped. The picture was of his fridge, and there stuck right in the middle of the door, like a beacon, was her magnet.

'I assumed you'd have thrown it away,' she said, her eyes stinging as emotion overwhelmed her.

'I intended to. I couldn't. I'm done with detachment and distance,' he said gruffly. 'I want to make memories with you, *amore mio*. I want to fill our life with clutter and light and love.'

'God, I've missed you.'

'You can't have missed me as much as I've missed you,' he said with the slightest of smiles that lit up her heart. 'My life meant nothing before you crashed into it. Now it means everything. *You* mean everything. You are my *anima gemella*, my soulmate.'

'And you're mine,' she said, everything she was feeling rocketing around inside her and making her giddy. 'But it's only been a couple of weeks. It's madness.'

'We have a whole lifetime to work on the details.'

'A whole lifetime?' she echoed as he took her in his

arms and pulled her as close as he could. 'I think I like the sound of that.'

'We'll figure it out together,' he said, bending his head and pressing his mouth to the sensitive spot on her neck beneath her ear and making her shiver.

'I think I like the sound of that too.'

'Il mio cuore,' he murmured, dotting a trail of kisses along her jaw.

'And that.'

And a kiss at the corner of her mouth. *'Ti amo.'*

'Especially that.'

And then he kissed her properly and carried her into her bedroom, and after that she gave up thinking at all.

EPILOGUE

Identical Strangers, 1.6 million views, a week ago

'So apart from looks,' came the voice of the interviewer off-screen, 'how similar are the two of you?'

'It's early days,' said Finn with an easy smile as he shifted in his seat and hooked the ankle of one leg over the knee of the other. 'But I'd say pretty similar. We're both great with numbers and mildly allergic to milk, so that's a start.'

'You're married, is that right?'

Finn gave a nod, a smile spreading across his face. 'That's absolutely right.'

'Any wedding bells on the horizon for you, Rico?' said the interviewer.

'I couldn't possibly comment,' said Rico with a smile half the size of Finn's but which lit up his face twice as much. 'All I will say is, watch this space.'

'We certainly will. Do either of you have anything else to add? Any message for your missing brother?'

'Just this,' said Rico, leaning forwards and looking seriously and directly down the lens. 'If you're out there and able to, please get in touch. Contact Alex Osborne of Osborne Investigations. We want to hear from you. And I can absolutely guarantee it'll be worth it.'

* * * * *

The Billionaire Without Rules

DEDICATION

For the parents at my kids' school, whom I shamelessly mined for info on many topics that pop up in this trilogy, from adoption to postpartum psychosis to how to get stranded in Venice to Caribbean floating bars to hacking into Times Square billboards. You know who you are!

CHAPTER ONE

'GREAT, ALEX, YOU'RE BACK. You'll never *guess* who's waiting for you in your office.'

Having shrugged off her jacket, Alexandra Osborne hung it and her bag on the coat stand and levelled her assistant and sometime associate, Becky, a look. She was in no mood for games. Or, right now, for Becky's perennially bubbly enthusiasm. She'd just ended yet another call informing her that a promising lead had gone absolutely nowhere and her gloom and anxiety were at an all-time high.

The absence of progress with regard to the case she'd been working on for the past eight months was both teeth-grindingly maddening and desperately worrying.

Last December, after discovering an adoption certificate while going through his late father's papers, billionaire hotelier Finn Calvert had hired her to look into the circumstances surrounding his birth.

Despite there being exceptionally little to go on, Alex had nevertheless eventually managed to trace the trail to a derelict orphanage on the Argentina-

Bolivia border, where paperwork had been found in a battered filing cabinet that suggested her client was one of a set of triplets. Finn had immediately instructed her to locate the others, and she'd poured considerable time and resources into it, to depressingly little avail.

One of Finn's long-lost brothers, Rico Rossi, had turned up six weeks ago, in possession of a letter that gave details of the agency his parents had used to adopt him thirty-one years before and, with the injection of new information, Alex had had high hopes. But the agency no longer existed and so far no one had been able to locate any archived records.

After a promising start she'd hit brick wall after brick wall. Even the interview that Finn and Rico had recently recorded, in which they'd entreated their third missing brother to come forward, had produced no genuine leads. It had been eight long months of precious little development and she desperately needed a breakthrough, because she could *not* allow this assignment to fail.

For one thing, she had a one hundred per cent success rate that her pride would not have ruined. For another, Finn Calvert was a hugely powerful and influential client who, upon successful completion of the mission, would be paying her not only the remaining half of her fee but a staggeringly generous bonus. His recommendation would open doors and his money would pay off debts that were astronomical since London premises and the kit required to do the job didn't come cheap.

Both, she'd realised when she'd accepted the case, would accelerate her expansion plans by around four years and all those people who should have supported and encouraged her when young, but who'd instead believed she'd never amount to anything and hadn't hesitated to tell her so, would be laughing on the other side of their face far sooner than she'd anticipated. Her success would be cemented and she'd have proved once and for all that she'd conquered not only the environmental obstacles she'd encountered growing up but also the fear that with one false move she could end up like her deadbeat family.

There was no way she'd *ever* pass up the chance of that, so she'd thrown everything at it, even going so far as to turn down other lucrative work in order to devote all her time and resources to this one job, which would secure her future and realise her dreams.

She'd assumed it would be as straightforward as other similar cases had been, that she'd easily track down the adoption paperwork and from there find the answers Finn craved. She'd never expected to be in this position all these months later. Having to admit the possibility of defeat and being forced to move on to different assignments in order to stave off the threat of looming bankruptcy made her want to throw up.

'Who is it?' she asked, mustering up a smile while reminding herself that it wasn't Becky's fault progress was so slow and she had no right to take her worry or her bad mood out on her assistant.

'Only our missing triplet.'

Alex stopped in her tracks, the smile on her face freezing, the floor beneath her feet tilting for a second. All her churning thoughts skidded to a halt and her head spun. Seriously? The man she'd invested so much time and so many resources in looking for was here? Actually here? After so much disappointment and despair, it was hard to believe.

'You're joking.'

'I am *not*,' said Becky, practically bouncing on her seat. 'His name is Max Kentala and he arrived about five minutes ago.'

'Oh, my God.'

'I *know*. I was literally just about to text you.'

'I was beginning to give up hope of ever finding him,' said Alex, a rush of relief colliding with the shock still zinging around her system.

'Well, technically he found you,' her assistant pointed out in an unhelpful way that Alex decided to ignore.

'He must have seen the interview,' she said instead, her pulse racing as she tidied her shirt and smoothed her skirt.

'Ah, so that I *don't* know,' Becky admitted ruefully. 'I tried to find out how he came to be here but he was incredibly tight-lipped. Impossible to read. And, to be honest, it was kind of hard to concentrate. He's every bit as gorgeous as his brothers, maybe even more so, although I don't see how that's possible, given they're identical give or take a haircut and the odd scar or two. We're talking not just hot, but *scorchio,*' she added, her expression turning dreamy as she gazed into the distance. 'I think it's the eyes. That blue… They kind of make you forget your own name… I wonder if he's single…'

'Becky.'

Her assistant snapped back and pulled herself together. 'Yes, sorry,' she said with a grin as she fanned her face. 'Phew. Anyway, I showed him into your office and made him a coffee. I'll move around the appointments you have.'

'Thanks.'

'Brace yourself.'

Used to Becky's dramatic tendencies—not entirely helpful in a trainee private investigator, she had to acknowledge—Alex ignored the warning and headed for her office, the adrenaline powering along her veins kicking her heart rate up to a gallop.

Max Kentala's hotness was irrelevant, as was his marital status. That he was actually here was very definitely not. On the contrary, depending on what information he brought with him, it could be exactly the breakthrough she was so desperate for. It could be game-changing. If there was the remotest possibility her current predicament could be reversed, she'd grab it with both hands and never let go, so she needed all her wits about her.

Taking a deep breath to calm the shock, relief and anticipation crashing around inside her, Alex pulled her shoulders back, fixed a smile to her face and opened the door to her office.

'Good morning,' she said, her gaze instantly landing on the tall figure standing at her window with his back to her.

A broad back, she couldn't help noticing as her stomach clenched in a most peculiar way. Excellent shoulders. A trim waist, lean hips and long, long legs. Then he turned and his eyes met hers and it was as if time had stopped all over again. The air rushed from her lungs and goose bumps broke out all over her skin. And was it her imagination or had someone turned the heating on?

Well, Becky certainly hadn't been exaggerating, she thought dazedly as she struggled to get a grip on the extraordinarily intense impact of his gaze. *Scorchio* was an understatement. Max Kentala was quite possibly the best-looking man she'd ever come across in her thirty-three years. Not that she particularly went for the dishevelled surfer look. In fact, when she *did* date these days—which was rarely since firstly she tended to work unaccommodating hours and secondly, with a cheating ex-husband in her background, she had a whole host of issues to do with self-esteem and trust—her dates were generally clean-cut and tidy.

This man's unkempt dark hair was far too long for her liking and he was badly in need of a shave. His faded jeans had seen better days, although they did cling rather lovingly to his powerful thighs, and the untucked white shirt he wore so well had clearly never been introduced to an iron.

No. He wasn't her type. So why her stomach was flipping and her mouth had dried was a mystery. Maybe it was the eyes. They really were arrestingly compelling. Blue and deep and enigmatic, they looked as if they held a wealth of secrets—catnip to someone whose job it was to uncover hidden truths—and she wanted to dive right in.

And to do more than that, if she was being honest. She wanted to run her fingers through his hair while she pressed up against what looked like a very solid chest. She wanted to plaster her mouth to his and urge him to address the sudden throbbing ache between her thighs.

It was bizarre.

Alarming.

And deeply, horrifyingly inappropriate.

This man was part of her biggest, most important assignment. He might well hold key information about it. It wouldn't do to forget that. However attractive she found him—and there seemed little point in denying she did—she could not afford to get distracted. So what if he wore no wedding ring? That meant nothing. And as for the throbbing, what was that all about? It hadn't been that long since she'd had sex, had it? A year? Eighteen months at most? And why was she even thinking about sex?

Snapping free from the grip of the fierce, very unwelcome desire burning through her and putting an end to all thoughts of sex, Alex gave herself a mental shake and pulled herself together.

'Alex Osborne,' she said crisply, stepping forwards into the room and holding out her hand for him to shake.

He gave her a brief smile and took it. 'Max Kentala,' he replied, a faint American accent tingeing his deep voice which, to her irritation, sent shivers rippling up and down her spine despite her resolve to withstand his appeal.

'I'm very pleased to meet you, Mr Kentala.'

'Call me Max.'

'Alex,' she said, withdrawing her hand from his and resisting the urge to shake it free of the electricity the contact had sent zapping along her fingers and up her arm. 'Do take a seat.'

'Thank you.'

See, she told herself as she walked round to her side of the desk and smoothly lowered herself into her chair. Cool and professional. That was what she was. Not all hot and quivery and ridiculous. Still, it was good to be able to stop having to rely on her strangely wobbly knees and sit down.

'I take it you saw the interview,' she said, sounding remarkably composed considering she still felt as if she'd been thumped in the solar plexus with a flaming torch.

He gave a brief nod. 'I did.'

'When?'

'Yesterday.'

And now he was here. He hadn't wasted time. Finn was going to be thrilled. 'Can I also assume you'd like me to set up a meeting with your brothers?'

'I set up my own,' he drawled. 'I've just come from seeing them.'

Oh? That wasn't right. In the interview, Rico had told anyone with any information to contact *her*. He and his brother protected their privacy and she'd known the interview would generate more false leads than real ones, as had turned out to be the case. So what did Max think he was doing, bypassing her carefully laid plans like that?

'You were meant to go through me,' she said with a frown, not liking the idea of a potential loose cannon entering the arena one little bit. 'Those were the instructions.'

'But I don't follow instructions,' he said with an easy smile that, annoyingly, melted her stomach. 'I make my own arrangements.'

Not on this, he didn't, she thought darkly, pulling herself together and ignoring the dazzling effect of his smile. Uncovering the truth surrounding the triplets' birth and adoption was *her* assignment. Right from the start, Finn had given her total autonomy. She'd set the rules and established procedure. She was in charge. However glad she was that Max had shown up like this, he had no business meddling. She was not having her entire future potentially snatched away from her simply because he'd decided he was going to do things his way. Her blood chilled at the very thought of it.

Despite the laid-back look and the casual smile, the set of his jaw and the glint of steel in his eye suggested he wasn't to be underestimated, but she wasn't to be underestimated either. She'd given up a steady career in the police force to set up her own private investigating business. She'd taken a huge risk and she'd worked insanely hard. She'd come far but she had a lot further to go. Her dreams were of vital importance. They drove her every day to do more and be better. At one point, as a confused and miserable teenager, they'd been all she had. They were not going to be dashed by anyone or anything. Almost as bad, if everything went to pot and she lost her business, she could well find herself having to re-join the police, where she'd run the risk of bumping into her ex, who'd been a fellow officer and was still in the force, she'd last heard, and no one wanted that.

She needed Finn's good opinion and she needed his money, which meant *she* had to be the one to find the answers. So from here on in the man lounging so casually in the chair on the other side of her desk, looking as if he owned the place when he absolutely didn't, would be toeing *her* line.

'Why are you here, Max? What do you want?'

Sitting back and eyeing the coolly smiling woman in front of him with deceptive self-control, Max could think of a thing or two.

For a start he wanted her to carry on saying his name in that low husky voice, preferably breathing it right into his ear while he unbuttoned her silky-looking shirt and peeled it off her. Then she could shimmy out of the fitted skirt she had on, hop onto the desk and beckon him close. In an ideal world, she'd tug off the band tying her hair back and shake out the shiny dark brown mass while giving him a sultry encouraging smile. It was the lamest of cli-chés, he knew, but hey, this was his fantasy, albeit an unexpected one when he generally didn't go for the smart, tidy professional type.

But he had to admit she was stunning. Beneath the fringe she had wide light blue eyes surrounded by thick dark lashes, high defined cheekbones and a full, very kissable mouth he was finding it hard to keep his gaze off.

The minute he'd turned from the window and laid eyes on her the attraction had hit. He'd felt it in the instant tightening of his muscles, the savage kick of his pulse and the rush of blood south. The intensity of his response, striking with the force of a tsunami, had made him inwardly reel. He couldn't recall the last time he'd been so affected by a woman he'd only just met. Ever?

Not that any of that mattered. The startling im-pact of her clear blue gaze on him, which he'd felt like a blow to the gut and the effects of which still lingered, was irrelevant. As were her trim curves. He wasn't here for a quick, steamy office encoun-ter, even if in an alternative universe Alex Osborne *had* decided to throw caution to the wind and do as he'd imagined.

He was here because of recent events.

Fifteen hours ago, all Max had known of fam-ily was a difficult, demanding mother who lived in New York with husband number four and a father who, after the bitterest of divorces, had abandoned him to move to Los Angeles, where he'd remained determinedly on his own for a decade until he'd suffered a fatal heart attack seven years ago.

To Max, up to the age of fourteen, family had meant endless disapproval and cold stony silences. It had meant constantly walking on eggshells in an environment devoid of true affection and respect, and bending over backwards to please yet failing every single time. It had meant a devastating awareness of not being good enough and living with the relentless guilt at never meeting expectations, all of which worsened after his mom had been granted sole custody of him in the wake of the divorce.

Since then it had involved coming to terms with having had a father who'd essentially abandoned him for good and managing a tricky, complex relationship with a woman who was needy, self-absorbed, hypersensitive and controlling. But he'd done it because she was his mother. Or so he'd always believed.

Then he'd seen the interview given by two men who were the spitting image of him apart from a few superficial differences, and what he'd understood of family had blown wide apart.

Max had been in his study at his home in the Caribbean when the video had been forwarded to him by his assistant with an instruction to click on it immediately. As a cyber security expert with global businesses and governments among his clients he never clicked on anything immediately, regardless of whence the recommendation came. When, at Audrey's insistence, he eventually had, yesterday afternoon, the shock had knocked the air from his lungs and drained the blood from his brain.

Pulse pounding, he'd watched the twenty-minute footage of Finn Calvert and Rico Rossi a further three times, pausing each time on the final frame in which Rico looked straight down the lens and urged their missing triplet to get in touch. He'd stared into the eyes that were identical to his own, the dizziness and chaos intensifying to the point he'd thought he was going to pass out, before gradually calming down enough to allow logic and process to take over.

In urgent need of answers to the myriad questions ricocheting around his head, he'd put in a quick, rare call to his mother, who'd confirmed that he had indeed been adopted from an orphanage in Argentina thirty-odd years ago and had then proceeded to try and make it all about her. Stunned and shaken to the core, Max had hung up before saying something he might regret, and had then hacked into the systems that would disclose as much information as there was about these men who could quite possibly be brothers he'd never known anything about.

Having established, among other things, that Finn and Rico shared his date of birth and were both currently in London, he'd booked himself onto the next flight. On landing this morning, he'd sent them each a message with details of where he'd be and when, should they be interested in meeting up.

Two hours later, the three of them were sitting in the bar of Finn's flagship central London hotel, swapping coffee for vintage champagne in celebration of having found each other after so long apart and firing questions back and forth, as if trying to cram half a lifetime into half a morning.

'Here's to long-lost brothers,' Finn said with a smile that could have been one of Max's own as he lifted his glass and tilted it towards his brothers.

'Saluti,' said Rico, following suit.

'Cheers.' Max tapped his glass against the other two and then knocked back half the contents, the fizz of the bubbles sliding down his throat adding fuel to the maelstrom of thoughts and emotions churning around inside him.

With the revelation that he was adopted, so many questions that had dogged him all his life had suddenly been answered. Such as how on earth he could ever be related to either of his parents, people who bore no resemblance to him either physically or in temperament. Such as why he'd always felt an outsider. Why nothing he'd ever done was good enough. Why his father hadn't fought harder for him in the divorce. The strange yet deep-rooted sense that he wasn't where he was meant to be and he wasn't with the people he was meant to be with.

These were the people he was meant to be with, he knew with a certainty that he felt in his bones. His brothers. Who shared his dislike of milk and his skill with numbers, and who, like him, had had encounters of varying degrees with the law. Who he instantly got and who instantly got him. With whom he felt more of a connection in half an hour than he ever had with either of his so-called parents.

'Any idea how we ended up in an Argentinian orphanage or why we were separated?' Finn asked him and he snapped back.

'None,' he said with a quick frown.

'Nor me,' said Rico.

'Alex has hit a brick wall.'

Max raised his eyebrows. 'Alex?'

'Alex Osborne,' Finn clarified. 'The private investigator I hired. Progress has been virtually non-existent lately, which has been frustrating as hell, but then there isn't a whole lot to go on.'

'How about I look into it?'

'Could you?' asked Rico.

'Sure,' said Max.

Having just come to the end of one contract and the next starting in a month, he had time. He also had resources. But, more than that, he needed to get to the bottom of this. He'd spent the last decade believing he knew exactly who he was and where he was going. The news of his adoption had turned his world on its head. It might have answered many of the questions and cleared up much of the confusion he'd always had, but it had also thrown up even more. Who was he? Where had he come from? How had he ended up where he was? And that was just the start of it. The need for an explanation, for information, burned inside him like the hottest of fires. 'I have an extensive data network and know where to look, so that's a start.'

'It would be good to get to the truth,' Rico said. 'Whatever it may be. Anything you need, let me know.'

'Here are Alex's details,' said Finn, handing him a card.

'Leave it with me,' Max replied.

And now here he was, his pulse beating a fraction faster than usual and his senses oddly heightened as Alex continued to look at him while waiting expectantly and somewhat challengingly for him to tell her what he was doing here.

'I want everything you have on the case,' he said, ignoring the awareness and the buzz of desire firing his nerve-endings, and focusing on what was important.

Her eyebrows arched, her chin lifted and the temperature in the room seemed to drop thirty degrees. 'Why?'

Because he'd worked hard to get over the traumas of his childhood and as proof had spent the last decade living in at least some degree of peace. Because yesterday that peace had been shattered and he badly needed it back. Because he valued his brothers' kinship, wanted their approval and their acceptance—old habits died hard, clearly—and would do anything to get it. And, frankly, because she hadn't exactly got very far.

'Because I'll be taking things from here.'

CHAPTER TWO

WHAT? NO. NO WAY.

Alex stared at the man oozing arrogance from the other side of her desk, the outrage shooting through her doing a very good job of obliterating the inconvenient attraction still fizzing along her veins.

She'd been absolutely right to consider him a loose cannon with the potential to wreak havoc. He clearly posed a greater danger to her plans than she'd originally assumed. But if he thought he could swan in here and take over the investigation, he could think again. She was *not* meekly handing him what little she had just because he demanded it. This was *her* assignment, and her reputation and her *future* were at stake.

'I'm afraid that's not possible,' she said coolly.

He arched an eyebrow and languidly hooked the ankle of one leg over the knee of his other. 'Why not?'

'The information is confidential and Finn's my client,' she said, determinedly not glancing down and following the movement, 'not you.'

'If I needed my brother's authority to act on his

behalf—which I don't—I'd have it. He was the one who gave me your card.'

Right. OK. So why had Finn done that? she wondered, her confidence suddenly plummeting for a moment. Was he unhappy with progress? Had he instructed Max to effectively fire her? She couldn't let that happen. She was *not* going to fail and have her dreams crumble to dust.

'You are not taking over this case,' she said, stiffening her spine and lifting her chin. Why would he even want to? She was the expert here.

'How long have you been working on it?' he asked with a deceptive yet pointed mildness that instantly put her hackles up.

'A while,' she said, wincing a little on the inside.

'Eight months, I heard.'

'It's complicated.'

'I don't doubt it.'

'Information is scarce.'

'Then you're looking in the wrong place.'

Really. She'd put in hundreds of hours of research and mined every database available. She'd built a network of operatives in Argentina and hired subcontractors of whom she asked a lot without enquiring too closely how they were going to get it. She'd looked everywhere there was to look. 'And what would you know of it?'

'Information is my business.'

'What do you do?'

'Cyber security.'

'And?'

'I have access to resources I imagine you can only dream about.'

The faint patronising tone to his words grated on her nerves even as his easy smile was setting off tiny fireworks in the pit of her stomach, and yet she couldn't help thinking, what kind of resources? Legal ones? Illegal ones? *Better* ones?

'But I have people on the ground and they're working hard.'

'They wouldn't be too difficult to find,' he countered with a casual shrug that didn't fool her for a moment because she could hear the implication and the threat behind his words. He didn't need her co-operation. There was nothing stopping him going ahead and embarking on an investigation of his own. He was just here to get a head start.

But if he *did* strike out on his own, *and* got the answers the brothers wanted, then where would she be? Bankrupt. Redundant. The failure that everyone had always expected her to be. And she wasn't having that. Max might not be the type to give up—that steely glint of his had sharpened, she saw—but then neither was she. Whether or not he had the authority to fire her or intended to do so, she was not backing down on this.

Quite apart from her professional pride and the monumental fee she was due to collect, she liked Finn and Rico. She wanted to track down every existing snippet of information about the birth and adoption of these triplets, piece together the story and give them the answers they craved. She'd started the job. She had every intention of finishing it, however hard. It was *her* responsibility, and that was all there was to it.

'I've pursued every avenue there is, Max,' she said, keeping the cool she'd developed over a decade in the police.

'I very much doubt that.'

Behind a casual smile of her own she gritted her teeth. She wasn't incompetent, despite what he clearly thought. 'I've looked into personnel records and bank accounts,' she said with what she considered to be impressive calm under very trying circumstances. 'I've examined company records and sent off freedom of information requests. Every lead has come to nothing. The orphanage was run by nuns and closed around twenty years ago. Everyone who worked there has either died or disappeared. There was a massive earthquake shortly after it shut and all the archives that were held in the town hall basement were destroyed. It was only by some fluke that your birth certificates, which were found at the actual orphanage, survived.

'The adoption agency, which was owned by a holding company, was originally registered in Switzerland,' she continued. 'It also closed down years ago. I've found no records relating to either entity. The only possible link I've established between the agency and the orphanage is three large payments that arrived in the orphanage's bank account around the time of your adoption, originally made in Swiss francs before being converted to pesos. Freedom of information requests have come back with nothing. Swiss banking secrecy at the time hasn't helped. The only end that isn't yet a completely dead one is a possible future DNA match. I sent Finn's off for analysis four months ago.'

'With no result to date.'

'No.'

'It's a long shot.'

At the dismissive tone of his voice, she bristled. 'I am aware of that.'

He regarded her for one long moment, then arched one dark eyebrow. 'So is that it?'

'I've done everything I can.'

'Except for one thing.'

Her brows snapped together. 'What?'

'Actually going there.'

She stared at him. 'To Argentina?'

'No. The moon. Yes, Argentina.'

OK, so, no, she hadn't done that, she had to admit while choosing to ignore Max's derision. She'd considered it, of course, in the beginning. At great length. But she'd come to the conclusion that it could well have been an expensive wild goose chase, which, if she'd found nothing, would have eaten substantially into the budget and, worse, damaged Finn's confidence in her. So she'd stayed in London and opted for a network of local operatives instead to do the legwork on the ground, and told herself that she could always go herself as a last resort.

And that was the point she was at now, she realised with a start. She'd reached the end of the road with what she could do from London. She was all out of options, bar one.

'That was my next plan,' she said smoothly, as if it always had been, while frantically trying to remember how much she had left to spend on her credit card. 'I'll be looking at flights this afternoon.'

'No need.'

The glimmer of triumph that lit the depths of his eyes sent a double jolt of alarm and wariness shooting through her that had nothing to do with the precarious state of her finances. 'Why not?'

'I'm leaving for La Posada first thing in the morning.'

What? *What?* She guessed he'd learned about the abandoned town in which the ruins of the orphanage were located from his brothers but God, he'd worked fast. 'First thing in the morning?' she echoed, reeling.

'Rico's put his plane at my disposal. I'm making use of it. So I'd like everything you have on the case, Alex. Names. Dates. Places. Everything. And I'd like it now.'

In the face of Max's implacability and the realisation that he'd done it again, Alex's brain swirled with frustrated panic and angry confusion. How dared he go behind her back like this? These decisions weren't his to make. Why wouldn't he play by the rules? Did he think they didn't apply to him? Was he really that arrogant?

Whatever his motivation, whatever his methods, whether or not he even *knew* about the rules, he'd backed her into a corner, she realised, a cold sweat breaking out all over her skin. Her least favourite place to be. She had no room for manoeuvre. She was trapped.

But she wasn't going down without a fight. In fact, she thought grimly as a plan to get out of the tight spot he'd put her in began to form in her head, she wasn't going down at all. However high-handed, disagreeable and infuriating Max might be, she was not letting him go off on his own and potentially snatching a victory that was rightfully hers from the jaws of defeat. He was unpredictable and a threat to everything she'd worked so hard for. He needed to be reined in and controlled. How would she be able to do that if he went to Argentina all on his own? And how was she supposed to know what he found, if by some miracle he did indeed find anything, if she stayed in London?

There was only one thing for it. She was going to have to go with him. It needn't be so bad. He might even turn out to be useful. She hadn't yet established what he knew about the past. He might hold crucial information. And what were these resources of his that she could only dream about? She'd be a fool not to enquire about those.

'All right,' she said, setting her jaw and snapping her shoulders back in preparation for battle. 'On one condition.'

'Which is?'

'I go with you.'

In response to Alex's demand, every fibre of Max's being stiffened with resistance. No. Absolutely not. What she was suggesting amounted to teaming up and working together. He did neither. He operated alone. He always had. He'd grown up an only child and had learned at a very early age that he could rely on no one but himself. Now, the highly confidential nature of his work meant he trusted few. Collaboration was something he'd never sought and certainly never wanted.

That Alex's performance wasn't as flawed as he'd previously assumed didn't matter. He didn't want her involvement. Or anyone else's, for that matter. The quest for the truth was going to be intensely personal. He needed to get a grip on the resentment and anger that the call with his mother had sparked and now simmered inside him. He had to find out whether he'd ever been wanted by someone, whether he'd ever mattered. Netting all the emotions that had escaped Pandora's Box and shoving the lid back on them could get messy and no one else needed to be along for that particular ride.

'Absolutely not,' he said curtly.

Her jaw set and her shoulders snapped back. 'Absolutely yes,' she countered with steel in her voice.

'I work alone.'

'Not any more.'

'I'll match what Finn's paying you.'

'It's not just about the money.'

'I find that hard to believe. The bonus he's offered you is exorbitant.'

He could practically hear the grind of her teeth. 'My fee structure is none of your business. If you want me to share with you the information I have,' she said bluntly, 'I go with you. Otherwise you get nothing. That's my offer, Max. Take it or leave it.'

The resolve flashing in the depths of her eyes and the jut of her chin told him she was adamant. That she wasn't going to back down. Which was absolutely fine. He didn't appreciate ultimatums. He'd had enough of those growing up and just the thought of them made his chest tighten and his stomach turn. So he'd leave it. He had no doubt he could get what Alex had already found. He'd never come up against a problem he hadn't been able to solve, family conundrums aside. He didn't need her. He didn't want her—or anyone—in his space and never had. His world was his and his alone, and he'd be far more flexible and focused if he pursued the mystery surrounding his birth on his own.

And yet...

He had to admit he found Alex's fiery determination intriguing. Why was this assignment so important to her? he couldn't help wondering. Why not just take the money and move on? What was she fighting for?

And that wasn't all that was intriguing, he thought, his pulse hammering hard as he let his gaze roam over her beautiful animated face. Her prickliness was having an incredibly intense and wholly unexpected effect on him. It was electrifying his nerve-endings and firing energy along his veins. Lust was drumming through him with a power he'd never have imagined when she was the polar opposite of what he usually found attractive.

She was so defensive, so rigidly uptight. It ought to have been a turn-off, yet he badly wanted to ruffle those sleek feathers of hers, to butt up against her defences. What would it take to break them down? How far would he have to push?

She wasn't immune to him, despite her attempts to hide it. He'd caught the flash of heat in her eyes the moment they'd met. He'd noted the flush on her cheeks before she'd pulled herself together and coolly held out her hand for him to take. She was as attracted to him as he was to her. How satisfying would it be to unravel her until she was in his arms, begging him to undo her completely? How explosive would they be together?

The urge to find the answers to all the questions rocketing around his head thrummed through him. The need to hear her panting his name while writhing beneath him was like a drug thumping in his blood. So what if, instead of rejecting her proposal, he accepted it? What if he did actually allow her to accompany him to Argentina in return for everything she knew? There was little point in replicating the work she'd already done. It would only waste time. Undoubtedly, two heads would be more efficient than one.

And while they investigated he could work on unbending her. They'd have to find *something* to occupy themselves in the downtime, and seducing her would provide a welcome distraction from the more unsettling aspects of learning he was adopted.

Alex need pose no threat to his goals. He had no interest in sharing with her anything other than hours of outstanding pleasure. He wasn't cut out for anything more. He'd witnessed first-hand how thankless and manipulative relationships could be and the unhappiness they wrought. He neither believed in nor wanted commitment. He needed that kind of toxicity in his life like a hole in the head, which was why the women he dated never lasted long. The shorter the encounter, the less chance there was of disappointment and dashed expectations, of having to accommodate the feelings that someone else might develop, of becoming trapped and gradually losing the control and power to end things when he chose. Alex, despite the novel intensity of the chemistry that arced between them, would be no exception. All he had to do was persuade her to agree to a fling. It wouldn't take long. He gave it thirty-six hours tops.

'All right,' he said with a slow smile as heady anticipation at the thought of embarking on a short, sharp, scorchingly hot affair with her began to surge through him. 'London City Airport. Jet Centre. Seven a.m. Don't be late.'

Alex, with her better-to-be-twenty-minutes-early-than-twenty-seconds-late approach to timekeeping, wasn't the one who was late.

After Max had left her office she'd thrown herself into rearranging her diary, issuing instructions to Becky—who'd agreed to hold the fort—and then going home to pack. After a couple of hours of research followed by an annoyingly restless night, she'd risen at dawn and arrived at the airport with her customary two hours to spare. She'd taken immediate advantage of the private jet lounge to fortify herself with coffee while going over the notes she'd made last night and the list of questions she wanted to ask him.

Of the man himself there'd been no sign, and there still wasn't. She supposed that one of the advantages of this kind of travel was not being beholden to a schedule but she'd been told the time of their slot for take-off and in her opinion he was cutting it extremely fine.

However, that was OK with her. The more time she had to brace herself against the frustratingly edgy effect he had on her, the better. To her despair, he'd been on her mind pretty much constantly from the moment he'd walked out of her office. His scent—spicy, masculine, delicious—had lingered on the air. The intensity with which he'd looked at her was singed into her memory and she could still feel a strange low-level sort of excitement buzzing in her stomach.

Last night's dreams hadn't helped. Every time she dropped off, there he was in her office, smouldering away at her, only when he eventually rose, it wasn't to leave. It was to pull her up off her chair and spread her across her desk, and then proceed to take her to heaven and back, thoroughly and at great length. She'd lost count of the number of times she'd jerked awake, hot and breathless and aching, with the sheets twisted around her.

Why Max should evoke this strong a response in her when his brothers—so similar in looks—left her completely unmoved she had no idea. He might be mind-blowingly attractive but he still wasn't her type and she still didn't trust him one inch.

That last smile he'd given her—slow, seductive and devastating—was particularly worrying. It spoke of secrets, of being privy to information that she wasn't, and if there was one thing she detested it was secrets. Her ex-husband had had many—mainly of the female kind—and when she'd found them out they'd crucified and humiliated her.

What did Max have to be secretive about? she wondered, draining her fourth coffee of the morning and setting the delicate porcelain cup in its matching saucer. She wished she knew. She had the disturbing feeling that it somehow involved her.

Not that what lay behind the smile really mattered, of course. She wasn't interested in any of his secrets, even less in ones in which she might feature. She was here to work, nothing more. And she could easily manage the strangely wild effect he might still have on her. As a thirty-three-year-old divorcee with a career like hers, she was no naïve innocent. She'd seen things, met all manner of people and been through her fair share of struggles. She'd become adept at hiding her true feelings beneath an ultra-unflappable surface and she saw no reason why that shouldn't be the case now.

It wasn't as if Max was similarly affected by her. It had been very clear that he wasn't interested in anything other than the information in her possession, which was a huge relief. The assignment was far too important to risk screwing up by either or both of them getting distracted.

As soon as he showed up she'd make a start by finding out what he knew. Assuming he was still intending to actually catch this flight, of course. Personally, she didn't know how he could operate like this. What was the point in stipulating a time to meet if you were going to completely disregard it? His website had revealed that he consulted for clients across the globe. Apparently he was some kind of computer genius, in constant and high demand. Truly, the mind boggled.

On the other hand, she had first-hand experience of how deceiving appearances could be. Look at the nonchalant way she'd sauntered into the private jet lounge as if she travelled this way all the time when she very much did not. Take her work, which proved it on a daily basis. Or her ex-husband, who'd been impossibly charming, handsome and initially doting, yet had also been a lying, cheating rat. And then there were her parents and siblings, whose willingness to break the law was staggering, who lied, cheated and stole as naturally as breathing while managing to maintain a perpetual air of injured innocence.

Just because Max chose to live life on the edge timewise, it didn't automatically mean he was reckless and rash. And just because he'd turned up in her office dishevelled and wearing crumpled clothes, it didn't mean he couldn't don a suit if necessary.

He'd certainly look good in one, she thought absently, staring out of the window and remembering the breadth of his shoulders and the leanness of his frame. A navy one, perhaps, to match the colour of his irises. With a crisp pale blue shirt open at the collar to reveal a wedge of chest. Although, frankly, he'd probably look better in nothing at all…

No.

This wasn't on. She had to get a grip. She really did. How Max conducted his affairs was none of her business. His attitude towards timekeeping and clothing was entirely up to him.

The reason her reaction to him yesterday had been so strong was because the shock and the relief at the breakthrough he presented, followed by the fear and panic that he intended to take the case over and cut her out of it, had momentarily rocked her foundations. Now, however, those foundations were solid, unassailable. Now she was prepared. She had to be.

Breathing deeply to ease the tension in her muscles and calm the annoying anticipation nevertheless rippling through her, Alex reached into her bag for her laptop. She flipped it open and determinedly concentrated on her emails, but barely two minutes passed before she felt the air around her somehow shifting. A prickly awareness washed over her skin and a pulse kicked in the pit of her stomach. Stiffening her spine and reminding herself of just how impregnable she was, she abandoned her emails and glanced up.

Max stood at the entrance to the cabin, being accosted by one of the two cabin crew on board, who seemed overly concerned with a desire to assist him. Alex mentally rolled her eyes, because how much help could an athletically built six foot plus man of thirty-one really need? But to her relief—because, quite honestly, she could do without having to sit through thirteen hours of simpering and flirting—he responded to the inviting smile with a quick, impersonal one of his own and a minute shake of his head.

'Good morning,' he said, heading towards her and

tossing his bag on one of the two soft leather sofas the colour of buttercream.

'Good morning,' she replied, reminding herself sternly that it was of no concern to her how he responded to an invitation. 'So much for not being late.'

At her arch tone, his dark eyebrows lifted. 'Am I?'

Well, no. Technically, he wasn't, but for some reason it felt as though a swarm of bees had made their home in her stomach and as a result everything had the potential to make her tetchy. 'You're cutting it extremely fine.'

'Let me guess, you've been here for hours.'

'There's no need to sound quite so dismissive,' she said, bristling at the hint of mockery she could hear in his voice. Admittedly, she might have been a tad overzealous with the two hours, but then she'd only ever flown economy. She'd never had the luxury of private jet travel, with its gorgeous gleaming walnut surfaces, cream carpet and real china. 'Punctuality isn't a bad thing.'

'Punctuality is the thief of time.'

Hmm. 'I think you'll find it's procrastination that's the thief of time. But, either way, mine is equally valuable as anyone else's.'

'I don't disagree. But, seeing as how I'm not late, the point is moot.'

Max folded his large frame into the seat opposite hers and buckled up. His knee bumped against hers and the jolt it sent rocketing through her could have powered a city for a week.

What was wrong with her? she wondered dazedly, her heart pounding like a jack hammer. One brief contact and she'd felt it like lightning. She was normally so steady and calm. Where was her composure? What was going on? Why him? Why now? More importantly, when was the air-con going to kick in? It was so hot in here.

Thankfully, Max was looking at his phone so couldn't have noticed her absurd overreaction to his touch. A minute later the engines started up and they were taxiing away from the terminal. As the plane accelerated down the runway, Alex gave herself a severe talking to. Her response to the gorgeous man once again sitting opposite her was not only ridiculous, it was wholly unacceptable. She had to pull herself together. How was she going to make any headway on the case if she couldn't work alongside him without turning into a quivering wreck? That wasn't who she was. And how dangerous would it be if he knew how strongly he affected her? That she'd been dreaming about him? He might well consider her unprofessional as well as incompetent and neither was the case.

By the time they were in the air, the slow steady breaths she'd been taking to calm her raging pulse and the pep talk had had the desired effect and she'd got herself under enough control to at least make a start on the questions she'd compiled.

'How was lunch?' she asked, determined to focus on the job. When she'd spoken to Finn yesterday af-

ternoon to subtly check that he wasn't intending to
fire her, he'd mentioned the three brothers planned
to spend the afternoon together. Max must have told
him that they were teaming up and heading to Argentina together because Finn had also, bizarrely and
unexpectedly, requested she take care of him. She
knew that both he and Rico had had issues concerning their adoption but, quite honestly, in Max, she'd
never met a man who needed taking care of less.

He glanced up and, despite all her efforts to control her response to him, her breath nevertheless
caught at the bright intensity of his gaze. 'Good,'
he said. 'Lengthy. It stretched into dinner and then
drinks. I ended up crashing in one of Finn's hotel
rooms.'

'You must have had a lot to catch up on.'

'We did,' he said with the quick flash of a genuine blinding smile.

'Do you get on well?' she asked, determined not
to be dazzled.

'Exceptionally.'

He was obviously over the moon at having found
his siblings, Alex thought, unable to prevent a dart
of envy lancing through her. She had three siblings,
with whom she had absolutely nothing in common
other than a mutual lack of understanding.

How great would it be to have or find just one person who instinctively got you? Who unconditionally
accepted you for who you were, warts and all. Not
even her ex had truly understood her, or genuinely

loved her for herself, possibly not even at all. But then, repenting at leisure was what came of marrying in haste. If she hadn't been so desperate for security and conventionality she could have saved herself years of heartache.

'Did you know you were adopted?' she asked, yanking her thoughts back on track since her relationships with her siblings and her ex weren't remotely relevant to the conversation.

'Not until the day before yesterday.'

'How did you feel when you found out?'

'Relieved.'

'Oh?'

'It's complicated.'

'In my experience, family generally is.'

His gaze sharpened and turned quizzical. 'In what way is yours complicated?'

Hers? Hmm. In what way *wasn't* it complicated? She was so different to the rest of hers that, ironically, for years she'd thought *she* had to be adopted.

She'd grown up on a rundown council estate, her parents and siblings largely relying on state support and the odd cash-in-hand job to keep them afloat. She'd been clever and wanted more, but aspiration had been thin on the ground both at school and home.

When she'd expressed an interest in university she'd been asked why she thought she was so special and told to get back in her box. In the face of such lack of encouragement she hadn't been brave enough to pursue that avenue, but had sought another way out instead. She hadn't fancied the army, with its olive drab and international danger zones, so she'd joined the police. Her family, who harboured a deep distrust of the authorities with whom they'd had more than one or two run-ins, had seen the move as a betrayal and never forgiven her.

She'd long since realised that their acceptance, their love, was conditional on conformity and it had been a price that ultimately she hadn't been willing to pay. But it still hurt, and she still wished things could have been different.

However, *her* family issues bore no relation to this case.

'I wasn't referring to mine,' she said, while thinking, well, not entirely. 'I simply meant that I've seen a lot of it through my work. Tell me about yours. It could be helpful.'

'It won't be,' he said with a frown, his jaw clenching in a faint but intriguing way.

'Let me be the judge of that,' she countered. 'Despite what you might think, Max, I am good at my job. There's a reason Finn hired me over one of the bigger, more established agencies. Not only was I highly recommended by an acquaintance of his, for whom I did some work, I leave no stone unturned. I'm tenacious like that. But I can only be the best if I have all the facts.'

He regarded her for a moment then gave a short nod. 'Fair enough. My father had a fatal heart attack seven years ago.'

'I'm sorry to hear that,' she said, feeling a faint twang in her chest, which was baffling when she hardly knew him.

'My mother lives in New York. They divorced when I was fourteen.'

'Have you spoken to her about your adoption?'

'Briefly.'

'What did she say?'

'She claims not to recall much of the detail.'

From across the table, Alex stared at him in shock. His mother didn't recall much of the detail relating to the adoption of her son? Was she ill? Had he not asked the right questions? 'How is that possible?'

'She can be difficult.'

Or could it be that his family was as dysfunctional as hers? 'I'd like to talk to her.'

'There'd be little point.'

'It's an avenue I can't leave unexplored,' she said, noting the tension suddenly gripping him and the barriers shooting up.

'It's too early to call now.'

'The minute we land, then.'

'Have you had breakfast?'

'No,' she replied, intrigued by the abrupt change in topic but letting it go until she figured out a way of bypassing the barriers.

'Well, I don't know about you, but I'm ravenous.'

CHAPTER THREE

UNBUCKLING HIS SEATBELT, Max got up and strode to the buffet bar, upon which sat a platter of cold meats and cheeses, bowls of fruit and a basket of pastries and rolls. He didn't want to talk about his mother to anyone at the best of times. He certainly didn't want to discuss her with Alex right now, he thought darkly as he took a plate and handed it to her.

Generally, he tried to think about Carolyn Stafford née Warwick née Browning née Kentala née Green as little as possible. He'd described her as difficult but that was an understatement. She was impossible and always had been. Everything was about her, nothing was ever good enough and her ability to find fault knew no bounds.

He could still vividly recall the time he'd broken his leg at the age of eight. She'd had to cancel a lunch date to take him to hospital and on the way there had let him know in no uncertain terms exactly how inconvenient he was being. The memory of the chilly silences she'd subjected him to as a child, when he'd failed to live up to one expectation or another, had had the ability to tighten his chest and accelerate his pulse for years.

Even now, she twisted words and situations for her own benefit and tried to manipulate and control him. The difference these days was that the armour he'd built over the years to protect himself from her—and from his father, for that matter—was inches thick and strong as steel. Everything now simply bounced off it.

So no, he thought, excising all thoughts of his mother from his head and piling breakfast onto a plate of his own, what he *wanted* to do was grab Alex by the hand, lead her into the bedroom he'd spotted at the back of the cabin and keep her there until they landed.

After departing her office yesterday morning, he'd put her from his mind and headed back to Finn and Rico, the need to reconnect with them before the flight out his number one goal. Lunch had extended into the afternoon and then to dinner and drinks late into the night, the conversation and his fascination with his brothers absorbing every drop of his attention.

Yet the minute he'd stepped onto the plane he'd felt Alex's gaze on him like a laser, and every single thing discussed and learned and every accompanying emotion that had swept through him had vaporised. It was as if he'd been plugged into the national grid. The tiny hairs at the back of his neck had shot up and electricity had charged his nerve-endings, the effects of which still lingered.

This morning she was wearing a smart grey trouser suit, her hair up in a neat bun, her glossy fringe not a strand out of place, but, once again, none of that was as off-putting as he might have assumed. On the contrary, it only intensified his intention to unwind her and find out exactly what lay beneath the icy cool surface.

Was it a concern that he was so tuned to her frequency? No. The tiny gasp she'd let out when his knee had bumped hers was merely encouraging. The hint of defensiveness and the faint stiffening of her shoulders he'd noticed when they'd been talking about complicated families was nothing more than mildly interesting, because he didn't buy for one moment that she hadn't been referring to hers.

Nor was the fact he found her obvious disapproval of him so stimulating anything to worry about. Sure, it was unusual and unexpected—especially given how much censure he'd grown up with—but it wasn't as if he was after anything other than a purely physical relationship with her. She'd already turned what he'd always considered he found attractive on its head and her opinion of him was irrelevant.

And, quite honestly, there was no need to overthink it.

'So, by my calculations,' said Alex, cutting through his thoughts and snapping him back to breakfast, 'if you factor in the change in time zones, we should be landing at La Posada some time this afternoon.'

'We're making a stopover in the Caribbean first,' Max said, breaking open a roll and drizzling olive oil onto it.

A pause. Then, 'Oh?'

'Isla Mariposa. It's an island off the north coast of Venezuela. I live there. We should land mid-morning local time. We'll leave for Argentina tomorrow.'

There was another, slightly longer pause. 'I see.'

At the chill in her voice, Max glanced up and saw that her eyes were shooting daggers at him and her colour was high, which was as fascinating as it was a surprise. 'Is that a problem?' he asked with a mildness that totally belied the arousing effect her glare was having on him.

'Yes, it's a problem.'

'We'll need to refuel and the crew will need a break,' he said, shifting on the seat to ease the sudden tightness of his jeans. 'I also need to pick up some clothes. It's cold where we're heading.'

La Posada stood three thousand four hundred metres above sea level and had a cold semi-arid climate. At this time of year, August, the temperature, which averaged seventeen degrees centigrade by day, plummeted to minus four at night.

'I know that,' said Alex somewhat witheringly. 'I checked. *That's* not the problem. Nor is refuelling and giving the crew a break, obviously.'

'Then what is?'

'You are,' she fired at him. 'You unilaterally making decisions that involve me without discussing them *with* me is the problem.'

In response to her unanticipated wrath, Max sat back, faintly stunned. 'If I'd known it was so important I'd have sent you the flight plan.'

'It's not just the flight plan,' she said heatedly. 'It's the way you set up a meeting with Rico and Finn when you were specifically requested to go through me. And then the commandeering of Rico's plane to fly to Argentina completely on your own.'

'Would you rather have flown commercial?'

'That's not the point. I'm the expert here. This is my field, Max. And it's *my* case.'

'No, it's not,' he replied, unable to resist the temptation to see how far she could be pushed.

'Yes, it is.'

'I prefer to think of it as *our* case.'

Alex threw up her hands in exasperation and he could practically see the steam pouring out of her ears, which would have put a grin on his face if he hadn't thought it would result in her throwing a croissant at him.

'But you're right,' he said a touch more soberly when it looked as if she was going to get up and storm off in vexation. 'I apologise. This is the first time I've worked with someone.'

Alex eyed him suspiciously for a moment but remained seated. 'Seriously?'

'I have a great respect for confidentiality.'

'You trust no one?'

'Not with work.' Or with anything else, but she didn't need to know that.

'Well, you're going to have to start,' she said, stabbing a chunk of kiwi with her fork. 'You'll soon get used to working with me.'

No, he wouldn't. This was a one-off and temporary. Joking aside, he didn't do 'our' anything and never would. A long-term relationship was way out of his reach, even if he had wanted one. Any hope he might have once had for love had been eroded so long ago he couldn't remember what it felt like, and thought of emotional intimacy, the kind he supposed might be required for such a thing, made him shudder. However, constant confrontation would hardly entice her into his bed.

'I'll endeavour to do better,' he said with what he hoped was the right amount of conciliation. 'And, with that in mind, my villa has a guest suite that I thought you might like to use, but feel free to book into a hotel if you'd prefer.'

The scowl on her face deepened for a moment, but then it cleared and she seemed to deflate, as if he'd whipped the wind of indignation from her sails. 'No, your guest suite would be great,' she said grudgingly. 'I wouldn't want to incur any unnecessary costs.'

'You're welcome.'

'Thank you.'

'This investigation means a lot to you, doesn't it?'

he said, deeming it safe to continue with breakfast and adding a slice of ham to the roll.

'Every investigation means a lot to me,' she said archly. 'And they all come with rules.'

Did they? 'I'll have to take your word for it.'

'So I'd appreciate it if you would respect them as much as you say you respect confidentiality.'

Respect them? She had no idea. 'No can do, I'm afraid.'

'Why on earth not?'

'Rules are made to be broken.'

'Mine aren't.'

'You seem very definite.'

'I *am* very definite.'

Max watched her neatly slice a pain au chocolate in half and thought that if that kind of a statement wasn't irresistible to someone who'd never come across a rule he hadn't instinctively wanted to trample all over, he didn't know what was.

His days of rebelling against authority and challenging the system were over long ago. A brush with the Feds at the age of twenty for hacking into the digital billboards of Times Square had made him reassess his need to foster anarchy and create chaos, but that didn't mean the urge had disappeared altogether. 'That sounds like a challenge.'

She looked up and glared at him warningly. 'Believe me, it absolutely isn't.'

'What's the attraction?' He took a bite of his roll and noted with interest that her gaze dipped to his mouth for the briefest of moments before jerking back to his.

'Well, for one thing,' she said with a quick, revealing clearing of her throat, 'society wouldn't function without them. They maintain civilisation and prevent lawlessness. Everyone knows what's what, and there's security in that.' She paused then added, 'But on a personal level I will admit to liking order and structure.'

'Why?'

'I grew up without much of either. I came to see the benefits.'

'The complicated family?' he said, catching a fleeting glimpse of disappointment and regret in her expression.

'Maybe,' she admitted with a minute tilt of her head. 'My upbringing was chaotic.'

'In what way?'

'It just was.'

Her chin was up and her eyes flashed for a second and he thought that if she didn't want to talk about it that was fine with him. Her family problems were no concern of his. He had enough of his own to deal with. 'Chaos can be good,' he said instead, reflecting on how it had got him through his teenage years before his arrest had given him the opportunity to reassess.

She sat back and stared at him, astonishment wiping out the momentary bleakness. 'Are you serious?'

'The most disruptive periods of history have produced the finest art and the best inventions. Think the Medici.'

'So have the quietest. Think the telephone. What do you have against rules anyway?'

What *didn't* he have against them? They stifled creativity. They put in place boundaries that were frequently arbitrary and often unnecessary. Mostly, though, they represented authority that he'd once seen no reason to respect.

Max had started hacking at the age of twelve as a way of escaping from the rowing at home, his mother's constant criticism and his father's lack of interest in him. Not only had he got a massive kick out of breaking the law; more importantly, he'd found a community to become part of, one that considered failure a valuable learning tool, celebrated the smallest of successes and accepted him unconditionally. It had given him the sense of belonging that he'd craved and that had been addictive.

His early talents had swiftly developed into impressive skills and by the age of seventeen he'd gained a reputation as being the best in the business. He'd had respect—of the underground type, sure, but respect nevertheless—and he'd welcomed it.

While some of his acquaintances had stolen data to sell to the highest bidder and others held companies to ransom by installing malware, the more nefarious paths he could have chosen to take had never appealed. His interest had lain wholly in breaking systems and creating chaos. He'd relished and needed the control and the power it had given him when home was a place where he had none.

Now he had control and power that he'd acquired through legitimate routes and chaos no longer appealed, but there was still part of him that missed those days and always would.

'I'm a rebel at heart,' he said, giving her a slow grin which, intriguingly, made the pulse at the base of her neck flutter.

'Well, just as long as you don't make it your mission to lure me to the dark side,' she said pointedly, 'we should get along fine.'

It was all very well for Max to dismiss her need for rules, thought Alex, smiling her thanks to the flight attendant, who was clearing away breakfast with an obligingly professional rather than flirtatious manner, to treat them as some kind of joke. He couldn't possibly understand the hunger for stability and peace that she'd developed growing up.

Home had been a noisy, disruptive place. There'd been six of them initially, living in a cramped three-bedroom flat on the eighteenth floor of a tower block decorated with graffiti, lit by dim, flickering light bulbs and littered with cigarette ends and fast-food packaging.

She'd shared a bunk room with her sister and then the baby, her niece, as well, when she'd arrived. Her older brothers, who'd shared another of the rooms, had come and gone at all hours, where and to do what she'd never dared to enquire. Her parents had considered discipline and regular meals too much of a challenge to bother with properly, and school had been optional. Somehow, though strangely, there'd always been enough money.

Since it had been impossible to study at home with the racket that went on, Alex had spent much of her time at the local library and it was there that she'd happened upon Aristotle and his thoughts on the rule of law.

What she'd read had been liberating. When she'd realised that there was nothing to celebrate about the reckless, irresponsible way her family lived, she'd stopped trying to mould herself into something they could accept—which was proving impossible anyway when she'd rejected the idea with every fibre of her being—and turned her sights on escape.

Rules had given her a path out of the chaos. She'd diligently followed the school curriculum despite little encouragement, taken every exam available and set her sights on a career in the police, which, with its hierarchy and methodical approach to things, had appealed to her need for structure.

Sticking to them was hardly an adventurous or daring course of action, but it was a safe one and one which she knew she could rely on. She'd experienced the fallout from zero adherence: the worry about where her father was and when he'd be back; jumping every time there was a knock on the door and knowing with a feeling of dread that the law stood on the other side; a diet so deficient it gave you anaemia that made you faint.

The knowledge that she shared her family's DNA was a constant worry. What might happen if she let go of her grip on her control? How quickly would genes win out and consign her to a future of petty crime and little hope? She couldn't let that happen. She didn't want to live the way her parents and siblings did. She wanted a steady, law-abiding, chaos-free existence, one in which she knew where she was going and how she was going to get there.

Max, on the other hand, for some reason evidently saw rules as something to bend and to break. A challenge. So what did that mean going forwards? Would he try and break hers? If he did, how many and which ones? How far would he go? And how would she respond?

Well, she'd fight back with everything she had, of course, because his love of breaking rules was not more important than her need to abide by them. That had been set in stone years ago and further cemented by embarking on a career as a woman in a man's world, which meant that she'd had to work twice as hard for her reputation.

Besides, she would not have him messing with her plans, her *life*, just because he felt like it. That tiny little thrill she could feel rippling through her at the thought of being the object of his focus could take a hike. It was wholly unacceptable and not to be indulged. She didn't want to be the object of his focus. Of *anyone's* focus, for that matter. She was very happy on her own, and had been since her divorce. She didn't need the stress and potential failure of another relationship, even if she ever could find it in her to trust again. The occasional date whenever she started to feel a bit lonely, where *she* called the shots, was more than enough.

Not that Max fell into the date category or ever would. Even if he had shown any sign of being attracted to her, he was too unpredictable, too much of a threat to her peace of mind. He was chaos with a capital C and therefore completely off-limits, despite the insane attraction she felt for him.

But he was also nothing she couldn't handle, she told herself sternly as she turned her mind to work. She'd come across far more temperamental personalities. He might have broken through her unflappable exterior with his decree about the stopover, but there'd been extenuating circumstances. She'd been provoked one time too many. It wouldn't happen again.

And, in any case, they'd be busy with the investigation. There wouldn't be time or space for Max to challenge her rules. There'd be no upheaval, no chaos. It would be fine.

While Alex set up a workspace at the table, Max grabbed his laptop from his bag, kicked off his shoes and stretched out on the sofa, still thinking of interesting and inventive ways to 'lure her to the dark side'.

It might not be as simple as he'd first imagined, he acknowledged, firing up the machine and revisiting their conversation. He hadn't counted on rules. But he didn't envisage too much of a problem. However mighty her will and however noble her intentions, the attraction they shared was a thousand times stronger. If it drummed through her the way it did through him—hot, insistent, all-consuming—it wouldn't take long for her resistance to buckle under the pressure. Maybe not quite within the thirty-six hours he'd so confidently predicted yesterday lunchtime, but well within forty-eight.

'Making yourself comfortable?'

At Alex's dry question he glanced over and saw that her gaze was fixed on his bare feet. No doubt she disapproved, which naturally made him want to do something even more unprofessional—say, strip off his shirt—just to see her reaction.

'Why don't you join me?' he said with a grin, briefly wondering what the chances were of her letting her hair down in both senses of the phrase and taking up a position on the sofa that sat at right angles to his.

'Thanks,' she muttered, returning her attention to her laptop, 'but I'm fine over here.'

As he'd thought. Minuscule. But that was all right. Now he was beginning to see how she operated, he could adapt his strategy to seduce her into his bed accordingly. 'What are you doing?'

'Emails.'

'Haven't you forgotten something?'

She frowned. 'What?'

'Your side of our deal. If I allowed you to accompany me this morning,' he said, his choice of words deliberately provocative, 'you'd give me all the information you have on the investigation so far.'

Her eyes narrowed for a moment and he felt a little kick of triumph. She was too easy to wind up. Less clear was why he found it so tempting to try.

'Sure,' she said with a disappointing return to her customary cool. 'I'll send everything over right now.'

The emails dropped into his inbox, one after the other, and as Max clicked on the attachments, opening up reports, birth certificates, a letter from Rico's adoptive parents to their son and even the analysis of Finn's DNA, his preoccupation with undoing Alex and pulverising her rules evaporated.

Reading the names of his birth parents, Juan Rodriguez and Maria Gonzalez, made his throat tight and his pulse race. Were they still alive? Who were they, what were they like, and did he resemble them in any way? What were the chances of finding them? And which of the three certificates was his? Would he ever get to know who he truly was? Would he ever find out why he'd been given up?

Rico's letter, a translation into English from the original Italian, was deeply personal and filled with loving thoughts as well as the name of the adoption agency. Somewhere deep inside Max's chest the words and the sentiments detonated a cocktail of resentment and pain that he hadn't experienced in years, followed hot on the heels by searing envy, which he wasn't particularly proud of since Rico's parents had died in a car accident when he was ten. But at least his brother had had a decade of affection and love, which was more than Max had ever had.

The analysis of Finn's DNA was less affecting but equally gripping. Their heritage was seventy-five per cent Latin American, twenty per cent Iberian, with a smattering of Central and Eastern European representing the remaining five per cent. Revelations included the low likelihood of dimples and the high possibility of a lactose intolerance. He scoured the data for similarities and found many.

Alex might consider this to be her field and her case, Max thought, methodically going through the reports supplied by her subcontractors, the details spinning around his head. But it was his history, his *family*. She could have no idea what it was like growing up sensing that somehow you were part of the wrong one, that you were unwanted but didn't know why. Nor could she know what it was like to obsessively wonder now how different things might have been if you'd grown up loved, wanted and happy in the right one. He'd spent thirty years not knowing his real parents. Thirty years apart from his brothers, with whom he'd shared a womb. So many memories unformed and opportunities lost...

'You mentioned having resources that I could only dream about,' Alex said, jolting him out of his thoughts, which was welcome when they'd become so tumultuous and overwhelming.

'You've been pretty thorough,' he said, clearing his throat of the tight knot that had lodged there. 'However, I can call in a few favours to see if we can't get round the Swiss banking secrecy issues and access Argentina's national archives.'

'Some favours they must be.'

'They are.' He'd once resolved the hack of a major Swiss bank and fixed a number of issues in systems controlled by the Argentinian government. 'But, other than that, I'm not sure what more I could legitimately add.'

'An interesting choice of words,' she said shrewdly. 'What about illegitimately?'

'It's a quick and efficient way of getting things done.'

Her mesmerising blue eyes widened for a second. 'Would you be willing to break the law for this?'

'I could,' he said, instinctively working through how he might go about it. 'And once upon a time I would have done so without hesitation. But not now. Now I have no intention of screwing up my career for a quick thrill.' These days he exerted his control and power in other ways, and accessing the systems to locate his brothers had been risky enough.

She looked at him steadily and he could practically see the pieces slotting into place in her brain. 'Were you a hacker?'

He nodded. 'A long time ago.'

'Is that how you got into cyber security?'

'It seemed like a good career move.'

Following his arrest, in an unlikely turn of events, Max had been offered a deal by the FBI: if he worked for them, he'd avoid jail. Initially he'd rejected the proposal. He hadn't even needed to think about it. Every millimetre of his being had recoiled at the thought of being employed by the authorities he despised. A sentence, however lengthy, would be infinitely preferable to selling out his principles.

But they'd given him forty-eight hours to reconsider, two days in a cell with nothing else to think about, and eventually he'd changed his mind. He was now on the authorities' radar. Escaping them in the future would be tough and actually he quite liked his freedom. The risks were beginning to outweigh the rewards, so maybe it was time for the poacher to turn gamekeeper.

From then on he'd been inundated with job offers, which ranged from finding weaknesses in firewalls and fixing them to providing advice on how to stay one step ahead of the hackers and disrupters in an exceptionally fast-moving field. None of his prospective employers had a problem with his brush with the law. His incomparable skills easily overrode what had gone before.

Despite being presented with some exceptionally generous packages once he'd paid his debt to society via the FBI, he'd opted to go it alone, to take his pick of the work. He'd never regretted the decision to be in sole control of his future, and not just because he had millions in the bank.

'How long have you been doing it?'

'Ten years.'

'I read you have clients all over the world.'

'I do.'

'Then I'm surprised you have time to work on the investigation.'

'I'm between contracts.'

'Handy.'

'I'd have made time regardless.'

Her gaze turned quizzical. 'It means that much to you?'

'Yes.'

'Why?'

There was no way he was going into detail about his upbringing, his efforts to overcome it and the emotional disruption the discovery of his adoption had wrought. He could barely work it out for himself. 'I'm good at solving puzzles,' he said with a casual shrug. 'I developed that particular skill while I was at MIT.' Or at least he had until his arrest, at which point he'd been stripped of his scholarship and kicked out.

'Computers are your thing.'

'They are,' he agreed, glancing at his laptop and feeling a familiar sense of calm settle over him. They were a damn sight simpler than people, that was for sure. They were devoid of emotion and didn't demand the impossible. They were predictable, easy to read if you knew what you were looking for and generally did what they were told. 'Like rules are yours.'

'Tell me more about the hacking.'

'What do you want to know?'

'Everything,' she said, getting up and moving to the sofa next to his, taking up a position that was too far away for his liking. 'Call it professional interest. There's a big gap in my knowledge of this particular area. How did you get into it?'

'I was given a computer for my tenth birthday,' he said, remembering with a sharp stab of pain how excited he'd been until his mother had told him in no uncertain terms that she expected it to improve his grades, otherwise it would be removed. 'I spent hours messing about on it, learning the language and writing programs, before discovering forums and chats. I got talking. Made friends. Things went from there.'

She leaned forward, avid curiosity written all over her face. 'How?'

'What do you mean?' he said, slightly taken aback by her interest in him and faintly distracted by the trace of her scent that drifted his way.

'Well, lots of people mess about on computers and chat online,' she said. 'Not many go down the hacking route.'

'Not many are good enough.'

She tilted her head. 'You say that with pride.'

'Do I?'

'You shouldn't.'

'Probably not.'

'What sort of things did you get up to?'

'The first thing I did was change a grade for a math test when I was twelve. I got an F. I should have got an A. I just hadn't studied. The F was a mistake.' More than that, though, he'd been terrified his mother would act on her threat and take his computer back.

She stared at him, appalled. 'How on earth could you not have studied for an exam?'

Because, since it was a subject he'd found easy, with the arrogance of youth, he'd assumed he'd wing it. 'Surely that isn't the point.'

'You're right,' she agreed. 'It isn't. What else?'

'I regularly set off the fire alarms and sprinkler systems at high school. I travelled round the city for free and was behind a handful of denial of service attacks. At one point I ran an operation cancelling parking tickets.'

'That's really bad,' she said, tutting with disapproval he'd come to expect. 'If the US authorities treat that kind of thing the same way the UK ones do, you risked years in jail.'

And that had been part of the appeal. The power, the control, the extremely high stakes and the respect he'd garnered that had made him feel so alive. It had given him a sense of identity, of purpose and he'd revelled in it. 'The commission I earned paid my rent while I was at college. I never caused anyone harm. I never even wanted to. Maximum disruption was my only goal.'

'And making money.'

'That was just a coincidence.'

'What did your parents think of what you were doing?'

'They never knew,' he said, hearing the trace of bitterness he was unable to keep from his voice and hating that old wounds he'd assumed were long gone appeared to have been ripped open. 'They were too wrapped up in themselves.'

'Ah,' she said, with a nod and smile he couldn't quite identify but which, for some reason, shot a dart of unease through him. 'Did you ever get caught?'

'Eventually. While I was at MIT, I hacked into the billboards in Times Square. I took down all the adverts and announcements and replaced them with my avatar.'

'Why?'

'Because I could. Because I was young and hubristic. Twenty-four hours later I had the FBI knocking on my door.'

'How did they find you?'

'A dark net contact of mine got sloppy and then did a deal to save his own ass.'

'Did you go to jail?'

He shook his head. 'I traded my principles for my freedom.'

'You got off lightly.'

'I was lucky.'

Very lucky, in retrospect. Forty-eight hours in the cells had been ample time to contemplate the journey that had landed him there. It hadn't taken him long to figure out that everything he'd done had been a reaction to the environment at home. His father's neglect, his mother's emotional vampirism. Operating in the shadows had given him the respect, approval and appreciation that he hadn't even known he'd been missing. His many successes had earned him recognition. His few failures had fuelled his determination to be better.

But he hadn't liked thinking about how weak and vulnerable he'd been as a kid. Nor had he enjoyed dwelling on why he'd carried on with his double life even when he'd escaped to MIT. He didn't want to admit to the fear that without it he didn't know who he was.

He'd never get the opportunity to work that out if he didn't give himself a chance, he'd eventually come to realise. And he had to stop being so angry. It didn't mean he'd forgiven his parents for the effects of their behaviour on him, but he could either allow the bitterness to take over or let it go. He'd chosen the latter, determinedly putting it all behind him, and gone on the straight and narrow, building his business and maintaining minimal contact with his parents. And everything had been going fine until he'd seen the video of his brothers and the fragile reality he'd created for himself had imploded.

'You'd get on well with my family,' said Alex with a dry smile that bizarrely seemed to shine through the cracks in his armour and light up the dark spaces within.

'In what way?' he asked, absently rubbing his chest.

'They have an unhealthy disrespect for the law too. Not quite on your level, admittedly. One of my brothers has a habit of shoplifting. My sister claims benefits but also works on the side. My father describes himself as a wheeler-dealer, but he treads a fine line.'

'Yet you went into the police.' Yesterday, he'd looked her up. The idea of a former law enforcement officer hooking up with a former criminal—albeit a non-convicted one—had held a certain ironic appeal.

'It was *my* escape.'

'How did that go down?' he asked, conveniently ignoring the comparison while thinking that she was way too perceptive.

'They've never forgiven me.'

'That I can understand. My mother's never got beyond my arrest.' Not even his subsequent success, which she tended to either diminish or ignore, could make up for that.

'I'm very much the ugly duckling of my family.'

'There is nothing ugly about you.'

'Nor you.'

A strange kind of silence fell then. Her cheeks flushed and her gaze dipped to his mouth. He became unusually aware of his heartbeat, steady but quickening. Her eyes lifted back to his, darkening to a mid-blue, and she stared at him intently, as if trying to look into his soul, which shook something deep inside him. The tension simmered between them. The air heated. He was hyperaware of her. The hitch of her breath. The flutter of her pulse at the base of her neck. He wanted to kiss her so badly it was all he could think about.

And then she blinked.

'Right,' she said briskly, snapping the connection and making him start. 'I'm going for a nap. Unlike some, I had a very early start. See you later.'

And as she leapt to her feet and fled the scene, Max had the oddly unsettling feeling that it was going to be a very long flight.

CHAPTER FOUR

NEVER HAD SHE been so glad of fresh air and space, Alex thought six hours later as she sat at the back of Max's speedboat, which was whisking them from Simón Bolívar International Airport, just north of Caracas, to Isla Mariposa, where he lived. She lifted her face to the glorious mid-morning sun while the warm Caribbean Sea breeze whipped around her, willing it to blow away the excruciating tension gripping every cell of her body.

So much for a nice refreshing nap. She felt as refreshed as a damp, dirty dishcloth, on edge and gritty-eyed, but then that was what came of not being able to catch up on a broken truncated night. She wished she could have blamed her tossing and turning on turbulence, but the flight had been smooth and uneventful. The only turbulence she'd experienced had been within.

She'd met many criminals in her time, but never a hacker and none as devastatingly attractive as the man standing at the wheel, handling the boat so competently. Beneath the blazing sun she could make out fine golden streaks in his dark hair. His eyes were even bluer in the bright mid-morning light. Once again he'd kicked off his shoes and once again she was transfixed.

Alex had never had a thing about feet before. If she'd had to provide an opinion on them she'd have said function over form was generally the case and the more hidden away they were the better. It would appear she had a thing about his, however, because they were things of beauty. She could stare at them for hours. She had, in fact, at length, on the plane, when he'd been talking about his early career and she'd been rapt. But at least it made a change from trying not to stare at his mouth, which was proving an irritatingly hard challenge.

What was the matter with her? she wondered, taking a sip of water from her bottle and surreptitiously running her gaze over him. Why were Max Kentala and his many physical attractions occupying so much of her brain? He really wasn't her type. It wasn't about his looks any longer. In that respect, it had become blindingly obvious that he was exactly her type, hair in need of a cut and jaw in need of a shave or not.

But with regard to everything else they were chalk and cheese. Their poles apart attitudes towards time-keeping notwithstanding, he'd been a law-breaker. She'd been a law-enforcer. He clearly embraced turmoil while she craved the security of stability and predictability. He considered engaging in criminal activity *a quick thrill*. They couldn't have more opposing values or be more different.

What she couldn't understand, however, was why she found this dichotomy so fascinating. The pride she'd noted when he'd been talking about the illegal ways he'd deployed his considerable IT skills, which had lightened his expression and made him look younger, more carefree and, unbelievably, even more gorgeous, wasn't something to be applauded. Hacking into the Times Square billboards wasn't cool or fun or imaginative. It was reckless, irresponsible and downright illegal.

The walk on the wild side he'd once taken was everything she abhorred, everything she avoided like the plague. That he'd so obviously enjoyed it should have dramatically diminished his appeal. But it didn't. Instead it seemed to have *augmented* it, which was baffling and more than a little concerning, as was the still unacceptable thrill that was begging to be indulged with increasing persistence.

Could it be that their many differences were somehow mitigated by their few similarities? They were both problem solvers who'd forged successful careers from nothing. They'd both had disapproving parents and had once upon a time sought an escape from their families. Both were equally invested in uncovering the truth, although she didn't quite believe that for him it was just a problem to solve.

So could their unexpected commonalities somehow explain her one-eighty swing from reproach to sympathy? *Something* had to account for that oddly heart-stopping moment they'd shared just before she'd legged it to the bedroom.

She hadn't meant to confess that she found him attractive. She was sure there was nothing to read in his comment along the same lines. Yet he'd suddenly looked so sincere it had caught her off-guard. Her gaze had collided with his and the intense heat she'd seen darkening the blue to navy had dazzled her. Her mouth had dried. Her pulse had pounded. She'd wanted to get up and move to his side. To lean down, pin him to the sofa and cover his mouth with hers. She'd very nearly done it too, to her horror, hence the sudden excuse of a nap.

She had to put the whole plane journey from her mind, she told herself firmly for what felt like the hundredth time in the past hour. She might not be able to make head or tail of her attitude towards Max but one thing was certain: his ability to derail her focus was wholly wrong. The unexpectedly sexy way he put on his sunglasses, pulling them from the V of his shirt and sliding them onto his nose, bore no relevance to anything. That the fine hair on his beautifully muscled forearms was a shade lighter than that on his head was not something she needed to concern herself with. And who cared that he'd been strangely monosyllabic and tight-jawed ever since they'd landed?

All she wanted was to crack this case and secure her future.

As they rounded a small headland Max slowed the boat and Alex turned her gaze to the shore. At the sight of the house that hove into view, her jaw dropped. Beyond the water that sparkled jade and turquoise and was so clear she could see right down to the bottom, above the curving swathe of palm-fringed white sand, the villa stood nestled among the trees that rose up behind. Four low-level triangular wooden roofs stretched out above huge glass windows and doors. In front, overlooking the sea, was a series of connected terraces. On one she thought she could make out a pool. At each end, a flight of wooden steps descended between the boulders to the beach.

Even from this distance she could see that it was a building sympathetic to its surroundings and stunningly beautiful. It was the kind of place she'd only ever seen in magazines, in which, incredibly, *she* was getting to stay. And yes, it was for work, just as the private jet had been, but that didn't stop her mentally sticking two fingers up at the teachers who'd told her repeatedly and scornfully that with her family she didn't stand a chance of ever making anything of herself. Nor did it stop her wishing her parents could see her now, not that there was any point to that at all.

Max brought the boat to a near stop and lined it up to the dock. He tossed a loop of rope over a mooring bollard with easy competence and a flex of muscles that, to her despair, made her stomach instinctively tighten, but she had the feeling that for the greater good she was just going to have to accept the way she responded to him and ignore it.

Displaying an enviable sense of balance, he unloaded their luggage and then alighted. He bent down and extended his arm. 'Give me your hand.'

For a moment Alex stared at his outstretched hand as if it were a live grenade. She couldn't risk taking it. If she did, she might not be able to let go. But she didn't have his sense of balance. One wobble and she could well end up in the sea, and quite frankly she felt jumpy enough around him without adding looking foolish into the mix.

'Thanks.'

After hauling Alex up off his boat and then dropping her hand as if it were on fire, Max grabbed their bags and strode up the steps to the house without bothering to see if she was following. He was tense. Tired. On edge.

As he'd suspected, it had been a very long flight. Once he'd rid his head first of images of Alex lying on the bed in the cabin of the plane alone and then of what would happen if he joined her, he'd found himself revisiting their conversation. Every detail, no matter how minute, appeared to be etched into his memory, and his unease had grown with every nautical mile, twisting his gut and bringing him out in a cold sweat.

Which was odd.

Generally he had no problem talking about his career or what he'd done to get there. He didn't have anything to hide. Most of it was in the public domain for anyone interested enough to go looking for it. It wasn't as if he'd given away a piece of himself or anything. He'd long ago come to terms with his mother's ongoing ignominy of having a son with a criminal background.

So why had their conversation unsettled him so much? Alex clearly disapproved of the things he'd got up to in his youth, but so what? Her opinion of him genuinely didn't matter. They were absolute opposites in virtually every respect, and he wasn't interested in her in any way except the physical.

Perhaps it was her curiosity in him which, despite her assertion to the contrary, had seemed more personal than professional. He couldn't recall the last time anyone had genuinely wanted to know what made him tick. Neither of his parents ever had. And these days most people just wanted to hear about his exploits. But Alex had wanted to know what lay behind them. She'd looked at him as if trying to see into his soul and it had rocked him to the core.

Or perhaps it had been that 'ah' of hers, the one she'd uttered when he'd told her that his parents couldn't have cared less about what he'd got up to. It suggested she'd caught the trace of bitterness that had laced his words and it smacked of sympathy and understanding, which he really didn't need. That they had parental disapproval and lack of forgiveness in common meant nothing. What did it matter that she was as much of a disappointment to her family as he was to his?

He was beginning to regret accepting Alex's ultimatum and allowing her to come with him. He should have stuck to his guns and listened to his head instead of his body. He had more than enough going on without her adding complications. He hated the confusion and uncertainty currently battering his fractured defences. He'd thought he'd overcome that sort of thing a decade ago. To realise that he might not have dealt with the past as successfully as he'd assumed was like a blow to the chest. At the very least he should have booked her into a hotel for tonight.

But there was nothing he could do about any of that now. However tempting it might be, he could hardly leave her here while he continued to Argentina alone. They'd made a deal and, for all his many faults, for all his crimes and misdemeanours, he'd never once gone back on his word. And booking her into a hotel now, when he'd already offered her his guest suite, would indicate a change of plan he didn't want her questioning.

At least where he was putting her up was separated from the main house, he thought grimly, striding past the infinity pool and heading for the pair of open doors that led to the suite. It wouldn't be too hard to ignore her for as long as it took for him to get a grip on the tornado of turmoil that was whipping around inside him. His plans for seduction could handle a minor delay while he regrouped.

'Here you go,' he said, stalking through the doors and dumping her bag beside the huge bed that stood before him like a great flashing beacon. 'Make yourself comfortable.'

'Thank you. This is an incredible house.'

'I like it.'

What he *didn't* like, however, was the fast unravelling of his control. Him, Alex, the bed... On top of everything else, the hot, steamy images now cascading into his head were fraying his nerves. The sounds she'd make. The smoothness of her skin beneath his hands and the soft silkiness of her hair trailing over him as she slid down his body.

He shouldn't be in here. He should have simply handed her her bag and pointed her in the right direction. He had to get out before he lost it completely. He whipped round to leave her to it, but she was closer than he was expecting. He slammed to a halt and jerked back, as if struck.

'Are you all right, Max?' she said with a quick frown.

No. He wasn't all right at all. 'I'm fine.'

'You don't look fine.' She put her hand on his arm and her touch shot through him with the force of a thousand volts. 'Your jaw looks like it's about to snap. You've been tense ever since we landed. Has something happened?'

What *hadn't* happened? Forget the fact that the last forty-eight hours had been more tumultuous than the last ten years. *She'd* happened. He couldn't work out why that should be a problem, but it was. As was the compassion and concern written all over her beautiful face. He didn't need that any more than he needed her sympathy or understanding. What he *did* need was space. Air to breathe that wasn't filled with her scent. Time to get himself back under control.

And yet he could no more move than he could fly to Mars. She was close. Very close. He could see a rim of silver around the light blue of her irises and he could hear the soft raggedness of her breathing. The concern was fading from her expression and the space between them started cracking with electricity, the air heavy with a strange sort of throbbing tension. Her pupils were dilating and her gaze dipped to his mouth and still her hand lingered on his arm, burning him like a brand.

The desire that thudded through him was firing his blood and destroying his reason, but he welcomed it, because this he understood. This he could command. She leaned into him, only the fraction of an inch, so minutely she probably wasn't aware she'd done it, but in terms of encouragement it was the greenest of lights and one he couldn't ignore.

Acting on pure instinct, Max shook her hand off him and took a quick step forwards. He put his hands on either side of her head and, dazed with lust, lowered his mouth to hers. Her scent and heat stoked his desire for her to unbearable levels and his ability to think was long gone, but he nevertheless felt her jolt and then stiffen and was about to let her go when she suddenly whipped her arms around his neck, pressed herself close and started kissing him back.

With a groan of relief, he pulled her tighter against him and deepened the kiss, the flames shooting through him heating the blood in his veins to bubbling. The wildness of her response, the heat and taste of her mouth robbed him of his wits. He was nothing but sensation, could feel nothing but her, could think only of the bed not a dozen metres away and the painful ache of his granite-hard erection, against which she was grinding her pelvis and driving him mad.

He deftly unbuttoned her jacket and slid a hand to her breast, rubbed his thumb over her tight nipple, and she moaned. He moved his mouth along her jaw, the sound of her pants harsh in his ear, sending lightning bolts of ecstasy through him. She burrowed her fingers into his hair, as if desperate to keep him from going anywhere, which was never going to happen—

And then a door slammed somewhere inside the house.

In his arms, Alex instantly froze and jerked back, staring at him for what felt like the longest of moments, her cheeks flushed and her eyes glazed with desire. But all too soon the desire vanished and in its place he could see dawning dismay. She shoved at his shoulders and he let her go in a flash, even though every cell of his body protested.

'What's wrong?' he muttered dazedly, his voice rough and his breathing harsh.

'What's wrong?' she echoed in stunned disbelief. 'This is.'

'It seemed very much all right to me.'

'It was a mistake,' she panted, smoothing her clothes and doing up the button of her jacket with trembling hands while taking an unsteady step back. 'I'm here to work.'

It very much hadn't been a mistake. It had been everything he'd anticipated. More. 'Work can wait.'

'No. It can't,' she said, swallowing hard.

'We're not leaving until tomorrow. There's no rush.'

'I'd planned to call your mother as soon as we landed. Now would be that time.'

At that, Max recoiled as if she'd slapped him. What the hell? If that door hadn't slammed they'd be on the bed getting naked just as fast as was humanly possible. She'd clung to him like a limpet. Kissed him as if her life had depended on it. And now she was talking about his mother? Well, that was one way to obliterate the heat and the desire.

Had that been her intention? If it was, she'd succeeded, because now instead of fire, ice was flowing through his veins, and instead of lust and desperate clawing need, all he felt was excoriating frustration and immense annoyance.

'Sure,' he said, reaching into the back pocket of his trousers and pulling out his phone, while his stomach churned with rejection and disappointment. He scrolled through his contacts and stabbed at the buttons. 'I've sent you her number,' he added as a beep sounded in the depths of her handbag.

'Thank you.'

'Call her whenever you like.'

'Don't you want to be in on it?'

'I already know what she's going to say.' And he didn't need to hear it—or anything else she might choose to add—again. What he needed was to get rid of everything that was whirling around inside him as a result of that aborted kiss, the agonising tension and the crushing disillusionment. 'Help yourself to lunch when you're done,' he said curtly. 'I'm going for a swim.'

Alex watched Max stride off, six foot plus of wound-up male, and sank onto the bed before her legs gave way.

What on earth had just happened? she wondered dazedly, her entire body trembling with shock and heat and confusion. One minute she'd been filled with concern for his well-being since he'd looked so tormented, the next she'd been in a clinch so blistering she was surprised they hadn't gone up in flames.

Touching his arm had been her first mistake, even though she'd desperately wanted to know what had been troubling him. Her fascination with the clench of his muscles beneath her fingers and the feel of his skin, which had meant she hadn't wanted to let him go, had been her second. Then she'd become aware that he'd gone very still and was looking at her with an intensity that robbed her of reason and knocked the breath from her lungs, and the mistakes had started coming thick and fast.

She shouldn't have allowed the enormous bed and the two of them entwined on it to dominate her thoughts. She should have spun on her heel and fled to the sanctuary of the terrace. But she hadn't. She'd been rooted to the spot, utterly transfixed by the inferno raging in his indigo gaze. Unguarded, fiery, havoc-wreaking heat, directed straight at her.

She didn't have time to wonder at the startling realisation that the attraction she'd assumed to be wholly one-sided could, in fact, be mutual. Or to even consider what was happening. A second later she'd been in his arms, her heart thundering so hard she'd feared she might be about to break a rib.

And, oh, the feel of him... The strength and power of his embrace and the intoxicating skill of his kiss. Her head was still swimming from its effect, her blood still burned. His mouth had delivered on every single promise it made. Heat had rushed through her veins, desire swirling around inside like a tropical storm. When he'd moved his hand to cup her breast the shivers that had run through her had nearly taken out her knees. If it hadn't been for that door, she'd have ended up in bed with him and she wouldn't even have cared. She'd have *relished* it, and that was so wrong she could scarcely believe it.

Where had that response come from? It had been so wild, so abandoned. Mortifyingly, she'd practically devoured him. So much for the professionalism she'd always prided herself on. She hadn't so much blurred the lines as erased them altogether.

What on earth had she been *thinking*? she asked herself, going icy cold with stupefied horror at what she'd done. Had she completely lost her tiny little mind? And where the hell had her rules been in all of this? Max had simply taken what he wanted and she'd let him. She'd had ample opportunity to push him away but she hadn't until it had been shamefully late. And before that she hadn't even thought about it. He might have taken her by surprise when he'd first kissed her but she hadn't for a moment considered not kissing him back.

God, she had to be careful. He was so much more dangerous than she'd imagined. He was such a threat to her rules, not because he saw them as a challenge necessarily, but because he made her want to break them herself. He made her forget why she had them in the first place.

But that couldn't happen. She couldn't afford to have her head turned or give in to the blazing attraction they clearly shared. Her future plans were at stake, and how good would it look if Finn ever got wind of what had just happened? He'd have every right to fire her after that lapse of professionalism.

If it happened again or, heaven forbid, went any further—which it absolutely wouldn't—and got out, her reputation would never recover.

A chill ran through her at the thought of how easily she could lose everything she'd worked so hard for. How precariously she teetered at the top of a very slippery slope. She couldn't allow another blip when it came to reason. Or make any more mistakes. She would not be governed by forces which threatened her very existence and over which she had no control. She would not turn into her family. She had an entirely different future to forge.

Three hours after Max had disappeared to go for his swim, Alex sat on a sofa beneath the shades that covered the terrace, nursing a glass of mint tea while largely ignoring the laptop open in front of her. How on earth could she concentrate on emails when she had so many other things occupying her mind?

Like that kiss…

No, not the kiss, she amended firmly. Hadn't she decided she wasn't going to think about it ever again? Wasn't she supposed to be completely ignoring the irritating little voice inside her head that demanded more of the delicious heat of it? She had and she was, and besides, it wasn't as if she didn't have anything else to think about. Such as the extraordinary conversation she'd just had with Max's mother.

As he'd told her, Carolyn Stafford had nothing to add to the investigation. With regard to Max's adoption, her then husband, the first of four and Max's father, had dealt with all the practicalities. He was the one who'd found the agency, arranged the payment and booked the flights to Argentina. She couldn't even recall filling in any forms. When it came to actually picking Max up, she had the haziest of recollections involving a woman whose name she couldn't remember, which struck Alex as very peculiar when it had to have been a momentous occasion.

The minute she'd established that Mrs Stafford could be of no further help, Alex should have hung up. The rest of the conversation had borne no relevance to anything. She didn't need to know about the issues in the marriage, the troubles they'd had conceiving and the belief that adopting a baby would somehow fix everything. The impact the divorce had had on Mrs Stafford was neither here nor there, although the way she hadn't spared a thought for how Max might have taken it was telling. She evidently held her son to blame for failing to repair the marriage, which didn't seem at all fair, and obviously considered him lacking in pretty much every other area. The digs and barbs had been well wrapped up and so subtle as to be easily missed, but Alex had noted them nonetheless.

But, to her shame, she hadn't hung up. Instead she'd listened to his mother's litany of complaints with growing indignation. She hadn't recognised anything about the man being described and at one point a sudden, inexplicable urge to put things right had surged up inside her, the force of it practically winding her.

But she'd known it would achieve precisely nothing.

Firstly, given that she'd only met Max yesterday, she was hardly qualified to provide an in-depth commentary on his character, even if she did have an extremely thorough knowledge of his mouth. Secondly, early on in her career with the police, Alex had done a course on psychopathic personalities and it sounded as if Max's mother was a narcissist. She'd come across as self-absorbed, condescending and unfairly critical. Everything had been about her. Any attempt to stand up for Max would have fallen on deaf ears, and that wasn't part of the job anyway.

She couldn't exactly start questioning him on it, she reminded herself, taking a sip of tea and staring out to sea, regardless of how much she might want to deep down. Not only was it none of her business, she was here to work, nothing more. She didn't need to know and, in any case, he wasn't around to ask.

And that was something else that was beginning to bother her, even though it surely shouldn't. Max had been gone for three hours. Wasn't that quite a long time for a swim? What if something had happened? Could he have been caught in a rip tide? What if he'd got a cramp and drowned? He might be a grown man who lived by the sea and presumably swam a lot, but maybe she ought to contact the coastguard. Just in case.

Trying to keep a lid on her growing alarm, Alex picked up her phone and opened up the browser to look for the number, when her gaze snagged on something moving in the water. A figure broke through the shimmering surface of the azure water, and she froze.

First to emerge was a sleek dark head, followed by a set of broad shoulders that she hadn't had nearly enough time to explore before. A swimmer's shoulders, she thought dazedly as she put the phone down, since there was clearly no need to contact the coastguard. Max, looking like some sort of Greek god, rising from the deep, master of all he surveyed, had not perished in the waves.

As he waded through the shallows, giving his head a quick shake that sprayed water off him like droplets of sparkling sunlight, more of his body was revealed. She was too far away to make out the details, but his bronzed shape was magnificent and by the time his long powerful legs emerged, undiluted lust was drumming through her, drugging her senses and heightening her awareness of everything. Her mouth was dry. Her breasts felt heavy and tight, and she was filled with the insane urge to get up and meet him and pull him down onto the sand with her and finish what they'd started back there in the guest house.

Having reached the shore, Max bent and picked up a towel off a lounger. He rubbed it over his head, slung it around his neck and started striding up the beach towards the steps, which gave her approximately thirty seconds to compose herself. It wasn't nearly enough, she realised, taking a series of slow deep breaths to calm her racing pulse and rid her body of the dizzying heat that she'd thought she'd obliterated hours ago.

But she managed it somehow, until he came to a stop right in front of her, blocking her view of the sea with an even better one, and she realised that her efforts had been in vain.

He didn't have an ounce of fat on him. He was all lean hard muscle. The depth of his tan suggested he spent a lot of time shirtless in the sun. Judging by the definition of his six-pack, he wasn't completely desk-bound. And she didn't need to wonder what might lie at the base of the vertical line of golden-brown hair that bisected his abdomen and disappeared enticingly beneath the waistband of his shorts because she'd felt it. She'd pressed her hips against it and wanted it hard and deep inside her, and that was exactly what would have happened if only that door hadn't slammed.

But she wasn't going to think about earlier. She certainly wasn't going to bring it up. If Max did, she'd brush it off as if it had meant nothing. Which it hadn't. And she was *relieved* that door had slammed, not disappointed.

But whatever.

Denial was the way forward here, even though she generally considered it an unwise and unhelpful strategy. In her line of work, knowledge was power. If her clients could accept what was going on, they could handle it. Right now, however, confronting what had happened when she was on such unsteady ground around him seemed like the worst idea in the world, and if that made her a hypocrite then so be it.

'How was the swim?' she said, nevertheless struggling to keep her tone light and her gaze off his chest.

'Good.'

'You were gone a long time.'

A gleam lit the depths of his indigo eyes. 'Were you worried about me, Alex?'

Maybe. 'No.'

He gripped the ends of the towel, which drew her attention to his hands and reminded her of how warm and sure they'd been, first on her face and then on her body.

'There's a floating bar the next bay along. I stopped for a drink.'

'A floating bar?' she echoed, determinedly keeping the memory of his kisses at bay. Was there no end to the incredibleness of this place?

'I'll take you for dinner there this evening.'

'I didn't bring a swimsuit.'

His gaze roamed over her, so slowly and thoroughly that she felt as if her clothes were simply falling away like scorched rags, and he murmured, 'That's a shame.'

No, it wasn't. The assignment didn't include swimsuits, dinner in a floating bar or the shedding of clothing. 'This isn't a holiday for me, Max,' she said, setting her jaw and pulling herself together. 'I was expecting to be heading straight to La Posada.' Which was situated six hundred kilometres inland. 'I didn't pack for a Caribbean island stopover.'

'All right. Forget the swimsuit,' he said, which immediately made her think of skinny-dipping with him in the gorgeous water beneath the moonlight. 'We'll go by boat.'

'No.'

'I apologise,' he said with a tilt of his head and a faint smile that lit an unwelcome spark of heat in the pit of her stomach. 'How would you feel about going by boat?'

The same. It wasn't going to happen, however he phrased it. She wasn't here for fun, and dinner out felt strangely dangerous. 'I'd rather you called in the favours you mentioned.'

'I already have.'

What? 'When?' she asked with a frown. How could he have wrong-footed her yet again?

'Earlier. On the plane.'

'What happened to working together?'

'What do you mean?'

'We had a deal, Max. You asked me to hand over everything, which I did. The least you could do is include me in your decision-making.'

'You were taking a nap.'

His reasonableness riled her even more than his unpredictability. 'Still,' she said frostily, not quite ready to accept that he'd done the right thing, given what had happened when the two of them had found themselves in close proximity to a bed. 'You should have told me.'

'I just have.'

Agh. 'You're impossible.'

His grin widened. 'Did you eat lunch?'

'No.' She hadn't felt comfortable raiding his fridge.

'Neither did I, and it seems neither of us is at our best on an empty stomach. So shall we meet back here in, say, half an hour?'

To her despair, Alex was all out of excuses. Any further protest and he might start questioning what was behind it. There was no way she wanted him guessing how much their kiss had unsettled her. Or how confusing she found the switch in demeanour when the last time she'd seen him he'd been all troubled and tense. And she badly needed him and his near naked body out of her sight. His mention of stomachs was making her want to check out his and she feared she wouldn't be able to stop there.

'Sounds great.'

CHAPTER FIVE

STALKING INTO HIS en-suite bathroom, Max stripped off and grabbed a towel. He secured it round his waist, rolled his shoulders to ease the ache that had set in as a result of his lengthy swim and, with a quick rub of his jaw, turned to the sink.

As he'd hoped, vigorous exercise, a cold beer and easy conversation had assuaged his earlier excruciating tension. It had taken a while, however. He'd been ploughing through the warm tropical water for twenty minutes at full speed before he'd been able to stop thinking about what would have happened had he and Alex not been interrupted.

His imagination had been on fire, and it had occurred to him as he'd cracked open a beer at La Copa Alegre that that was unusual because, despite his mother constantly telling him that his was very vivid whenever he'd tried to correct her memory about certain things as a kid, he'd never thought he had much of one. His ability to see outside the box and apply lateral thinking to problem-solving was second to none, but it was always done in the context of data. Facts. Systems, processes and algorithms. Lurid was not a word that had ever applied to his thoughts. It was now.

On emerging from the sea he'd intended to head straight for the house. But he'd felt Alex's eyes on him like a laser and had instead deviated towards her as if drawn by some invisible force. She'd taken off her jacket, he'd noticed once he'd been standing in front of her. The pale pink T-shirt she'd had on had been tight. The alluring curve of her breasts had not escaped his notice, and as a bolt of heat had rocketed through him at the memory of how she'd felt in his hand, tightening his muscles and giving him an erection as hard as granite, he'd been grateful for the loose fit of his shorts.

She might have chosen to opt for denial with regard to the chemistry they shared, he thought now, lathering up his jaw, reaching for a razor and setting about methodically cutting swathes through the foam, but he wasn't. That kiss had blown his mind. He wanted more. A lot more. And so did she. She'd barely been able to keep her eyes off his bare chest just now. The hunger in her gaze had been illuminating. It gave him ideas. Would it be playing dirty to capitalise on her interest in his body? Might it not simply lead her to realise that little bit faster that making out with him hadn't been a mistake?

He couldn't deny that the idea of pushing more of her buttons appealed. He liked the way her eyes narrowed and flashed when she was riled. It gave him a kick, as did the thought of demolishing her barriers and persuading her to break her own rules. The end would more than justify the means. Based on the wild heat of the kiss, he had little doubt the end would be spectacular.

There was no need to dwell on the other ways in which Alex bothered him, he told himself as he rinsed his face. He wasn't interested in any similarities in their upbringings. Or their myriad differences in outlook. He'd never meet her family. It didn't matter that she'd looked very comfortable sitting on his sofa on his terrace drinking his tea. Or somehow *right*. No one had been or ever would be right.

Love didn't exist, in his experience—certainly not the unconditional kind that people banged on about—and he was through long ago with trying to conform to someone else's expectations in the futile hope of reward. But even if he had believed in it, even if he had deserved it, he would have steered well clear.

Love, he'd decided while cooling his heels in that prison cell all those years ago, was likely to be unpredictable and tumultuous. It would follow no formula and the outcome would not be dependent on the input. If love were a flowchart, it wouldn't be nice and neat, with square boxes and straight arrows. It would be a mess of thought bubbles filled with dramatic declarations and angst amidst a tangle of wiggly lines, a constant state of confusion and turmoil, and who needed that kind of hassle?

Sure, he'd had a few wild and wacky girlfriends as a youth, but he'd subsequently come to the conclusion that it was far safer to focus on his own world and his place in it. To be in total control of his actions and opinions and emotions, and responsible for those alone. Relationships meant having to take someone else's feelings into account, and he'd never been shown how to do that. He wouldn't know how to do such a thing even if he'd wanted to.

No, when it came to women, he was supremely content with keeping things short and simple, one or two nights, a week at most, avoiding emotional involvement and unmeetable expectations, and how he felt about Alex was no different. The strength of his desire for her might be unique, but she wasn't. All he wanted, he thought as he stepped into the shower and switched on the water, was her in his bed. Anything else was totally irrelevant. So tonight he'd focus on that.

La Copa Alegre was as fabulous as Alex had imagined. The two-floor wooden platform was anchored to the seabed three hundred metres offshore and floated on the surface of a literal sea of cerulean. In the centre stood the grass-roofed bar. At one end, giant sails of fawn fabric shaded the deck, upon which sat half a dozen double sunbeds. At the other was the grill that had cooked the sublime seafood platter which had arrived at their table twenty minutes ago. Strings of softly glowing lights looped around the structure and sultry Latin American beats thumped out of the speakers situated on the top floor that was a sun deck by day and dance floor by night.

So in no way was it the venue making Alex regret not being firmer in putting her foot down about dinner. That was all down to Max, who for some reason had decided to switch on the charm.

It was hard enough to resist him when he was being irritatingly unpredictable and immensely frustrating. It was almost impossible when he kept up a flow of easy conversation while flashing her devilish smiles. And then there was the revelation that he was fluent in Spanish. She didn't speak a word, so she could only take an educated guess at what he actually said when he issued greetings and ordered drinks and food, but the sexy accent and the deep timbre of his voice when he rolled his 'r's were spine-tingling.

So much for her intention to stick to mineral water and keep a clear head, she thought exasperatedly, taking a sip of her drink and despairing of how badly wrong this whole occasion was going. She'd given in to his suggestion of a margarita with embarrassing speed. But then she'd needed something strong to dampen the insane heat and desire that had been rushing along her veins and repeatedly knocking her sideways ever since he'd reappeared on the terrace on the dot of the appointed hour.

That he'd been on time had been a surprise. The fact that he'd shaved was another. On the one hand it was rather exciting to be able to gaze at the strong line of his jaw, but on the other she missed the stubble that had, only this morning, grazed the ultrasensitive skin of her neck and whipped up such a whirlpool of sensation inside her.

And then there were all the tiny touches that had happened along the way. The warm palm at the base of her spine as he'd led her to the boat, burning through the fabric of her top and scorching her back. The firm grip of his fingers around hers when he'd helped her first board and then alight on arrival at the bar. Why hadn't he let her go as abruptly as he had this morning? Why had his hand lingered on hers? More annoyingly, why couldn't she stop thinking about the kiss?

Under any other circumstances, with the attention Max was paying her, this evening might feel like a date. Yet it wasn't. It couldn't be. Nor was any of it remotely relaxing. The margarita was doing nothing to assuage the desire flooding every inch of her being. Her pulse thudded heavily in time to the music vibrating through her. She'd changed into a sleeveless top and a pair of loose trousers, but her clothes felt too tight. Every time she moved, the fabric brushed over her body and her hypersensitive skin tingled.

She was overdressed, that was the trouble. The rest of the select, beautiful clientele were far more scantily clad, and that included Max. He was wearing a pair of sand-coloured shorts and a white shirt that he hadn't bothered to button up, and that was yet another source of discomfort. His bare chest, just across the table, was insanely distracting. She couldn't look away. She wanted to lean over and touch. To put her mouth to his skin and see if she could taste traces of salt from his swim. At one point he'd lifted his bottle of beer to his mouth and a drop of condensation had landed on his right pec. It had sat there, not going anywhere, snagging her attention, and she'd wanted to lick it off. She'd wanted to trace her tongue over the ridges of his muscles and run her fingers over the smattering of hair that covered them.

The clamouring urge to do all this—and more—was not only crazy, it was intolerable. She would never give in to it. It would not be professional to embark on anything with someone who was part of an assignment. If she did and it got out, her reputation would be destroyed. But even if there had been no assignment and they'd met under entirely different circumstances, Max would still be off-limits. Firstly, he'd never allow her to call the shots and, secondly, he posed a huge threat to her control and could easily give her a push down the genetic slippery slope she feared so much.

No, she had to focus on work and stay strong. Her resolve must not weaken, however great the provocation. She had to call a halt to the nonsense going on inside her.

She set her glass down with rather more force than

was necessary and determinedly pulled herself together. 'So I spoke to your mother,' she said, taking a prawn from the platter and peeling it. 'You were right. She doesn't have anything to add to this case.'

'I thought not.'

Max appeared to have nothing further to add to that, but she needed to pursue this line of questioning if she stood any chance of keeping her thoughts out of the gutter. 'Aren't you interested in what she did have to say?'

'I can't think of anything I'm less interested in right now.'

His languid gaze drifted over her, electrifying her nerve-endings, and the prawn she'd just put in her mouth nearly went down the wrong way, but she was not to be deterred.

'You said she was difficult,' she said, clearing her throat and ignoring the sizzling heat powering through her veins. 'I can see what you mean.'

'Have I told you how lovely you look this evening?'

At his compliment her temperature rocketed, despite her best efforts to stay cool. 'We only met yesterday,' she said, determined not to let it or the unsettlingly alluring gleam in his eyes detract her. 'I look like this all the time.'

'And still very professional.'

Now that was a compliment she could get behind. If he recognised that their relationship was to remain purely professional it would make her life a whole lot easier for the next week or two. 'Thank you.'

'Do you ever let your hair down?'

She frowned. What did that have to do with anything? 'Literally or metaphorically?'

'Either. Both.'

'Metaphorically, I run. The generally wet, perpetually grey pavements of London aren't a patch on your lovely Caribbean waters, but I like them.' And literally, her hair was tied back in a ponytail this evening, which was really rather relaxed for her. But they were getting off topic. 'So. Back to what I was saying, I—'

'Alex.'

'Yes?'

'Stop.'

'Stop what?'

'I'm not going to talk to you about my mother,' he said, the cool evenness of his tone totally belying the shutters she could see slamming down over the gleam. 'Not this evening. Not ever.'

Why not? What was the story there? She badly wanted to know, because there definitely was one, and these days she couldn't come across a mystery without needing to solve it. But his jaw was set and his shoulders were tight, and what could she do? Wrestle the information out of him?

'All right,' she said, suppressing the instant vision of exactly how that wrestling might play out and parking the topic of his mother until later.

'Good.'

'Have any of those favours you called in produced anything useful?'

'Not yet.'

'It's insanely frustrating.'

'And far too nice an evening to be talking about the investigation,' he said, his eyes glittering in the candlelight and the faint smile now curving his lips doing strange things to her stomach. 'There'll be plenty of time for that when we arrive in La Posada tomorrow. Why don't you take a break tonight?'

Take a break? He had *no* idea. 'I haven't taken a break in years,' she said, flatly ignoring his effect on her.

'All the more reason to do so now.'

What did he know about it? 'How much time do you take off?'

'Three or four months a year.'

Seriously? 'What do you do?'

'I surf. Hang out with friends. Travel.'

Alex stifled the pang of envy and then consoled herself with the realisation that he'd been his own boss twice as long as she had. 'Has your business never given you a moment's concern?'

He leaned forwards and regarded her thoughtfully for a second. 'Honestly?' he said, turning his attention to the seafood platter. 'No. Ever since I was arrested I've had so much work come my way that I've been able to pick and choose.'

'An unusual outcome to an arrest, I imagine, but lucky you.'

'It's not luck. I'm exceptionally good at what I do.'

And what else might that be? she couldn't help wondering as her gaze snagged on his hands, which were deftly dealing with a lobster claw. How skilled would they be on her? Not that they'd ever *be* on her again, obviously. The kiss had been a never-to-be-repeated aberration, and he was still talking.

'Your website says that you were in the police for ten years before you started up your own agency five years ago.'

'That's right,' she said, ruthlessly removing the scorching images of his hands on her body from her head and biting into the slice of lime that garnished her margarita in the hope that the sharp acid hit might jolt some sense into her.

'What made you swap?'

This was better. A conversation about work she could handle. 'Years ago, when I suspected my then husband was cheating on me, I hired a private investigator to find out what was going on and report back to me. Which he did. But not with a whole lot of sympathy or tact. I saw a gap in the market for a more sensitive approach and decided to fill it. We started off investigating cases of suspected infidelity, then expanded to work on missing persons and fraud. There's very little we don't now cover.'

'Impressive.'

She put down the slice of lime and sat back. 'I

have big plans, which I will allow nothing and no one to ruin,' she said pointedly.

'I'm surprised that you'd take the risk.'

Oh? 'Why?'

'You said you liked order and structure. A career in the police reflects that. Setting up your own business doesn't.'

Hmm. So that was true. She'd never really thought about it like that. She'd only ever focused on her need for security. But maybe she was more of a risk-taker than she'd thought. Professionally, at any rate. Only time would tell whether hers would pay off, but if it didn't it wouldn't be because she hadn't tried her hardest.

'Yes, well, there was also the complication that my ex worked for the police too,' she said, hauling her focus back to the conversation. 'We met on the training course and were posted to the same area. The divorce made things difficult. I was under no obligation to leave but it was hard. Especially when he started dating another colleague.'

'He should have been the one to go,' Max said bluntly.

'I agree,' Alex replied. 'But once I got my head around it and started making plans it was exciting. I wanted to move on anyway. From everything.'

'What went wrong?'

So that was none of his business. That strayed from the professional into the personal, and it was a step she wasn't sure she wanted to take. She didn't like to talk about the mistakes she'd made or even think about how naïve and foolish and desperate she'd once been.

And yet, if she shared more of herself with Max, maybe he'd feel obliged to do the same with her. Her curiosity about his relationship with his mother was killing her. She wanted to know everything about it, for the case, naturally, but she suspected it would not be forthcoming without serious leverage. Perhaps not even then, but she had to give it a try, and since she'd got over the disaster of her marriage long ago, it wouldn't exactly be traumatic.

'I got married far too young and far too quickly,' she said, twirling her glass between her fingers and resisting the urge to down the remainder of her drink. 'I'd already left the chaos of my family behind. A solid relationship seemed to me to be the next step and I guess I thought that in one I'd find the emotional connection I'd been missing at home. I was embarrassingly desperate to go down the conventional route. I thought I'd found a partner for life and we were engaged within three months.'

'So it was a whirlwind romance.'

'Hardly,' she said dryly. 'He broke our vows within months of the ink drying on the certificate. Yet it took me five more years of trying to fix things before realising that I had to end it for good.'

'That's a long time.'

'Far too long, in hindsight. God knows where my self-respect was. But I hated the thought of failing. I gave him endless chances and believed too many of his promises. I tried to change, more fool me. I even turned down a promotion because it meant more time away from home and he wasn't happy about that.'

'You left no stone unturned.'

'Exactly. But none of it worked.' She shook her head and gazed at the shadowy horizon for a moment before giving herself a quick shake. Regrets were futile. All she could do was ensure that if she ever did get over her trust issues enough to embark on another relationship, she wouldn't make the same mistake again. 'Looking back, I don't know what I was thinking. I guess I was going through some kind of identity crisis. Police officers are supposed to have sound judgement. Mine was a disaster.'

'The man was an idiot.'

'Well, he was young too,' she said, a little confused by the ribbon of warmth that was winding through her at Max's terse pronouncement. 'And my career was moving faster than his, which I think he found intimidating. He used to make these sly little comments to undermine my confidence and belittle me.'

'Like I said, an idiot.'

'The only good thing to come out of the whole sorry mess was that I made a promise to myself that never again would I try and be what someone else expected me to be. I've learned to be exceptionally resilient on that front. Very little shocks me these days.

Except people's propensity for self-centredness. That still floors me every time. I don't know why.'

'What did your parents want you to be?'

'Definitely not a police officer,' she said, unable to prevent a quick stab of hurt and regret from piercing her heart. 'I grew up in a very working class area of east London, except "working" class is a bit of a misnomer. It was a sink estate with lots of crime and many social problems. My school had a forty per cent truancy rate. No one cared. I once told my teacher that I wanted to go to university and she first just stared at me and then burst out laughing. At that point I realised that if I wanted to achieve anything I'd have to do it on my own. Joining the police was a way out.'

'Do your parents still live there?'

'Yes.'

'Your job must have made visiting tricky.'

'It made it impossible. But then I wasn't welcome anyway. I'm still not.'

'Do you want to be?' he asked, something about the intensity of his expression suggesting that he was really interested in her answer.

'I'm not sure,' she said with a sigh. 'Sometimes I think I do, which is nuts, right?'

'Not at all. As we've already established, families are complicated. Yours is probably jealous.'

She stared at him for a moment as that sank in. 'Do you think so?'

He shrugged. 'It's a possibility, I guess, although

I'm no expert. But, ultimately, whatever lies at the heart of it, it's not your problem. You can't change anything. You'd be better off letting it go.'

Easy for him to say. 'And how do I go about that?'

'I wish I knew.'

A shadow flitted across his expression and she wondered suddenly if perhaps it wasn't easy for him to say. Could it be that he wasn't as laid-back as he liked to portray, and was, in fact, far more complex a character than she'd thought? It was a more appealing idea than it should have been. 'Let me know when you figure it out.'

'Likewise. But, for what it's worth,' he said, 'I think that what you've achieved under the circumstances is remarkable.'

Did he? She scoured his face for signs of insincerity but found none. Well, well, well. A little boost to her self-esteem from a man who was her opposite in almost every way. Who'd have thought? 'Thank you.'

'You're welcome. Would you like some dessert?'

Yes, was the answer on the tip of her tongue. For dessert she wanted him. A little salt, a little sweetness, a whole lot of spice. However, since that wasn't going to happen and she was full of shellfish and margarita, she ought to decline. But, for some bizarre reason, she couldn't get the 'no' out. Despite how very on-edge she was feeling, she didn't want the evening to end. And, besides, he owed her now, and this time she wouldn't be letting the debt go unpaid. 'Dessert would be lovely.'

CHAPTER SIX

MAX DUG HIS spoon into a bowl of coconut sorbet and thought that he could easily understand Alex's determination not to conform to someone else's expectations. How many times as a kid had he tried to do the exact same thing, with equally disappointing results? How long had he spent pointlessly trying to figure out what it was his mom wanted from him and then attempting to provide it, to no avail? It had never ended well. The inevitable failure ate away at a person's confidence and crushed their spirit until either they were ground to dust or got out. Like him, Alex had chosen the latter. He wondered if, also like him, she inwardly recoiled at the word 'compromise'.

Her ex-husband was the biggest fool on the planet. She was beautiful, intelligent and capable. To be cherished, not cheated on, if a long-term relationship was your thing. Any idiot could see that. How pathetically insecure must he have been, to handle her successes with such disparagement. How difficult that must have been to live with. Max had experienced both, having been on the receiving end of endlessly crippling insincerity and belittling while growing up, and his admiration for her grew.

Not that Alex's marriage was any of his concern, beyond the fact that it had ended and she was now single. How much he admired her was irrelevant. The stab of sympathy he'd felt when she'd been talking about disappointing her family had been wholly unnecessary.

What was important here was that his plan to get her into bed worked and, infuriatingly, with the way things were going, it didn't look as if it was going to. All evening he'd been as charming as he knew how—which had had great results in the past—and he'd deliberately left his shirt undone, but she'd seemed remarkably unmoved by his efforts. She'd generally responded to his flirting with an arch of an eyebrow and a glare of disapproval and hadn't ogled his chest once.

He, on the other hand, was anything but unmoved by her. She'd changed out of the trouser suit of earlier into a pair of loose-fitting trousers and a sleeveless top and looked effortlessly chic, which was a result he was sure she hadn't intended. The breeze had loosened her ponytail so that tendrils of hair fluttered around her face. He wanted to peel the clothes from her body and pull the band from her hair with a need that bordered on desperate.

While eating, she kept making all these appreciative noises, even groaning at times, and he'd instinctively contemplated all the ways *he* might be able to make her groan, should the opportunity arise. Desire was drumming through him and he was so hard it hurt and all he could think about was what it would take to erode her resolve. What more could he do? The not knowing, the possibility of failure, was driving him nuts.

'What you've achieved is remarkable too,' she said, cutting through his frustration and making him glance up at her.

'What do you mean?'

'It doesn't sound like you had the easiest of childhoods either.'

He didn't want to talk about that. He wanted to talk about the chemistry they shared that she seemed determined to ignore, or, better still, act on it. And what did she know of his childhood anyway? How long had her conversation with his mother lasted?

'As I told you before,' he said so smoothly she'd never guess how churned-up inside he was feeling, 'that subject is off-limits.'

'Was it that bad?'

It had been traumatic and difficult and he had no wish to take a trip down that particular memory lane. 'It bears no relevance to anything.'

The look she levelled at him was pointed. 'Neither did mine.'

Now what was that supposed to mean? That because she'd talked to him he was under some sort of obligation to reciprocate? To hell with that. He'd hardly forced her to spill out the details of her marriage. He hadn't even been that interested. He owed her nothing.

And yet…

Maybe it wasn't such a bad idea. What if opening up to her succeeded where the flirting and his bare chest hadn't? What if she was the sort of woman to be lured into bed with sincerity and connection rather than flattery and visuals?

He wanted her more than he'd wanted anyone and failure hadn't been an option since the moment he'd left the police station a reformed character. So perhaps he should take a leaf out of her book and leave no stone unturned in his quest to seduce her.

Any connection created would hardly be deep and it sure as hell wouldn't be binding. It wasn't as if his experiences were any great secret. It was just that he'd never felt the need to share before. He'd never had a conversation where this aspect of his past came up. But it had now, and if he continued to deflect she might suspect there was more to it than there really was, and for some reason that didn't appeal. Besides, with her background, she'd hardly be likely to judge.

'All right, fine,' he said, nevertheless bracing himself as he set his spoon into his empty bowl and met her gaze. 'The environment I grew up in was a toxic one.'

She sat back and regarded him steadily, and he was strangely relieved to see in her expression no sign of victory that she'd succeeded where no one else ever had. 'You said your parents argued.'

'It was more than just that,' he said darkly. 'It was frequently a full-on war. My mother is obnoxious.'

'Your mother is a narcissist.'

At her blunt observation, Max frowned. 'What makes you say that?'

'Well, I'm no expert, obviously, but I once did a course on psychopathic personalities and, from what I recall, she fits the profile.'

'Which is?'

'A constant demand for praise and attention, ignoring the needs of others and a belief of being special, for a start.'

That sounded very familiar. 'How about an inability to tolerate criticism, never-ending attention-seeking and an obsessive need to control the lives of others?'

She nodded and took a sip of her drink. 'All that too.'

'Then you could be right.' He'd always known his mother was utterly self-absorbed, but he had to admit now that was probably the least of it.

'The conversation I had with her earlier today was extraordinary.'

'What did she say?'

Alex tilted her head and regarded him for one long heart-stopping moment. 'I thought you didn't want to know.'

Well, no, he hadn't then. But he did now. Because,

THE BILLIONAIRE WITHOUT RULES

to be quite honest, he was sick to the back teeth of
being in the dark. The dark was where a man could
get hurled off course, where doubts set in and chaos
reigned, and three days of it was more than enough.
'Humour me.'

'It's not pretty.'

'I can take it,' he said, thinking that that was
hardly news. Nothing about his family background
was pretty. How bad could it be?

'You won't shoot the messenger?'

He had entirely different plans for the messenger
if this strategy of his played out. 'No.'

'OK, then,' she said, taking a deep breath, her
gaze unwavering. 'She told me that the marriage
was in trouble and that she'd decided a baby—you—
would fix things. Your father initially refused but
she told him that if he loved her he'd do this for her,
and fast.'

Even though he'd been expecting the worst, the
information still struck him like a blow to the gut.
Yet another ultimatum, he thought, acid and bitterness swilling around inside him. How he hated them.
So he really *hadn't* been wanted by his parents. He
didn't know why it was such a shock when the evidence had always been there, but it was nonetheless.

'She said she doesn't remember anything about
picking you up,' Alex continued, oblivious to the
turmoil he was experiencing, 'and I don't know if
that's genuinely the case or if, once it had been done,
it had served its purpose and didn't require any more

thought. Given her narcissism, I suspect the latter. She laid a lot of the blame for things at your feet, wholly unfairly. That kind of behaviour can be very destructive. I'm so sorry.'

He loathed the pity in her eyes and wished he could shrug casually, but he couldn't. 'It's not your fault,' he said, thinking that the old adage 'be careful what you wish for' had never been more appropriate.

'My father should have stood up to her. He should have been stronger. He should have said no.'

'Narcissists can be very persuasive and manipulative.'

She was right about that. To the outside world, his mother was beautiful and charming. It was only with her family that she showed her true monstrous self. Appearances were everything, which was presumably why their disaster of a marriage had limped on for so long. But still.

'He was weak. He was worse than I was in his efforts to please an unappeasable woman.'

'A toxic environment indeed.'

'And yet he left me there.' For which Max had never forgiven him. But perhaps the adoption explained that. Perhaps he'd never considered Max his true son.

'Didn't they share custody of you?'

'My mother was keen to keep control over me and my father couldn't have cared less.'

'How devastating.'

'It wasn't great.'

'Did you see much of him before he died?' she asked, her voice cracking a little and her eyes shimmering.

'Twice.' That was it. Neither visit had been a success. He'd harboured a lot of anger and his father had clearly just wanted to put everything behind him. 'He moved to Los Angeles after the divorce,' he said flatly, ruthlessly clamping the lid down on all the old memories and feelings that were bubbling up.

'The other side of the country.'

'It wasn't a coincidence.'

'And you choosing the Caribbean as your home, which is what, two thousand miles from New York?'

She was too clever by half. 'That's not a coincidence either.'

'I didn't think so. What about your stepfathers?'

'They were never around for long.'

'Used and then discarded?'

'Either that or they swiftly saw through the deceptively beautiful facade and got the hell out.'

She shook her head. 'I can't imagine what it must have been like.'

He was glad she couldn't. He wouldn't wish it on anyone. 'It wasn't much fun,' he said with staggering understatement. 'My dad couldn't have cared less about me while my mom was obsessed. She had to control everything. My friends, my clothes, even the music I listened to. Weakness and failure weren't allowed. They reflected badly on her. Expectations were impossibly high and I rarely met them, and the criticism was relentless. Nothing I did was ever good enough and she had no problem with letting me know that. If I put a foot out of line, she'd go very still and very quiet and then simply walk out of the room. In the end I figured it was less hassle to keep my opinions and feelings to myself. She wouldn't let me stay out of her way, so I just bided my time and bit my tongue until I got accepted at MIT.'

'How on earth did you get through it?'

'I had the hacking and its community.'

'Like I had studying,' she said with a slow nod of what looked like understanding. 'I spent most of my time at the library. That was where I realised my family chose to live the way they did and that I could choose not to.'

'Hence the rules?'

'Via the classics.'

'Everyone needs some form of escape.'

'And everyone has expectations to face,' she countered, 'although in my case, they were low rather than high. I still don't meet them and I've come to terms with that, so I have no idea why I still feel guilty about it.'

Her too? 'I was angry for a very long time.'

'I think I still am.'

'You should try a couple of days in jail. There's nothing like it for reflecting on what's going wrong and why. Break a law or two. It's a lot cheaper than therapy.'

'I'll bear that in mind,' she said with a faint smile.

'But you do realise your parents' behaviour is none of your fault, don't you?'

'In theory, yes. In practice, it's complicated.'

'As I know only too well. So is all that why you're so keen to track your biological parents?'

'I need to know who I am and where I come from,' he said, once again struck by her perception as much as the effect of her smile on his lungs. 'How I ended up with parents who didn't give a crap about me. With a mother who can't even remember travelling halfway across the world to pick me up and a father who barely spared me a thought. I've spent the last decade believing I'd dealt with it and living in relative peace. But one twenty-minute interview three days ago blew that peace to smithereens and I need it back. I hate not knowing what's going on. With so much information about my history missing, I suddenly feel like half a person. I need that information. I need answers.' Deep down, he also desperately hoped he'd find out that, whatever the circumstances that had led to his adoption, he'd once been wanted, but there was no way in hell he was going to share that with her. Exposing that level of vulnerability to another human being was never going to happen. Instead, he said, 'You have no idea what it's like to have your life so suddenly torn apart.'

'Well, I do have some idea,' she said with a tilt of her head. 'When I first found out my husband was cheating on me, my world collapsed. Not just my marriage, but everything I'd been working towards.

Structure. Normality. A life of conventionality. It took me a while, too, to get back on track, and God knows it wasn't easy, but I did, and nothing will push me off it again.'

'Which is why the success of this assignment is so important to you, why you wouldn't just take my money and move on.' She was fighting for her future like he was fighting for his identity.

She nodded. 'When I was young I was repeatedly told I'd never amount to anything. I've worked hard to overcome that. You were right about the importance of the fee Finn's paying me. It does matter. But his good opinion is invaluable. Much of my work comes via word-of-mouth and his recommendation would open all kinds of doors. I have big expansion plans and I won't have them derailed.'

Yeah, well, he had big plans too and didn't want them derailed either. He was done with talking about the past. It was all water under the bridge anyway. He was infinitely more interested in the present and the imminent future. The conversation had taken an unexpectedly heavy turn but that didn't mean it couldn't now be steered in a different direction. It was still early and he wanted her as much as ever. It was time to wrap things up here and move on.

'Are you done?' he asked, wiping his head of the conversation and everything it had stirred up and contemplating his next step instead.

'Yes. Thank you.'

'Then we should head back.'

* * *

The boat journey back to Max's house was conducted in silence, the warm dark night acting like a sort of blanket that prevented further conversation, which was more than all right with Alex, who was feeling all churned up inside by what she'd learned about his upbringing, such as it had been.

She couldn't get the look of torment that had appeared on his face when she'd revealed what his mother had said to her on the phone out of her head. Or the shock and the hurt that had flashed in the depths of his eyes, even if he had got it all under control with remarkable speed.

Should she have told him? was the question that kept rolling around her thoughts. If she'd known the effect it was going to have on him, she might have thought twice. But, on the other hand, if they asked, didn't everyone deserve to know the truth, however messy, whether it was to do with a faithless spouse, an embezzling employee or a narcissistic mother? Hadn't she always believed that ignorance wasn't necessarily bliss?

One of the things she recalled from her course on psychopathic personalities was that the effects of narcissistic behaviour on those around the narcissist could include feelings of not being good enough, a deep-rooted need for approval and the suppression of emotion. Before this evening, if she'd put much thought to it, she'd have remembered Max's pride in his former life as a hacker and his general air of supreme confidence and assumed that he'd overcome any suffering he might have experienced or even escaped totally unscathed.

But she'd have been wrong.

How could he not have been affected? she reflected, her heart wrenching at the thought of it, while the Caribbean breeze whipped at the scarf she'd tied around her head to protect her hair. He'd essentially been bought by a pair of people who didn't deserve to be parents, and then shamelessly used by one while being wholly neglected by the other. It was hard to know which one of them had been worse. An insecure, manipulative mother or a father who'd bailed on him and left him to the cruel whims of a woman who only thought of herself?

What a horrible, wretched environment he'd been brought up in. He'd had no siblings, no one who was going through the same thing to talk to. What must it have been like to grow up knowing that his father didn't want him? That while his mother had been physically present, every interaction she'd had with him had had an ulterior motive? Where had the love been? The affection? Not that she knew much about it, having had little of either herself.

No wonder he'd sought out an online community among which to find what he'd been missing at home. She couldn't imagine it would have been the place for a discussion of the kind of angst his upbringing must have generated, but the comradeship he had clearly found there had to have been the only way to survive, just as studying and a plan to escape had for her. If there'd been anything remotely amusing about any of it she'd have thought it was funny how they'd both drawn the short straw on the family front, but really there wasn't.

Once they were on dry land and heading up the steps to the house, Alex wondered how he felt about it all now and what effects still lingered in a way that had nothing to do with the filling of a gap in her professional knowledge. She was intrigued by the many complicated layers to him and the insanely tough journey he'd had. She couldn't imagine what he was going through now, having had his world turned so upside down by the discovery of his adoption. Her identity crisis wasn't a patch on the one he had to be undergoing.

'Nightcap?' he offered as he headed for the outdoor bar, his deep voice making her shiver despite the balminess of the evening.

'No, thank you,' she said, managing to muster up a smile to mask the thoughts rocketing around her head. 'I think I'll head to bed.' Where she would no doubt revisit their conversation at the bar and wonder if there was some way she could help him deal with everything. Where she would ponder his insight into her family's possible jealousy and her blamelessness for it instead of the way he made her feel. Where her resolve to stay strong and resist him wouldn't be challenged by the burning desire to know more about him and the dark, sensual intimacy of the terrace that was softly lit by hundreds of tiny discreet solar-powered lights.

'The night is young.'

'But today's been a big day,' she pointed out, slightly dazed by how eventful it had been, 'and tomorrow's an even bigger one.'

He turned to face her and leaned against the work-top of the bar. 'Just one drink.'

'Jet lag is catching up with me.' It was a lie. She'd never felt so energised. But she didn't trust herself. The intensity of his gaze was a threat to her reason. Where was the flirting? Where was the charm? That she could bat away. This sudden serious intent of his, on top of the intimate conversation they'd had earlier, felt so much more dangerous.

'Coward.'

She went very still. His eyes were dark, his expression unsmiling and her pulse skipped a beat. 'What makes you say that?'

'Your determination to ignore what's between us.'

Her heart thumped and her mouth went dry. So they were doing this, then. 'There's nothing between us.'

The fire burning in his gaze nearly wiped out her knees. 'Our kiss this morning would suggest otherwise.'

'Like I said, that was a mistake.' And the less said about it the better.

'I disagree,' he said, his voice low and rough. 'It nearly blew the top of my head off. If that door hadn't slammed when it did, you know we'd have ended up in bed together. And you know we'd probably still be there.'

She envied how easily he could accept what he wanted from her. He was so sure, so confident. In this, she was quite the opposite and, despite the envy, she couldn't help wishing that he'd opted for denial like she had.

She swallowed hard and fought for control. 'I know nothing of the sort.'

'I'm very attracted to you, Alex,' he said, running his gaze over her so slowly and thoroughly that a wave of heat rushed over her, tightening her nipples in a way she desperately hoped he wouldn't notice. 'As you are to me. You can carry on burying your head in the sand if you want, but that won't make it go away.'

Wouldn't it? He was probably right. The pressure crushing her was immense. How much longer could she stand it? Perhaps if she confronted the attraction, the intoxicating mystery of it would disappear and along with it the heat and the desire. Denial wasn't working and facing up to things was something she encouraged in her clients, so maybe she ought to put her money where her mouth was.

'All right,' she said, mentally crossing her fingers and wishing her heart would stop hammering quite so hard. 'It's true. I want you. A lot. And I'm not in the slightest bit happy about it.'

'I know you aren't,' he said, the tension in his shoulders easing a fraction and the ghost of a smile curving his mouth. 'But do you have any idea how rare the chemistry between us is?'

'Not really,' she admitted, thinking that if she was in for a penny she might as well be in for a pound. 'I imagine I'm considerably less experienced than you.'

'We'd be explosive together.'

Like phosphorus and air. There she was, happily sitting surrounded by water, all nicely inert and safe, and then along he came, luring her to the surface and encouraging her to break through it, at which point things would go bang.

'It's not going to happen,' she said, having to believe that for the sake of her future.

'Why not?'

'There's a huge conflict of interest.'

'As we've established, I'm not your client.'

'That's not the point,' she said, struggling for a moment to remember quite what the point was when her head was filling with images of the two of them being explosive together. 'Finding the truth about your adoption is too important to me to screw up by fooling around and getting distracted.'

'Who says we can't do both?'

'I do.'

'You want me.'

'That doesn't matter.'

He regarded her for one achingly long moment. 'You know I could prove you wrong, don't you?'

In a heartbeat. Desire was flooding through her, weakening her knees and her resistance. All he'd have to do was touch her and she'd go up in flames. 'I'd hope you have more integrity than to try,' she said, inching back out of his mind-scrambling orbit and wondering if she was expecting too much from a criminally minded former hacker.

'On any other occasion, I'd say I absolutely do,' he said with an assessing tilt of his head. 'Right here, right now, however, I'd put it at fifty-fifty.'

Her heart gave a lurch and for one appalling moment she couldn't work out which fifty she wanted. But then she pulled herself together. 'I have rules about this sort of thing.'

'Of course you do.'

'Don't mock me.'

'I'm not. But would it really be so bad if they got broken?'

'Yes,' she said firmly, squashing the little voice in her head yelling, *Would it? Really?* The risks vastly outweighed any potential reward. She couldn't allow herself to think about possible explosions.

'Why?'

'I've worked insanely hard to get where I've got and my reputation is everything to me. I would stand to lose a lot if it got out that I fraternise with people involved in a case.'

'Who would ever know?'

'I would.'

'But think of the fireworks.'

'There'd be fireworks?' What was she saying? Of course there'd be fireworks. Mini Catherine wheels were spinning in her stomach and they weren't even touching.

He ran his gaze over her yet again, as if he *knew* the effect it would have on her, and those Catherine wheels nearly took off. 'I know what I'm doing.'

That didn't help one little bit, because now all she could think about was how spectacularly good in bed he would be. 'I wish I did.'

'You do,' he said. 'You're successful and well-respected. Finn sang your praises. He described you as tenacious and determined. He wouldn't have hired you if you hadn't come highly recommended. Your reputation would be in no danger from sleeping with me.'

Maybe it would. Maybe it wouldn't. But, actually, that wasn't the real issue.

'You're wasting your time, Max,' she said with a shake of her head, although who she was trying to warn she wasn't sure. 'We are totally different. Sleeping with you would bring chaos to my life. You're unpredictable, a loose cannon. And I don't want that, however briefly. I need to stay in control of everything. My rules aren't just about order and structure. They keep me focused. On the right track. Every morning I wake up with the feeling that if I'm not careful I could well end up like the rest of my family. That all it will take is one slip, one "it'll be fine just this once", and genes will take over and I'll lose everything I've worked so hard for. You can't have any idea what that's like.'

'I know exactly what that's like,' he said, his

eyes dark and glittering. 'I've done everything in my power not to turn out like either of my parents. Doesn't matter that we share no genes. Nurture trumps nature in my case.'

'I won't risk it.'

'Some risks are worth taking.'

'Not this one.'

He took a step towards her, and her breath caught while her heart hammered. 'I don't want anything long-term, Alex,' he said, his gaze so mesmerising she couldn't look away. 'I'm not cut out for that. I simply want you, for as long as we're working together.'

'And then what?'

'We go our separate ways with no regrets.'

But she would have regrets. She knew she would. She wouldn't be able to help throwing herself into it one hundred per cent, the way she did with everything, and while it would undoubtedly be fabulous while it lasted, the fallout would be huge. He was too overwhelming, too potent—too everything. The impact of a fling with him would be immense and she didn't want to have to mop up the mess afterwards. She wasn't willing to make that mistake again and that was all there was to it.

'This might be some kind of game to you, Max,' she said, the thought of history repeating itself injecting steel into her voice, 'but it isn't to me.'

'It's no game.'

'Then have some respect for my rules. Have some respect for me. And back off. Please.'

CHAPTER SEVEN

WATCHING ALEX SPIN on her heel and head off in the direction of the guest wing, Max grabbed a beer and cracked it open, disappointment and frustration coursing through him like boiling oil. Her resolve was stronger than he could have possibly imagined. Under any other circumstances he'd applaud it. Under these circumstances, tonight, he hated and resented it.

Not that that was her fault, of course. She had every right to turn him down and she'd given a perfectly reasonable, understandable explanation for why she was so reluctant to yield to the attraction that arced between them. He knew what it was like to fear turning into your family. He'd spent half his life concerned that both his father's general weakness of character and his mother's manipulation could be hereditary and had done everything in his power to avoid both.

But right now all he could think was that he'd given it his best shot with Alex and he'd failed. The physical attraction, although mutual and scorching, wasn't enough. Opening up and allowing her a glimpse into parts of him that hadn't seen the light of day for years wasn't enough. *He* wasn't enough.

Rejection spun through him at the idea of that, leaving the sting of a thousand darts in its wake and stirring up memories of his childhood that he'd buried deep long ago. Such as seeking out his father's attention for help with a school project, only to be dismissed with a glance of irritation and a mutter of 'later'. Such as once making a birthday cake for his mother, who'd showered him with thanks before telling him that she was watching her weight and tossing it in the trash. But he shoved aside the memories and ignored the tiny stabs of pain, loathing the weakness they represented.

The impact on him of Alex's rejection was ridiculous, he told himself grimly as he lifted the bottle to his mouth and necked half its contents. It wasn't as if she were the only woman on the planet he'd ever wanted, and it wasn't as if he'd never want anyone else. There were plenty of other women in this world who would be only too pleased to spend a night or two in his bed.

Why had he tried so hard with her? What made her worth an effort he'd never had to make before? Had he really been so keen for a distraction from the disruption caused by the discovery that he was adopted? Didn't that somehow make him a bit of a coward rather than her?

Well, whatever his motivations, whatever they made him, the result was the same. Despite the sizzling chemistry that she'd even acknowledged, she didn't want him. So he'd back off. He had no interest in pursuing someone who didn't want to be pursued and she'd made it very clear that she was that someone.

Starting now he'd withdraw the smiles and the charm she disdained and channel the pure professionalism that she valued so highly. He'd prioritise the investigation, the way she had. He'd get the answers he so badly needed and haul his life back on track. It was faintly pathetic that it mattered so much. He was a grown man of thirty-one, for God's sake. Professionally, he was at the top of his game. He was envied by the best of the best. Personally, however, the events of the last few days had revealed that he languished somewhere at the bottom, unable to claw his way up, and it was frustrating as hell. He needed to get to the truth, whatever it might be, so he could move on.

None of this was a game to him, despite Alex's accusation. It mattered. A lot. And that was all there was to it.

Max and Alex had arrived in La Posada late the following evening, having landed at the airport in La Quiaca in the afternoon and picked up a top-of-the-range four-by-four to cover the hundred-and-fifty-kilometre distance by road.

The Quechuan town, home to six thousand inhabitants and situated on the eastern edge of the Andes, stood on the top of a dramatic ridge. It had been rebuilt after a devastating earthquake twenty years before, some thirty kilometres from the original site. The air was dry and dusty. The surrounding landscape was rocky, the vegetation was sparse and the sun was harsh. The contrast to the sparkle and lushness of the Caribbean could not have been sharper.

But it wasn't the lack of humidity, the aridity or even the altitude that accounted for her irritability, Alex had to admit as she breakfasted alone on coffee and bread in the restaurant of the only hotel in town. It was her apparent and alarming contrariness.

Despite knowing she'd done absolutely the right thing by laying her cards on the table, bidding Max goodnight and marching off into the house, she'd still spent a large part of the night fretting about how things between them would turn out come morning.

What would she do if he completely ignored her plea and launched a concerted effort to change her mind? she'd agonised as she'd stared at the ceiling and listened to the chirrup of the crickets that inhabited the thickets beyond the terraces. Realistically, how long would she be able to resist his considerable charms? She'd like to think for ever, but she was only human, the attraction was impossibly strong and it had been so long since she'd had any attention.

And why had he set his sights on her in the first place? She was nothing special. Surely he had to know far more appealing women than her, gorgeous, interesting ones who were totally on his wavelength and shared his approach to rules. No doubt she was merely convenient, popping into his life at a moment when he was in between contracts and looking for a challenge to fill the time. It could hardly be anything else. Despite the intimacy of the conversation they'd had at La Copa Alegre, he was so out of her league he might as well be on another planet.

In fact, her concerns had become so troubling that at one point she'd actually considered telling him to go to Argentina on his own and simply report back, which was so baffling and downright wrong that she'd had to give herself a mental slap to get a grip while reminding herself at length that never again was she going to allow how she felt about a man get in the way of work. Nor was she going to keep on wondering how explosive was explosive.

However, she needn't have worried. Max had clearly taken on board what she'd said. The smiles had gone and had been replaced with polite distance. He hadn't touched her once since they'd met on the deck to catch his boat to the airport. He'd barely even looked at her. On the plane he'd been professionalism personified. He'd opened his laptop the minute they'd taken off, and had only stepped away to make some calls.

Alex, on the other hand, had hardly been able to concentrate on anything. She'd been restless, as if sitting on knives, and the plane had felt oddly claustrophobic. Even Becky, with whom she'd checked in somewhere over north Brazil, had queried her distraction, for which she hadn't had much of an answer.

Bizarrely, with every nautical mile, she'd found herself growing increasingly irritated by Max's aloofness. Surely it was over-the-top. Surely they could have settled on somewhere in between flirty and frosty. To her confusion and consternation, that irritation still lingered.

None of it made sense, she thought frustratedly, taking a sip of freshly squeezed orange juice to wash down the last few flakes of delicious buttery *medialuna*. She should be glad he'd backed off. She shouldn't be feeling piqued that he'd done what she'd asked. And as for the disappointment that had lanced through her yesterday evening when the hotel he'd booked had had another room available, which he'd accepted without a moment's hesitation, what on earth had that been about? She didn't want to be put in a situation where they had to share a room. Or at least she shouldn't. And she ought to have been delighted not disappointed when, after checking in, he'd ordered room service before heading off, not to be seen again for the rest of the evening.

She couldn't work out what was wrong with her. Max was showing respect for her rules, for *her*, so where was the satisfaction? Where was the relief? Why was she missing the smiles, the conversation and even the dangerous edge of the night before last? Why did she keep willing him to actually meet her gaze for longer than a fleeting second or two? When exactly had she become so obsessed with his hands that she could practically feel them on her body?

She'd had nearly twenty-four hours to ruminate these baffling questions but, to her exasperation, she was no closer to an answer. But at least his imminent arrival at her table would give her a welcome break from that particular madness.

God, he was gorgeous, she thought, watching as he made his way across the room, weaving through the tables, all lithe grace and powerful intent. This morning he'd foregone the shave and her fingers itched to find out whether the light stubble adorning his jaw was as electrifying as she remembered. His hair was damp and, as a vision of him in the shower, standing beneath the jets while hot, steaming water poured over him and ran in rivulets down the contours of his body, flew unbidden into her head, she felt a throb between her legs.

'Good morning,' he said with a quick impersonal smile that she'd inexplicably grown to loathe.

Was it? It seemed very hot for this time of day. And she clearly hadn't got used to the altitude because she was suddenly finding it hard to breathe. 'Good morning.'

'Did you sleep well?'

To her surprise she had, but maybe it shouldn't have been unexpected, given the restlessness of the nights that had gone before. 'Like a log. You?'

'Same.'

Hmm. He didn't look as if he had, she thought, assessing him carefully as he took the seat opposite her and poured himself some coffee. Despite the tan, his face was slightly paler than usual, and drawn. Faint lines bracketed his mouth and the frown creasing his forehead looked as if it had been there a while. But his expression was unreadable and his eyes revealed nothing.

She wished she knew what he was thinking. It took no great leap of imagination to suppose this had to be hard on him. By his own admission, the discovery that he was adopted had turned his life on its head. She couldn't even begin to envisage what kind of upheaval it must have generated.

And now here they were in the country of his birth, the land of his heritage. Not only that, they were half an hour from the orphanage where he'd spent time before being taken to the US. It had all happened a long time ago, certainly, but surely it had to be having some kind of effect on him. He'd acted so swiftly on hearing the news and then moved so decisively. Those weren't the actions of a man who was largely indifferent. So could it be that deep down he was all over the place emotionally, and stoic detachment was his way of handling it?

'How are you feeling?' she asked, wondering if there was any way she could help, if there was indeed something troubling him.

'About what?'

'Well, everything, really,' she said, watching him

closely for a reaction or a sign, however minuscule. 'But principally, being here in Argentina.'

'I'm feeling fine. Why?'

'I was thinking that today's visit to the orphanage might be difficult for you.'

'Not in the slightest,' he said as he reached for a roll.

'Are you sure?'

'Yes. It'll be fine.'

Right. So that was two 'fine's in a row. In her experience, nothing suggested a problem more. 'What time shall we leave?'

'There's no need for you to come.'

So that wasn't happening. For one thing, she wasn't being cut out of the loop. For another, his shoulders were tight. His jaw now looked as if it was about to shatter. He was very much not 'fine'. There was no way she was letting him go through whatever he was going through alone. Her chest tightened and her throat ached at the mere thought of it and he'd had to deal with enough on his own.

'I disagree,' she said with a tiny jut of her chin as resolve surged inside her.

'Too bad.'

'This is my case too, Max. I've been working on it exclusively for eight months. I'm as invested as you are.'

His eyes met hers finally, incredulity shimmering in their indigo depths, along with a good deal of scepticism. 'You couldn't possibly be as invested as I am.'

Debatable, but also possibly an argument for another time. 'Consider me moral support then.'

'I don't need support,' he said flatly. 'Moral or otherwise.'

Yes, he did, despite the waves of rejection and denial radiating off him. She could understand why he might want to push her away. For him this had to be intensely personal. They weren't friends. They certainly weren't lovers. They were colleagues at most and she'd told him to back off. Why on earth *would* he want to share the experience with her?

But he could protest all he liked. Just because she'd put an end to the chemistry and the flirting, it didn't mean she didn't care. What if he *did* turn out to need the support? She was the only person to provide it right now and, in her admittedly biased opinion, she was also the best. A large part of her job was handling the fallout of her investigations with perceptiveness and sensitivity, and she excelled at reading emotionally fragile situations, instinctively knowing when to step in and when to stay back. She'd also learned to look beneath the surface, and beneath Max's, beneath the outward stoicism and steely control, she sensed great, seething turmoil.

'You have it, whether you want it or not.'

'You once asked me to back off, Alex,' he said warningly. 'Now I'm asking you to do the same.'

'This is different,' she said, having no intention

of getting into a tit-for-tat. 'I'm worried about you, Max, and I have lots of experience in picking up pieces, should there be any. So I'm coming with you.' If he continued to reject her offer, then so be it, but if he said 'fine' again she'd know it was the right thing to do.

He let out a deep sigh of defeat and gave a shrug as if he couldn't care less. 'Fine.'

The drive to the Santa Catalina orphanage took longer than expected. Not only was the road riddled with potholes and strewn with rocks, they had to keep stopping for meandering alpaca. It was taking every drop of Max's concentration to avoid the hazards, yet with every passing kilometre his pulse thudded that little bit faster and his stomach churned that little bit harder.

Despite what he'd told Alex, in the hope she'd stop her damn prodding and leave him alone, he'd been feeling off-kilter ever since they'd landed. At first the unease had been vague, a mild cocktail of anticipation and uncertainty. But overnight the pounding of his head had intensified and a tight knot had lodged in his chest.

He didn't appreciate that he hadn't been as successful at hiding the mess of his emotions from Alex as he'd hoped, but he couldn't deny she'd been spot-on about the reasons for it. The minute he'd set foot on the land of his birth, he'd been rocked in a way he could never have anticipated. Arriving in La Posada, knowing that the orphanage he'd spent time in was so close, had compounded the unsettling sensation that his foundations were cracking.

But why any of that should be the case, he couldn't work out. Argentina was a country like any other. Largely destroyed in the earthquake, the orphanage was just a pile of stones. He'd read a report and seen a photo of the place in one of the attachments Alex had forwarded him. How traumatic could the reality actually be?

Nevertheless, he recognised that he was standing on shaky ground, metaphorically if not literally. He had been for days now. He'd held the chaos at bay by focusing on getting Alex into his bed, but, thanks to her determination to resist the attraction, that shield had shattered and, without it, havoc prevailed. The emotions he thought he'd got a handle on over a decade ago now crashed around inside him, fierce and volatile. If he didn't keep a tight grip on them, they could all too easily result in the hot mess of an eruption he'd once predicted, and he wanted no witnesses.

So why had he caved and allowed her to accompany him today? He could have simply taken off without her. He hadn't had to wait for her to meet him at the car. Yet his resolve, already weakened by the tempest whipping up a storm inside him, had crumbled to dust with petrifying speed.

Why did the idea of her support appeal so much? He'd survived perfectly well without it—or any support, for that matter—previously. The last thing he wanted was her picking up his pieces in the event there were any to pick up. And what did it matter if he couldn't recall the last time anyone had worried about him? He was totally used to being on his own and worrying about himself, well, *himself.*

For all he knew, Alex's concern and the support were just an excuse, and for her it was all about the job anyway. She'd made it blindingly clear how important the assignment was to her, so of course she wasn't going to give up the chance to find any more evidence for herself, or, if there wasn't any, closing down that line of enquiry once and for all. If he had any sense at all he'd be focusing on that instead of allowing himself to get side-tracked by contemplating other, more unsettlingly appealing motivations she might have, such as simply wanting to be there for him, which he knew, after their post-dinner conversation, couldn't be the case.

However, regardless of everything going on inside him, he was oddly relieved that she hadn't been deterred by his attempts to push her away. He was glad she was here, whatever her reasons. And because that was confusing as hell when she'd so flatly rejected him, and because he didn't have the wherewithal to analyse it right now, he thrust it from his mind and focused instead on navigating a patch of vegetation that had encroached onto a section of the road.

After consulting the map that the hotel receptionist had sketched out, Alex directed him off the main road and along a track lined with the remains of what looked like houses.

'It must have been quite an earthquake,' she said, gazing at the devastation all around.

'Seems risky, building a new town quite so close.'

'Better materials and modern methods, I suppose. There it is,' she said, pointing at a dilapidated building a couple of hundred metres ahead on the left and effectively cutting off his attempt at a distraction.

Max parked up, the hammering of his pulse and the thumping of his head more intense than ever, and got out. A dry, dusty wind was whistling down the abandoned streets and around the ruins. The only signs of life were a couple of goats, wandering about and nibbling on the odd wrecked tree. It was bleak and desolate and eerie, and there was a chill in the air despite the warmth of the midday sun.

Barely aware of Alex now, he walked on, as if being pulled in by some invisible force. The front door had long gone, as had the windows. Most of the walls had fallen in and there was no roof.

How on earth had he and his brothers wound up here? was the thought pummelling away at him as he moved from one destroyed space to another, numbly picking his way through the rubble. Who had left them here? Why? Had they been happy? Well-fed and cared for? How could they have been separated? What kind of adoption agency would have allowed such a thing?

In the absence of memories, speculation flooded

through him, blurring his vision and quickening his breath. Babies. Kids. The noise, the bustle, the nuns. He could be standing on the very spot where he and his brothers had once slept…

But there were no clues here. This place had been stripped of anything useful or valuable long ago. The rusty filing cabinet that was bolted to what was left of a wall had already been emptied of documents by Alex's on-the-ground contact, who'd found his birth certificate and those of his brothers within. Nothing else remained.

He didn't know what he'd expected to find, he realised, his throat aching and his chest tight. Or why he'd come, when the place had been thoroughly searched already. The rashness of the decision, the uncertainty and the confusion indicated a weakness that he hated. If he'd somehow hoped to find a connection with his past, it had been a hugely self-indulgent move.

In fact, this whole experience was making him feel sick. His hands were clammy and his head was swimming, the nausea rolling through him threatening to overwhelm him. The world seemed to be spinning around him and he could hardly breathe. The blood was draining from his head and the strength was leaching from his limbs.

What if he never got the answers he sought? What if neither he nor Alex ever uncovered the truth? How would he be able to get a grip on everything that was going on inside him and figure out what his life really meant? What if he never recovered a sense of peace? What if this chaos was for ever?

He needed to get out, away from the thoughts and the emotions ricocheting around him. His control was unravelling faster and more wildly than ever before, and it was terrifying. He couldn't handle any of this any longer. It brought back unwanted memories of vulnerability and desperation, and it was making him unhinged.

Forget wanting to find out who he might have once been. He didn't need to know that to work out who he was now. The future was his to decide. This trip had been a mistake. For a decade he'd been all about looking forwards with a single-minded focus that had not wavered once. So what the hell had he been *doing* this last week?

'Alex?' he yelled, summoning up some strength from who knew where and striding off in the direction of the exit, the car, sanity.

'Over here,' came the response from somewhere to his left.

'We're leaving.'

CHAPTER EIGHT

'ARE YOU ALL RIGHT?' said Alex, a little breathless as she half walked, half jogged to keep up with Max's long quick strides and a lot concerned with the way he appeared to have the hounds of hell at his feet.

'No, I'm not all right,' he muttered, a deep scowl darkening his face, his jaw clenched and his hands curled into fists.

'What's wrong?'

'I'm through with this.'

Her chest squeezed in a way that had nothing to do with the burn in her lungs. She shouldn't have left him alone, she thought, her throat tight and her pulse galloping. She'd wanted to give him space and privacy and so had taken herself off, which had clearly been an error of judgement, but at least she was here now, to help him navigate this stage of his journey.

'This has to have been a lot to deal with.'

'I don't just mean today,' he said curtly, unlocking the door of the car and yanking it open. 'I mean the entire bloody investigation.'

Alex opened her own door and clambered in, her mind reeling with shock. 'What?'

'I'm done.'

Having buckled up, he fired the engine, released the handbrake and hit the accelerator with such force that the wheels spun and kicked up a cloud of dust so large it completely obscured the ruined town that he seemed intent on putting as far behind him as possible.

'What are you talking about?'

'I'm leaving,' he said tightly, his gaze on the road, his fingers gripping the steering wheel as if his life depended on it. 'Going home.'

She clung to the door handle, for a moment too stunned for words. 'No, you can't do that,' she said once she'd regained the power of speech.

'Keep the plane. I'll make my own way back.'

What had happened? What was going on? 'But why?'

'Work.'

That made no sense. Hadn't he told her he was between contracts?

'You said all you needed to work was your laptop,' she said, thinking of the device he'd been so occupied with on yesterday's flight.

'You don't need me here.'

'I do.'

'In what possible way?'

Well, quite. She'd managed on her own for eight months. It was an entirely fair question. She didn't need him here, in truth. But her mind had gone blank. She couldn't think. All she knew was that she didn't want him to leave. She'd got used to having him around. They were supposed to be working *together*. Besides, he clearly wasn't in a good place at the moment and how was she supposed to keep an eye on him for Finn if Max went home on his own?

'I don't speak Spanish,' she said, her head spinning as she grappled for an excuse.

'You're competent and driven. You're more than capable of finishing up here. You'll manage.'

'I know, but this isn't right, Max.'

'It's my call.'

'I have a plan.'

A muscle hammered in his jaw. 'I'm sure it's great.'

It wasn't particularly, but at least it was something. 'Step one is checking out all the hospitals within a hundred-kilometre radius of here. Step two is taking a gamble on your biological parents living close by. It's you parading around town on the off-chance that someone might recognise you. That can't happen if you're not here.'

The brief glance he threw her way was incredulous. 'That won't happen even if I am.'

'It's worth a try.'

'It's even more of a long shot than a DNA match.'

'I am aware of that,' she said, determined to keep her cool so she could work out what to do. 'But I am also aware that the three of you reuniting after thirty years apart has little to do with me. Rico found out about Finn because of a photo he'd seen in the financial press, and you showed up because of the interview, which was originally suggested by Carla.' Rico's fiancée. 'Even the feelers we have out with the Swiss bank and the Argentinian government are yours. Nothing *I've* tried has worked and I'm not ready to give up.'

'Has it occurred to you that we might never discover the truth?'

'Yes, it has,' she said, her heart giving a quick lurch at the thought of defeat, of failure. 'But I can't dwell on that. I have to see it through.'

'I'm not stopping you.'

'You need to see it through too.'

'No, I really don't,' he said, his jaw tight. 'I'm done with digging around in the past. It can't be changed. I'm going to focus on the future. That's how my brothers have handled things. They're all about looking forwards, not back.'

Yes, well, they had partners to help them and children in various stages of development to focus on. Max had no one. And while he might not think it at the moment, he needed to deal with this. The truth was what he sought. She wouldn't let him throw away the chance to find the answers because of what could quite possibly be a knee-jerk reaction to what had to be a very stressful set of circumstances. Not without further consideration anyway.

'They've had far longer to process things,' she

said, her heart in her throat as the car swerved violently. 'And it wasn't easy for either of them at first.'

'Then all I need is time.'

He needed more than that. 'Pull over.'

'What?'

'Stop. Please. You're in no fit state to drive.'

'I'm fine.'

'You nearly hit an alpaca just now.'

'What alpaca?'

'Exactly.'

She could practically hear the grind of his teeth,
but a moment later he'd pulled over, killed the engine
and tossed her the key. They got out and swapped
seats and Max did up his seatbelt, but Alex had other
plans. She twisted to face him and it tore at her heart
to see the torment he was trying so hard to contain.

'The key goes in the ignition, Alex.'

'Let's look at this calmly,' she replied, ignoring
his sarcasm as much as the sizzling effect of his
proximity on her.

'I am calm.'

No, he wasn't. He was anything but calm. The tension gripping his whole frame buffeted hers. There
was a wildness to his movements and his words that
suggested he was a man fast reaching the end of his
tether.

'What's going on?'

'Stop trying to psychoanalyse me, and drive.'

'In a moment.'

'Am I going to have to get out and walk?'

'If that's what you need.'

'What I need is to get back to the hotel so I can start packing.'

That was the last thing he needed, in her opinion. But how was she going to keep him here? If he was determined to go, there was nothing she'd be able to do to stop him. Could she appeal to his better nature? Did he even have one? What incentive would work? He was so wound up. How could she get him to relax enough to be able to realise she was right?

But hang on…

'Why don't we take some time out?' she said as the idea of relaxing triggered a memory from dinner at La Copa Alegre and inspiration struck.

He whipped round and stared at her as if she'd sprouted a second head. 'Some time out?'

'The last few days have been incredibly intense for me,' she told him, steeling herself against the blaze of astonishment and turmoil she could see in his eyes. 'I can't imagine what they've been like for you. I read that there are some salt flats not far from here, just across the border. They could be worth a look.'

'Are you mad?'

She'd never felt saner in her life. 'We'll go out there,' she said, more convinced it was the right thing to do with every passing second. 'After lunch. Check out the nature. Take advantage of the new moon and gaze at a few stars once the sun has set. There's even a luxury lodge. We could stay the night there and come back refreshed tomorrow.'

'*Refreshed?*'

His disbelief was fierce but she refused to quail. 'You did say I should take a break.'

'You don't need me for that.'

'And you don't need me for anything,' she said, reminding herself that this wasn't about her. This was about him. And even if it hadn't been, she ought to be glad he thought he didn't need her for anything because that was exactly what she wanted. 'I get it. But I won't let you mess this up, Max. You need to give it a chance. For the sake of your brothers but, more importantly, for yourself. I know what it's like to not know who you truly are, and I know how petrifying it can be to have to work that out. But I also know the relief that comes when you're through it. You'll regret it if you leave. Running away doesn't solve anything.' She let that sink in for a moment then leaned forward a fraction, keeping her gaze firmly fixed on his. Injecting as much persuasion into her tone as she could, she said, 'So let's be tourists for a while. We won't talk about the case. We'll just take the opportunity to relax and forget ourselves for once. We can start again tomorrow. It would be less than twenty-four hours. What do you think?'

Max didn't want to hang out in any salt flats and relax. He couldn't think of anything less appealing than doing the tourist thing and stargazing with a woman who'd so ruthlessly rejected him yet to whom he was still wildly attracted. He'd have to be some kind of masochist to agree to it when all he wanted to do, but couldn't, was reach out, pull her tight against him and run his hands all over her, before kissing her until neither of them could think straight.

He didn't want conversation of any kind with her. They'd talked plenty—too much, in fact—and they were already staying in a perfectly good, if basic, hotel in La Posada. And what did she know about relaxing anyway? Could she even do it? Not once in the brief but impactful time he'd known her had she shown any evidence of it. The kiss they'd shared, the one that she'd been able to dismiss so easily but still tormented him night and day, hadn't been in the slightest bit chilled. Even during dinner at La Copa Alegre her conversation had been laced with wariness, her body gripped with tension.

And what the hell gave her the right to tell him that he'd regret it if he left? he wondered, his stomach churning and his head pounding. She knew nothing about anything. He wasn't petrified. He wasn't running away. He'd just had enough. He was completely overwhelmed by everything that had happened recently, that was all, and God, he was tired. He'd barely slept recently. He'd hardly been able to breathe. He wanted to go home, crash out for a month and wake up to the realisation that the last week had been nothing but a bad dream.

But it wasn't. It was reality. His new reality, in

fact, and much of it—namely the discovery of his brothers—he was delighted about. The rest of it, not so much, but, if he was being brutally honest, he probably wasn't going to be able to escape that by simply going home. No matter how much he tried to convince himself that the past was of no interest or importance to him, it was, and it would follow him wherever he went, evermore festering away inside him and corroding his identity and his self-worth the longer it went unaddressed.

He needed to track down his biological family in order to find out whether he'd been wanted. If he'd once mattered to someone, to anyone. It was only on meeting his brothers and feeling somehow anchored by them that he'd realised how adrift he'd always been, how unsure of his place in the world at large, knowing somewhere deep down inside that he was entirely on his own.

But now he had the chance to make sense of it all, so what choice did he have but to stay and see it through to the bitter end? Whatever the outcome, and he was aware that he might not get the results he so badly hoped for, at least then he'd know he'd given it everything. At least then he could process it and, somehow, move on.

Whether she knew it or not, Alex's point about not letting Finn and Rico down had struck him deep in the gut. He shouldn't need their approval, or anyone's, but he craved it nonetheless. He liked them, he valued the relationship they were developing, and he'd do nothing to jeopardise it. He'd told them he'd do what he could to get to the truth and, while he was all for breaking rules, he didn't break promises. How could he have forgotten that?

He hadn't been thinking straight for days now. Could it be that he wasn't thinking straight now? Could Alex be right and he *did* need a breather? The thought of handing over even the minutest modicum of control made him want to recoil in sheer horror, but perhaps he'd be wise to concede to her on this. The tumultuous news of his adoption and all it entailed sat like a rock on his chest, crushing him with its ever-increasing weight, and his judgement wasn't exactly firing on all cylinders at the moment.

And, in any case, this wasn't just about him. It was about Alex too. Her career and her future. He'd agreed that they'd work together and so far she'd kept her end of the bargain. In fact she'd gone beyond it. She hadn't let him push her away, no matter how hard he'd made it for her. She'd been resolute and unshakeable. He'd never had that kind of steadfast unconditional support. He didn't know quite what to do with it, but at the very least he owed it to her to stick around a little while longer.

Besides, maybe she *did* know how to relax. Despite the stress and turmoil storming his defences, he couldn't deny that he found the idea of it intriguing and alluring, a tiny beacon of light piercing the dark maelstrom of chaos. He'd failed to entice her into his bed, but if he could get her to lower her guard and ease up, he would at least be able to claw back some kind of pride.

'The salt flats it is.'

They set off after lunch and spent two hours driving along huge, wide, empty roads that bisected great swathes of desolate rocky landscape before reaching their destination. En route they passed cactus fields, a stretch of bubbling geysers and abandoned towns made entirely of salt. The jagged mountains that rose majestically in the distance were awe-inspiring. In every direction, as far as the eye could see, bright white salt sparkled in the sun, the light reflecting off it dazzling. They came across flocks of flamingos, wild vicuña and ruby-red lagoons. The sky was cloudless and the air clean and raw. It had to be one of the most isolated, most beautiful places on earth.

Heading out here had been the best idea she had had in ages, Alex reflected as she and Max sat on the viewing platform attached to the one dome-shaped pod-like cabin that had been available, watching the sun dip beneath the horizon, having dined on a feast of yucca soup followed by grilled *paiche* served with a delicate risotto and then, to finish, an exquisite mousse of dark chocolate and eucalyptus. She had to admit that she needed the break. It felt so wonderful to throw off the shackles of work for a while. To put aside her worries, even temporarily, and lose herself in the wonders of the world.

As agreed, she and Max hadn't talked about the

case or family or anything, really, of a personal nature. Instead, the conversation had meandered through a wide variety of largely neutral subjects— travel, food, books. It had hardly been scintillating but, even so, she hadn't been able to get enough of it. She wanted to know everything about him, and she didn't even bother to try and convince herself that her interest was professional. It wasn't. It was entirely personal. Those complex layers of his that she'd identified during the floating dinner, that she'd caught a glimpse of at the orphanage, drew her attention like the brightest of beacons and were impossible to ignore.

But now, with the fire crackling in the pit that stood in front of them, the conversation had petered out. Max seemed to be as lost in thought as she was and she wondered whether he too had been struck dumb by the mesmerising reflection of the sun on the mirror-like surface of the ground and the staggeringly beautiful streaks of reds and gold slashing across the vast blue sky or if he could possibly be thinking the same thing she was, namely the fireworks he'd mentioned.

Despite her best efforts, she hadn't been able to scrub them from her mind, but that was what came of spending so much time cooped up with him in a car, however large and luxurious. The distance between places here was immense. Five minutes was all it took for her to become achingly aware of him sitting beside her, his shoulder mere centimetres from hers, and then she found she spent the rest of whatever journey they were on trying not to lean into him and keeping her eyes on the scenery and not on his profile, which inevitably was agony.

And then there was the lodge. If she'd known it was billed as a honeymooners' paradise and that the half a dozen domes came with a king-size bed only she'd never have suggested staying the night. The air of romance was everywhere, from the double shower in the en-suite bathroom to the intimacy of the tables set for two in the dining room to the cosy sofa they were sitting on out here. Not only did she feel like a fraud, she couldn't stop thinking about how exciting their kiss had been, how desperately she wanted more and how nearby and enticing the bed was.

Max, on the other hand, clearly wasn't suffering from the same kind of struggles. He hadn't batted an eyelid about there only being one dome available. He'd dismissed her suggestion they drive back, saying it was too far, and told her he'd take the floor, as if it didn't bother him in the slightest that they'd have to share a room. He still hadn't touched her. His distance was polite. His smiles were entirely impersonal. She both envied and resented his ability to simply switch off the attraction. How did he do it? she wondered for what had to be the hundredth time in the last hour.

And what would it take to switch it back on again?

It was a question that shouldn't have been of the remotest interest but, despite everything, she badly

wanted to know the answer. The longer he obeyed
her request to back off, the more she wanted him
to dishonour it. She desperately yearned for him to
deploy that rebellious streak of his and break every
single one of her rules, which made no sense at all.

Or did it?

As she gazed up at the vast canopy of stars that
now spread out above them like a giant glittering
blanket, her heart began to thump that little bit harder
while her head began to spin that little bit faster. The
sky was so big out here, the universe so huge. She
could make out the Southern Cross and the Milky
Way and suddenly she felt very small and very alone.
At least Max had his brothers now. She had no one.
No one on her side, no one to turn to for support.

She'd been so lonely for so long and just for one
night, maybe a few more, she didn't want to be. She
was so tired of keeping how she felt about Max at
bay. Constantly fighting it when she was achingly
aware of every movement he made, every breath he
took, his scent, his warmth, the impact of his gaze
on her, took more effort than she could possibly have
imagined and she was running on fumes.

Why shouldn't she sleep with him? she thought,
her mouth going dry and her entire body heating as
the last of her defences bit the dust. Why shouldn't
they have the fling he'd proposed the night she'd
told him she would never act on the attraction they
shared? It needn't be complicated. Sex with him

wouldn't mean anything beyond a release of tension and, she hoped, outstanding, mind-blowing pleasure.

He'd certainly be a boost for her self-esteem, if the kiss was anything to go by, and God, she could do with one of those. How she hated the angst and insecurity she'd developed about her body, thanks to her ex. She wanted to feel good about herself, physically as well as professionally, and if Max was as skilled as he said he was she knew she'd feel amazing.

But what about her rules?

Well, those no longer seemed quite as important as they once had. As he kept reminding her, he wasn't a client. Neither of them was looking for anything long-term and, as he'd pointed out, no one else need ever know.

So what if she let a little bit of chaos into her life? She could handle it. She'd spent years building up her armour against precisely this sort of thing. She didn't need to worry about possible heartbreak and misery. There'd be no regrets. Things would never get that far. It wasn't as if she wanted a relationship with him. Or anyone, for that matter. Even if she could overcome the major trust issues her husband's many infidelities had engendered, the possibility of failure, the potential upheaval when it all went wrong was too distressing to contemplate and deeply unappealing. But a fling? With Max? That she would welcome. That she wanted with an all-consuming hunger that was fast becoming unbearable.

So what was she going to do? Was she brave

enough to find out whether, despite the discouraging signs, he still wanted her too? Was she prepared for the very real yet faintly sickening prospect that she'd killed the attraction he'd once had for her? If she had, could she somehow manage to rekindle it?

Whatever the outcome, she had to try, she thought, her heart hammering as desire and longing rushed through her blood. She had to know. Because she couldn't go on like this. She didn't want to for ever wonder, what if. She'd had enough of the loneliness and the constant battle to ignore how he made her feel. And, above all, despite what he might think of her, she wasn't a coward.

'Look,' said Alex, wonder tingeing her voice as she pointed up at the sky. 'A shooting star.'

In response, Max just grunted. He didn't trust himself to speak right now. If he opened his mouth, there was every possibility it would be to beg her to change her mind about sleeping with him, because he was finding it increasingly hard to remember her rules and respect her wishes.

With hindsight, he should never have agreed to this whole ridiculous taking a break thing. What had he been thinking? Had he gone completely mad?

The afternoon had started off great. He'd never been to Bolivia. The landscape was stunning and fascinating. Alex was an amusing and interesting travelling companion, and with the investigation and the drama of the last few days firmly, if temporarily, put to one side he'd felt the chaos recede and a modicum of calm descend. It might have taken every ounce of strength he possessed but he'd ignored her proximity, and dismissed the fanciful idea that he could listen to her talk about nothing for ever, and had instead forced himself to concentrate on nature in all its vast and varied glory.

Things had started to fall apart for him when they'd arrived at the lodge and there'd only been one dome available to book. It had been too late to head back, he'd realised, deep unease setting in as the consequences dawned. The roads were unlit and wildlife with a death wish had a tendency to appear out of nowhere.

He'd briefly toyed with the idea of leaving Alex to occupy the dome while he slept in the car, despite the temperature dropping to sub-zero overnight. But he'd pulled himself together and reminded himself that his control wasn't that unreliable. He didn't have to face hypothermia. Alex could have the bed. He'd take the floor. She'd viewed that as an acceptable compromise and, quite honestly, how hard could it be?

Then he'd walked into the sumptuously furnished, seductively lit room, which was mostly bed and very little floor, and realised he was in for a night of pure, agonising hell.

'And there goes another one,' she said, yanking him back to the deck and the dazzling display of stars. 'You're meant to make a wish.'

That was a joke. The only thing he wanted right

now wasn't going to happen, and the frustration was excruciating.

'Yeah, well, you were meant to be relaxing.'

'I am.'

No, she wasn't. She was huddled up at her end of the sofa, as far from him as she could get, practically clinging to the arm of it as if it were a lifebelt.

'I don't bite,' he muttered, loathing the fact that she didn't trust him.

'That's a shame.'

What the hell did she mean by that? he wondered, whipping his head round to find her watching him in a way that had his pulse suddenly racing. She'd loosened her death grip on the sofa and turned to face him, but why was she looking at him like that, sort of nervous yet hopeful? What was going on?

He was about to ask precisely that when she suddenly reached up and back, pulled off the band holding her hair back and, to his utter shock, shook out her hair. It fell in great, soft, dark brown waves around her shoulders, the tendrils framing her face shining in the light that came from the firepit, and it was every bit as exciting as he'd imagined.

'What are you doing?' he said, shock and desire turning his voice into almost a growl.

'I thought I would let my hair down.'

'It's beautiful,' he said before he could stop himself.

'Thank you.'

'All of you is beautiful.'

'Do you really think so?'

How could she possibly doubt it? Her smile, her eyes, everything about her, was lovely and he liked it all. He also liked their conversation, their differences and their similarities, not to mention her interest in him and the support she offered, but he couldn't go there, not even in his head. All that mattered, all that ever mattered when it came to women, this woman in particular, was the physical. 'Yes.'

She took a deep breath and leaned forward an inch, dizzying him with her scent and confusing him beyond belief, because what was she doing? 'You're the most attractive man I've ever met,' she said, the words coming out of her mouth in a rush. 'And the most dangerous.'

His heart gave a great lurch. 'In what way?'

'You make me want to break my own rules.'

Yeah, well, he knew that. But he'd failed. And he'd had enough of this. He was tired and turned on and in for eight hours of agony.

'We should call it a night,' he said gruffly. 'You in the bed. Me on the floor.'

Her gaze dropped to his mouth and the chilly air between them thickened with heat and tension. 'Is that really what you want?'

'Not by a long shot,' he said, the truth drug he appeared to have taken continuing its effect.

'Neither do I.'

He went very still, his gaze locking onto hers, his heart hammering as her intentions became clear, but he wasn't taking anything for granted. Not this time. 'What are you saying?'

'I want us in the bed together.'

God. 'You know where that will end up.'

'I know where I'd like it to end up,' she said, the desire and heat shimmering in her eyes stealing the breath from his lungs. 'I want you, Max. So much I'm going out of my mind. And I'm sick of trying to convince myself otherwise.'

Not giving in to the need drumming through him and reaching for her was taking every drop of control he possessed. His head was spinning. He was so hard he hurt. But he couldn't get this wrong. He didn't think he could take yet another rejection.

'You have rules.'

'They don't seem very important at the moment.'

'Prove it.'

CHAPTER NINE

ALEX DIDN'T EVEN HESITATE. Max had flung open the door she'd feared might be permanently shut and she was going to head on through it before she thought better of it. Excitement and anticipation rushed through her, obliterating the nerves and the doubt. In a flash she tossed aside the blanket, and with one quick move she was astride him, sitting in his lap, wrapping her arms around his neck and crushing her mouth to his.

And oh, the *relief* when he instantly started kissing her back, clamping his hands to her hips to hold her in place while the kiss burned hotter than the fire in the pit. Tongues tangled and teeth clashed and when he ground her pelvis against his, the rock-hard length of his erection rubbing her where she ached for him so desperately, she actually whimpered.

That seemed to trigger his inner caveman because suddenly he tried to take control of the kiss, but she used the advantage of her weight on and above him to push him back and increased the pressure because *she* was in charge right now. She had something to prove and she wasn't going to stop until she absolutely had to, so it went on and on, battering every one of her senses with the most delicious of assaults.

He filled her vision. He tasted of chocolate and whisky, dark and wicked. His touch set her alight and his scent dizzied her head. The desire that was sweeping through her was intense and undeniable, which was absolutely fine because she didn't want to deny any of this any more.

'Is that enough proof for you?' she said huskily when they finally broke for breath, noting with satisfaction that his eyes were glazed and a flush had hit his cheekbones.

'Are you sure about this?' he muttered, his voice spine-tinglingly low and gravelly.

'I've never been surer about anything.'

'You're not going to tell me it's a mistake or a conflict of interest?'

'No,' she said with a tiny shake of her head and a faint smile. 'Well, it's probably both, but I don't care.'

'Good.'

Without breaking contact, Max surged to his feet, his arms like steel bands around her back. She wrapped her legs around his waist and tightened her arms around his neck, and felt as light as a feather as he strode into the dome. He kicked the door shut and then fell with her onto the bed in a tangle of limbs before rolling her onto her back and pinning her to the mattress with *his* weight.

He didn't seem to have a problem with her attributes, judging by the hardness of his erection and the fierce intensity of his gaze that was locked to hers. He wouldn't care that her boobs were on the small side and she didn't have much in the way of hips. This was going to be everything she'd hoped for, she could tell.

And then she stopped thinking altogether because his head came down and his mouth landed on hers and once again she was nothing but a molten mass of need.

'I've wanted you since the moment we met,' he muttered against her jaw while he slid his hand beneath her clothes and up her side, making her shiver and shake.

'Really?' she breathed raggedly, clutching at his shoulders and wishing he wasn't wearing so many layers.

'I took one look at you in your tight skirt and neat top and I wanted to strip them off you then and there.'

'Likewise. Only in your case it was your worn jeans and crumpled shirt.'

'It made no sense.'

'I know. We're so unalike.'

'You can't imagine the agony I've endured.'

'I do have some idea,' she panted as he reared up to whip the clothes off his upper body. 'That kiss… I haven't been able to stop thinking about it, and that's been driving me nuts.'

Having hurled his clothes onto the floor, he set about hers. 'Your willpower is both awe-inspiring and frustrating as hell,' he muttered, removing her layers with flattering speed and throwing them in the general direction of his.

He undid her bra with impressive dexterity and tossed that to one side too. Her spine seemed to have dissolved because all she could do beneath the heat of his gaze was lie back, as if granting him permission to look, which he did for one heart-stopping moment, and then touch, which, to her relief, he decided to do too.

When he bent his head to her breast and swept his tongue over her nipple she nearly jack-knifed off the bed. He held her down and did it again and she moaned. After what felt like far too short a time, he transferred his attention to her other breast, whipping up such staggering sensations inside her that she could scarcely breathe, and she jammed her fingers in his hair to keep him there for ever.

But Max obviously had other ideas and, true to form, he simply did what he wanted. Just when she thought she couldn't stand the electric shocks stabbing through her any longer, he moved lower, sliding his mouth down her stomach, the hint of stubble setting her achingly sensitive skin aflame.

When he reached the waistband of her trousers and pants, she instinctively lifted her hips and he eased them down and off. Then he settled back between her legs, holding her thighs apart, and put his mouth to where she was so hot and needy.

Her entire world centred on what he was doing to her and, at the sparks zinging through her, her head fell back while her fingers tightened in his hair. The tension was unbearable, the pleasure so intense she felt as though she were on a roller coaster, going faster and faster and higher and higher. He slid two long, strong fingers inside her and she moaned and gasped. And then he did something clever with them and quite suddenly that roller coaster left the rails and soared into the ether and she broke apart into a million tiny glittering pieces, wave after wave of ecstasy washing over her.

'I knew you'd be good at this,' she managed once the world had stopped spinning and she'd got her breath back.

'Alex, sweetheart, we've barely begun.'

He levered himself off her, his face dark and intense and his jaw so tight it could have been hewn from granite, and he jerked away to locate his wallet. Having found what he was looking for, he stripped off his jeans and shorts and ripped open the foil packet. Her breath caught as she watched him roll the condom onto his impressively long and thick erection with hands that seemed to be shaking, and her entire body trembled.

And then he was back with her, parting her knees and positioning himself before thrusting inside her, filling and stretching her so sensationally that she thought she might pass out with the indescribable pleasure of it.

When he began to move, she lost the ability to think altogether. She moaned and he kissed her hard. She clutched at his shoulders, feeling the flex of his muscles beneath her fingers and revelling in the masculine strength and power of his body. Her hips rose and fell instinctively to meet his movements and the pressure inside her swelled unbearably.

'Don't hold back,' she breathed on a sob, and it was like putting a match to a touch paper.

He moved harder and faster, his increasingly wild, fierce thrusts driving her higher and higher, their kisses becoming frantic and desperate until, without warning, she shattered again, the waves of pleasure hitting with such intensity that she cried out. Max followed her over the edge moments later, lodging hard and deep and groaning as he pulsated inside her before collapsing on top of her, his chest heaving and his entire body shaking.

For several long moments they lay there recovering, and then Max eased out of her and shifted onto his side.

'So,' she said with a giddy grin once she'd got her breath back. 'Fireworks.'

His gaze, as he looked down at her, was glittering and wild. 'Told you.'

'I saw stars.'

'That'll be the glass roof.'

'Not just the glass roof. You certainly know how to give an ego a boost.'

'Was yours in need of one?'

God, yes. 'When someone cheats on you repeatedly you find yourself…doubting your attractions.'

He frowned at that. 'You have many, as I think I just made pretty obvious,' he said, reaching out and running a hand slowly over her, making her sensitive skin shiver and her breasts tighten. 'But if you're still not convinced, I'd be more than happy to prove it again.'

'You know what?' she said huskily as fresh desire began to thud through her. 'I'm not sure I am.'

Yesterday, the overnight timeout suggested by Alex had felt to Max like aeons. At two in the morning, however, after the events of the last six or so hours, it didn't seem like nearly enough.

He'd never had sex like it, he thought, wide awake and staring up at the billions of stars through the roof made up of glass equilateral triangles while beside him Alex slept. She'd been insatiable and he'd been beyond desperate and they'd already got through half the box of condoms located in the drawer of the night stand, thoughtfully supplied by the lodge that clearly catered to honeymooners.

The edge of sexual tension and frustration he'd been living with since he'd met her had gone and, whatever the reason for her volte face, he couldn't be more satisfied with the way things had turned out.

He'd known she'd be unable to resist in the end. It had taken longer than he'd anticipated but if there was one thing he *could* be sure of at the moment it was the power of chemistry.

He had to hand it to her, though. There was definitely something to be said for taking a break from reality, especially when that reality sucked. He felt he could breathe out here. Some of the chaos had calmed. Getting the answers he needed was still a top priority, despite the blip at the orphanage, but this little bubble that he and Alex were in at the moment didn't suck at all and, if he was being brutally honest, he wasn't quite ready for it to burst.

She'd suggested they head back to La Posada today to continue with her plan, which, frankly, didn't seem a particularly solid one, but what was the rush? There was plenty more to see and do here, and not just inside their dome. What would be the harm in staying another day or two?

It wasn't as if the investigation was moving apace and required their immediate attention, and it wasn't as if he hadn't chilled out with women before in a heavy-on-the-sex, light-on-the-conversation kind of way. None of them had been anything like Alex, it was true, but that didn't mean anything. All this was, was sex. Spectacular, head-wrecking sex, but just sex, nonetheless.

And sticking around a bit longer would do her good too, he thought as she turned in her sleep and sort of snuggled against him, which he found he didn't mind at all. Everyone needed a holiday, however brief, and by her own admission she hadn't taken one in years. He understood why she had an issue with letting her hair down, but she ought to do it more. Because he had to admit he liked the relaxed version of Alex, with her guard lowered and her inhibitions history. He liked her a lot.

Well, wasn't she full of good ideas at the moment, Alex thought with a wide satisfied grin as she sprawled across the bed and ogled Max, who was standing at the coffee machine wearing nothing but an open shirt and underwear, his hair damp from the shower.

Last night, and this morning, had been unbelievable, better than her wildest dreams, and God knew she'd had a few of those. The things he'd done to her... The things she'd done to him... Her confidence, so badly knocked by her lousy ex, was back with a vengeance and her self-esteem was higher than it had been for years. Max didn't seem to have an issue with any part of her body. In fact, he couldn't seem to get enough of it, and he'd made her feel like a goddess.

Taking up the challenge of proving that her rules no longer mattered had been a risk, but it had paid off in spades, and as she watched him stick a pod in the coffee machine, close the lid and stand back to let the machine do its thing, she wondered if maybe she ought to be a bit braver in other areas too. Maybe she ought to have it out with her family once and for all, and tell them exactly how she felt about the way she'd been brought up, how damaging it had been. It wouldn't change anything when the chasm between them now was wider and deeper than the Grand Canyon and equally unbridgeable, but at least then she'd have closure and the grip the past had on her would ease.

She knew now that she had what it took to be a success. As Max had pointed out yesterday when they'd been talking about work in a very vague sort of way, given the confidentiality that governed both their fields, she was still in business after five years, which was no mean feat when most start-ups failed within the first twelve months, and word-of-mouth recommendations were still coming in.

If this trip was the end of the road with regard to the investigation—and she had to face the fact that it could well be, because not only had Max heard back from his contacts, who'd come up with nothing, she didn't want him breaking the law and hacking into whatever systems he'd have to when he'd put such things behind him—would that really be the disaster she feared so much?

OK, so perhaps her track record would be broken and her expansion plans might have to be put on hold, but what was the hurry? Wasn't it a bit pathetic to still be trying to prove something to people who couldn't care less? After all these years? During dinner at the floating bar, Max had suggested she just let it go and perhaps it really was as simple as that.

It would be no reflection on her if this investigation ended now. She'd done everything she could. She badly wanted Max to have the answers he sought for his own peace of mind, but in reality there were no avenues left to pursue. The three brothers had found each other after thirty years apart and were intent on forging a relationship going forward, and that was huge.

So wouldn't everyone be better off by simply moving on? In her considerable experience, not to mention her own *personal* experience, answers didn't always fix things. Look at all the investigations she'd run. Look at the mess of her marriage. Sometimes, success resulted in more unhappiness, more uncertainty and often innumerable other problems. Even if they did by some miracle get a breakthrough, it could well be the case that the truth was harrowing, more so than anyone could have imagined, and hadn't Finn, Rico and Max suffered enough? Didn't they need some sort of closure too?

Max handing her a cup of coffee snapped her out of her thoughts, and as her gaze fixed on his bare chest, which she'd explored at great length and now knew in exquisite detail, she flushed with heat.

'What is it with you and buttons?' she said huskily, taking a sip and feeling the welcome hit of caffeine suffuse her blood.

'What do you mean?'

'You have a habit of forgetting to do them up.'

'No, I don't.'

Her eyebrows lifted. 'You mean it's deliberate?'

'It might be,' he said with the hint of a grin as he grabbed a coffee of his own and stretched out on the bed beside her.

'At dinner the other night too?'

'I don't know what you mean.'

He knew exactly what she meant. 'It wasn't that warm and there were mosquitoes. You had an ulterior motive.'

'I didn't think you'd noticed,' he said, shooting her a look of pure wickedness.

'I noticed.' Oh, how she'd noticed.

'And it bothered you.'

'I didn't think it was very professional.'

'Perhaps this is simply how I roll on holiday.'

'You were showing off.'

'I was getting desperate.'

At the thought of how much he'd wanted her, desire flooded every inch of her body. 'It worked.'

'Ever play poker?'

'No. Why?'

'You'd be very good at it. No one would ever be able to tell what you were thinking.'

'Can you tell what I'm thinking now?'

'You're thinking what I'm thinking,' he said, his gaze dropping to her mouth, and it was so tempting to lean in for a kiss that would blow her mind and lead to another hour of outstanding pleasure, but it was getting late and check out was looming.

'Sadly, I don't believe I am. I was thinking we should be getting going and heading back,' she said with real regret because, even if they carried on sleeping together back in La Posada, there was something magical and special about this place.

'I disagree.'

'Oh?'

'I think we could do with more refreshing.'

Her heart began to hammer. 'What do you suggest?'

'Another couple of nights here.'

Her willpower was no match for the excitement beginning to ripple through her. If she were stronger she'd insist on leaving now, as had been the plan. But being out here, just the two of them with no cares, no work between them, was intoxicating. There was something about the freshness of the air and the vastness of the scenery that made everything else seem very insignificant. Max had eased up yesterday afternoon while they'd been exploring the landscape and she longed to see more of the man behind the assignment, to burrow further beneath those layers of his. Besides, after eight months, what was another couple of days?

'I could get behind that.'

'And then we head back to La Posada. Where the investigation will resume and this,' he said, indicating the both of them, 'will continue.'

'Until either we find the answers we seek or we decide to call it quits,' she said, for some reason feeling it needed confirmation.

'Exactly.' His expression sobered then and his smile faded. 'You should know, Alex, I don't do long-term. I don't do relationships.'

She understood where he was coming from but she needed no warning. She was entirely on the same page. She wasn't in danger of being swept up in the romance of the place and mistaking this for something it wasn't, no matter how many of his layers she managed to peel back. People didn't change, even if they promised over and over again to try, and in any case she didn't want him to.

'Neither do I.'

'Because?'

'Oh, you know,' she said lightly. 'A number of trust issues, thanks to a cheating ex. Not wanting to experience the monumental chaos of a breakup ever again. That kind of thing. You?'

'I witnessed the fallout of a disintegrating marriage,' he said, a shadow flitting across his face. 'Nothing would ever persuade me to go there. And, as I may have mentioned once or twice, these days I prefer my life free from chaos too.'

'Have you ever had a relationship?'

'Not since I went on the straight and narrow.'

'Why not?'

'I don't need the hassle. One night, one week, maybe two, suits me fine.'

'Me too.' Although she could count on one hand the number of dates that had ended up in the bedroom since her divorce and have fingers left over.

'A woman after my own heart.'

'Your heart is of no interest to me,' she said, even as hers gave a quick lurch. 'Nobody's is.'

'You don't believe in love?'

'It's not that I don't believe in it,' she said, thinking with a shudder of the potential pain and devastation a badly broken heart could cause. Hers had merely been dented by her ex, but even that had been difficult enough to recover from. 'On a theoretical level I can understand that true love exists, but the only kind I've ever experienced is conditional.'

'I haven't experienced any kind. What my parents felt for me was not love.'

No, it most certainly wasn't.

'Girlfriends?'

'They're never around long enough.'

'Deliberately?'

'It's just the way things pan out.'

Hmm. That didn't exactly answer the question.

'My family has always made it perfectly clear that unless I conform to their standards they want nothing to do with me,' she said. 'I know now that that's not a price I'm willing to pay.'

'Nor me.'

'Just as well that we're in this just for the sex then, isn't it?'

His eyes glittered, the look in them turning predatory, and as he took her cup off her and set it and his own on the night stand, his intention clear, desire began to sweep through her. 'I couldn't agree more.'

By the following morning, Max and Alex had taken a trip in a hot-air balloon, had a picnic lunch on a shimmering sea of white and bathed naked in hot springs. Once again, the day had been warm and sunny, the night cold, clear and starry. And, once again, the minute the door of the dome closed behind them after dinner, clothes were shed and hands met skin and the temperature hit boiling point.

Unlike the day before, however, the talk had been anything but small. A thousand feet above the ground, catching Max at a moment his defences had been blown away by the sheer magnitude of the view, she'd drilled down into the nitty-gritty of his up-bringing and rewarded him with details of her own. Over lunch he'd found himself telling her about why the need to find his biological family burned so much more intensely in him than in his brothers, how badly his self-worth needed him to have been wanted by somebody, and she'd reciprocated by confessing how she'd hated the insecure, needy woman she'd become after she'd found out about her husband's cheating, which had made him want to hunt the man down and throttle him.

The glimpses Max had caught of the woman be-hind the rules were fascinating. Who'd have thought Alex had such a dirty laugh? If someone had told him the day they'd met that she couldn't pass a bottle of glittery nail varnish in a shop without buying it and that her collection was now in the hundreds he'd have scoffed in disbelief.

But then who'd have thought he'd find her beams of appreciation so addictive? Who'd have thought he'd do pretty much anything to elicit one of her blinding smiles of approval, whether it was simply building and lighting a fire in the pit, helping her climb into the hot-air balloon or closing down the hot springs site so they could have privacy?

She was like a drug running through his veins and making him feel invincible, and while part of him was all for the high, another part of him was troubled by the growing sense that things were heading in a dangerous direction. The connection between them didn't feel purely physical any longer. Feelings were developing, he could tell, and his subconscious shared that unease because in the middle of the night he'd woken abruptly from the most erotic yet unsettling dream of his life.

He'd been sitting in his study back home, staring at his screens and trying to figure out how to fix a piece of code that wasn't quite right. Alex had sidled in wearing nothing but a half open shirt and a smouldering smile and had then planted herself between him and his desk. From there she'd proceeded to blow his mind several times over and he hadn't even had to leave his chair.

But when, still trembling in his arms, dream Alex

had held him tight while murmuring that she was there and everything was going to be all right, an odd chill had swept through the room, freezing the blood in his veins and sending icy shivers down his spine. The more she'd continued to whisper reassurances and soft words of support in his ear, the more he'd wanted to get up and run. But he couldn't because firstly she was sitting in his lap, pinning him to the chair, and secondly his arms were wrapped around her and wouldn't loosen, no matter how much he ordered them to.

Now, he was sitting on the terrace in front of their dome, watching the most stunning sunrise he'd ever seen while tapping his phone against his thigh and remembering how, at dinner last night, a warm light seemed to have taken up residence in her eyes and her smiles had been somehow different, although he couldn't put his finger on quite why, and that added to the apprehension because he didn't know what to make of them.

His foundations, already on shifting sands, seemed to be cracking. His stomach churned with a low-level sort of anxiety and his mind wouldn't rest. He felt as if he could skid off the rails at any moment and he didn't know how to stop it.

'What are you doing out here?'

At the sound of Alex's voice behind him, husky with sleep, the anxiety ratcheted up a notch.

'Watching the dawn.'

'Are you all right?'

Why did she keep asking him this, as if she cared? Why did he hope she did?

'Fine.'

'You look a little tense.'

'I've had a text from Rico.'

'Is everything OK?'

'It's our birthday next month,' he said, telling himself that this was what was bothering him, with its stirring-up of unwelcome memories of birthdays gone by. 'He wants to know whether I'd be up for a celebratory dinner.'

'And are you?'

He wouldn't miss it for the world. 'I guess. I haven't celebrated my birthday for years.'

She pulled the blanket around her tighter and came to sit beside him, which simultaneously made him want to shift closer and leap to his feet. 'Why not?'

'When I was a kid, my mother chose my friends, what I wore, what I ate. That didn't let up on my birthday.'

'My birthdays weren't much fun either,' she said dryly. 'No one ever even remembered. At least you got presents.'

'Only because they could be repurposed as weapons. She used to use the threat of taking them away as a punishment for whatever I did wrong.'

Her eyes shimmered. 'What a bitch.'

'Yup.'

'You're so lucky to have found your brothers,' she

added with a wistfulness that, for some bizarre reason, made his throat tighten.

'I know.' He'd filled her in on the conversations they'd had and how much meeting them had meant to him. Now he came to think of it, there'd been a wistful look on her face then too.

'You now have family that cares about you. That gets you. You have an instant connection with people you met a week ago. I've known my family for thirty-three years and have no emotional connection with them at all. I have no such connection with anyone.'

She had an emotional connection with him. The thought spun into his head before he made it spin right out again. That couldn't be the case. The only connection they shared was a physical one. All that was between them was sex. He wasn't the one for her, even if she had wanted something more. He wasn't the one for anyone. Ever.

But he didn't like the clench in his chest at the thought of her all alone in this world, and he liked even less the jealousy that speared through him at the thought of her with someone else.

The dream, still fresh in his mind, was unsettling. He couldn't work out what was going on and he didn't want to, so it was a good thing that just then her phone, which she'd brought out with her to take pictures of the dawn as she'd done the morning before, beeped to alert her of an incoming message.

She focused on the device for a second or two,

hitting a button there, scrolling up and down there, and then she gasped, 'Oh, my God.'

'What?'

When she lifted her gaze from the screen and looked at him, her eyes were wide and stunned. 'Remember I told you Finn had sent his DNA off for analysis?'

As if he'd ever forget anything he'd learned about his new-found family. 'Yes.'

'So it turns out it wasn't such a long shot after all.'

He went very still at that and his heart gave a great crash against his ribs. 'What are you saying?'

'There's a match.'

CHAPTER TEN

As Alex's pronouncement hit his brain, each word detonating on impact, time seemed to stop. Max's head emptied of everything but this one massive revelation and then began to spin as questions started hurtling around it. His pulse thundered, his stomach churned and he couldn't seem to make any of it stop.

The facts. That was what he had to focus on. The facts.

'Who is it?' he said, his voice sounding as though it came from far, far away, even to his own ears.

'I don't know,' she said, sounding as dazed as he felt. 'A woman. A Valentina Lopez. The message is in Spanish.'

She held out the phone and for one moment he just stared at it as if it were about to bite. Valentina Lopez? That name hadn't come up in any of Alex's research. So who could she be? He ought to be snatching the phone out of her hand to find out, and yet he hesitated. There was an odd unexpected security in uncertainty. Once he read the message there'd be no going back. He could be on the brink of finding out everything he needed to make sense of his life, his value and who he was, or he could be opening a whole new can of worms.

But then he pulled himself together. This was precisely why he'd made the snap decision to fly from the Caribbean to London in the first place. Why he'd taken up Rico's offer of his plane and agreed to work with Alex, who'd been right that morning she'd stopped him leaving. He had to investigate this. For his brothers and, more importantly, for himself.

Bracing himself, he took her phone and glanced down at the screen. The details were blurry so he blinked, gave his head a quick shake and forced himself to focus.

'It would appear we have a first cousin,' he said a moment later, his limbs suddenly so weak he was glad he was sitting down. 'She's twenty-five. She's a marketing assistant and lives in Salta.'

'Oh, my God,' Alex breathed. 'That's five hundred kilometres south of La Posada. Does she say anything else?'

'That she'd like to meet.'

'Do you think she might know something?'

'I have no idea.'

'What are we going to do?'

As with so much that had happened over the last week, Max didn't have a clue. That he had more blood relatives was blowing his mind. His parents had both been only children, his grandparents long dead, so it had always been just them. But if he had a cousin here then he had an aunt and uncle and who knew how many more. He might have biological parents and grandparents. More siblings. An instant family, with the relationships and history and everything that entailed, things he'd never had. Or he might not. The chaos that had receded over the last couple of days was back with a roar, expanding and intensifying with every passing second, and it was making it impossible to think.

Or maybe that was Alex, who was sitting looking at him with a combination of wariness, hope and excitement, who still managed to stir up desire in him, even now, with this, and who, he realised with a jolt, confused the hell out of him.

What on earth had he been *doing* lately? he wondered wildly as he tapped out a reply, which took an age since his fingers were shaking so much he kept hitting the wrong letters. What had he been thinking?

All the things he'd told her... His angst over his parents, the doubts he had about who he was and the reasons behind his drive to get to the truth... None of that was in the public domain. None of that she'd needed to know for the case. And what about the compromises he'd made, the lengths he'd gone to to please her, all so she would think more of him, better of him? He'd vowed never to change, to never again mould himself into being something someone else wanted, but that was exactly what he'd been doing.

For some reason his guard hadn't just lowered, it had disappeared altogether, and he felt as though he were on the edge of a precipice and about to hurl himself off it. She hadn't robbed him of the control and power he valued so highly and needed so much. He'd handed both over to her on a platter, without blinking an eye. He'd allowed her to break all the rules he hadn't even known he had. She'd pierced his armour. He was beginning to feel things he didn't want to feel, couldn't allow himself to feel, didn't deserve to feel.

He should never have allowed it to happen, he thought as panic began to set in. Hubris had been his enemy once again; in his arrogance he'd assumed he'd have this fling with Alex firmly under his control. But he'd been weak and foolish in his need for her and she'd sneaked beneath his defences. He'd become too involved. Their affair was supposed to have been a purely physical thing. It was never meant to have involved the discussion of innermost thoughts and emotions.

He shouldn't have indulged himself by analysing how alike they were, or wondered how the hell she couldn't see it, he realised, his throat tight and his head pounding as he hit the send button on his reply to Valentina Lopez. He shouldn't have granted her access to so many fragments of himself that she'd seen the whole.

But it wasn't too late to put a stop to it. To get some breathing space and perspective and regroup. He was going to Salta on his own. He was more than capable of handling whatever he found there alone. He'd spent thirty-odd years doing precisely that. He didn't want Alex there for any fallout. She'd already seen far too much of him and the thought of exposing any more of his vulnerabilities to her made him feel physically sick. It was now a question of survival.

'Well, I don't know about you,' he said bluntly, throwing up a shield of steel behind which he could restore his strength and fortify his defences, just the way he had as a kid whenever his mom had been particularly vicious or his father particularly uninterested, 'but *I'll* be leaving for Salta just as soon as possible.'

What the hell?

Stunned and confused, for one heart-thumping moment Alex just sat there watching as Max leapt to his feet and strode back into the dome. One minute she'd been desperately hoping that he would invite her to his birthday dinner—which was insane when what they were doing together firstly stayed in Argentina and secondly definitely did *not* involve birthday dinners—the next she'd been receiving a text from Becky with the instruction Check your emails!!!!!!, which she'd done and received a shock that had knocked her for six. As if all that wasn't enough to make her reel, Max's blunt declaration that he was flying solo on this whipped the air from her lungs and the strength from her limbs.

But, whatever was behind it, it wasn't happening.

They were beyond unilateral decision-making. He had to be in shock. She'd noticed that his fingers had trembled as he tapped out a reply and the tension in his jaw. That was what this was about, she was sure, and as a result he needed her more than ever.

Filling fast with energy and determination, Alex sprang into action and ran after him. 'Wait,' she said, faintly alarmed by the frenzy with which he was gathering up his things and tossing them into his bag.

'What?' he snapped distractedly.

'Don't you mean *we* will leave as soon as possible?'

He didn't even look at her. He looked as if he was somewhere else entirely and her chest tightened with sympathy and alarm.

'No,' he said flatly. 'I mean "I".'

He sounded resolute and tension radiated off him like some kind of force field designed to keep her out. And as it dawned on her that he was not going to yield on this, was not going to talk to her about what he was feeling, hurt sliced through her.

'You want to cut me out of the loop now?' After everything they'd talked about? Everything they'd done?'

'It's nothing personal.'

The sting of that lodged deep in her chest and twisted. 'It is to me, Max,' she said, her throat tight, her voice cracking. It was deeply personal for a whole host of reasons she couldn't begin to unravel right now. 'This is *my* success,' she said, going for the simplest. 'I've waited eight months for a breakthrough like this. I need to be part of it.'

'It's *my* family. There's no point in you coming. You don't speak Spanish. You literally wouldn't understand.'

Another arrow pierced her heart, dipped in envy for the family, the connections, the love and acceptance he might find, and yet more pain. No, she didn't speak Spanish, but she could be there, in the background if necessary. She *would* understand. She could see what he was going through. She wanted to help him. But he wasn't letting her and that was more agonising than she could ever have imagined.

'I'd like to be there for you.'

'I don't need you to be there for me, Alex,' he said, his horribly and bewilderingly blank gaze finally meeting hers. 'I don't *want* you to be there for me. That isn't what this is. You knew the score. You *agreed* with the score.'

Yes, she had, but still. Wow. Just wow. It was as if he'd punched her in the stomach and sliced her heart in two. Her head was spinning and she couldn't breathe.

'We'll head back to La Posada now,' he said, tossing her bag on the bed and then striding into the bathroom. 'I'll drop you off at the hotel and then go on to the airport. I'll be back this evening and fill you in on the details then. Get packing.'

Max wouldn't be filling her in on the details this evening, or at any other time, Alex thought dully as the powerful four-by-four ate up first the Bolivian and then the Argentinian kilometres. She wasn't sticking around when she clearly wasn't wanted. What did he take her for? Some kind of sap he could use when it suited him and discard when it didn't? Well, that wasn't her.

She understood that the news that he had a cousin—and therefore quite possibly more relatives—must have come as an almighty shock, but how could he dismiss her so brutally? Didn't she deserve more than that?

If she was being completely honest, the thing between them had never been purely physical. She'd been fascinated by him from the moment they'd met and not just because of his devastating good looks. Somewhere along the line she'd started thinking that maybe it was the same for him. The things he'd told her had been freely shared. She hadn't had to prise anything out of him. She'd sensed his trust in her in his touch, in the strength of his need for her.

Yet the security she'd been starting to feel with him had been entirely false. One huge toss of the sea and Max had retreated behind his feet-thick walls, keeping her well and truly out, more determinedly, more successfully than before, and now everything was falling down around her like a house of cards.

How could she have been such a fool? What on earth had made her think her support, her help, would count for anything? He'd never asked for it. He clearly didn't want it. And why would he when he'd never had either before, and had presumably adapted to that? Where had that arrogance of hers come from?

This was precisely why she didn't get involved, she reminded herself, the blood in her veins chilling at the thought of how close a shave she'd had. This was why she had rules. To protect herself from hurt. To ward off weakness. To prevent the kind of emotional turmoil that could destroy her focus and threaten her future. She ought to be grateful that Max had revealed his true self before she'd tossed aside what remained of her rules and found herself in too deep. Before she wound up trying to find ways to prolong the investigation and therefore their affair too, believing that it could turn into something it wasn't.

As soon as he dropped her at La Posada and left, she'd make her way home. Her work here was done. Once she was back in London, free of Max's impact and the cruelty of his whims, she'd focus on the fact that, after all these months of nothing, her long shot had paid off. She'd had the breakthrough she'd so badly needed. In terms of progress, she'd gone from zero to a hundred. Because of a recommendation *she'd* made. Once the implications had fully registered she'd be on cloud nine. She was sure she would.

To hell with what Max discovered in Salta. If she wanted to know she'd find out from Finn. She would not wonder how he got on or how he dealt with whatever it was that Valentina Lopez had to say. She would not regret that she couldn't be there to share the joy or the sorrow he might feel. She would not allow the pain of his rejection to linger or indulge the many what-ifs she could feel crowding at the edges of her mind.

In fact, she wouldn't think of him at all.

Max arrived back in La Posada at midnight, wrecked and battered by the events of the day, to discover that Alex had checked out. She'd left a brief note at Reception, informing him that she was closing down the investigation and going home and wishing him luck for the future, before signing off with her full name and professional title.

And that was absolutely fine, he told himself, his chest aching and his stomach churning as he strode into his room, kicked the door shut and cracked open the bottle of bourbon he'd procured from the bar on his way up, the words of her bald little note ricocheting around his head. Better that she wasn't around to see him like this, actually, and what had he expected anyway?

He'd had plenty of time to reflect on this morning's conversation. He hadn't handled the news of the match well, he knew now. In his mind's eye he could still see the hurt on Alex's face when he'd told her he was going to Salta alone, could still hear her gasp of shock when he'd told her why. That he'd been both knocked for six by the news that he had a cousin and thrown into a spin by various realisations about the nature of their affair was no excuse.

He'd planned on apologising and explaining, as well as confessing that he deeply regretted rejecting her support because all too soon he'd realised he could have done with her there, even though he wasn't entirely sure why. He'd have got on his knees to beg her forgiveness, if it had come to that. He'd have done whatever it took to calm the storm that was raging through him.

But none of that was necessary now, he reflected numbly, splashing bourbon into a glass and swallowing it in one. There'd be no grovelling, no recounting of the meeting he'd had with his cousin and no forgiveness and acceptance. No arms around him when he broke down over the fact that his biological mother had died six years ago and, his father had been a one-night stand she'd had when she was sixteen, and no soothing insight into how he might go about dealing with the heart-breaking fact that he would never know if he was like either of them or who he truly was.

But at least there was also no risk of him crashing through his shield of steel and begging Alex to agree to continue their fling even after the case closed, which was not only impractical when they lived half a world apart and unprecedented when he rarely reversed a decision once made, but also so very, very dangerous.

He wasn't good enough for her, he told himself,

pouring himself another glass of liquor and again downing the contents. He wasn't good enough for anyone. How could he have forgotten that? Wanting to be wanted by her would lead to nothing but misery and disillusionment. Even if this morning had gone differently and by some miracle she'd agreed, how long would it be before he screwed up so badly that her approval and appreciation turned to disappointment and regret?

No. As he'd always known, he was far better off free from the emotional havoc of a relationship that he'd inevitably mess up through ignorance and inexperience. He neither wanted nor deserved the responsibility of Alex's happiness and well-being. He wouldn't know how to take care of them. He could scarcely believe he'd even contemplated it. Hell, he didn't even know who he was. The confused, unwanted, unloved kid? The cocky, rebellious hacker? The cool-headed cyber security expert? Or a man being torn apart by pointless feelings for a woman he could never have?

He'd survive. He always did. And he had his brothers now. He'd take the bundle of unopened letters Valentina had given him to England. He'd read them with Finn and Rico instead of with Alex. It was much more appropriate that way anyway.

He had no doubt that tomorrow he'd realise that things had turned out for the best today. He'd treated Alex appallingly and the regret and shame scything through him were nothing more than he deserved.

He'd been wise to put a stop to their affair before it had got out of hand and he'd done even more damage. He didn't think he could bear it if he made her unhappy, which he inevitably would.

He picked up the bottle for the third time and figured that since the bourbon was doing such a good job of dulling the pain he might as well finish it off. In the morning, with hindsight, he'd see that he'd had the luckiest of escapes and, more importantly, so had she.

But if he'd had such a lucky escape, thought Max three tumultuous days later as he sat with his brothers in Finn's drawing room in Oxfordshire, the letters strewn across the vast coffee table that sat between two enormous sofas, why was Alex all he could think about? Why did the fact that she'd sent her invoice to Finn the day she'd got home, as if she hadn't been able to wait another minute to sever the connection they'd once had, cut him up so painfully?

He'd assumed, an inch from the bottom of the bottle, he'd have no trouble wiping her from his head. He'd told himself that he had more than enough to worry about and did not need either the confusion she wreaked or the hassle she caused. He'd deal with what was going on inside him somehow. He'd done it before. He could do it again. She was out of his life and it was a relief.

But, if that was the case, why was he still feeling so out of sorts?

Outwardly, he was just about holding it together, but inside he was falling apart. Every time a memory from the time he and Alex had spent together slammed unbidden into his head, the impact of it nearly wiped out his knees. When he recalled the way she'd smiled at him, warmth spread through him like a blanket seeping into every corner of him, even those parts that had always been so cold and empty, before it was whipped away by regret.

He was untethered, adrift, and he itched to return to his old ways. He wanted to break laws and hack into a system or two, just to claw back some kind of control and power over what was happening to him. He wanted to immerse himself in the dark web and find out what his former colleagues were up to and maybe lend a hand. It was only the thought of Alex's disapproval that stopped him and that was baffling, since her opinion of him was neither here nor there any more.

It wasn't as if he didn't have anything else to occupy his mind. Once he'd sobered up he'd gone home, where he'd spent two days translating the letters their mother had written, and what a weekend that had been.

The letters, which ran to dozens of pages each, detailed a history of her life and as much of theirs as she'd known. They were filled with explanations and reasons and the hopes she'd had at first of finding her sons and then, when that had looked less and less likely, the dreams she'd had for them. Her anger, her sadness, her love poured from the lines, and reading them, analysing them as he'd translated them, had completely wrecked him.

It seemed to be wrecking his brothers too. For two hours they'd been studying the letters, largely in silence, and jaws were tight and brows were furrowed. The struggle for self-control seemed to be as tough for them as it had been for him.

'Bit dusty in here,' said Finn gruffly, clearing his throat as he put down the final page, the one in which their mother's heartbreak at knowing she was going to her grave without ever finding them had ripped Max to shreds.

'I appear to have something in my eye,' said Rico, looking as if swallowing was hard.

Finn rubbed his face and got to his feet. 'I think I'll go and find Georgie.'

Rico shoved his hands through his hair and did the same. 'I'm just going to call Carla.'

They exited the room, leaving Max alone with nothing more than a pounding head and a racing pulse. His chest ached. His vision blurred. He could hardly breathe with emotions that were crushing him on all sides, one in particular scorching through him like lightning.

It was envy, he realised with a jolt as the room began to spin. He envied his brothers. For the relationships they had and the women they loved. How did they do it? He wished he knew. Because, deep down, he didn't want to be alone. He wanted Alex, in the way Finn had Georgie and Rico had Carla. Not only to help him navigate the choppy waters he was in, but to sail along with him even when they weren't choppy. In other words, all the time.

Which meant what? That he'd been the biggest fool on the planet to turn her away? Well, that seemed pretty much spot-on. Despite his attempts to convince himself otherwise, Alex *was* different to the other women he'd hooked up with over the years. Quite apart from the fact that what they'd been doing was far more than 'hooking up', they'd travelled similar paths. They understood each other. Until he'd been spooked into falling back into bad habits and internalising his fears, everything had been going great.

So could he have pushed her away deliberately, sabotaging something good before it blew up in his face? Had it been his way of maintaining control over a situation that was fast slipping out of his grip? It wasn't beyond the realms of possibility. But what if it didn't blow up in his face? What if he'd thrown away the best thing that had ever happened to him because of some ridiculous concern that he might not survive it?

He had to take responsibility for his behaviour, he realised suddenly as he sprang to his feet and began to pace the length of the drawing room. His hang-ups about the past might be valid, but his response to what happened now was his own. He had a choice, and he could either continue to allow it to eat him up with bitterness and resentment or he could let it go.

He was fed up with dwelling on the past. Shouldn't he take a leaf out of his brothers' book and start looking forwards rather than back? It would be charting new territory and that was scary as hell, but that was no excuse not to do it. That smacked of cowardice.

Could the future hold Alex? He desperately wanted it to, because he could see her in it. He wanted her in it. Was he in love with her? How would he know? Where was a flowchart when he needed one? But *something* had to account for the gaping hole in his chest and the tightness in his throat. The ache in his heart and the spinning of his head whenever he thought of her, which was pretty much all the damn time.

He had to be in love with her, he thought, going dizzy at the idea of it. He probably had been from the moment they'd met. That was why he'd found it so much fun to provoke her. That was why he'd been so determined to make her his. Why he craved her smiles and wanted to make her happy.

Their mother's letters proved that he and his brothers had once upon a time been loved. Very much. He'd mattered and been wanted. And now he realised that he wanted to matter to Alex, as much as she mattered to him.

And all those worries of his? Pathetic. He hadn't changed. He hadn't moulded himself into anyone. He'd made no sacrifices. She'd demanded nothing of him. The compromises he'd made had made him happy too. He had nothing to fear from love or a relationship. It didn't have to be toxic or manipulative.

Who he'd been was of no importance. What was important was the sort of man he wanted to be, and that was a man who deserved her, and if she had expectations of him, well, he wanted to spend the rest of his life attempting to meet them.

This morning Finn had asked him if there was anyone he wanted to invite to their birthday dinner on Saturday. He'd flatly said no, but here, now, he'd changed his mind. He wanted to invite Alex. He wanted a second chance. He could only hope it wasn't too late.

CHAPTER ELEVEN

When Alex had arrived back on UK soil, she'd hit the ground running. Finn had settled her invoice with much appreciated efficiency and she'd wasted no time in paying off her debts before hiring a recruitment consultant and calling up a commercial estate agency.

In the midst of the flurry of activity she'd paid her family a visit, which had been a tense and unpleasant hour, not least because her elder brother had put in a request for ten grand and then spat at her feet when she'd refused. In that moment, any qualms she might have had about cutting them out of her life for good had evaporated, and once she'd got everything she wanted to say to them off her chest she'd left with no looking back and no regrets. She was wholly on her own now, but she was independent and strong, utterly content with who she was and her place in the world.

True to his word, Finn was already recommending her agency, and Becky, who'd done a great job of holding the fort while she'd been away and whom she was on the point of promoting, was taking more calls than she could handle. The plans for expansion were once again within touching distance and the new kit Alex had ordered was scheduled to arrive imminently. The future looked bright and brilliant and she was marching straight into it.

She didn't have time to think about Max, nor did she care to. She'd been so upset, so angry at the abrupt, careless way he'd dismissed her and, for some unfathomable reason, so damn sad, but by the time she'd landed in London after a lengthy journey that involved a number of changes and a lot of analysis, she'd been totally over it. And him. She couldn't believe that at one point she'd actually been hoping their affair might turn into something more. Anyone who could be that cruel didn't deserve her and wasn't worth her head space, no matter how many times he'd rocked her world.

And that was why, when the invitation to the triplets' black-tie thirty-second birthday celebrations at Rico's house in Venice had dropped into her inbox, Alex had seen no reason not to accept. She hadn't dressed up in months. She'd never been to Venice. She might even make a long weekend of it. Besides, she'd like to see Finn and Rico again and meet Georgie and Carla and it wasn't as if she was going to go all dewy-eyed over Max. That was the very *last* thing that was going to happen. Thank God she hadn't done anything stupid like gone and fallen in love with him. That really would have been recklessly insane.

If she'd made the guest list, she was, no doubt, one of a hundred guests, so she'd probably hardly even see him. And in the unlikely event she did, well, her unflappable facade was in place and these days it was impregnable. There'd be no shock, no thundering rush of lust, just polite professionalism and cool distance.

So what if she'd bought a new dress? She could hardly wear a trouser suit to a black-tie dinner. Her hair was loose tonight but that was because the style suited her outfit, not because Max liked it like that. The fact that she'd brought him a present had nothing to do with wanting to show him they could be given freely, without any strings attached. It was merely polite. She'd brought gifts for Finn and Rico too, although the books she'd selected for them were far less personal than the tiny bag of Bolivian salt she'd had sent over at vast expense for him. And if her heart was pounding so hard she feared it was in danger of escaping her chest…well, that was entirely down to the exhilaration of the boat ride across the lagoon.

But when Alex's water taxi approached the jetty and she saw Max standing there, tall, solid and so handsome he took her breath away, frowning out across the water as if looking for her, she realised, with a nosedive of her heart, she'd been kidding herself.

Everything she thought she'd successfully buried

shot to the surface, all the hurt and misery she'd felt on the plane home, and she knew, with a sinking of her spirits, that she was no more over him than she could fly to the moon.

How on earth had she managed to ignore the X-rated dreams she'd had, which woke her up on a regular basis in a tangle of sheets and a puddle of lust, her heart aching with regret and sorrow?

How many times had she had to stop herself calling him up to tell him how well her business was going and to find out what he was up to?

How much had she wished he'd been there to hold her after she'd cut her family out of her life, which had been hard, even if completely the right thing to do?

Taking a couple of deep shaky breaths, Alex ordered her galloping pulse to slow and pushed the memories and the flush of heat that came with them aside. It was only natural that her subconscious would remember the best sex she'd ever had and miss it. It meant nothing. She could handle it. And how could she have missed *him* when he'd been so horrible? Her plans for the future were of no interest to him and he wouldn't have been there to hold her anyway. That wasn't what their affair had been about and she mustn't forget that.

'Hi,' he said with the ghost of a smile that annoyingly melted her stupid soppy heart.

'You look awful.' His face was gaunt, she noted as she alighted. There were bags under his eyes, his cheekbones were sharp and the black suit he was wearing fitted a little more loosely than she suspected it should or indeed than she'd once imagined.

'You look beautiful.'

Well. She wasn't going to be distracted by that, no matter how much of a flutter it sparked in her stomach. She was still so angry. 'Thank you.'

He thrust his hands in the pockets of his trousers and she refused to notice how lovingly the fine fabric pulled across the powerful muscles of his thighs. Nor would she think about how much she'd missed wrapping her arms around his broad, strong shoulders, or how heavenly he smelled.

'How have you been?'

'Good.' He didn't look it. He looked as if he'd been to hell and back, and yet there was something remarkably calm in his indigo gaze, something sort of settled, which she just couldn't put her finger on. 'You?'

'Very well,' she replied, intent on keeping her tone impersonal. 'Busy.'

'Work going well?'

'Work is going very well, thank you,' she said coolly.

'I'm glad you're here.'

'I can't imagine why.'

'You left without saying goodbye.'

He'd given her no option and what did he care anyway?

'The case was closed, Max. My work was done.

Once you'd gone to Salta there was no need for me to stay.'

He tilted his head, his gaze turning quizzical. 'Don't you want to know what happened?'

She did. She badly did. She deliberately hadn't asked Finn. She'd worried she wouldn't be able to stop herself from asking about Max too, which was pathetic when this case had taken up nearly nine months of her life.

'All right, fine,' she said with a casual shrug, as if it were neither here nor there. 'What happened?'

'I met with Valentina,' he said as they started walking up the jetty to the magnificent villa she could see peeking through the towering cypress trees.

The early autumn sun was low in the sky and the heat of the day still lingered. That was why she was so warm. It had nothing to do with the man walking with her, so close that he was taking up all her air, so close that she'd barely have to move her hand to be able to hold his. She had to focus and stay strong if she stood any chance of getting through this evening which she was beginning to regret with every passing second.

'Did she know anything?'

'Not a lot. She never met our mother, whose name, by the way, was Silvia Solana, contrary to what appears on our original birth certificates.'

'Was?'

'She died in Buenos Aires six years ago. Pancreatic cancer.'

She tried not to care but it was impossible when her chest ached for him. He had to have been *so* disappointed. 'I'm so sorry.'

'It's fine.'

'How can it be?'

'She left us letters.'

'Letters?'

'Twenty-six of them. She wrote to us once a year on our birthday and then one last one a few weeks before she died. In them she explains everything.'

'What happened?'

'She had a one-night stand with a guy she met in a bar when she was sixteen. She didn't know who he was and she never saw him again.'

'What was she doing in a bar at the age of sixteen?'

'Rebelling.'

'Like mother, like son.'

He cast her a quick startled glance and then grinned, and he looked so carefree that she found she could hardly breathe. 'I guess so,' he said. 'Perceptive as always.'

He made it sound as if he knew her, which he didn't or he'd never have treated her so badly, but, before she could tell him that, he continued, 'Her parents were deeply religious and when they discovered she was pregnant they sent her to a convent. We were removed from her by the nuns when we were two months old. She was never told where we were taken or what ultimately happened to us. She escaped the convent, went to Buenos Aires to find work and never spoke to her parents again. When they died, she established contact with her sister, but by then she was ill and didn't have much time left.'

'That's so sad.'

'She never stopped looking for us.'

'She must have loved you all very much.'

'She did.'

Alex cleared her throat to dislodge the knot that had formed there against her will. 'Do you have other relatives?'

'We have aunts and uncles and cousins galore. Some in Salta, some in Buenos Aires. One cousin lives in New York, oddly enough.'

'Will you visit them?'

'Some time.'

'That would be good.'

'Would you like to read the letters?'

God, yes. But the case was closed. They were done. 'I've moved on to other things.'

'Have you?'

'Very much so.'

'I'm sorry I didn't take you to Salta with me, Alex. I needed you there.'

She steeled her heart not to melt. His apology came far too late. 'Don't worry about it,' she said with an airiness that she didn't feel at all. 'It's all water under the bridge. No hard feelings. We agreed to a short-term thing that was going to last just as long as the investigation and it ended. It's completely fine.'

'Is it?'

Something in his voice made her meet his gaze and her pulse skipped a beat at the dark intensity that shimmered within. It wasn't fine, she thought with a sudden surge of alarm. It wasn't fine at all. 'Absolutely.'

'What if I told you I loved you?'

The world stopped for a second and then began to spin, but she couldn't let herself go there. She was in such a good place at the moment and she'd worked hard for it. The risk of upending everything for a man who played fast and loose with her emotions was too great. 'I'd say we've known each other for less than two weeks and ask what you were on.'

'I know it's been quick but I *am* in love with you, Alex. I think I have been since the moment we met.'

'You could have fooled me.'

'The only person I've been fooling is myself.'

She badly needed a drink and to mingle, to be able to remove herself from his presence in order to be able to think straight, and they'd reached the pretty terrace now, which overlooked the lagoon and was decorated with strings of light. But where was the party? Why was the table set for six?

'Where's everyone else?' she asked, confused and alarmed by the absence of other people.

'Finn and Georgie are putting their son to bed.

Rico and Carla are in the kitchen doing something clever with pasta.'

And that was it? This wasn't a party. This was an intimate dinner. A family dinner. What did that mean? She couldn't work it out. All she knew was that Max had whipped the rug from under her feet yet again and coming here had been a mistake.

'I'm sorry,' she said as panic swept through her like the wildest of fires. 'I can't do this. I should go.'

Of all the responses Max had expected to his apologies and his declaration of love, Alex spinning on her very sexy heel was not one of them. Yet she was charging back down the steps towards the jetty and he was so stunned it was a full ten seconds before he sprang into action.

'Stop,' he said, even though, this being an island and her water taxi having left some time ago, she couldn't actually go anywhere.

'No.'

He caught up with her and put a hand on her arm which she threw off, but at least she stopped and turned to face him, even if the torment on her face sliced straight through his heart. 'What's wrong?'

'This is.'

'In what way?'

'We had an agreement,' she said wretchedly.

'I know.'

'You don't do love.'

'It turns out I do, with you.'

'Then how could you have pushed me away like that?' Her eyes filled with sadness and he felt physically sick at the knowledge that he'd put it there.

'I'm so sorry I did that,' he said, his chest aching with regret. 'You'll never know how sorry. I guess I was trying to protect myself. I learned early on in life to suppress my emotions. The only way to survive was not to care and so I didn't. I grew up believing I was worthless and unwanted, which was compounded by the discovery that I was adopted, and that's a hard habit to break.'

'You hurt me badly.'

The ache turned into pain of the sort he'd never felt before. 'I know and that guts me. Not that it's any excuse, but I was struggling to work out who I am.'

'You should have just asked. I know who you are.'

'You're the only person in the world who does,' he said, not taking his eyes off her for even a second, willing her to believe him because his entire future depended on it. 'You came along and crashed through my defences, Alex, and it was terrifying at first and now it isn't at all. You knowing me and me knowing you makes me incredibly happy. I love you and I'd like to spend the rest of my life proving it to you.' He took a deep breath, his entire world now reduced to this woman and what she said next. 'The only question I have is, how do you feel about me?'

Alex didn't know. Max had stirred up so many emotions inside her and she couldn't unravel any of them.

But he was waiting for an answer and, with the way his gaze bored into hers, it mattered. A lot.

'Volatile,' she said, wishing she was better at explaining it.

He jerked back as if she'd struck him and she wanted to hug the shock out of him, but if she did that she might not be able to stop and they'd have resolved nothing. 'Volatile?'

'Like I'm on the top of the world one minute and at the bottom of a pit the next. It's not the way I want to be. It's not the life I want to live. I need stability and security. I always have.'

'I'll give it to you.'

No doubt he thought he could, but it was impossible. That wasn't who he was. 'How?' she said desperately, all pretence of control gone. 'You are chaos and unpredictability. You don't want to change who you are any more than I want to change who I am, and that's fine because I wouldn't want you to.'

'It's far too late for that,' he said, his gaze on hers steady and sure. 'I already have changed and I'm OK with it. I'm done with the chaos. I figure it's a choice and I choose, well, not that. I choose you. I've always feared the idea of being responsible for someone else's feelings. But I want to be responsible for yours. Trust me with them, Alex. Take a risk with me. You won't regret it.'

Wouldn't she? How could he be so sure? How could anyone? He was so calm, while she was the one who felt wild and out of control, and yet the longer she stared into his eyes, the more she could feel the wildness ease. It was as if they'd swapped roles, as if she'd rubbed off on him and he'd rubbed off on her.

Could she do it? That was the thought ricocheting around her head, making her breath catch and her heart race. Could she take the risk? Did she even want to?

Yes, yes and, God, yes.

Because she was in love with him too, she realised as the walls she'd built around her heart on the plane home crumbled to dust. Madly and irreversibly. She'd been so miserable these past couple of days, so sad. Just being here with him, colours were brighter, sounds were sharper. When he pushed her buttons she loved it. She never felt more alive than when he was challenging and provoking her. He was the polar opposite of everything she'd ever thought she wanted but she'd been wrong. They were like two sides of the same coin.

'I've missed you,' she said, her voice shaking from the force of the emotions rushing through her.

'I've missed you too.'

'I cut all ties with my family.'

'That was brave.'

'It had to be done, even if I am now all alone. I could give you tips, if you want.'

'You aren't alone, Alex. You have me. If you want me. You need never be alone again.'

She did want him, desperately, but... 'What if it all goes wrong?'

'It won't.'

'You don't know that. It did for me before.'

'I do know that,' he said with quiet certainty that filled her with confidence and brushed away the doubts. 'I won't allow it. I don't want you to be anyone other than who you are, Alex. Why would I when you are absolutely brilliant?'

'You are *not* worthless,' she said, her throat thick.

'I know. Silvia's letters prove it. I love you and I will always be there for you, the way you've been there for me.'

She had to trust him. She wanted to trust him. All she had to do was take a risk, and it wasn't even that much of a risk. This might have been quick, but she'd never been surer of anything in her life, and they could work out the logistics later.

Her heart was pounding and her eyes were swimming as she took a step forwards, but nothing was going to stop her telling him how she felt now.

'I love you too,' she said, winding her arms around his neck, her heart so filled with happiness it felt too big for her chest.

He pulled her close and she lifted her head as he lowered his, and their mouths met in a kiss that was hot and tender and went on and on until the sun dipped beneath the horizon.

'Happy birthday,' she murmured raggedly when he finally lifted his mouth from hers.

The smile he gave her was blinding. 'It's a *very* happy birthday.'

EPILOGUE

Christmas Day, three months later

THE NORDIC FIR standing in Finn and Georgie's drawing room in their sprawling mansion situated in the Oxfordshire countryside was so tall it nearly touched the ceiling. Strings of fairy lights were draped over thick wide-spreading branches from which gold and silver baubles hung, and tinsel sparkled in the bright winter sunlight.

Outside in the snow, under a cloudless blue sky, two-and-a-half-year-old Josh was building a snowman with his mother, Georgie, and his aunt, Carla. Alex was searching for sticks, presumably to be turned into its arms. Inside, the rich aroma of roasting turkey and stuffing filled the house and carols rang out from speakers hidden in the ceiling.

This year the dining room table was set for seven. Next year, wherever they chose to spend it—London or Oxfordshire, Venice or the Caribbean—there'd be more. Georgie and Finn were expecting a daughter via surrogate in May. Carla was due in August, and only this morning Alex had told Max that come September they too would be welcoming the patter of tiny feet.

Before the roaring fire, the brothers stood side by side, each nursing a glass of Scotch as they gazed out of the window at the activity outside.

'I'd like to make a toast,' said Max, raising his glass and thinking how unbelievably lucky he was, how unbelievably lucky all three of them were, to have found each other and have the love of incredible women.

'To the best Christmas in thirty-two years?' said Rico.

'To many more in the future?' said Finn.

'To family.'

* * * * *

Keep reading for an excerpt of a new title
from the Modern series,
HEIR ULTIMATUM by Michelle Smart

CHAPTER ONE

LONDON'S SKYLINE, Sebastiano Russo grudgingly admitted, looked spectacular that evening with the soft glow of the setting sun creating a shimmering golden haze around its iconic rooftops. The helicopter he was travelling from Edinburgh in swooped down and landed on one of the most magnificent London buildings of all, the elegant home to the world's most exclusive private members' club.

As usual Lazlo, the unobtrusive manager of the Diamond Club, was there to greet him on the roof and whisk him inside.

Being in no mood for small talk and with no inclination to seek the company of the other club members in residence that evening, Sebastiano headed straight to his private suite. Losing a billion euros of his fortune in one fell swoop had a way of making a man not want company, especially when the reasons for losing said billion euros was down to your own mindlessness.

At least here he could switch the world off.

The Diamond Club's facilities and services along with its innate alluring ambience gave him everything he needed when wanting to let off steam during his business trips in London. As the face of Russo Banca Internazionale, image was everything so any potentially scandalous behaviour was kept strictly behind closed doors. For centuries, the Russo family had owned and steered the glamorous private banking institution with discretion and a touch of glamour. Its high-end customers—clients had to deposit a minimum five million euros to open an account—valued the high returns paid out even during world economic turbulence and the faultless, personalised service. Since Sebastiano had taken the helm, he'd prioritised expanding its wealth management arm and enhancing its digital services without losing any of the little touches that made their clients feel so valued. Under Sebastiano's stewardship, RBI's profits had doubled in five years. If Sebastiano's loss should be made public then his reputation and his bank's reputation would be decimated. Who would trust a man to take care of their wealth if that same man couldn't take care of his own?

For this one night he would allow himself to brood in solitude. Come the morning, he would summon his core team and talk damage limitation strategies.

It had been three months since he'd last visited the Diamond Club. Three months since he'd thrown that spontaneous party in his suite which had ended in the most unexpected way. It was the longest he'd spent between visits since Raj Belanger had invited him to join the club.

There would be no partying that night. The only company Sebastiano wanted was the bottom of a bottle of bourbon and someone prepared to fade into the background pouring it for him.

Lazlo remained silent until they arrived at the double doors of Sebastiano's suite. With a respectful nod, a bow of his head and a murmured wish for Sebastiano to have a peaceful evening, he disappeared with his usual unobtrusiveness. This was one of the many things Sebastiano liked about the Diamond Club. It wasn't just that the staff were all highly trained with discretion practically embedded in their DNA, it was that they all had the ability to judge their guests' moods with nothing more than a look and adapt their own personas to suit what they intuited was wanted from them. In all his years as a member there, the staff had always intuited his mood perfectly.

Having given pre-instructions that only a bar tender was required that evening, Sebastiano shrugged off his suit jacket in the small reception area of his suite and slung it on the back of an armchair, then ripped off his tie and chucked it on the jacket. The cufflinks were the next to be removed before he headed into the suite's main living area rolling the sleeves of his shirt up, only to take one look at the bar tender and come to an abrupt halt.

A long beat passed before the willowy dark blonde woman greeted him with a respectful smile. 'Good evening, Mr Russo.'

Chest tightening, eyes narrowing, he bypassed the pool table and football table that never failed to make a billionaire of any age light up like a child, and pulled up a stool at the long, dark red-wood bar. 'Layla,' he acknowledged with a taut nod to match the tautness in his voice. 'I thought you were moving on.'

If he'd known her notice period hadn't ended, he would have made sure to notify Lazlo of his wish for a different dedicated bar tender.

The last thing he'd wanted was to be confronted by the one member of the Diamond Club's staff that he'd spent the night with.

She flashed the smile that accentuated her high cheekbones. 'Still here, just,' she confirmed lightly, in exactly the same tone with which she always served him. 'Bourbon, one cube of ice?'

He narrowed his stare again, searching her beautiful features for even a hint of reproach or peevishness but found nothing. Nothing to suggest Layla would behave with anything less than the intuitive professionalism that had led to him requesting she always serve his bar when he was in residence.

'Forget the ice,' he said gruffly, 'and make it a large one.'

Her brief smile this time was sympathetic, as if she'd peeped into his mind and seen the colossal mistake that had blighted his day and had the potential to blight the rest of his life.

She poured his drink and placed the crystal tumbler before him.

He drank it in one swallow. 'Another.'

The process was repeated. Only once he felt the liquid start to work its soothing magic did he slow his pace and sip his third glass. Rolling his taut neck, he said, 'Music. Anything of your choice but no jazz.' A cousin had once bored him for an entire Sunday afternoon with a lecture on jazz appreciation. If there was anything to appreciate about it, Roberto's monotonous, droning voice had put Sebastiano off for life.

'Something upbeat?'

Layla's musical voice could never be described as monotonous or droning, he thought, taking another large sip.

He nodded.

She tapped on a tablet and within moments rhythmic beats pulsed lowly through the vast room.

In the two years Layla had worked at the club she'd proved herself the most intuitive of all the staff to his needs and wants, and as the bourbon, helped by the music, continued to soothe the edges of his angst, the tightness in his chest that had formed at seeing her manning his bar loosened a little too.

Post-coital promises were never meant in the way real promises were, he told himself. Everyone knew that. Layla was an adult and there was nothing in her body language to suggest she was upset at his failure to call her. Now that he was a little more settled and a bit more clear in his thinking, the only impression he was receiving was that of a woman pleased to see him.

Well, it *had* been a great night that they'd shared together. The kind of night that lingered.

Relaxing even more, he raised his glass at her. 'Join me?'

Something sparkled in her forget-me-not-blue eyes. Pretty white teeth grazed the bottom lip of a wide mouth with a cupid's bow in the top lip and which three months ago had trailed kisses over every inch of his skin. 'Maybe later.'

He raised an eyebrow at the suggestiveness in her tone and the sweep of her long eyelashes.

She didn't miss a beat, arching her own eyebrows in return.

A frisson raced through his veins.

He recognised that look. It was one they'd shared three months ago in the hours before he'd thrown his guests out of the suite.

Maybe he wouldn't have to forget his troubles in a bottle or two of bourbon after all, he mused as anticipation roused. There were other, far more pleasurable ways to shake off a bad mood and if there was a pleasure greater than Layla wrapping her long legs around his waist and scraping her nails down his back while he plunged deep inside her, he was yet to experience it.

The sparkle deepened into a gleam and she leaned over the bar to top up his glass. For a moment her smart black, V-necked top gaped open, giving him a glimpse of the small, high breasts that had fitted perfectly into his mouth.

As she saw the direction of his stare, her mouth quirked in the corner. When she leaned over the bar again, this time resting her chin on her closed fist, and murmured, 'Can I get you anything else?' there was no doubt in Sebastiano's mind that the gape allowing him to see her black lace bra was deliberate.

The frisson deepened. He was close enough to smell her soft, subtle perfume, his mouth filling with the remembered taste of those perfect breasts, tongue tingling to remember the texture of her large raspberry-coloured nipples. Gazing into her eyes, he murmured back, 'Maybe later.'

Her lips widened into the lopsided smile that was her only flaw. And it wasn't even a flaw. Without it, her face would just be jaw-droppingly beautiful. Her smile turned her beauty into something spectacular. And sexy. It was a smile that promised erotic, hedonistic nights and by God had the reality matched up to the promise. To breathe in her perfume and the heat of her skin and to know that very soon those long legs could be wrapped around him again…

'How come you're still working here?' he asked after taking another long sip of his bourbon.

She gave the lightest shrug. 'My plans changed.'

'So you're staying?'

'No.' Another lopsided smile and sweep of the long lashes. 'This is my last shift.'

Now he was the one to sweep his gaze, taking another open peek at the small breasts wrapped in black lace before meeting her stare again and raising his glass. 'Then fortune is shining in my favour.'

Her elbow inched a little closer to him. 'It didn't look as though you thought fortune was on your side when you walked in here,' she observed.

Her intuition really was exceptional.

'Trust me,' he said ruefully. 'Today has been the day from hell.'

Sympathy brimmed. 'Want to talk about it?'

'No.' In his next breath he said, completely unbidden, 'I lost a billion euros.'

The Diamond Club's staff were the best in the business, from the level of service they provided, to their discretion, to showing no reaction whatsoever at any of the snippets of gossip or state secrets they became privy to in the course of their work, but even Layla's forget-me-not eyes widened at this.

He swallowed what was left in his glass and wiped his mouth with his thumb. 'Want to know how?'

Straightening, she reached for the bottle. 'Only if you want to tell me.'

What the hell? Layla had proved herself an excellent sounding board over the years. The best sounding board. What he told her went in one ear and out of the other. 'A company I'm the majority shareholder of in a personal capacity went into administration last night. On paper, I am now one billion euros poorer.'

She made an 'ouch' face and refilled his glass.

He drank with a grimace. 'I should have sold. The warning signs were there.'

After a day spent berating and raging at himself for his idiocy, he was still none the wiser as to where the lethargy in his brain that had prevented him acting on his instincts had come from. Anyone with an ounce of nous had known to sell and dissociate from a company that had turned toxic.

'I'm not used to screwing up,' he added after another drink.

'You're human,' she said softly. 'Screwing up happens to the best of us.'

'Not to me.'

She stared at him meditatively then put her elbow back on the bar and her chin back on her fist. 'Want to know what I think?'

Surprised—Layla rarely commented on the stuff he confided in her—he stared back and then shrugged. He supposed there was a slim possibility that a bar tender who doubled as a waitress was capable of an insight into his psyche that he hadn't considered. 'Sure.'

'I think you work too hard.'

'I have a lot of responsibility.' An understatement.

'I know, but when did you last take a break?' she challenged, eyeballing him in the sexiest manner imaginable.

'I take plenty of time off,' he said eyeballing her right back.

She leaned a little closer. 'I mean a proper break. A holiday, something like a trip around the Med on your yacht but without your PA, lawyer and accountant in attendance... I bet if you were to call them and order them here, they'd be knocking on the door within minutes.'

He couldn't help grinning at how on-the-nail her observation was, and was rewarded with another of her sexy lopsided smiles.

'I doubt you ever fully switch off,' she continued, her musical voice pitched low and sensuous. 'I bet you even check your emails on Christmas Day.'

'Think how much more money I'd lose if I didn't check them every day,' he riposted.

'You could afford to lose a billion euros a day for a month and still have billions left over.'

'I'd like to keep *all* my billions, not be left with scraps.'

'Then take my advice and take a break. A proper break. Recharge your batteries.' Their faces were now only inches apart. 'You know another thing that's good for stress?'

'Bourbon?'

She gave a short, soft laugh and leaned closer still. A lock of her silky hair tickled against his cheek as she whispered, 'A deep tissue massage.'

'Hmm… Now that sounds like something I'd be up for.'

'I just bet you would,' she said knowingly before another gleam lit her eyes. 'Shall I call the spa?'

He tilted his face. Their lips were a whisper

away from brushing together. The sweetness of her breath filling his senses only added to the intoxication firing through his veins. Spearing his hand into the mass of thick, wavy tresses, he murmured, 'I can think of someone else I'd rather do it.'

Her lips parted against his. The sweet tongue that had explored him with the same passion as her mouth flickered against his lips but before he could mould his mouth to hers, she'd slithered back and out of reach. The hair he'd been holding fell like a waterfall around her shoulders.

Eyes full of cat-like sensuality, she gave her lopsided, oh, so sexy smile. 'I'll get some massage oil. Go and make yourself comfortable in your bedroom.'

Sebastiano stripped his clothes down to his briefs, hot blood pumping hard through him.

This was not an outcome he'd anticipated when he'd decided to end his day from hell by drowning his sorrows at his private club. The only outcome he'd anticipated was a banging hangover.

The last time his blood had pumped this hard was that night three months ago.

He'd fantasised about Layla for two years.

Her beauty had blown his mind from the first look. The tall, willowy blonde who could have graced the cover of any glossy magazine had entered his suite carrying a box of champagne for a small party he'd been hosting, and when she'd smiled at him all he'd been able to think was that there could be no sexier creature on the planet.

But she was staff. Not *his* staff, but still staff, paid to serve and cater to his every whim, part of his world but not of it. To seduce her would have been an abuse of his power. That didn't mean he couldn't request that she always tend his bar when he was in residence and enjoy feasting his eyes on her. Enjoy her company. Enjoy being able to unwind and confide things about his life with her and enjoy the sensation that she was listening because she was genuinely interested and not just because she was being paid. It helped that he doubted she retained much of what he confided.

The frisson that accompanied their talks when they were alone together was, he'd long been certain, mutual. And then she'd told him while lining up the glasses in preparation for the party he'd been throwing three months ago that it would probably be the last of his parties she worked at because she'd handed her resignation in.

The look that had flowed between them at those words...

Sebastiano's intention to party until the sun

came up had been thrown out of the window, as had all his guests when midnight struck and he'd sent them home. He'd sent all the staff out too. Everyone except Layla.

There had been no doubt about what would happen the moment they were alone together. The last of the guests couldn't have left the corridor before she was locked in his arms. It had been the most thrillingly sensuous night of his thirty-five years, so thrilling that he'd taken her number and promised to call after his meeting and arrange a proper date. At the time he'd even meant it.

Which was why seeing her behind his bar had at first been such an unwelcome surprise.

Enough time had passed that he'd thought it right to assume he would never see her again and now, with anticipation burning so brightly inside him, he could barely remember why he'd changed his mind about calling her.

One more night with the woman who'd spent two years weaving through his fantasies...

He was sitting on his bed propped against the headboard wearing only his black briefs when she appeared in his open doorway holding a small bottle of massage oil.

Pressing her cheek against the door's frame, she slowly, unashamedly, swept her stare over his naked torso, all the while grazing her bottom lip with her teeth. It was enough to send the blood straight into his loins and relight his arousal.

With the face of a Hollywood siren in its golden age and the body of a supermodel, Layla wasn't hot, she was scorching and when she moved from the frame and stepped out of her heels, moisture filled his mouth.

Honey-blonde hair spilled around her shoulders, she walked seductively towards him, her short black skirt displaying her long, toned golden legs for his delectation, hips gently swaying. When she reached the foot of his bed she lightly ran her fingers over his calf.

'Turn over,' she murmured.

He obeyed, resting his cheek on a pillow. Anticipation thudded through him.

Why the hell hadn't he called her?

The light was dimmed. The mattress dipped. Air moved as she made herself comfortable beside him. The shock of cold oil poured down his spine. His flinch was automatic. Her musical laughter was soft.

It was the single most erotic moment of his life.

Her knees pressed against his side, she spread her palms and smoothed the oil over his back and shoulders, and then she got to work, kneading at his muscles with the whole of her hands, gripping the bicep closest to her and stretching his arm out so she could work her magic on his forearm too. So damn good did it all feel that if her breasts hadn't made the occasional brush against his back when she stretched herself to massage his other bicep, he might have relaxed enough to fall asleep. As it was, Sebastiano found himself caught on the cusp between pleasure and pain: the pleasure coming from her clever hands, the pain from his unrelenting arousal.

The deepening of Layla's breaths as she worked on him told Sebastiano that he wasn't the only one aroused.

Lips brushed the nape of his neck.

He groaned, would have twisted round onto his back if she hadn't pressed the tips of her fingers into his skull and kissed the rim of his ear before whispering, 'Close your eyes and don't move.'

Used to being the seducer, he found the novelty of being the seduced heightened the eroticism, heightened the thrums of desire pulsing through him.

He'd had no clue that the worst day of his life would end in such glorious eroticism. It was almost worth losing a billion euros for.

He heard a rustling beneath him but there was no time to wonder what she was doing for now she was straddling his lower back, mouth hot in the arch of his neck.

'Keep your eyes closed,' she commanded seductively. 'No moving.'

With her incredible body draped over him and the heat of her breath dancing sensation over his skin, Sebastiano had no wish to do anything but continue to obey.

Hands smoothed up his right arm. A breast covered in too many layers whispered against his cheek. He groaned again, resisting the compulsion to open his mouth and—

A shock of cold metal wrapped around his wrist. In the split second it took for him to open his eyes, Layla had leapt off him and parked herself at the foot of the bed.

It took another split second for him to register that she'd handcuffed him to the bed post.

BRAND NEW RELEASE

Don't miss the next instalment of the Powder River series by bestselling author B.J. Daniels! For lovers of sexy Western heroes, small-town settings and suspense with your romance.

RIVER JUSTICE

—R—

A POWDER RIVER NOVEL

Previous titles in the Powder River series

September 2023

January 2024

In-store and online August 2024

Subscribe and fall in love with a Mills & Boon series today!

You'll be among the first to read stories delivered to your door monthly and enjoy great savings.